Five For Freedom

Michael Eckers

Five For Freedom is a work of fiction set in a background of history. Public personages, living and dead, appear in the story under their right names. Their portraits are offered as essentially truthful, though scenes and dialogue involving them with fictitious characters are invented. Any other usage of people's names is coincidental. Any resemblance of the imaginary characters to actual persons living or dead is unintended.

To the men and women who sacrifice

so much that we may enjoy

freedom.

Contents

"I remember it like it was two days ago. That basket from near mid-court was a gift alright. Bruce was a wonder himself; not too tall, easy to block against. But get him in the clear, well sir, he wasn't going to miss. I've seen him make fine shots before, but never one like that. There was only three seconds left, no time to get the ball in closer to Bobbie or Jim. They were the forwards you know; Bruce, he was a guard. Well, that ball arched up and out of his hands like a meteor... didn't even make the net move as it went in and through. A one-point victory over a team them experts picked to win. Sure, we'd been undefeated, but coming from a small town and all; well, we sure showed those Des Moines folks. Then they hoisted that trophy up, all five of them holding tight to it. Smiles big as the moon; ran around the court showing it off. Finished their last year at school like Hollywood stars, they did. Then they all went their own ways until the war started. It just happened that they all joined up right away; and in different branches at that. Bruce? He got hurt in a car wreck just before graduation; had some kind of fit or shakes or something. Anyway, he got a job writing for a small newspaper in New York since he'd been the yearbook editor and all back in school. The rest you've probably heard from the others. Tonight, will be the first time they've all been together since graduation I expect. Don't know of any other time since then. Well, go and talk to other folks, I've taken enough of your time."

At that, the man with a farmer tan line across his forehead ambled away. The reporter finished jotting in his notebook and looked for another local to interview. He still wasn't sure why his paper had sent him from Chicago to this 'one road town' in Iowa to cover the anniversary of a basketball game. There were dozens played every week back home he could cover without having to travel. He was intrigued by some of the people here; he'd already noticed an Air Force General and one high ranking Navy officer. He spotted a woman in a dress that didn't speak of a small town, standing alone carefully balancing a china teacup and saucer... seemed a bit out of place with everyone holding paper cups of punch; might be interesting to talk to...

Chapter 1
January 1942

The editor's office at the Daily News was nothing special; even the gilded lettering on the door was cracked and beginning to peel. Bruce Hollins, one of the newest writers for the paper, sat in a chair that had seen the bottoms of far too many others since its manufacture. He thought for a moment just what shape behind would fit exactly in the chair, certainly not his. Glancing around the office, Bruce saw a framed award the paper had received more than a decade ago. The frame was hung askew with a discernable layer of dust on it. A trashcan overflowed with crumpled balls of paper on the floor surrounding it like Indians around a circled wagon train. A few had actually succeeded in entering the container. Bruce made a mental note that his editor had never been a basketball player, at least not a very accomplished one. He chuckled to himself; thinking one day he'd have his own office, complete with a wastebasket mounting a miniature backboard, hoop and net. This was the first time Bruce had been inside the room; he'd passed by the closed door often in his three months here. His initial interview had been held by phone; the call coming to his folks' home back in Ames, Iowa.

G Gordon Bennett, editor, strode in without even noticing Bruce. He dropped into his chair and plopped his coffee cup on the desk, spilling some of the too dark liquid on a pile of papers. A string of unmentionable mutterings rang out as he tried to rescue the top couple of pages. Looking up, he noticed his reporter seated across the office.

"Hollins... glad you're here bright and early. I know the war's only started, what, three weeks ago... I've already got more stories than people to cover them. Know anyone that needs a job? Send him my way; better yet, if it's a dame... definitely send HER my way." He let out a blast of a laugh, like a sudden alarm going off. Bennett always thought his own jokes were the best; never seemed to notice no one else laughed along.

"Seriously Hollins, I've got a huge job for you. Small pool of reporters, all the rest married and all... don't supposed you'd like the chance of your life? I've been given... hell, thrown a juicy bone... I need someone to get on a ship loaded with the first of our guys heading to Europe. Boat leaves Thursday with the 34th Division; National Guard unit from Minnesota and Iowa. They'll be the first Americans to get to bonnie old England. I thought of you because you're from back there somewhere and speak their language; not England, of course... aren't you from Iowa or Utah or out west someplace?"

"Iowa, boss; Ames, Iowa to be exact. There were even guys from the Red Bull Division, the 34th, in my hometown that fought in the first war. I'd really love the chance to do this.... really." The genuine excitement showed on his face.

"Wonderful, look them up on the ship as you head over. That'd make a great story... we could even get it printed in your hometown paper. Make you famous in two places and double our subscriptions." Another fog horn of a laugh erupted from the depths of G Gordon Bennett. "The boat, let's see... the *USAT CHATEAU THIERRY*; an Army transport will be sailing from Pier 90 along with a British ship called.... uh, the *HMTS STRATHAIRD* in two days. You'll get your berth assigned when you show up. Let them know you're from the Daily News; there'll probably be a few other reporters on board as well. Maybe enough to get a good poker game going. Write down everything and send it back when you get to England; mail it back. I don't imagine anything will be important enough to cable or call through; way too expensive. We'll figure out how to get your wages over there once you arrive. Here's a couple hundred bucks to see you for a while; I don't have a clue what the exchange rate is for British pounds. It'll all work out I'm sure. This is a good chance for you to write like you want; I promise we won't chop it up too badly. Being young like the soldiers will be an advantage; they won't feel like they're talking with their old man."

Bruce was stunned at all he'd heard in the past few minutes. England? The war in Europe? He was going to be able to get there after all?

#

Bruce spent the next day making arrangements for his departure; getting another newspaper staffer to check his apartment and collect his mail, shopping for a new suit he thought he'd need in England. He also bought two sets of coveralls, similar to what soldiers might wear; they would certainly come in handy on the ship going over. He packed his typewriter, a 1940 Royal Quiet Deluxe that was his pride and joy; a gift from the Ames school superintendent when he graduated. The gesture was especially appreciated because Bruce had not been able to attend the commencement of his class; he wasn't discharged from the hospital until a few weeks later. Altogether he was careful to load only one steamer trunk since he figured he'd probably be carrying his own gear. Late that afternoon he called his folks back in Iowa to carefully let them know what was going on; he didn't give any details about the ship or date of departure or anything he thought might be information somebody could use. In his mind, he was already thinking of how easy it would be to give away secrets by just having a conversation. The paradox did not escape him; he was a reporter telling people about things, important things, and yet he had to be guarded in precisely what he was telling them...

#

Wednesday, the 14th, he was at the pier by the Brooklyn Navy Yard before the sun had come up. It was chilly and a light snow was falling. Two large ships were tied to the docks, both painted gray from the waterline up; different shades of gray he noticed. One flew a British ensign and the other American. Bruce hefted his trunk on his shoulder and strode toward the gangplank leading to the American vessel. Setting it back down and showing his boarding papers Bennett had given him the day before to a ship's officer on the pier, Bruce introduced himself.

"First mate Anderson, Mr Hollins. Pleased to meet you; you'll be bunked with two other news people coming aboard. Main deck just forward of the after-crew station on the port side. In case you didn't get that, sir, just go up and across the ship. Turn left and head about two thirds of the way to the back of the ship. You'll see a door open to a compartment with three bunks in it. Take your pick, you're the first to arrive. I might add there will be quite a crowd on board when we sail; be a good move to keep your door locked when you're not in your compartment. You'll be eating in the officer's mess; one deck up and forward, just aft of the bridge. Ask a crewman if you need anything. We'll be running drills once we're at sea. I think you'll find quite a show starting about two bells; that'd be 1300 hours or 1:00 this afternoon. I'd advise not going below decks after that time; at least until the troops get settled in. You can feel free to get off the ship later today if you need to; just be sure to be back well before we leave at first light tomorrow."

Bruce thanked Anderson and made his way up the gangplank, grateful for the wooden crosspieces as the snow was making footing difficult. As he reached the main deck he saw that walkways were covered in a different kind of paint; it had what looked like sand in it and made for better walking. He crossed the deck and turned left. There was hardly room for him with the trunk on his shoulder; from the wall to his left to the ropes on his right, separating himself from a long fall and watery landing, was barely three feet. He noted how easy it would be to fall overboard at any time, especially in rough weather or at night.

He passed a wider area with another walkway leading back across the ship. Must be the crew station Anderson spoke of; a few steps later and he saw the open door. Looking in he saw a

6

compartment not much larger than Bennett's office. There were three bunks stacked atop one another in the far corner. Three metal lockers lined another wall with a small desk and one chair completing the contents of the room. Not too bad, he thought, for just three of us. I could be bunked below with the soldiers; have to go down there later and see what their accommodations are like.

That afternoon the Army did put on quite the show. Thousands of troops stood in long, straight lines several ranks deep the length of the pier where the *CHATEAU THIERRY* was moored. The sight was most impressive and Bruce was kicking himself for not bringing a camera along; so much for relying on press photographers. The men began filing up three gangplanks leading into the cavernous insides of the ship. As a rank was depleted another moved forward in its place. It seemed the ship would surely sink or, at least, settle in the water under the weight of the men boarding. All the while, great cranes were lifting piles of crates and loads of barrels off small barges tied alongside the ship on the opposite side. Giant nets would be loaded on the barge and hoisted up, swinging and swaying higher, over the railings and into a large hold in the ships mid-section. Bruce could hardly believe his eyes at how many men he watched being swallowed up by the ship.

When the men were nearly all loaded and the cargo stowed he did notice the deck crew onboard adjusting the mooring lines, an indication that the added weight did settle the ship a bit in the water. After enjoying a simple meal of clam chowder, salad and a piece of Atlantic cod, washed down with strong coffee; and meeting more officers than he could possibly remember the names of, Bruce took leave of the ship for a couple of hours to walk along the Hudson River fronting the city. He'd always wanted to enjoy the view from the Brooklyn Bridge and took the opportunity now. While standing far above the water with the bright lights of New York behind him, he realized how easy it was to see things in great detail far off. It was still bright as day and Bruce wondered what it would be like in London, where total blackouts were observed every night because of the German bomber attacks. The British had been in the war with Germany since September of 1939.

Bruce returned to the *CHATEAU THIERRY* after a few hours of touring the waterfront. He was pleased to meet his two roommates who had arrived and moved in during his absence. Roy Coffee worked as a reporter for a Kansas City paper and was well known by the men of the 34th Division, having covered them extensively over the years, most recently during the large Army maneuvers of the past summer in Louisiana. Frank Summers was a freelance writer who sold his pieces to various papers and magazines throughout the country. Both had been writing longer than Bruce had been alive. Still, the two were excited about the upcoming trip 'across the pond' and expressed their willingness to help Bruce develop his own skills. They were both quite envious of his typewriter when he showed it to them.

"I remember Hemingway has one just like that; in fact, he says it's his favorite and the best he's ever worked with." Frank had made the comment, not in a boastful but more matter of fact way.

"You've met Ernest Hemingway?" Bruce was thunderstruck by the idea he'd be bunking with someone who had.

"Well, most who have met him will tell you they can't remember many of the details afterward." Frank answered, while tilting his head back and downing an imaginary drink.

"Mr Coffee, how long have you been writing about the Red Bulls?" Bruce queried.

"It's Roy, my father is Mr Coffee, even though he's been dead for two decades. I first met these boys when they came up from Mexico and sailed for France back in 1917. In fact, if you look right there, you'll see the pier we left from then." Roy stood and pointed out the door toward another part of the Navy Yard. "They were called the Sandstorm Division back then. Their patch had the 'bolla', a Mexican water jug with a dead bull's skull on it. During the war the skull was stitched with red thread; that's how they got the name Red Bulls."

Bruce reached in to his pocket and pulled out a note pad and pencil. As he began taking notes, Frank snorted and said, "You're going to need more paper than that to take notes on everything Roy knows about these soldiers. Plenty of time to get it all down before we arrive 'Over There'.

The next couple of days passed quickly as time was fractured by the various drills necessary to ensure the safety of all onboard. Everyone learned where their muster stations were located in the event abandoning the ship became a reality; the waters they traveled through were infested with German submarines, U-boats, which had recently begun harvesting a crop of death along the eastern seaboard of the United States. The lights that Bruce had enjoyed on his trek to the Brooklyn Bridge days earlier served as a brightly lit backdrop for the subs to spot freighters plying their way up and down along the coast. The night he was standing in awe at those lights, a British tanker had been sunk only a hundred miles away, off the southern coast of New Jersey. Had the night been dark with an enforced blackout the chances were good that Bruce would have seen the glow from the explosion and subsequent inferno as the tanker was engulfed in flames, killing the entire crew of twenty merchant seamen. America had much to learn about safety and security along her own coasts.

After the activity of drills subsided, the time began to move more slowly. By the end of the first week minutes seemed to drag and hours turned into days. Bruce began the habit of visiting the soldiers quartered below decks. He had introduced himself to several and found many that loved to talk with him about their own times in high school and college. He met one corporal that had been on the opposing team in a regional basketball game when they were both juniors back in Iowa. They spent nearly an hour happily reliving the game; one which Ames had won, but only barely. The soldier told Bruce he'd met a couple of other basketball players and would gather them up for a talk the next morning. That night the two ships, escorted by a pair of U S Navy destroyers, caught up with an Atlantic storm. The winds howled and the seas freshened until the boats were riding up, then down and side to side. Bruce's stomach seemed to be moving to the same rhythm but on a different beat. He was thankful the railing was only three feet from the door now. Holding on tightly to a rail stanchion he could barely make out the surface of the sea, but had the distinct feeling that looking straight out was nearly straight down. How he wished he hadn't enjoyed that second helping of spaghetti for dinner. His discomfort only got worse when, after lying down on his bunk, he had to listen to Roy recalling his trip across to England back in 1917. It was the intimate detail used to describe the smells coming from the berthing compartments on that trip that finally eased Bruce's sufferings.

Breakfast the next morning, for some, consisted of dry soda crackers. Bruce was one who appreciated their calming effect on his insides as they worked overtime soaking up the liquids already threatening to abruptly leave. He was feeling much better as he grabbed his notebook and pencil to head down to the meeting of the basketball group. He swallowed hard, a couple of times, when he opened the hatch leading to the berthing below. Roy had been dead on in his description of the smell...

The corporal from the day before greeted Bruce as he navigated between the floor to ceiling stacks of bunks, five and six high in some sections. He was introduced to a couple of players from other Iowa schools and two from up in Minnesota. The corporal said there was one more that would be showing up, if he wasn't glued to his rack. Bruce sat on the edge of a bunk to wait with the others, spending several minutes reminiscing about the past glory of their high school days. He glanced down the passageway, stared and jumped up like something had bit him on the bottom.

"I don't believe it! Fred Howard, what in the world are you doing here?" Bruce shouted.

"Bruce? Whad'ya mean me? What the hell are you doing here... and what kind of uniform is that anyway?"

Their reunion was full of back slapping, grins, questions and even a few answers. The other guys watched, enjoying the show. It had been only seven or so months since they'd seen each other; it just seemed like years and they were a world away from Iowa as well.

"You wouldn't have known, I suppose; still in the hospital when I joined the Guard. I heard from my mom you'd gotten out, but I was already on my way to maneuvers by then. What do you hear about Jim or Stan? I know Bobbie joined the Marines a few weeks before Pearl Harbor. I suppose he's just about done with boot camp by now."

They talked and talked for hours, catching up on what they each knew about friends, family and the area they grew up in. Bruce learned all about what the graduation he'd missed was like; the ceremony and party in the high school afterward. He felt bad he hadn't been part of it, but was grateful now that he knew what all had gone on. A sergeant came by and directed several of the soldiers, including Fred, to gather for squad training. Bruce told his friend goodbye and promised to come down again the next day.

That night he wrote a letter to his folks relating the meeting up with Fred and asking what they knew about Bobbie Milliken, Stan Larson and Jim Hartke of the basketball team. He'd mail the letter the second he arrived in England. Bruce drifted off to sleep to the thrum of the engines and the gentle rocking of the sea.

The weather turned colder and foggy the next day. Bruce was standing along the rail with Roy and Frank talking about the start of the war and what opportunities there might be in the near future for news reporters. He told them about his friends Fred and Bobbie. As they stood in the crew muster station, the wider area near their cabin that was out of the cold wind, one of the escorting destroyers came into view through the fog, making a sharp turn that was heeling her over until the ship seemed about ready to tip. They could hear a 'whoooop – whoooop' sound as the small ship picked up speed in the turn. It disappeared into the fog and soon an enormous explosion was heard off in the distance. Then another and a few seconds later a third reverberated down the side of the transport. They could feel the deck under their feet rumble as the engines of the *CHATEAU THIERRY* increased revolutions to make more speed. They could sense they were turning, though not at the severe angle the destroyer had.

"Submarine!" Roy shouted as he headed back to the cabin. In an instant, their own ship's alarm sounded; Bruce and Frank quickly followed Roy to the cabin, getting there just before the ship's crewmen came racing along the deck to their few gun positions.

Bruce caught his breath once he was seated on his bunk. Roy and Frank's faces wore very worried looks; Bruce was sure his mirrored their own. Now they were glad for the drills in the first days out of New York. They had been instructed to head for their cabin and not to get in the way of the crew. But sitting through a possible U-boat attack was probably worse than actually doing something. They felt the concussions of three more depth charges from further away and then the ship began a turn to starboard, this time leaning a bit further as the speed had increased.

"I sure would like to be on a destroyer someday, making turns like that; and those explosions... man, they really pounded my chest." Bruce was over his initial fright now, adrenaline pumping.

"You can have them; I spent two weeks on a 'tin can' a few years ago. I never puked so much in my life; never did get used to bobbing up and down like a damned cork on the ocean. No sir, I'll take a big old tub like this transport any day." Roy continued to talk about an assignment he'd had in the Gulf of Mexico, sailing with the Navy for a short time, writing about a new class of destroyer coming into service. "That boat wasn't even as fast as the newest ones just being launched this year. Nowadays you'll have to love riding roller coasters to serve on one."

The next hour was spent returning to their talk about 'writing the war'. Roy was very interested in Bruce's tale of the five friends winning the state basketball championship a year ago and now two of them running into each other in the middle of the Atlantic. He encouraged the young man to find out if the other three were in the military and to work hard at convincing his editor to let Bruce write a series of stories about them.

"You know, son, there's always plenty of reporters around to gather nameless facts and statistics and dates and places to tell about. But only once, maybe, in a guy's life does a chance to do a REAL story crop up. When we get to England, take the initiative and wire what you've written to your editor; make sure it's good stuff, though. When he gets it, he won't give a damn about the expense; he will be able to scoop all the other papers in town. Well, in New York, he'll beat a few others, anyway. Point is, when you write what you like, people like what you write. It's a fact most reporters never really get a handle on. I pump out stories like a hen laying eggs; but the one or two that got noticed have been the ones about the Red Bulls because I care about these guys and have lived with them, probably more than with my own wife.... seems that way lately."

"I agree wholeheartedly", chimed in Frank. "Roy and I will be covering the war from London because it's safe, dry and English gin isn't too bad. Not that we're too old to go out in the field; it's just less fun than it used to be. You've got a real chance to cover this war from right alongside the guys fighting it. Hell, even if all you end up with is a ground pounder in the 34th Division and one Marine; I'd put money on them seeing a lifetime's worth of action before this thing is over. Maybe Roy and I should write your editor and threaten to come work for him if he doesn't give you this chance..."

A knock at their cabin door and a young steward's head popped in. Word was the destroyer picked up noises on its acoustic gear and wasn't taking any chances. Might have been a Nazi U-boat or maybe a whale; breakfast would be ready in fifteen minutes regardless. Oatmeal and the last of the real eggs, poached.

13

After eating, Bruce headed back down to visit with Fred; they spent most of the morning together as Fred answered Bruce's questions about his time in the 34th. Bruce had the chance to interview several other soldiers as well. Spending time with the men in Fred's platoon gave him a real taste of how close these guys were to each other, much closer than Bruce and Fred had been on the basketball team and in school. The top sergeant in the group explained it to Bruce.

"When you go into combat, the real deal, you have to almost think like the guy next to you. After all, if he's got your back when it gets rough, you want him to know what you're going to do, too, right? That's precisely why the Army teaches us to do things just so... everybody the same, get it? Fred does the same thing in a situation that I'm going to do so I know what he's going to do. It's part of what makes us close, we begin to all think alike. At the same time, what sets us apart from other armies is that we CAN think differently and react on our own if we need to. Your average Nazi just does exactly what he's told and no more, no less. At least we hope that's what he does... it's what we've been told."

Bruce went through his notes each night, making sure to remember the comments and personalities he planned to include in the article that was beginning to take shape in his head. He knew most of what he was going to send back to Bennett at the Daily News would have to be finished when they arrived at their destination; he wouldn't have time to write the whole thing from scratch when they docked. He wanted this story to arrive in New York before anyone else had the chance to scoop him.

#

Three more days, thankfully a mix of calm seas and sunshine, brought the convoy into Belfast in Northern Ireland. The three correspondents were among the first off the *CHATEAU THIERRY*; there was quite a crowd to greet the ships as they docked. British Army officers, Red Cross workers, firemen and even a military band striking up a tune that sounded rather like "The Star

Spangled Banner". The three men were brought over to an area that contained several other reporters and photographers, including a few Americans. The crowd's cheering intensified as the first of the soldiers began making their way down the gangways out of the transports. Bruce was quick to get the names and titles of the various dignitaries and officers that would be speaking and welcoming the Americans before he made his way through the crowd and onto a quieter street. He found a policeman, easily identified by his tall "Bobbie" hat and inquired where he might be able to cable his story to New York. The officer said he'd be pleased to escort him to the AP office personally. By the time the welcoming ceremony was finished back at the pier, Bruce's story was already in the hands of G Gordon Bennett; who was thoroughly enjoying what his young, cub reporter had sent him. It began:

"The fabled green of this part of Britain cannot be overstated. Even the fog, which turns our hometown landscapes a common gray, is tinged with a bit of an emerald hue. Add to it now a new shade of green; that of olive drab, as the first American soldiers have arrived. A generation ago we sent our boys 'over there' to fight the Hun; their sons are here now, starting with William H. Henke of Hutchinson, Minnesota, officially recognized as the initial drop in what will become a torrent of soldiers against the Nazi..."

Chapter 2
February 1942

The American infantry officer directed the young man on the bicycle up the hill further to a collection of tents in a small patch of woods. Peddling hard the messenger was nearly there when he tired and had to dismount and walk the bike the rest of the way. It was a bit steeper than he was used to in the city. He walked to the nearest larger tent and stood, softly calling to see if anyone was in.

"Excuse me... anybody there? I have a telegram for someone and an officer said I should find a Mr Hollins up here... anyone about?"

"What... huh? Hollins? Oh, yes... come on in. Just waking up... sorry. I'm Bruce Hollins, you have something for me?"

"Aye, if you're Mr Bruce Hollins, I do sir. I have a telegram from America for you, sir. From New York, it is; I've never delivered one from America before. I suppose I'll have to get used to this."

Bruce smiled at the boy; he was, perhaps, fifteen or so. "Here you are; I'm not sure just what an appropriate tip is and the money here confuses me to no end." Bruce held out a handful of coins for the boy to choose from.

"Well, me mum would box my ears if I cheated anyone, so... there's another. I'll take two coppers if you don't mind."

"Here, take this one, too. It looks a bit more impressive and has a king's face on it." Bruce guessed he was giving the youngster far too much, but he hoped this telegram would be worth it.

"Half a crown? Thank YOU, sir. I'll be sure to nab any more telegrams that come in for you Yanks, that's a certain." The boy whirled around with his bike, mounted and was off.

Bruce shook his head to clear it a bit more. The morning's hike had taken everything he had; what time was it now, anyway? He looked at his watch; three thirty. Well, he hadn't slept through chow anyway. He'd 'volunteered' to go with Fred's platoon on an overland march. A piece of cake they called it; fifteen miles up and down the damn rocky hills and back. Bruce didn't complain, much, at the time; he simply said he should go shower when they got back. That was nearly two hours ago and he'd been sleeping the whole time. His feet did not want to go anywhere near the boots he'd gotten from the army; obviously, it took a lot more than fifteen miles to break in a pair of them.

Sitting back on the edge of his cot, also provided by the army, he carefully opened the envelope, took a deep breath and began to read:

MATERIAL RECEIVED. PICKED UP BY ASSOCIATED PRESS. RESPONSE FROM ACROSS NATION TREMENDOUS. SEND MORE OF SAME. BENNETT

Suddenly his feet didn't hurt at all; that is until he finished dancing around the inside of his tent. Across the country; his article had made it around the country on the Associated Press lines! He would have to get into town tomorrow and send a telegram to his folks, or call them if that was possible from here. He put on his regular shoes and walked out to find Fred and tell him the good news. Now he could write more about the soldiers themselves; not just what they were doing here, which wasn't much considering the war in the rest of the world. A couple more articles like the first one and the Daily News would have to let him find the other guys on the team, wherever they were.

Twenty minutes later he finally caught up with Fred, who was behind the kitchen peeling potatoes, with a thoroughly downtrodden look on his face.

"Hey, soldier, what do you have to do to get a great job like yours?" Bruce asked as he walked up.

"Pipe it, Bruce. Three of us tied as the last to roll call after the hike. They only needed two for KP, you know, Kitchen Police. Can you believe I can't even win with odds like that; I mean, 1 in 3 chance of winning and I don't get it. Anyhow, it's only for tonight. Peeling spuds is not the worst, we could be having something with tons of onions in it. Besides, it's the first time on KP; had to try it out one day, I suppose. So what's going on in the world of news reporting? Pull up a stool and tell me."

"I just might do that, this time anyway. It so happens your friend, the guy sitting with you right now, just got a telegram from New York about the article he wrote on the way over here on board the transport."

"They can fire you by sending a telegram?" Fred could not pass up the opportunity.

"Ho, ho, what a jokester; you ought to be in pictures, bub. Not only did I not get fired, yet... my article was picked up by Associated Press for national distribution. How about that?"

"I take it that's a good thing, right? Don't forget, I barely learned to read in school, let alone know what happens when you write."

"Yes, it's a good thing; great in fact. I have an idea I'd like to bounce off you. You told me Bobbie joined the Marines, remember? Well I'm going to suggest that my paper send me to find him, Stan and Jim, if they enlisted too. I mean, if the whole team, besides me, is fighting? That's got to be a story people back home would want to hear about, right?"

"You think folks would want to read stories about a high school basketball team from a town in Iowa, for Pete's sake? How bored do you think people are?"

"Not about the basketball, knucklehead. It's about the war and fighting and what all you are doing in it. Sure, I think people in America will like following the four of you; what you're doing,

18

where you are and all that. Course I will have to work things just right with the censors and all that, but it'll be okay, I know it will. First, though, I've got to get more stuff on you and the 34th. What's on the schedule for tomorrow?"

"Oh, tomorrow it's our rotation on the rifle range. Another battalion set it up while we were enjoying our stroll around the whole county of Cork, or wherever we are. In the afternoon we'll be firing the .30 caliber Garand; maybe you'll have a chance to shoot, too."

"I'll sure jump at the chance to do that! Listen, I'm going to go talk with the other correspondents for a bit; I'll see you later tonight or in the morning. See ya."

"Yeah, see ya. Now it's just me and my spuds..."

Bruce went looking for Roy; Frank had already left for London to find out what was happening with American commanders who would be setting up their offices in the capital. He was told that Roy had left the base along with the Division Commander for a meeting with British officials and would not return for some hours. As he walked back to the correspondents' tent Bruce considered his position as, perhaps, the youngest reporter to be covering the newest participant in this world war. There was a sort of comfort in that realization; after all, he was an upstart writing about what was considered an inexperienced army not yet baptized by fire. By the time he reached his quarters Bruce knew how he was going to approach his next article. Taking a fresh sheet of paper, rolling it under the platen of his typewriter, he began to write:

"Life is full of newness; from a baby's first breath to the arrival of an army from the new world to the old. I'm surrounded by thousands of men, young and not-so-young, many of whom are sharing the new experience of being in a foreign country. One of them, Fred Howard of Ames, Iowa happens to be enjoying his very first assignment at Kitchen Police, or KP as it's called here, dutifully peeling mounds of potatoes for tonight's meal..."

The next morning Bruce was up early, sipping a steaming mug of hot coffee as the division's public affairs officer read his article; in lieu of official censors, it was his job to make sure nothing was written that could jeopardize military security. Bruce was focused on the Captain's face as he read; he seemed to be enjoying it and wasn't scratching out anything at all.

"I can see why Roy has high hopes for you, Bruce. You write well and are certainly careful not to include things we'd rather not have revealed. I'd like to add that your structure is also very good; you're a very gifted writer."

"Thanks, Captain. Let's hope my editor thinks so as well. I have to say I'm a bit surprised that you'd offer a critique on the structure; it's going a bit beyond censoring."

"Well, son, not all of us were born for soldiering. Remember, the 34th is a Guard unit. It happens I'm an English teacher from Rochester; activated just before maneuvers in Louisiana last summer. First teaching I'll miss in quite a few years. If you have any questions, come see me. In the meantime, I think we'll be fine if you keep writing like this. I see no real need for you to have papers 'graded' in the future. But I would like to see one on occasion before I have to wait for a copy from back home to get here, know what I mean?"

"Sure do and thanks. I'd better be getting myself into town and get this article on its way to New York; show my boss I'm not just freeloading on the army over here. I'll swing by now and again with what I'm writing so you can have first crack."

Bruce headed over to the divisional motor pool to catch a ride into town; a supply truck was leaving in just a few minutes. He took the opportunity along the way to find out the driver was from Sioux Falls and drove a cab there before he was shipped out with the 34th. Bob Adkins was his name and he actually preferred driving the large truck; he said he'd not been stiffed for any fares yet, but it was only a question of time. Bruce was having fun getting to know little bits about the different backgrounds of the soldiers. He considered it a gold mine of good personal stories to write about.

When the two arrived in town Bruce directed Bob to the office where he could cable the story out. Bob offered to pick him up in half an hour if that worked; Bruce thanked him and headed into the building to take care of his own business. Twenty minutes later he was waiting outside when Bob pulled up and took him back to the division. Bruce headed straight for the rifle range; when he arrived Fred's platoon was up on the firing line shooting. Bruce approached a lieutenant and spoke with him, explaining who he was and asking if he could observe the men in their practice.

"Mr Hollins, I've heard from my men that you've become quite a fixture among them. You're more than welcome to join them practically any time. The only exception is when they're involved in training that involves real danger or when your presence may not match up as well with security. Have you ever fired a military weapon? Care to try?"

"No, sir... never have shot anything other than a shotgun for pheasants and ducks. I've never even fired a rifle or pistol, only my dad's 12 gauge. I'd like to try; though I may be a bit of a slow learner."

"Sergeant, why don't we set up Hollins here with a Springfield and see how he does?"

"Yes, sir. Right over here, Mr Hollins." The sergeant led Bruce to a bench behind the firing line. Fred noticed his friend and gave a barely discernable wave; Bruce nodded and smiled in return. The next ten minutes was a very abbreviated lesson in the 1903 Springfield; the rifle used by the army since before the First World War. It was a clip fed, bolt action single shot .30 caliber rifle, very much like weapons used by most of the world's militaries, including the 34th Infantry. One battalion in the division was now equipped with the M-1 Garand, a semi-automatic rifle that fired eight shot clips as fast as you pulled the trigger. It was the rifle of the future, quickly replacing the Springfield as numbers of them were produced back home.

Bruce learned how to shoot standing, sitting, lying down and even how to fire from the hip, not using the sights. By the end of a long couple of hours, his hands were a bit numb from shooting, his shoulder hurt a lot and his mind was tired from remembering a thousand things he didn't know the day before. All in all, he considered it among the most fun and memorable things he'd experienced. Sergeant Miller, the instructor, told him he'd done a fine job and had learned faster than most. Bruce then asked the sergeant about himself, what he had done before the army.

"Me? I was a police officer just outside Des Moines for a number of years. Joined the Guard back in 1937; they made me an instructor right out of my basic training. Now I head up a machine gun squad and teach here on the range. So how come you're not in the army or another branch yourself. We can use guys that shoot and learn fast."

Bruce told him about the basketball team and being injured in a car accident and now he was a war correspondent for a New York paper. Miller gave him an approving nod and words of encouragement.

"You know, I'm sure the folks back home enjoy hearing about us and what we're doing; though, right now it's mainly practice and learning how to survive in England. We'll be going into the fight sooner than later, I suppose. So Fred Howard was on your team, too? And you won the state championship last year? I don't follow basketball much; now, if you'd won in football I'd have heard of you without doubt. Good luck, Bruce, and remember what you've learned today; you never know when you'll be in a situation where a gun is mightier than your pen, to change up an old saying a bit."

During the next several weeks Bruce took many opportunities to continue practicing at the rifle range and became rather good friends with Sergeant Miller. He even had the opportunity to fire one of Miller's .30 caliber Browning machine guns; after he was made to carry the gun, its stand and other equipment up to the line. Normally there were two other men helping with this job. Miller explained that, at times, a single soldier might be needed to set one up and fire it; not a simple task. Bruce gained great respect for the men in the platoon as he became more aware of all that soldiering encompassed. He was even presented with a complimentary helmet when the Division was issued the new, decidedly better, headgear. These were the M-1 model and now the GIs would no longer resemble their English comrades with their flatter, soup bowl helmets. Bruce accepted the gift with a statement that he'd always remember the guys whenever he wore it, which would be very seldom if he had his own way.

Another telegram was delivered by the same messenger, this time on a new bicycle; purchased with the earnings he'd made running back and forth to the division's base. Bruce smiled as the lad approached and dug in to his pocket searching, by touch alone now, for a half crown to give him. To this he added a pack of Wrigley's chewing gum; the boy's face lit up when he got them.

"Thanks, Mr Hollins. My brother's going to get one piece of this. Mum says it's always nice to share."

"Your mom's right on that one. Nice bike you got; bet that was hard to find?"

"Right'o it was. But I paid 'top dollar' as you Yanks put it. Well, I gotta be going, see you later."

Bruce laughed as the boy rode away; it was funny how GI's found it hard to understand the language here when this young one was so quick to learn to speak American. Boys, new bikes, chewing gum and money; it was just like being back home, the way kids grow up. He smiled again as he thought, adding shooting guns can easily be on the list now. Then he remembered the telegram. He opened the envelope and took out the yellow Western Union form; just like home alright.

YOUR WORK A HIT EVERYWHERE. FLIGHT
BOOKED FOR YOU LIVERPOOL TO LONG ISLAND ON
YANKEE CLIPPER ON 18 MARCH. BENNETT

At first Bruce was genuinely disappointed at the prospect of leaving the 34th division. He'd established friendships among the troops and felt completely a part of them. At the same time he wanted to continue his new found quest for the rest of the team from Ames. He knew he'd found a type of writing he enjoyed; telling the stories of boys from anybody's hometown, now half a world away and facing unknown perils in the future. He vowed to himself that nothing would stop him from rejoining the 34th guys again in that future.

Bruce left his quarters; the original tent having been replaced weeks earlier by a rounded metal hut, shaped like a common can cut lengthwise and placed on the ground. Easy to put up and much warmer, less drafty than a tent; the huts had been constructed just in time to welcome an uncommon snowfall, much to the enjoyment of these Midwestern Americans and their penchant for snowball fights. Now he was leaving this 'home away from home' to return to New York and his job at the Daily News. He wondered just what G Gordon Bennett, his boss, had in store for him.

Bruce found Fred walking quickly in his direction, two newly sewn stripes on his sleeve. Pointing to them, Bruce gave his friend a quizzical look.

"What, these? It's about time the army figured out I look better with a couple stripes on my arm. Just found out this morning and you were almost the first person I wanted to show them off to. Now it's Corporal Howard, newest assistant squad leader in second platoon. Going to find someone with a camera to take a picture to send home."

"Hey, how about I phone your folks when I get back to New York? A letter would probably take longer to get there."

"What are you saying; you going back? You look like you're already packing in your mind. When do you leave?"

"The paper has arranged a ticket for me on the Yankee Clipper out of Liverpool on the 18th... I'll be in New York a couple days later. Just got the telegram and my boss doesn't say why, just to come back. I'm excited but don't want to leave right now, you know."

"Well, I doubt we'll be doing any real fighting for some time anyway. Hey, maybe he likes your idea about finding Stan, Jim and Bobbie. Anyhow, you've got your typewriter and that new helmet. You're ready for just about anything now; you even know how to shoot."

"Yeah, well, I've still got a few hours before I have to head down to Liverpool. Sailing over on a ship was a new adventure; flying over the ocean is something I've never done either. Fact is, I've never even been inside an airplane, even one parked on the ground."

"Me neither; you'll have to write about that so's I can read how sick you get. Be sure to use lots of good adjectives to describe it."

Bruce packed up his gear; it took more than the one steamer trunk he'd come over with, and hired a 'hack' to take him to the ferry terminal in town. He was thankful for a nice calm ride on the ferry from Belfast to Liverpool. Along the way he realized he'd been in Britain for nearly two months and had not seen much at all of the country outside of the ride from the division's camp into town. Now he was on water again, traveling past the only other land he'd see on this trip, the Isle of Man, sitting in the middle of the Irish Sea. As the boat sailed through the wisps of fog Bruce thought about the bright greens of Ireland, now becoming a bit drabber as war torn England approached.

#

Arriving at the ferry dock in Liverpool, Bruce found a taxi to take him to his room at a hotel a block or so from the Britannia Adelphi, probably the most luxurious hotel outside of London in the whole country. Bruce wanted to see it, but knew he couldn't afford to stay there, even for one night. After checking into his own room he walked down the street to the Adelphi. Bruce promised himself that one day he'd get a room there, as spectacular as it was. A more somber note was struck in his mind as he walked further and found a higher point overlooking the port and city. Liverpool was the main artery for supplies arriving from the United States and Canada; supplies that were keeping the nation alive. The Germans had bombed it so often in 1940 and early 1941 that it was second only to London for damage and deaths.

He had seen how large the port was on the ferry ride in; had noticed dozens of large freighters and other types of ships, some moored to the piers and others waiting in the harbor, flags from several different countries flying over them. He wasn't surprised at the attention Germany and its Luftwaffe had paid to Liverpool. He was not prepared for the vistas of destruction he saw in the town itself over the two days he had before his flight on the Yankee Clipper.

What did surprise him was the fact that the Clipper, a Boeing model 314, was a flying boat. It took off and landed on the water. Bruce learned that there were no land runways long enough for a plane of its size to take off from; which he understood when he saw the size of the plane as the taxi dropped him off at the landing. Flying boat was a good description; maybe flying ship was more accurate. A motor launch took him to the plane where it was anchored in the harbor. The closer he got the bigger it seemed. As he was welcomed aboard and led to his seat, Bruce marveled at the interior size as well. He was beginning to worry about the ability of the engines to lift it out of the water, let alone keep it in the air across the Atlantic to Long Island.

A steward, in white coat, told Bruce that dinner would be served in the dining area two hours after they were in the air, handing him a menu as he spoke. The menu listed five courses for the meal. With the overstuffed seats that also functioned as beds at night, Bruce wondered if, perhaps, he might not have stayed in the

Adelphi and charged the room to the Daily News. He was delighted to meet a couple that would be sharing his seating area; every four to six seats were grouped in a compartment on the plane. Mr and Mrs William Coldwell were from Los Angeles; Coldwell worked in the movie industry and was on a business trip to England, trying to get the British actor Leslie Howard to commit to making a film for his studio.

"The Leslie Howard, from *Gone With The Wind?*", asked Bruce.

"None other than..." replied Mr Coldwell. "Too bad, though; he's tied up working on a film over here... maybe next year, he said. And you, young man, flying on the Clipper, what is it you do for a living, if you don't mind my asking."

"Actually I'm a correspondent for the New York Daily News. I've been covering the 34th Division; the first American troops to arrive here in Britain. My editor wants me back in the states and sent me the ticket."

"Either you've got a very wealthy editor or you're a hot commodity yourself. What's your name?" Coldwell was looking Bruce over very intently at this last question.

"I'm sure you don't know me, sir. I've only been at this a short while. My name is Bruce Hollins."

The mention of his name didn't stir anything in Mr Coldwell, but his wife seemed to recognize it. "Did you write a column when the soldiers first arrived in Belfast, sort of a home town, this is their name and what they did before the army kind of story? I remember reading it in the Times; dear, you remember.... I even read it to you and said how different it was, sort of gets you right here"... She said this as she lightly patted herself on the breast.

"Really, Samantha! Oh, you mean the heart. I do recall you reading it; not my sort of thing, though."

"Excuse me, ma'am... did you say the Times? My article ran in the New York Times?" Bruce was getting light headed as he said it.

"Perhaps, but I read it in the Los Angeles Times. Maybe they're owned by the same people? Anyway, I liked it and think you write very well indeed."

Anything more said by either of his flying companions was lost to Bruce as his thoughts were consumed by the reality of his writing being read across the country. He'd never really believed Bennett's lines about that; did he? So completely absorbed was he that the takeoff of the Yankee Clipper happened without him even noticing. The steward passing through their compartment announcing dinner brought Bruce back to the present. He took off his glasses, carefully wiping them with his handkerchief, as he thought about his plans for meeting up with his other former team mates. He knew he must be firm with Bennett; must convince him of the legitimate desire of the public to know about their sons in the military. Mrs Coldwell helped drive that idea into his heart; the way she had brightened up and mentioned the personal stories he'd written of the 34th Division men.

He would start back in Ames, Iowa. Finding the information from the mothers themselves would be a nice beginning and it had been more than six months since he'd seen his own parents. A break would be nice to gather his thoughts. Besides, Iowa was right on the way to California and Bruce figured a new Marine was bound to go there for basic training before heading into the Pacific Ocean.

Dinner was an elegant affair for a news reporter; white linen, crystal and real sterling flatware. Five courses of the best food he'd ever eaten; ever. From the fresh spinach and tomato salad to the steak tartar to the wonderful chocolate torte for dessert; the quality and quantity were perfect. Bruce topped it off with the signature 'Clipper Cocktail'; Jamaican rum, extra dry vermouth and grenadine with a lemon twist. He returned to his compartment to find a steward had already turned his seat into a comfortable bed, complete with privacy curtains; it was very similar to a Pullman berth on a railroad train. He enjoyed one of the best night's sleep since leaving New York months before.

Morning brought fresh coffee and a single page of news highlights from overnight; written from radio broadcasts and printed right on board the flight. Bruce marveled at the immediacy of it, making sure to slip his copy into a pocket to show Bennett a piece of the future. Breakfast was a close rival in quality to last evening's dinner. Afterward, Bruce was invited by a steward to visit the flight deck on the upper level, if he cared to. Even if he hadn't been a news reporter, he'd have jumped at the chance. He was introduced to the flight crew, consisting of the pilot, co-pilot, navigator, radio operator and flight engineer. The cockpit was as large as the bridge of the troop ship Bruce had sailed to England on. The pilot shook his hand and said he considered it a privilege to meet the writer of the articles he'd read recently reporting the personal stories of the soldiers now in Europe. Mrs Coldwell had mentioned the young man to the crew. Bruce swallowed hard, his throat and mouth suddenly dry with embarrassment. He thanked the pilot for his kindness and for the tremendous service he'd experienced on the flight.

"Well, we didn't advertise the fact, but this is the last flight on this Clipper. This plane, along with others in the fleet, has been requisitioned by the government. They'll probably start doing their part for the duration after a tune up, refitting and a paint job. In a real way, you've been a part of history. By the time the war is over, we'll probably have bigger and faster planes crossing the oceans."

"I honestly cannot imagine anything bigger than this in the air, sir. And faster might be what some people want; I'll take a leisurely flight with fine food and good sleep any day. I'll be getting back to my seat now; thanks so much for the tour and the whole experience. I certainly hope I'll have another chance to fly a Clipper when the war is over."

"Good luck to you, Bruce. I hope you'll keep writing those articles. I know people need to hear about who the sons and fathers and brothers are in this fight. We'll get tired soon enough about the battles and such. I've already got my orders to report to the Army

Air Corps; I'm trading passengers for other cargo soon. I've always wanted to fly to Berlin; maybe I'll get my chance. If we meet again later, you can write about Bill Young from Baltimore dropping bombs on Adolph."

"You bet I will, Mr Young. Good luck to you, too."

Chapter 3
March 1942

"Damn glad to have you back, Bruce. You cannot believe the letters, phone calls and even telegrams we've been getting in response to the articles you've written... from all across the country, no less."

G Gordon Bennett was leaning forward in his chair with a look in his eyes Bruce had never seen on him before; like that of a track sprinter looking down the track at a finish line, just before the starting gun goes off. Bruce was still a bit tired after a night of celebratory parties on his return from England. One of the other staff reporters had picked him up at Port Washington out on Long Island when the Yankee Clipper had landed. Being aboard the final flight of the flying boat from Europe made Bruce a minor celebrity in its own right; with the accolades he was earning from his writing, a night on the town was certainly deserved.

"You know, when I got your first article from Belfast, by wire no less, I was a bit perturbed. I'd told you not to go the expensive route, just mail it across. After reading it though, and getting a phone call from Frank Summers, no less... well, I felt we had to go out on the AP with your story. Very unusual for a cub reporter like yourself, but what the hell... it sure stirred things up. You've probably gotten as much fan mail as Joe DiMaggio." Bennett lit up a Lucky Strike as he continued, "What I want to know is, what's next; in your mind, where do you go from here? You gonna quit and freelance like Summers or try for a bigger paper like The Times?"

"No, sir. I haven't even thought of working anywhere else. I had no idea what was going on here... the response to my articles, I mean, until I was on the Clipper flying back. A couple of days is not enough time to think about things like this; but I have given thought about what I'd like to write next."

"Out with it, Bruce. Strike while the iron's hot; that's what my old man always said. What's on your mind?"

"Well, Mr Bennett... I met up with a friend and basketball team mate on the ship going over; you know, I wrote about Fred in my first article. He told me one of the other guys on our team, Bobbie, joined the Marines around the time of Pearl Harbor. I'd like to call my folks, see if they know about the other guys, too. Maybe do a couple of shorts on what they're doing. It probably sounds lame, but it's what I think I'd like to do next."

"Well, it'd sure beat having you write obits or some of the other stuff I used to assign you to. You seem to have gotten the pulse of people somehow; putting names and faces to the war, you know. Take a couple of days; you look like you need some sleep anyhow. Why don't you start by putting a call through to your folks from here, now.... I'll go grab a bite to eat. Let me know, say... Thursday, what you've dug up on your old team. If it's anything worth covering, I think the Daily News just might have a new war correspondent on its payroll. That'd be a first."

Bennett got up, came around the desk and actually shook Bruce's hand. The gesture, with its sincerity made the young man think; that's the handshake of someone who actually likes me. He'd never thought of his boss that way before. Even Bennett's foghorn laugh didn't seem annoying; Bruce realized a boss need not be someone distant. He sat down at Bennett's desk and picked up the phone, dialing the operator. "Could I have long distance, please?"

The next days showed Bruce that while he'd gotten fan mail, he was sure it wasn't as much as DiMaggio; unless the baseball great only got three letters a week. He was surprised as he read a few, though, that he had really struck a chord with those who wrote him.

Some were from mothers and fathers of boys from the 34th; others from families of boys in different branches, beginning to spread out around the world in the new war. Bruce had also picked up news from his own parents. Bob Milliken had indeed joined the Marines. He was about finished with his first part of training at the new Camp Kearney out in southern California, near San Diego. He also learned that Stan Larson and Jim Hartke were in the military as well. His mother said all the boys' moms got together on Tuesday mornings to catch up on what the boys were doing and where. Just like they met each week while the team was playing in high school; it was his mother's idea. They had tea at his house and shared letters the boys had written. Stan was in the Navy and Jim had joined the Army, trying to get into the Air Corps. Those two had enlisted in the days right after Pearl Harbor; so all four of the others were serving. Bruce began formulating a plan to put before his boss.

"Just making sure I understand this... all four are in the service, in different branches? So.... small town basketball team, state champs no less. War starts, four enlist, one's a writer.... they're all over God's creation, fighting against our enemies. You're the thread tying them together.... and all their mom's are at home, living lives, waiting for letters, praying together for their sons... I think it just might work, Bruce. I like it a lot, I really like it a lot. Let me get to work with seeing how the paper can afford the travel and all... and I'll have to clear you through the military; have to get you proper credentials and all. Yeah, yeah this could turn into something big alright."

G Gordon Bennett was glad for the chance to regain the energy and drive for which the Daily News had once been known. The years of the Depression had taken the wind out of her sails like the rest of the country. Now he felt the paper was ready for a new start; new war, new correspondent to cover it, the timing was perfect.

"Bruce... I'd like you to take this one and run with it; all the way through. Find your friends, write about them, their buddies;

what they're doing and where they are. I've got a good starting place for you, I think, before you leave New York. Out in the Navy Yard is the newest battleship being built. It won't be finished and commissioned until sometime next year; hopefully it won't be flying a Japanese flag the way the war in Asia is going. Anyway, go and write a story on her…. she's the USS *IOWA*. While you're there, be sure to have the Navy issue you a war correspondent ID card; word came down a couple of weeks ago that you'll need one from now on. Here's a letter from me you'll have to give the guys at the issuing office. Let me know tomorrow what your plans are; a timetable and costs for train tickets to Iowa. Once you're there we can talk over where you'll be going next."

Bruce took the envelope with Bennett's letter to the Navy, picked up his hat and headed out the door. He felt like he had a real job now, a mission to accomplish. He knew the things he'd learned on the trip to Europe would serve him well in the days ahead as he left the Daily News building to catch the subway that would bring him within walking distance of the Navy Yard. This small town Iowa lad was certainly learning his way around the big city; not to mention through life. His mind was working on a list of things he needed to do; booking a sleeper for the train trip home, getting his typewriter cleaned and oiled before he left, arranging for someone to sublet his apartment since he'd be gone awhile.

When he arrived at the Yard, a dozen or so blocks from the subway, Bruce asked a Marine at the gate where the public affairs office was. The sentry directed him to a brick building across the parking lot and told him to check in there. He headed over, walked in and found the office listed on the directory in the lobby. Finding the door marked Public Affairs, he entered and told the sailor behind a counter what he needed. Bruce was directed to take a seat and the PAO would be right with him. Soon an officer in a khaki uniform came in; he had the insignia of an Army captain on his collar points.

"Good afternoon, I'm Lieutenant Mason; can I help you?"

34

"Lieutenant? Sorry, sir, I've been with the Army for the past couple of months… aren't those Captain bars?"

"You'll get used to the different service ranks if you're looking to be a correspondent… I've actually got a small booklet that'll help; remind me to get you one before you leave. Did you bring a letter from your editor?" Bruce handed him the envelope from Bennett and Mason continued, "Good. We need to get you photographed and finger printed. Won't take more than a few minutes; follow me."

Bruce and the Lieutenant had a good conversation during the time it took to process his ID card. The picture wasn't portrait quality, but it would suffice. While they talked, Mason told Bruce he had personally enjoyed the articles he'd read in the Daily News about the 34th Division in England and the trip over. He was looking forward to Bruce writing some about the Navy if that was in the future. Bruce explained the other part of his trip to the Navy Yard. Mason paused and thought for a moment.

"We don't usually allow civilian non-workers on the construction site here. Besides the security issues, it can be a pretty dangerous place. Lots of very large, heavy objects swinging about. I haven't been to the *IOWA* for several weeks myself, though…. why don't we head over there now? You've got valid identification and, hold on, let me grab one of those booklets I told you about. This will give you some help on ranks, structure and such in the different branches."

"Thanks, Lieutenant. And thanks, too, for bringing me to see the battleship. She's named for my home state."

"You, too? I'm from Muscatine myself. Went to Navy ROTC at the University of Illinois and became an officer almost two years ago. I'm actually hoping to get a billet on the *IOWA* when she commissions next year. What part of Iowa are you from, Bruce?"

"Ames; my dad manages a small bank there. I wanted to go to college but I landed a job writing here in New York before classes

35

began. Figured I'd start going at night but with the war on that will have to wait I suppose."

"You keep writing as well as you do and you shouldn't have to worry about college. The experience of covering this war will probably qualify you to teach writing, if you live through it…"

The two talked as they walked toward the construction site. Bruce could not believe the size of the ship. He'd thought the *CHATEAU THIERRY* was a big ship; this thing dwarfed the transport. Mason pointed out where the gun turrets were being placed. You had to imagine the finished product; at this time only the keel and first three or four decks had been built. Still, the immensity of the battleship was evident; her main armament would be nine 16" diameter guns in three turrets, two forward of the superstructure and one aft. Bruce learned that there were to be several more ships like her built in the next few years. The *IOWA* would be the fastest, most powerful ship the country had ever built. He told Mason that the ship looked fast just sitting there, with her sharply angled bow jutting skyward. She was beautiful; Bruce fully understood why an officer would want to serve on board.

As Bruce was riding the subway back toward his apartment he began to write in his notebook the beginning of his next article. This one was about a Lieutenant Mason of Muscatine, Iowa who was serving his country well alongside the newest addition to the Navy; one with a familiar name that would avenge those named after sister states that had been attacked at Pearl Harbor.

The next day Bruce reserved his tickets to Des Moines; he'd be traveling on the Pennsylvania Railroad's Broadway Limited to Chicago. The Limited had recently set a new standard in travel times with 16 hours on their line. At Chicago he'd change trains and pick up a Burlington Route train to Des Moines, sleeping in a Pullman for that stretch; after nearly 24 hours he would arrive in Iowa at eight o'clock in the morning where his father would pick him up at the station. The excitement of the trip began to grow as he hung up the phone; he missed his home more than he'd thought.

Bruce tried putting a call through to his folks but the operator told him the lines were all tied up. He sent a telegram instead, letting them know when he'd be arriving in Des Moines and asking his dad to pick him up. One of the new city reporters at the Daily News had posted a need for a room on the bulletin board in the paper's lounge so the second item on his list was also checked off. The reporter was from out of state so Bruce told him he could use the furniture and everything else in the apartment as well. He had dropped his typewriter off at a shop around the corner on his way to work that morning; he'd pick it up that afternoon. Everything seemed set for his departure. His paychecks would be deposited in a New York bank that would wire him whatever he needed around the country as he looked up his former team mates.

Typing out his article on the battleship, and Lieutenant Mason, took most of the rest of the afternoon; fortunately, he'd written quite a bit in long hand during the subway ride home from the Navy Yard. It felt oddly nostalgic sitting at his Daily News desk again. The typewriter he'd borrowed from the copy editor was badly in need of an oiling. Bruce ran the article by Bennett before he headed out for his new adventure; the editor liked what he read and sent it to be included in the next day's edition after making only a few minor corrections.

"Bruce, you keep writing this well and you'll put me out of my job as editor... I'll just be reading it and handing it to layout. Best of luck on your trip home and be sure to let me know exactly what's going on when you get there." Bennett grabbed his hand and pumped it hard while he said goodbye. With that he was on his way.

After picking up his own typewriter Bruce headed home; the last night in his apartment for 'the duration'. He packed his clothes and the few personal things he wanted, along with some items he'd be leaving with his folks in Iowa. One box full of books and odds and ends marked "Bruce's – Don't Open" was left behind on the floor of a closet. He slept surprisingly well that night; when he woke early the next morning he was up, showered and shaved with more than enough time to catch a cab to Pennsylvania Station. He hopped out of the cab, gave the driver a nice tip and strode into the cavernous landmark. The enormous clock hanging beneath the high windowed domes overhead showed a few minutes after six o'clock. Bruce figured he had time for a bite to eat as he headed to the ticket window. On the way to the restaurant Bruce couldn't help but notice all the men in uniform; even at this early hour of the day. He hadn't really considered the whole impact this war was having; the scale of it. But here he was, heading halfway across the country just to find out where he would be going next. He stopped and picked up a copy of the Daily News at a stand. There was his article, lower left on the front page, with his own byline. He still was not used to seeing his name on the outside of the paper; historically it was buried back around page six or seven with an obit or something about a local fire or petty robbery. He ordered two eggs, sunny side up with toast and bacon; coffee to drink. He knew he could eat on the train, but it would cost about double on board. He settled back and began to read what he, himself, had written...

Bruce was working his way through the rest of the Daily News when he heard the announcement over the public-address system: "Westbound Broadway Limited, service to Chicago and points between, boarding on Track 2". He got up, folded the paper and headed to the main stairway leading down to the track level. As he approached the train he showed his ticket to a steward who pointed to the third car in line. Bruce thanked him and walked down the platform along with several other passengers. Finding his seat, he stowed his bag on the rack above him. He was getting comfortable when the conductor came along to validate his ticket. As he was punching the stub, the conductor saw Bruce's copy of the Daily News.

"You know, I never read the News before they started running those articles", pointing to Bruce's own as he said it. "The way that Hollins writes, it makes you feel like he's talking about your own friend or neighbor, not just another soldier. Good way of getting everyone in on the war, you know?"

Bruce nodded in agreement without divulging that he was the writer of the column. He wanted to finish reading the paper and focus on his plans for the days ahead. The news from Europe contained nothing new; another American division had arrived in the United Kingdom and a Soviet offensive in Crimea against the Germans seemed to be stalled. The fighting in the Pacific was getting grimmer by the day; Japanese troops were now in Rangoon following the British withdrawal from the city. It meant Tokyo now controlled Java, Burma, New Guinea and the Dutch East Indies. No one had been able to stop their advances since December and the American situation in the Philippines was no better; our forces were squeezed onto the Bataan Peninsula and word was that General MacArthur had arrived in Australia, leaving behind all the troops and equipment to the mercy of the Japanese. Bruce thought about the depression that most Americans must be feeling and felt a surge of emotion that his style of writing allowed a sort of optimism to creep into people's lives. He knew that while he was searching out and finding his friends, he'd also continue to write about the everyday soldiers and others he encountered along the way.

#

The trip to Des Moines passed quietly as the rhythmic motion and sounds of the train lulled him into a sleepy sort of daze. The hours melted away and it didn't seem possible that sixteen hours had passed when the train pulled into Chicago. His change over to the Burlington went smoothly, leaving him time to eat in the station; again he spent half of what dinner on the train would have cost. He regretted booking a sleeper, however, as he was not tired in the least and spent the night in an observation car alone, staring at the occasional lights flashing by as the train sped through the rural areas of Illinois and into Iowa, stopping once in the Quad Cities area of Moline and Bettendorf.

As Bruce exited the train at the Des Moines station he heard a familiar voice call his name and, looking up, spotted his parents just beyond the gate. Their smiles were matched by his own as he half ran with his suitcase to greet them. After hugs and kisses, the three all walked hand in hand through the station to the car. The hour drive up to Ames passed quickly as his mother spoke of how proud the entire town was of his articles and how everyone, simply everyone, wanted to see him while he was home. She also invited him to the weekly tea that the other mothers were part of; a sort of renewal of how they gathered while the boys were playing basketball. Each Tuesday morning, they would get together at the Hollins' home to have tea and spend time praying for their boys; that they wouldn't get hurt in practice or games, that they would continue to study hard in school and that they would be good examples to the younger boys in the basketball program at Ames. After the championship, the ladies stopped meeting and the families began to drift away. Mabel Howard, Fred's mother, had been the catalyst drawing them together again when Fred's first letter had arrived from England.

"What do you hear about Jim Hartke and Stan Larson? I know Bobbie joined the Marines just before Pearl Harbor; Fred told me that when we met up on the ship."

"Well, it so happens that Olive, Edith and Clara joined Mabel and me just last week so now all five of us are meeting again. I've got it all written down at home but I'll try to tell you now....." His mom ticked the boys off a finger at a time with the hand she held up from the back seat. Bruce's dad grinned at the determined look on her face. "Fred is in the Army... with the Red Bulls in England. Jimmy, uh... James, is in the Army Air Corps studying engine mechanics... he's going to Florida next... in April or May. Bobbie is a Marine in San Diego, nearly finished with his training and his mother is worried he'll be leaving for Hawaii soon. Stan is in the Navy and will finish basic training in Maryland any day now and is supposed to go to gunnery school out west next. He and Bobbie will both be in San Diego, unless the Marines leave before Stan gets there. And you're here, right now, with us." She gave Bruce a hug around the neck as she said the last. Bruce smiled and patted her hands, feeling like he loved and missed her more than ever at the moment.

As his mother sat back in her seat Bruce began to tell them of his own plans. He hoped to connect up with all of his friends as they served the country in their widely different jobs. He also said he no longer felt like appealing his doctor's wrong diagnosis concerning the seizure he had after his accident.

"You know, with the doctor saying I have epilepsy, even though I never had more than the one episode in the hospital... I feel like I can contribute to the war effort best from right where I'm at as a correspondent. I'll be able to write about the guys fighting and working; to let everyone know what their sons and brothers and husbands are doing. Roy Coffee told me he thinks it's about the best thing a reporter can do, to write in a way people can really understand and feel good about. That's what I want to do, too."

"Roy Coffee? When did you meet him; isn't he the writer from Kansas City?"

"Yeah, dad, he is. We sailed across the Atlantic together, along with Fred Summers, another writer. We were on one of the transports with the 34th; I wrote you about that, didn't I?"

"Not that we got; nope, not a letter from you. Had to read about the 34th in the newspaper; that was quite a surprise you know. A nice surprise, but what a way to hear from you. It'd be nice to get a letter once in a while, maybe along with the news stories."

"Gosh, dad, I'm really sorry. I get so caught up in writing and interviewing; I guess I forget the most important people when I meet so many interesting ones."

"That's alright, son. Your mother and I understand; we really do. Besides, it is kind of a thrill to hear about you from others in town. I almost feel like I have to read the paper earlier in the morning just so I can keep up with my customers at the bank. Well, here we are; safe and sound at the old homestead."

As he pulled the car around the corner up the block from their house, Bruce's dad pointed ahead. In front of their house people had gathered in the cold morning air; a huge banner, nearly as long as the street was wide, proclaimed 'Welcome Home Bruce".

"Didn't I tell you everyone wanted to see you, son?" beamed Louise. "Tomorrow morning we're having tea; a chance for you to speak with all the moms. When we get in the house I'll show you the map your father hung for us in the parlor; we plan on using it to track where all you boys are."

Bruce and his parents were practically mobbed when they got out of the car. People from his past were there to greet him; fellow students, teachers, neighbors and some he didn't know. He was especially glad to see Mr Hopkins, editor of the Ames Daily Tribune; it was his recommendation that landed Bruce the job in New York. Mr Hopkins presented Bruce with a framed copy of his first article, the one written aboard the *CHATEAU THIERRY*. In the frame with the clipping was a thank you note from G Gordon Bennett to Hopkins about the new cub reporter he'd sent to the Daily News. Bruce was genuinely touched and completely at a loss as to what he should say. A couple friends noted it was the first time they had ever known him to be so quiet.

Louise invited everyone in for tea and coffee; most accepted though a few had to leave to get to their jobs. The next couple of hours were full of memories and Bruce shared with everyone his idea of locating and writing about the team. Every person there thought it a grand idea and wished him the best of luck and safe travels. When the last visitor was gone, his folks were washing up the cups and saucers. Bruce sank onto one of the kitchen chairs and nearly fell asleep chatting with them; the lack of sleep on the train had definitely caught up with him; not to mention how good it felt to be home...

The ladies were excited to see him the next morning. Seated around the table were the mothers of his best friends from high school. Olive Larson's husband Bill was the manager of the Feed Mill up in Ellsworth, though they lived in Story City; their son, Stan was now a sailor. Bobbie Milliken, the new Marine, was the son of Edith and Bob, Sr. Mr Milliken owned a carpentry business in Jewell Junction. Clara and Sidney Hartke farmed a few miles outside of Ames. Their son, James had been accepted into the Army Air Corps as a machine gunner. Fred Howard, Bruce's subject in the article on the 34th Division was the son of Mabel and Frank, also farmers; though Frank had just built a new hog barn and was contracting with Hormel, providing pork for the military. These mothers had committed to meet weekly and pray for their sons while the boys were in school. The entire families were supportive of the boys and their basketball; those who lived outside of Ames provided transportation to and from school every day so they played on the same team. Now they had renewed that bond by gathering once a week to support their sons in a new chapter of their lives. The map on the wall had five pins stuck in it; two in San Diego, one in Texas, one in New York and the last across the Atlantic Ocean in England. Louise giggled as she jumped up and quickly moved Bruce's pin to the middle of Iowa. Clara said how nice it was that they didn't have to wait for a letter to move it.

Most of the morning was spent helping Bruce with the information he needed to help him locate each of his friends; units, duty stations and dates they may be moving on. It confirmed his plan to head to California first; Bobbie was due to ship out in a few weeks and Stan was just starting gunnery training in the Navy. His mom had remembered all the details in the car very well.

Chapter 4
April 1942

As late March snows gave way to early April rains, Bruce was anxious to finish up here in Iowa and be on his way again. He'd met with 'simply everyone' in his home town and had even taken part in a basketball game between the current high school, which had finished their season before the playoff rounds, and an assortment of alumni. It was fun; Bruce made two of his signature long shots and then managed to foul out of the game, vehemently denying it had been intentional. The time he spent with his friends' mothers had been the highlight of his visit. During the tea all of the women shared how their own sons had felt the year before when Bruce had not been able to attend school the final weeks and missed graduation because of the accident. Now the other boys were the ones absent and they all promised to pray for his ability to connect with their sons.

Bruce knew he had, perhaps, two weeks at the outside before Bobbie would be leaving Camp Kearney to embark on a ship destined elsewhere. With Stan in San Diego as well, that was his first destination. He would be able to meet up with both of them and write his articles before heading back to the east coast to catch Jim down in Florida before returning to New York. After that Bruce hoped his editor would send him back to England where he could rejoin the 34th Division. By then, perhaps another three months from now, they'd be getting ready to see some real action. Though the news from the fighting front in Asia had been discouraging thus far, Bruce felt most Americans were hopeful that things would be better once the country was completely on a war footing. He wondered if the states would have to institute rationing like he saw in England; he didn't think folks would like being tethered close to home without gasoline. The military would be sure to need all the fuel it could get.

Arranging his railroad travel this time involved taking a ride on the Burlington to Omaha where he connected with the Union Pacific to Los Angeles. From there it was another short hop the hundred or so miles to San Diego. With fewer stops along the way the trip wouldn't take much more time than his journey from New York. He made sure to book a sleeper on the long haul from Omaha to the west coast and wouldn't drink quite so much coffee before that part of the trip.

Bruce received a packet from the Navy about the uniform requirements of an authorized war correspondent. Though he didn't have time to arrange to buy them in Iowa, the packet had the address of a store in San Diego that carried everything he'd need. The idea of wearing a uniform surprised him, especially one resembling a commissioned officer. He had also called and reserved a spot for himself in the indoctrination course he was required to attend when he arrived. He wondered if the other guys felt like he did as they prepared to 'join up'; he was excited and apprehensive at the same time. When he mentioned it to his dad, he got a nod of the head and "Yep, perfectly normal".

His parents drove him to Des Moines again to catch his train. He thought they would just drop him off but his mom insisted on seeing him to the platform. After picking up his tickets the three walked through the station; Louise began to cry just a bit. Bruce stopped and gave her a hug.

"You know, of all the guys, I'm the one you'll be seeing the most. I'll be sure to swing through here on my way every time I can. I'll do better at writing letters to you, too. I think what you and the other moms are doing is great; I'm going to write about you on my ride to California, starting in about a half hour. Look for it; I have a feeling my boss will put this on the wire for certain."

He hugged her tight and gave her a goodbye kiss, then turned to his dad and shook his hand.

"Good luck, son. Keep your head down."

"Thanks, Pop. Be sure to thank Mr Hopkins for me again, will you? It was one of the best things for me to get the Daily News job."

"You're absolutely right, Bruce. Do him proud like you do us; and don't forget to write... often."

The porter took his bags; Bruce kept his typewriter case with him. He boarded, found his berth and opened the window to wave to his folks. A few minutes later the train started to move; he unlatched the case and set the Royal on the small table that folded out from the wall. Rolling in a clean sheet of paper he began to weave the story of a group of mothers whose support of the war took a decidedly different course from many others.

By the time he'd finished his article the train was speeding its way across southern Wyoming. At Ogden, Utah it would head south a bit to Salt Lake City. Bruce found out from the conductor that they would stop there for about an hour; plenty of time to mail it back to New York from the station. He grabbed a sandwich and cup of coffee from the lounge car and took it up to the observation deck above. There he enjoyed the view of the mountains to his south, highlighted in the late afternoon sun, their snow covered peaks jutting high out of the dusty colored basin flatlands the train was heading through. He imagined lines of covered wagons and Indians galloping their ponies with the cavalry hotly pursuing them on their larger horses. The land had changed so little out here it didn't take too much to conjure up the scene in his mind. He had always enjoyed reading stories of Kit Carson, Wild Bill Hickok, Sitting Bull and General Custer; as a boy he and his friends had played 'Cowboys and Indians' any time they weren't shooting baskets together.

The memory brought Stan and Bobbie to his mind; he took out a pencil and his notebook and began jotting down a list of the things he'd have to get done when he arrived in San Diego. His orientation with the Navy was important, doubly so because it took care of both sailors and Marines. Bruce figured he would order his uniforms right away and then report for the Navy class; that would give the tailor time to finish any alterations before he was ready to wear them when reporting to the training bases. He continued with his list as he smiled at the notion of writing an article on how to become a War Correspondent.

When the train slowed to a stop coming into the Salt Lake City station, Bruce got off, headed into the depot and posted his envelope at the service counter. Then he placed a phone call to New York, leaving a message with the copy desk alerting Bennett to expect its arrival and letting his boss know he'd be getting to California the next day. He stretched his legs walking on the platform for several minutes and boarded the train again when the conductor was leaning out announcing the departure to Los Angeles and continued service to San Diego. Bruce noticed a large group of soldiers getting on board a few cars back; he would make a point of going and talking with them in a little while.

Returning to his own room Bruce took out paper and began to write a letter to Mr Hopkins, his old boss in Ames, thanking him for the gift and the great visit they'd had when Bruce was home. Finishing after a couple of pages, he was reminded to also pen a quick note to his folks, both to thank them for the great time he had and to satisfy their desire to hear from him. He sealed both envelopes, applied postage, glad he'd picked up some stamps before he left Ames, and put them in his briefcase to mail from San Diego. Patting his pocket to make sure he had his notebook, he headed back towards the car he saw the soldiers enter; the slight swaying of the train reminded him of the ship's motion on a calm day crossing the Atlantic and the plane flying back. Train whistles, aircraft engines and ship horns may sound different but they all felt alike to his inner ear.

Bruce found the car full of soldiers enjoying the complimentary coffee and doughnuts, courtesy of their host, the Union Pacific. He approached a couple of sergeants and introduced himself; they invited him to sit down and have a cup of rio and a dunker. The coffee was strong and the doughnut was too sweet and greasy; no wonder the guys were wolfing them down. The sergeants hadn't heard of him or the Daily News, but couldn't fault him for asking. They told him to go ahead and ask questions. When he did they were freely flowing with the information that their detail was the first group heading to an area further down in Utah called Topaz; it was to be the site of an internment camp for Japanese that were living along the Pacific Coast. One of the non-com's thought they were coming from San Francisco. The inmates wouldn't be arriving for some time, maybe a couple of months. The camp had to be built and it would take some time for all the materials to arrive. He did say it was about the most inhospitable place he'd ever been and he'd grown up in a hotter and drier part of Colorado. The soldiers were part of the National Guard from that state and would be the camp guards and personnel once the internees arrived. Bruce was surprised and more than a bit shocked to hear that citizens of the US were being forced to move to these camps from areas they had lived in for generations; but he understood the security reasons behind the government's decision.

"Really?" piped a corporal that had joined them. "I grew up in Denver; my best friend in school is full blooded German; you don't see anybody throwing Krauts into camps, huh? How about all the Italians in New York? You seen them being taken away; you work there yourself?"

"No", Bruce replied, "and I don't know of any plans to relocate them, or any of the Irish either. When I was in England this winter, there sure were a lot of hard feelings about them by the

British. Ireland is neutral but buys weapons and supplies from Germany, not England. Sign of the times I guess."

"I guess, too. Anyway, it's supposed to take care of espionage along the coast. Hell, most of the Japs there are farmers, raising food for us Americans to eat. I suppose there won't be much trouble having some friends of the government guys taking over their farms and making money off their hard work."

A sergeant added, "So you see, Hollins, we're going to have a good fun time doing our duty at the Topaz relocation camp, right? We all get along ourselves and the Japs haven't even started coming yet."

Bruce was sure he'd have plenty of material for an article by spending the evening in this car. He circulated among the soldiers, getting comments along with names and home towns. He planned on picking up several Los Angeles and San Diego newspapers when he arrived to gather good background info on the 'relocation program', as it was being called. Followed by shouts of "Don't forget to write" and "remember me in the funny papers", Bruce made his exit after stopping to thank the sergeants on the way back to his own car. It took him quite some time to get to sleep that night; he wasn't sure if it was the coffee, the doughnuts or the news about the relocation.

A porter knocked on his door, announcing their arrival in Los Angeles in thirty minutes. Bruce rose, dressed and headed down the corridor to a restroom to freshen up for the day. He enjoyed a good breakfast in the dining car; fresh fruit, eggs, ham, toast, coffee and tomato juice. His hope for a view of the city as they arrived was forlorn; too much early morning fog to see much of anything. The train stopped for twenty minutes before starting again on the final leg to San Diego. Most of the way the fog still prevented any real sightseeing, but he managed to catch a quick view of the coast with a sharp drop down to the ocean with waves rolling up on large rocks, throwing foam spray high into the air. There was a small patch of sandy beach, covered with big brown lumps that were moving; a couple at the next table voiced excitement at the chance to spot some sea lions! It was certainly a fine introduction to a new world for the young man from Iowa.

Bruce's first impressions of San Diego, gathered as the train rolled in along the huge bay that made it such an important military site, were of sand colored ground, towering palm trees and thousands of people entering and leaving a huge aircraft plant just before arriving at the station. There were lines of giant double tailed bombers parked along a runway, all covered by enormous nets to camouflage them. It was the first hint, visually, to him that the nation was at war from coast to coast; battleships in New York to bombers in California.

Bruce gathered his things, quickly packed his bag and headed for the platform, thanking and tipping his porter on the way. As he stepped outside the train, he was immersed in the gentle, warm breeze with a wonderful salty, slightly fishy smell that is San Diego. The sunshine warmed him to his bones, but not in an oppressive, desert kind of way. He stopped, closed his eyes with his face to the sun and sighed. A fellow passenger commented as he passed by, "Yes sir, there's another newcomer... you can always tell the first time in San Diego."

The porter had told Bruce the U S Grant Hotel, where he'd be staying, was only a six or seven block walk up Broadway from the depot. Bruce set out with his suitcase in hand and his coat over his arm. He hadn't gone one block before he stopped, rolled up his sleeves a bit, and continued on. The sun felt so good, so different from the chill of New York, Northern Ireland and Iowa. He noticed a large percentage of military uniforms among the other people walking. About half way to the hotel, he couldn't help noticing a large store across the avenue called "The Seven Seas"; it's advertising claiming it to be THE place in San Diego to buy uniforms. Bruce reminded himself to head back down this way after he'd checked into the room the Daily News had arranged for him.

A few more blocks and he saw the large gray and tan stone building, fully seven or eight stories tall, up ahead. It was the tallest structure in view and looked to be about as opulent as he'd likely find in the city. He walked into the lobby through the massive brass door held open by a handsomely dressed doorman. A clerk greeted Bruce with a smile and asked for his name on the reservation; upon hearing it she smiled again and mentioned how much she had enjoyed his last article, about his encounter with the Navy and the battleship *USS IOWA*. While trying to take the compliment in stride, Bruce managed only to mumble a broken "Th-th-thank you, miss." He felt like he'd never get used to being recognized by folks; not him, really, just his name.

Bruce followed the bell hop from the elevator to his room on the seventh floor; he tipped the boy a dollar once he got in the room. "Thanks, mister. Thanks a lot." The room overlooked the downtown area including the Spreckels Theater across and up the avenue; his view looked over buildings to the Naval Air Station at North Island across the expanse of San Diego Bay. To the west rose the high bluffs of Point Loma with the lighthouse out at the end, hundreds of feet above the water. It was a wonderful view; Bruce hoped he could find time to enjoy it from the balcony.

First things first; he had the hotel operator connect him with one of the editors at the San Diego Union newspaper. He wanted to make arrangements to use their wire service to send his articles to the Daily News back in New York. The editor, who knew G Gordon Bennett personally, went far beyond granting Bruce's request. He put a car and driver at his service to help him while he was in town; it was not at all what Bruce expected. He'd be picked up first thing the next morning to bring him to the main Naval station where his indoctrination class as a new correspondent would be held. Bruce sincerely thanked the editor, hung up the phone and started unpacking. He would spend the rest of this afternoon getting fitted for the uniform items he'd need and finding out where Stan and Bobbie were stationed. He'd have to think on how to go about the second task; he was sure there would be hundreds of possible sites where they could be.

After taking a nice long shower, Bruce got dressed and walked the few blocks to the Seven Seas, back toward the waterfront. Entering the store he was struck by the size of the place; it was much bigger than it looked from outside. Palm trees reached to the ceiling a full three stories above his head. Nets full of merchandise were hung between the trunks like hammocks. There were thatched roof huts scattered around filled with uniform tops and bottoms for the various services, mostly Navy and Marine. Hawaiian music was playing, a little too loudly. There were hundreds of men and women shopping, picking up belts, buckles, shoes, socks and the myriad of patches and pins that adorned the uniforms. There were even more racks full of the latest civilian attire as well. A sales clerk asked Bruce if she could be of assistance; he told her he was a War Correspondent and would be working with the Navy and Marines. She led him to a private room off the main floor and said a tailor would be there in a few moments. Bruce sat down in a very comfortable chair; his first thought was to wonder how he could get it to New York as a gift for Bennett's office. A minute later the door opened and an older man walked in, tape measure around his neck and glasses perched on the end of his nose.

"War correspondent, I hear; don't see too many of you. Not yet anyway. My name's Saul; we'll get you measured up and then start picking out what you need. Did you plan on picking the packages up or would you prefer them delivered? It shouldn't take more than a few days to have everything finished."

"I'm staying at the Grant Hotel up the street. If it's not too much bother to have someone bring them there, I'd appreciate it. I'll be pretty busy finding a couple of my friends here I'm sure; must be a million new recruits and trainees around San Diego."

"You have no idea; we haven't been this busy since the end of the last war. I suppose that's as it should be, though. What's the name, so we get your things to the right room?"

"Bruce... Bruce Hollins, I'm in room 718 at the Grant."

"Hollins; H-O-L-L-I-N-S, I suspect? Fine; first name Bruce. That name rings a bell, huh..." Saul looked over the top of his glasses with a searching expression. I've got it; you wrote that article about the Yankee Clipper's last flight? I'm hooked on those flying boats; took one myself a couple years ago from Hawaii all the way to Hong Kong. Anyway, I'd be surprised at someone young as you writing an article that showed up in The Times."

"Not nearly as surprised as I was when I first found out. I wrote my first one while I was crossing over to England and my editor in New York sent it out on the AP wire; apparently it was picked up and printed practically everywhere."

"Well, no wonder, if it was as good as the one I read. You've got quite a talent for getting people and things described just right; almost like I was riding along right beside you, know what I mean? So, if I was you... I wish... I'd just ask the help of the Public Affairs guys that'll be teaching your class at the main base on 32nd Street. They'll know the easiest way to get hold of your buddies, I'd guess. Especially since they're both Navy; I know, one's a Marine... it's really pretty much the same thing. Both are the Navy Department; same folks working most of the records."

"Thanks, Saul. I'm sure you just saved me hours of phone calls. I'll ask tomorrow at my class. Any good advice on where to get a taste of some local food?"

"Well, Bruce, that all depends on the size of the bankroll. The Hotel del Coronado has a fabulous restaurant with an equal price. My favorite seafood place is down at the foot of Broadway, by the water. You can buy shellfish right off the boats if you want to. If you like Mexican, I'd go to a new place, opened just over a year ago. It's over off the west side of Balboa Park up on the mesa; the place is called El Indio's. Best tortillas and beans you've ever tasted. Don't go during shift change at Consolidated Aircraft; the line gets to be too long. Let's see... when we get finished here you could grab a cab, couple of bucks will get you there and back to the hotel, no problem."

"You know, this place should be called the information center; a guy can get clothes tailored and plan his whole stay in town at the same time. I really appreciate the info, Saul."

"Well, Bruce, it's the kind of service I expect from all my employees."

"Wait... you OWN this place?"

"What? Did you think I'd just work in a joint like this? My dad, also Saul, started it long ago; he taught me what I know about tailoring and sales. I own it now." Saul winked and the corners of his mouth turned way up at the last line. "What say we finish up with you so I can get on with some real customers?"

Bruce knew at that moment where he'd be buying all of his clothes from now on. He was out of the store in just over an hour, in a cab on his way to grab the best Mexican lunch in town; of that he was sure. The driver of the cab took Bruce a little out of the way when he learned his fare had just arrived for the first time in San Diego. Bruce was treated to the views of beautiful Balboa Park, including the zoo and the old Exposition site of 1915. The buildings were fantastic, nestled among huge tropical trees and shrubs. He wondered why he'd never heard how beautiful this city was; the whole country would find out after his next article.

Bruce enjoyed his first Mexican food immensely. He tried a dish that was spicy chicken with rice, tomatoes, black beans and a sauce that defied definition. It was called a burrito; Bruce asked if he could have a menu to take with him. The food was hot enough to require a cold beer to wash it down. When he asked the owner if he knew 'Saul the tailor', the man pushed his glasses down his nose, looked over them and said, "Si, Saul el sastre". Bruce laughed and ordered Saul's favorite lunch. When the cabbie dropped him off back at the Grant Hotel, Bruce asked him to deliver the food to the

Seven Seas and handed him a large tip. The cabbie was more than willing to comply.

The next morning Bruce was in the hotel dining room enjoying his second cup of coffee when a young man, about his own age, approached the table. He was medium height and build, blond hair and walked with a pronounced limp.

"Excuse me; are you Bruce Hollins? I'm Sam West of The Union; I'll be your driver while you're here in San Diego. I've got to admit I was expecting someone much older than myself."

"Morning Sam; care for a cup of coffee? They make it pretty well here. I'll be ready to go in a minute; just finishing catching up on the news. You work for a good paper; much larger than the one I write for in New York."

"Yeah, but my boss would say they've got one reporter that's worth the whole bunch of us. He really likes the way you write, Bruce. We all do; it'll be a real pleasure helping you get around."

"Thanks; I can't believe I've been writing for only six months. I guess I've seen more this year than most folks. It's been kind of a whirlwind. Anyway, do you know the main Navy base on 32nd Street? That's where I need to be in an hour."

"I sure do. My dad was stationed there up until a year ago; I've been there more than a hundred times I'd guess. I can drop you at the main admin building; it's where everyone starts. They'll be able to show you where you need to go from there. I don't suppose I'll be able to drive on base, though; security is bound to be tighter than before Pearl Harbor."

"Well, today is indoctrination for me as a Navy Correspondent. I don't know if my class will be more than just this afternoon. How will I let you know when to pick me up later?"

"I'll give you the phone number of my sister; she lives less than a mile from the base. I'll go visit her while you're on base; it'll work for today at least."

"Great; do you mind if I ask how you injured your leg?"

"Naw, I don't mind. I was with a bunch of friends at The Cove up in La Jolla. It's a rocky place where we love to swim; diving from the rocks takes good timing. You've got to hit a wave or the water's pretty shallow. My timing wasn't so good. I broke my leg pretty bad. The doctors say I'm lucky not to be riding a wheelchair the rest of my life."

"Ouch. I was in a car wreck last year myself; missed my graduation. No serious injuries, but I had a seizure. The doctor said I could have more of them so I can't join up to fight. I just hope it won't keep me from writing about the guys who do."

"We do what we can do; that's what my dad says. He's on an aircraft carrier somewhere in the Pacific now. I expect he's one you could write about. Well, we'd better be going; don't want you tardy the first day of school."

With that the two headed out into the downtown bustle of San Diego. The morning fog was just giving way to another sunny day. Bruce sat up front with Sam as he drove along the waterfront of the bay towards the Navy base. They passed shipyards where Bruce could see workers climbing and crawling among the huge skeletons of steel being fashioned into warships and merchant vessels. Gigantic cranes swung their long arms around, pieces of hull plate or prefabricated sections the size of a house hanging down from wire cables as thick as a man's leg. Bruce was impressed with the scale of it all, and with the thought that this is only the beginning. What will America be like when its industry really gets geared up to full capacity? He was aware of President Roosevelt's hopes and plans for the nation to become the 'arsenal of democracy' for the whole world.

"That's National Steel and Shipbuilding, one of the larger employers in San Diego besides the military itself. Then there's Consolidated Aircraft, of course. When you get to 32nd Street, try to imagine how busy it was when the whole fleet was here. Most of it, the battleships and carriers and all, were moved to Hawaii just over a year ago. A lot of people around here wonder if the Japs would have dared to come all the way here to attack, if the fleet hadn't been moved so much closer to Tokyo."

A couple of minutes later Sam brought the car to a halt outside a large gate, guarded by several armed Marines. He pointed out a large building across a vast parking area that Bruce took for the admin building. Sam handed over a note with a phone number and the name Susan written on it. Thanking his driver, Bruce got out of the car and headed for the guards, pulling out his wallet and removing his identification card from the Brooklyn Navy Yard. A Marine corporal looked it over and directed him to the large building Sam had pointed out. Walking there Bruce smelled the air, a mixture of saltwater and diesel fuel. It reminded him of Liverpool, though here it was coupled with bright sunshine and palm trees; not the dreary gray dampness of an English winter.

Bruce entered the admin building and asked a sailor at the information window for directions to his class. He was given a pass to another, smaller building a few hundred yards down the street. Bruce felt rather conspicuous walking along; he was the only person in civilian clothes in a world of uniforms. Everyone was wearing khaki or Navy blue or white or Marine green. He hoped Saul's promise of a few days to get his own uniform was true.

"Bruce? Bruce Hollins; hey Bruce, wait up?"

He was startled to hear his own name called from across the street. He stopped and recognized the officer approaching. "Lieutenant Mason?"

"Hi Bruce, I'd say 'long time no see' but it's not been very long at all; and it's Lieutenant Commander Mason now.... oh, forget it. Why not just call me by my first name, Dixon; Dix for short."

"Wait.... Dixon Mason. I bet the Navy has a good time with that. Don't you all go by last name THEN first name? Doesn't that make you..."

"Yeah, yeah....Mason, Dixon. I know; that got old the first year of ROTC back in Illinois. I'm glad rank settles a lot of those old lines." They both laughed as they continued their walk, both asking the same question; 'what are you doing here'?

Bruce explained he was still looking for his basketball buddies and Dix told about his promotion to Assistant Public Affairs Officer for San Diego. He would be teaching, for his first time, the class of War Correspondents as he started his new job. His desire for assignment to the new battleship, USS IOWA, was still strong; there was just no need yet for an officer of his rank onboard until the ship was actively commissioned. Dixon was in San Diego for only a short time until the IOWA was fitted out and fully manned.

As they walked, Dixon suggested that Bruce contact a Chief Yeoman Wolff in the Personnel Office, located next door to the main admin building. Their class wouldn't begin for another half hour and Bruce took the opportunity to hurry back the way they'd just walked to see Chief Wolff. Unfortunately the Chief wasn't in his office; his assistant wrote down Bruce's name and said Wolff would swing by the class later in the day to speak with him. It was another hurried walk back and Bruce was entering the room just as Dixon was introducing himself to his new class.

"And making a grand entrance is someone you've probably heard of lately.... Bruce Hollins will be another of the new War Correspondents. Good to have you here, Bruce."

Bruce was a bit embarrassed but took the kindly ribbing in stride. The next few hours were full of information on Navy protocol, censoring rules and a hundred little differences between each branch of service a Correspondent would experience. During their only break, to stretch a bit and "hit the head", an older man in a khaki uniform approached Bruce. It was Chief Yeoman Wolff.

"Mr Hollins? Yeoman Ross told me you need some help... something about locating a sailor and a Marine? Got to be honest with you, sir. I can sure do it, but it may take a couple of days, if that's ok? Write their names and home towns and I'll have one of my men get right on it. Alright if I bring the info back here? Commander Dixon said you'd be in his class through the week."

"That would be perfect, Chief. Thanks; I mean it." Bruce wrote down Fred and Bobbie's information and handed it to Wolff.

"Fine, sir. I'll get to it right away… and, by the by, I really enjoy your articles, sir. That one on the IOWA was very well written. Anything I can do to help, just shoot me a line or stop by when you're in port."

"I'll be sure to do that, Chief. Do me a favor and thank Yeoman Ross for his help, too."

When the class had ended for the day, Bruce declined the offer to go tilt a few beers with some of the other Correspondents. He needed to get back to the hotel to continue working on his article about the War Relocation Camps; he was also thinking of another on the hustle and bustle that San Diego had become.

He asked to use a phone at the main admin building and dialed the number Sam had given him earlier. The voice that answered was decidedly not Sam.

"Hi, this is Bruce Hollins. I'm calling for Sam; you must be his sister, Susan?"

"Hello, Mr Hollins, I am Susan. Sam's been telling me about you. I'll have him pick you up in, say, fifteen minutes? Traffic gets a little heavy around the main base in the afternoon. Should he meet you at the main gate?"

"That'll be fine, thanks. Goodbye, Susan."

Bruce stopped by a mobile canteen that was parked just outside the gate. It was a YMCA truck serving doughnuts, coffee or soft drinks. He picked up two of the doughnuts and a Coke. It would hold him over until the hotel; he'd not eaten since breakfast and was hungry… learning was hard work.

Sam's car pulled up as he finished the last swallow. Bruce opened the back door as he noticed someone sitting next to Sam in the front. She was in green overalls with her hair pinned up short under a baseball cap.

"Hey, Bruce, come up front… plenty of room. I didn't think you'd mind if we gave Susan a lift to work? She's on the evening shift at Consolidated and it's just a bit past the hotel; saves her an hour ride on the bus."

"Sure, Sam. Hi, Susan… I'll just put my case on the back seat and get in."

"Well, Mr Hollins… I was sure expecting someone a little older when Sam told me he'd met you. He had me read a couple of your articles while you were busy at the base. How'd your class turn out, if I may ask?"

"I'd guess it'll take a while for all the ranks and rules to soak in, but I think I'll fit in pretty well. Writing is writing, I suppose. What's your job at Consolidated, Susan? By your work clothes, I'd guess you're not the receptionist."

"Oh, that's good. No, Bruce, I only answer phones for my kid brother here. I'm a wire puller… I climb into tight spots big guys can't fit in and run wiring and control cables. You cannot imagine how many there are in a bomber… little spaces that all of it has to go through. I suppose there's a mile or more in each plane, seems like. I got the job because the foreman knows our dad; used to work with him in the Navy. Sam says you're staying at the Grant? A nice place I've never been in. Looks fancy from the outside."

"Why don't you and Sam join me for dinner one evening? I'd love some company; you are about the only people I've really met in San Diego, other than for business. Do you get any days off work, Susan?"

"Actually tomorrow is my evening off; you sure it's ok?"

"Let me check with my boss… yep, he says it's fine. How about you come along when Sam picks me up again tomorrow and you can show me some of San Diego before dinner?"

Sam dropped Bruce off at the Grant and left to bring his sister to work. As he walked into the lobby he saw the clerk motioning to him from the front desk. Bruce nodded and headed to the counter.

"Good afternoon, Mr Hollins. I've got several telephone messages for you, sir. Hope your first day in our city was a pleasant one."

"Yes, it was, thanks. Plenty of business to do, I hope to see some of the local sights while I'm here as well."

"If there's anything I can do to help, it would be a pleasure, Mr Hollins. My name is Bernice; please ask if there's anything you'd like." It was the smile and look in her eyes that shook him up.

"Uh, yeah, thanks. I'll keep it in mind, Bernice. Do you suppose I could have those messages now?

"Oh, certainly… anything to help, Mr Hollins. Anything at all."

This was completely new and unnerving; Bruce had never had a girl talk to him like that. And the look she gave him…

An hour later Bruce headed back out through the lobby, purposely avoiding any glance toward the front desk, and Bernice. He walked up Broadway a few blocks and then turned south to the Library. At the information desk, he spoke with a librarian about his desire to read up on the Relocation Program in California. She directed him to a table and brought out several copies of the more recent LA Times and San Diego Union newspapers covering the topic. Bruce spent the better part of two hours reading up on moving thousands of Japanese Americans from their homes on the West Coast to a dozen camps located inland. The camps were in several states, all the way east nearly to the Mississippi River. The closest was up in the Owens Valley, a couple of hundred miles north and east of San Diego. Bruce hoped one day to visit Manzanar Camp as it was being called. For now, he'd write an article about the soldiers from the train in Utah and the work they were doing on the camp there. He realized limitless ideas and places existed he could easily write about; he had to focus on his assignment, particularly since it was his idea to begin with. After he found Stan and Bobbie, hopefully here in San Diego, he'd call the Hartle's and find out where James was in the Air Corps. Bruce returned the papers to the desk, thanked the librarian and went outside into the pleasantly cool evening. The sun was setting over Point Loma and the air had a salty, ocean smell and feel to it. He smiled to himself and realized how much he liked the variety of places he'd already visited in a few short months.

The next morning Sam was right on time; time for another cup of coffee that is. The two laid plans to visit a few sites that evening, with Susan, before returning for dinner at the hotel's restaurant. Bruce gave Sam the copy of his article for the Daily News and asked if he'd wire it to New York. Then it was off to another day of military expectations and regulations. At his request, the hotel had prepared a couple of sandwiches for Bruce; no more growling stomach this afternoon before class was finished.

At the afternoon break, Sam shared his lunch with a couple of other Correspondents; one from Portland and the other from Salt Lake City. Chief Wolff approached as they were enjoying bacon with lettuce and tomato on white wheat.

"Mr Hollins, sir. Yeoman Ross came through for you; both the sailor and the Marine you're looking for are still here. Seaman Larson is at the Gunnery School out on Point Loma and Private Milliken is at Camp Elliot; it's about fifteen or twenty miles north of town, near Camp Kearney, sir. I've got the information and directions to each place in the envelope."

"Thanks, Chief. I am impressed at the efficiency, really."

"Yes, sir; I've got to say, Mr Hollins, I was nearly a hero at the supper table at home when I told my wife and kids who I'd met. We all like your writing, like I said yesterday. Anything I can do to help."

Sam and Susan were already at the gate and honked the horn to get his attention. He walked past the Marine guards and climbed in the car. Susan was not in overalls, on the contrary, she was in a very pretty cotton skirt and white blouse that accented her shoulder length blonde hair. Her lipstick was red, but not too red.

62

"Hey, what happened to the Susan that was here yesterday?" It was the best he could blurt out as he sat down next to her.

A slight blush colored Susan's cheeks. "Oh, she's here, somewhere… hiding under all these dress up clothes. Ready to see some of our home town before we eat?"

Sam drove while Susan told about the places they visited. Driving through Balboa Park, which Bruce had seen from the taxi, Susan narrated the history of the Exposition. Then the original Spanish mission in the valley, followed by the Presidio on the bluff between the valley and San Diego bay and on to Ocean Beach, a quiet community along the far shore of Point Loma. They hoped to get out to the lighthouse at the end of the Point, but the road was closed because of security; Point Loma was home to many military schools and the gun installations protecting the main harbor. Coming back from Ocean Beach, Sam drove up and over the hump that begins the Point, offering a beautiful view of the lights of the city along the bay. Susan pointed out where the Marine Corps Recruit Depot and Navy Recruit Training Center were located, close by Consolidated Aircraft. Bruce was impressed by the size of it all. He asked Susan if she thought he might possibly be allowed to tour the aircraft production site while he was in town. She promised to check the next day before she started work.

Their drive took a bit more than two hours and all were ready to eat when they returned to the hotel. The restaurant was nearly full; almost every table sporting a customer in uniform. The maître d'hôtel showed them to a quiet table back a bit from the noisy main seating area. The three enjoyed a relaxing dinner with easy conversation about their personal pasts and family. Susan and Sam's mother had died a few years earlier from an infection; she had cut her leg on something outside and developed blood poisoning. Their father was currently serving on *USS HORNET*, an aircraft carrier in the Pacific. Both were worried about the fighting and his safety, naturally, but they also had a confidence in the Navy. Susan lived in one of the two small houses her father owned; she shared it with two renters who both worked at Consolidated. Sam lived in the other house alone; he was considering getting a boarder since their dad would probably be at sea for a long time.

Bruce told of his growing up in central Iowa, the basketball team and their state championship the year before. He spoke of his own incredulity at the events since that game; how the car accident caused a college to cancel his full scholarship, the decision to take a job in New York that Mr Hopkins had arranged for him to get. He quickly went over his travels the past couple of months; Susan and Sam both sat with eyes wide open as he related his ocean crossing on the transport and return on the Yankee Clipper.

"Bruce, you've undoubtedly traveled further in two months than anyone I've ever known. What an exciting life; sleepy old San Diego must be a bit dull after all you've seen lately. And all that way by yourself; I'd be scared out of my mind."

"No, no, no... Susan, I think San Diego is wonderful. The sunshine, warm air and delicious smells here. I don't think I've ever seen a more beautiful city; New York is noisy and busy and I never made it to London. I think crossing the states on trains is probably my favorite part. We live in a country that is an amazing mix of colors and trees, lakes and deserts. I hope someday to be able to travel through it slowly, to enjoy each little part of it. Right now, though, I have my own mission in this war, I think... People tell me all the time how much they like what I write; I need to keep it going... sort of letting them see a bigger picture of what all of us are doing, I don't know. Sometimes I'm living in a dream, or a Walt Disney movie or something. I just like to meet people, talk and listen, then write down what I've heard. To me it's just what I do; I'm really surprised and honestly embarrassed when they think I'm special or..."

"Bruce, you are special and you write things that are easy to read. People like that... I know I do and I've only read a couple of your articles. I hope you find your friends quickly so you can continue to write what people want to read. Meanwhile, I hope my knucklehead brother gets you around San Diego safely. I hate to end the evening, I've had a great time. Sam needs to get me home and a bit of sleep would be good for all of us."

"Agreed. I've had the best day in a while myself. Thanks for the tour, please see if I can get into Consolidated… I'd love to write something about that. Sam, I need to be at the base by eight o'clock tomorrow morning."

The three stood to say good night and goodbye. Bruce was surprised and thrilled as Susan gave him a kiss on his cheek when they separated in the lobby. He also noticed a scowl on the face of Bernice, the hotel clerk as he walked past to the elevator. Then he heard the song, "Stormy Weather", coming from the hotel lounge.

"Perfect."

#

Bruce joined the others in the Correspondents' classroom in bombarding Mason with questions about reports of a bombing attack on Tokyo that had made the papers overnight. Taking all the frenzied queries in stride, the new Public Affairs Officer replied that President Roosevelt himself had the best answer. The bombers had come from a secret American base called "Shangri La" and the raid had been the first strike back at the Japanese since their attack on Pearl Harbor back in December. He assured the men it would not be the last; that the Navy, along with the other military forces, were preparing to "take the war to the enemy". After the hubbub settled down, their final day of orientation to their jobs as War Correspondents began. Hours later Mason congratulated each attendee as he handed them their new identification cards, authorizing them access to a host of previously unknown opportunities. He gave the example of now being able to board Navy warships, even at sea, to observe and report activities, under the "guidance and direction of appropriate command authority".

"What this means, gentlemen, is you'll be allowed to tag along on military missions; but you'll also listen and obey those in charge. You're not to carry arms or engage in the fighting; you are reporters, not combatants. This must be made absolutely clear; as it has been throughout your orientation. It's been an honor and privilege to get to know each and every one of you. My office will always be here, even if not occupied by myself personally, to assist you. Now go let the world know what we can do!"

Sam picked Bruce up at their usual spot and the two headed out to Point Loma to find Stan Larson at the Navy Gunnery School. Stopping at the entrance to the training facility, Bruce showed his new identification card to the Marine guard and was passed through without comment.

"I guess that card of yours works for more than just yourself, Bruce. The guard didn't even ask to see my driver's license, for crying out loud. I suppose I'm just part of the car, like an extra steering wheel or something."

"Well, Sam, you've sure been more than that the past week. I'll be sure to tell your editor how much help you've been. A couple more days and you can go back to being busy, instead of just waiting for me."

The two entered the door marked 'Main Office' and approached the sailor behind the counter. Bruce noticed the man's rank as a Yeoman Second Class, two red chevrons below crossed quill pens under the large white eagle; same as a Sergeant in the Marines.

"My name is Bruce Hollins. I'm a War Correspondent with the New York Daily News. I'm trying to locate a Seaman Stan Larson; I was told he's a trainee at the gunnery school here." Bruce handed the Yeoman his ID card.

"Yes, sir. If this man is your driver, he'll have to wait in the car or here in the office."

"Yep, just another spare part", said Sam as he backed over to a chair in the waiting area.

Bruce smiled at him as he tucked his identification back in his wallet. The Yeoman came back from his desk with a binder, open to a page listing names of those in training. His finger traced down the page, then another and one more until it stopped.

"Larson, Stanley… Seaman. Class 42 dash 2 Bravo. Let's see…" He opened another folder, shuffled a few papers and said, "Bravo class is on the 5"/38 mount. Sir, if you'll wait a moment, I'll get someone to guide you to the site."

"Thanks, Yeoman. I'll wait with my driver."

Bruce looked at Sam, who was holding his hands like he was driving. Avoiding an outburst of laughter, Bruce just shook his head and smiled. The two made small talk about some of the places they'd seen on the tour the day before when the Yeoman announced a guide was available. Bruce thanked him again and was introduced to a Seaman Nelson, dressed in a light blue shirt and dungaree pants, with carefully polished "boondockers". They were the black, ankle height shoes every sailor wore. The toes glistened and Bruce wondered just how a person could get them so shiny. Nelson guided him out the back door and through a maze of sidewalks, buildings and various sized guns mounted on railings or tripods and some so big they looked like telephone poles sticking out of steel shacks.

The two approached a group of a dozen or so sailors around one of the mounted guns, this one about eight feet tall with a barrel of the same length. Shells that looked to be about three feet long stood lined up behind it. A Chief Petty Officer was instructing the class on how to load a shell into the gun. Seaman Nelson approached the Chief and said something in a low voice. The Chief glanced at Bruce and said, "Larson, someone to see you."

"Aye, aye, Chief", was heard from inside the group of trainees and out stepped Stan, staring with wide eyes at Bruce.

"What the hell are you doing here? I mean… it's great to see you, but how did you find me and what….?"

So began the end of the search for his second teammate. Bruce and Stan sat down, just out of earshot of the training class, and caught each other up on what had 'gone on' since graduation, nearly a year ago. Stan had started classes at the University of Iowa and had enlisted a few days after Pearl Harbor, to the great consternation of his Hawkeye basketball coach. No amount of logic or badgering could convince Stan to remain in school. He'd been in San Diego for boot camp and went straight to this school; he'd be finished here in two weeks and then would be reporting to the *USS LAFFEY*, a new destroyer that just finished her own fitting out, having been commissioned the month before in San Francisco.

"The Chief says it's great, and a surprise, for me to get assigned to a brand new ship. Most of us will be going to older tin cans… destroyers, to start with. One guy will be on a cruiser out of Pearl. All of us want to get to a battleship some day; those 16 inch guns are really something, that's for sure."

"Fred told me you'd joined the Navy. I ran into him on a troop ship crossing the Atlantic back in January… we were on the way to England. I'll be looking for Bobbie after the weekend; he's in the Marines up at Camp Elliot. I guess that's just north up on the mesa."

"You know Bruce; it's hard for me to think that a newspaper in New York would spend the money to send you all over the place looking for a bunch of high school buddies like this… what gives anyway?"

"Well, when I wrote an article about meeting Fred and his being part of the first Americans to get to England to fight the Nazis, a lot of people back home here just loved it. I still can't believe how many tell me they read the articles I write and think they're great for morale. I just write what I see and hear, especially when I talk with soldiers and other people. But, hey, I'm getting to travel and see my buddies. So, what else is happening; met any girls or got one back home?"

"You kidding? Between one semester and all the Navy training since, I haven't had time to go anywhere… let alone meet anyone. What about you?"

"I don't know. My driver's sister is nice… she gave me a tour of San Diego yesterday; her dad's on an aircraft carrier, the

HORNET. I don't think it'll come to anything, though…. after I meet up with Bobbie, I have to find Jimmy. Last I heard from his mom, he's supposed to be getting to Florida this month or next. Then I suppose it'll be back to New York to find out what my boss wants me to cover next."

"Well, buddy, you've sure had a nice trip so far. Hey, maybe you could arrange for us three; you, me and Bobbie to get together for a picture or something here in San Diego. The papers might like that."

"That's a great idea! Wish I'd thought of that; you know, I didn't even bring a camera on the ship when I met Fred. Some reporter, huh?"

"I remember a time when you ran out of the locker room on to the court without your shoes…"

"I completely forgot about that…"

Bruce and Stan spent most of the next hour making plans to get together a few days later, after Bobbie had been located at Camp Elliot. The Chief Petty Officer in charge of Stan's training was cooperative in allowing the time away from his training for a possible reunion of the three friends. Bruce said goodbye to Stan and rejoined Sam in the admin office.

"Sorry that took so long, Sam. Next time we'll have to get you a book to read or something to do during a wait like this."

"That's ok, Bruce. The yeoman let me look through the last couple of "Life" magazines. I think I actually learned a few things." The two shared a laugh as Sam drove the car out the gate and headed back toward downtown.

"You can drop me off at the hotel, Sam. I've got a lot of things to do, some calls to make. Would you ask Susan if she's had a chance to see about a tour of Consolidated?"

"Sure. I can swing by her place on my way back to the Union. Might be better if you called her yourself, though. You've still got her number?"

"You bet I do; I'll call her from the hotel, thanks." Bruce was a bit flustered thinking about Susan; he really liked her but found it hard to balance the feeling with knowing he had, maybe, a week left in San Diego.

Sam pulled the car to a stop in front of the hotel. Bruce thanked him and got out. As he was walking through the lobby to the elevator, Bernice approached with a large package, wrapped in paper.

"Mr Hollins, this came for you earlier today. I wanted to deliver it to you personally."

"Thank you, Bernice." The card on the package said it was from the Seven Seas. "Great, these are my new uniforms... good timing."

"Uniforms? I thought you're a reporter; have you joined the Navy or something? I love a man in uniform."

"What? Oh, these are for when I'm on a base. War correspondents are supposed to wear these now so everyone will know we've been through military training."

"Well, if you need them ironed or hung up... or laid out on the bed." She smiled and winked at him as the elevator door closed. Bruce found himself staring at the closed doors with his mouth hung open. The elevator operator just smiled and looked up at the ceiling as they started up.

The clothes fit perfectly; khaki pants and shirt, with a "WC" patch on the left shoulder. Saul included a pamphlet from the Navy on the regulations telling how each item was to be worn. It was the same one he'd gotten in his indoctrination course from Lieutenant Commander Mason. The black necktie and shoes were the only part not khaki; Bruce had a mental image of falling down on a beach and only being seen because of the tie. He carefully hung all the items in his closet, noting that they were all carefully folded and didn't need pressing... poor Bernice.

Bruce changed into more comfortable clothes, sat down and rang the hotel phone operator. He asked her to connect with long distance to New York and gave her Bennet's number. A minute later he heard the familiar voice.

"Bruce, how the hell are you? Found time to lay on the beach yet?" Even over the phone, that laugh still sounded like a foghorn.

"No, sir, too busy working... did you get the articles I had wired through the Union?"

"Sure did... you might want to read a paper or two once in a while to find out, though. Your first one on these Relocation Camps was good... think you'll have time to get up to the Owens Valley and see Manzanar? More first-hand accounting, you know. Can you find out anything about this attack on Tokyo? It's what everybody's covering right now... Washington's not saying much. Anybody you've met got more on that?"

"I just read about it this morning. The Navy Public Affairs Officer talked with us at our final class; didn't say anything about them being involved. I'll see about a trip up to the Relocation Camp, probably on my way back east. I found Stan Larson, my buddy in the Navy, and spent time with him this afternoon. Tomorrow I'll look up Bobbie Milliken, the Marine at Camp Elliot. I hope to get the two together soon for some photos; I'll see if the Union will loan a photographer. I'm also working on a tour of the Consolidated aircraft plant out here; my driver's sister works there. They build big bombers and Navy patrol aircraft."

"I see no moss grows under your tail. Keep the articles coming and see what you can get on this Tokyo attack. Say hello to Dave Rupert at the Union from me."

"Sure, will do."

Bruce hung up the phone and thought for a moment. He picked it up again and asked for a local call to Susan's number. One of her boarders answered and said Susan had just left for work. Bruce left a message and thanked her. He ordered some coffee, black, from room service and sat down at his typewriter.

"It's a long way from an Army camp in Ireland to a Navy base in California; so great a distance that the term World War takes on new meaning…

Hours later, far past what his bedtime was in high school, the phone rang. Bruce got up from his writing, now several pages in length, and answered it. Susan's voice brought him back to the here and now.

"Hi, Bruce… Bonnie, one of my renters, said you called earlier. She just started her shift here and I'm on a short break… thought I'd call. Can you make it here tomorrow night, around nine o'clock or so? Our office will have someone here to guide you around the plant and answer questions… I'll be there, too."

"Sure, thanks… I wouldn't want to make this tour without you there. Maybe we could get a bite to eat after, together?"

"I'd like that, but it'll have to be breakfast. My shift doesn't end until nearly dawn. How do you like pancakes?"

"Love them… I also want to say how much I enjoyed last evening."

"Me, too. Listen, I've got to go. My breaks don't last long. See you tomorrow at the plant. Bye."

The sound of her voice lingered in his head. He looked at the clock; it was nearly midnight. Maybe another hour, he thought, then to bed. Plenty to do tomorrow, too.

#

Bruce and Sam were on their way to Camp Elliot the next morning. Low clouds slowly gave way to the emerging sunshine as they headed inland and up on to the mesa north of the city; the promise of another beautifully warm spring day.

"Predicting weather here must be about the easiest job in town. Onshore breezes with patchy fog until midday followed by warm temperatures and clear skies. Low clouds returning in the evening with cooler air. I'd bet we have days like this about 300 times a year."

72

"I wouldn't complain... folks back in Iowa are probably just beginning to dig out from the winter snow about now. I'll take the warm sunshine anytime."

They approached the gate; armed Marine sentries motioned for them to stop. Bruce showed them his identification and the car was passed through. Sam mumbled again about being a spare wheel as he pulled up to the large building the sentries had directed him to. Bruce smiled as his driver pulled out a book to read while he was waiting. They walked into the administrative office and Bruce approached the front counter while Sam found a comfortable place to sit.

A Marine clerk wrote down Bobbie Milliken's name and promised to be back in a few minutes with information on where he might be. Bruce took the time to study a map of Camp Elliot on the wall next to the counter. The Camp was part of a massive area of land dedicated to both Marine and Naval training, focusing primarily on aviation. At least two airfields were here on the mesa with barracks and facilities for thousands of sailors and Marines. He couldn't imagine it all being built in such a short time and correctly surmised the base had been used in the First World War as well. The building he was in was certainly new.

The clerk returned and showed Bruce where Bobbie's platoon was located; at least where they were billeted. He explained that they could be almost anywhere on the base in training; there would be someone at the barracks who could give him more information. Bruce thanked the young Marine and told Sam, who drove them there in short order. The barracks were filled with men in green dungarees getting gear ready for a day long hike through the mesquite brush of the mesa. Bruce found a sergeant and gave him Bobbie's name, explaining why he wanted to speak with him.

"Milliken, front and center. Looks like you get lucky today."

Bobbie trotted up, rifle in hand and stopped. "Bruce... what are you doing here?"

"Thanks, Sergeant. I'll need to speak with him for an hour or two."

"Well, sir, he's yours for most of the day. Milliken, when you're done… report to Corporal White in the clerk's office."

"Yes, Sergeant."

Bobbie led Bruce to where his bunk was, stowing his gear and putting his rifle away. The two sat and caught up on the past months; Bruce told him about his assignment with the Daily News.

"Well, if you want a picture with Stan and me, you'll have to be quick. We're shipping out day after tomorrow; don't know where we're heading but the scuttlebutt is we're going to Hawaii before we see action. Today's hike was our last before we board ship."

"Day after tomorrow? I'd better get moving on things. I've got to bring Stan up here…" Bruce was thinking about tonight's tour of Consolidated and breakfast with Susan afterward. "We'll have to talk with your Corporal White and see if I can get you away for a short time tomorrow afternoon for the picture."

They walked to the clerk's office in the adjoining barracks. Corporal White checked the duty roster and saw that Bobbie wasn't assigned to any specific duty the next afternoon; he'd be standing guard that evening. Bruce arranged for the picture to be taken around 1400 hours, two o'clock in the afternoon. The two friends each grabbed a cold Coke and sat down to finish their own conversation.

An hour later, Bruce left Bobbie with Corporal White and found Sam asleep in the car in the shade of a lonely scrub oak. The two headed back to San Diego where Bruce would have to arrange to pick up Stan the next day, borrow a photographer from the Union and, somehow, manage to get a little shuteye himself before the Consolidated plant tour. He gave Sam the article for the Daily News when they reached the hotel.

Susan and Sam picked him up at the Grant just before nine o'clock that evening. Sam would drop them off at Consolidated and meet them again in the morning. Bruce had managed to get an hour long nap after his phone calls. They arrived at the plant a few minutes later; Susan led Bruce to the security office. A Fred Burns met them there to give Bruce the tour and a history of the company. Bruce was surprised to find out this was the location where Lindbergh's plane, "The Spirit of St Louis" was built. The plane had actually been tested up near Camp Elliot. Some of the men who built that plane were working here, building flying boats and the B-24 Liberator bombers. Bruce was introduced to one of the design engineers who had recently been recruited from North American Aviation, up in Los Angeles. North American made the other twin tailed bomber, a smaller two engine plane called the B-25. In conversation, Susan remarked that her father was serving on an aircraft carrier in the Pacific, the *HORNET*. The engineer surprised her by saying that he'd been on the *HORNET* a month or so earlier when it was still in the Atlantic near Norfolk, Virginia. They had been testing a theory about taking off of a carrier in a B-25. He wasn't aware that the *HORNET* had returned to the West Coast. Nothing more was said of that subject as the tour continued, though an idea connecting the conversation with the bombing of Tokyo began to form in Bruce's mind.

Bruce was shown the main production floor, where huge four engine B-24s were assembled, starting with the hollow bodies at one end of the building and continuing on until a completed bomber rolled out the other end. This single factory was able to manufacture ten to twelve bombers each day, along with other planes. It was a huge and impressive sight to Bruce. Susan showed him her own work station and introduced Bruce to several of her coworkers. They crawled up into one of the bomber wings, where Bruce was too large to fit. Ahead was a girl of Susan's size, deftly guiding wires and cables through holes Bruce could never hope to reach.

"We may be small, but these big brutes couldn't fly without us", the girl said as Bruce watched her work. The entire tour filled his mind with words to write. As they finished, Bruce was reminded that security was important. His articles couldn't contain any information that might be important to the enemy. Here was his challenge; to make reading about this place interesting without giving away anything. He knew he'd need Dix Mason's help on this.

His tour ended in an area foreman's office. Bruce thanked all those who had taken time to guide him around the plant, explaining and answering questions. Susan used the phone in the office to call her brother, letting him know they were ready to be picked up. In the time it took to walk the length of Consolidated's assembly building, Sam was waiting outside Gate Two. A hazy eastern sky was beginning to brighten and sounds of reveille could be heard from the Marine Corps Recruit Depot; another day was starting in America's effort to win back the Pacific from Japanese control. Susan had Sam drive them to a small café along the San Diego waterfront. A breakfast of pancakes and eggs with crispy fried potatoes was enjoyed while watching tuna boats leaving the harbor on their quest for a good day's catch.

After enjoying his meal, and Susan's company, Bruce asked Sam to drop him by the hotel. He needed a shower and change of uniform before another busy day. Today's reunion pictures of himself with Stan and Bobbie would provide a good accompaniment for what he planned to write this evening. His article for the Daily News would go out by wire from the San Diego Union offices tomorrow and he would enjoy a weekend of rest, somewhere warm on a beach... with Susan. After all, it was her idea.

The day went off without a hitch. Bruce and Sam picked up Stan from Point Loma, drove to Camp Elliot and met Bobbie. The three friends took time to reunite, walking and talking among themselves. Bobbie and Stan both encouraged Bruce to find James, wherever he was in the Air Corps. Photos were taken of them together and individually. Bruce even posed for one with Bobbie's sergeant, on request.

"Someday, when you're famous, that picture will be worth money", he said, to the accompanying laughter of the group. The photographer promised to send him a copy, writing down his military address. The sergeant was careful to spell out his last name... Basilone.

After dropping Stan back at his gunnery school, Bruce and Sam headed downtown. They stopped at Seven Seas, where Bruce bought some needed beach shoes, swim trunks and other clothes. He also picked up a larger suitcase to hold his uniforms and expanding wardrobe. Saul spotted him and came over.

"Good morning, Bruce. I'd like to thank you for the lunch you sent over your first day here... very thoughtful."

"Hi, Saul. It was really nothing compared to the help you were, and continue to be. You're welcome."

"Say, young man of the world, you wouldn't be interested in doing some fishing this weekend? I've got a boat, a few other friends and the albacore tuna are biting strong just off the coast. Might be fun."

"Thanks, but I've been invited to the beach for some sun and relaxation. I'd love to take you up on the invite, if the paper will let me spend more time here. I'm almost done in San Diego and have to make plans to get to Florida soon."

"You do get around. You mind if I send a list of friends there over to the hotel? I know folks, and have family, from Pensacola down to the sleepy little village of Naples. Any of them would be glad to lend you a hand."

"That would be great; you really are a help. I'm sure I could use some contacts while I'm there. Thanks again."

"You keep writing, Bruce... and don't get in the way of any bullets while you do it."

Bruce thought the last words were a bit strange. What danger could there really be in finding one last member of a basketball team? After Florida, his search would be over and Bennet would probably have him writing obituaries again.

"I've got us a small beach house up near Del Mar. The race track just closed because of the war and we may see a few Marines around. They use the area for some sort of training. My dad's best friend owns the place; sort of an uncle to Sam and me. He said it's no problem using it this weekend. The surfing at the beach is great, too. Things to do with lots of quiet. I've been here with a few of the other girls at work to relax and forget about long hours of crawling inside bombers."

They were sitting in a train car, suitcases above them in a rack. Del Mar was about twenty miles north of San Diego and their train ride would take less than an hour. Bruce was already beginning to unwind; maybe it was the afternoon sun coming through his window. Maybe it was her smiling face and long blonde hair highlighted in the same sunshine.

Hearing their stop announced by the conductor, Bruce and Susan made their way out of the car. Bruce had both suitcases as Susan led them down the street and around a corner. Ahead was a single story stucco house with a white railing around one end of the roof. Pointing to it, Susan said that was her favorite place to sit when the fog hung on the beach.

"I imagine it's like sitting on a cloud sometimes; the fog is so close to the ground you can see over it. I've never flown in a plane but cloud tops must look the same."

"I've only flown once myself, but I know the sky above the clouds is so blue it almost looks like it's not real." Bruce liked the look of the outside; small palms grew alongside prickly little cacti. It was so different than Iowa elms, oaks and green grass. He wondered how close they were to the beach.

"Well, let's get settled in, shall we?" Susan unlocked the front door and walked in; Bruce followed with the luggage. The inside of the front room was decorated in a nautical theme. There were glass globe floats in reds, greens and blues hanging in fish nets alongside a mirror mounted inside an old ship's wheel. Lamps made from brass ship fittings sat on tables fashioned out of driftwood. Bruce was intrigued with the way it all blended so well. He set the suitcases down as Susan showed him the other rooms. A simple kitchen, inside bathroom and two bedrooms completed the floor plan. She had him put one suitcase on each bed and led him out the back door. A walkway made of weather beaten gray planking went over the thinning grass out to an area of short dunes, some twenty or so yards away. Bruce could plainly hear the sound of the surf beyond and the scent of fresh, salty air tickled his nose.

The two strolled along the wood pathway, sun still warm as it slowly dropped toward the horizon in front of them. Gulls flew lazy circles in the sky and a few puffy white clouds made their way inland. Looking to their right and left the two saw no one; not a person was on the beach today. Other than the sound of the waves and the occasional squawking of a gull there was no noise. Bruce felt his body, then his mind, relax further. This was going to be a wonderful weekend.

"There's a market down the street. I'll go buy some food, would you mind gathering some of the driftwood for a fire on the beach? Make sure you get the dry stuff." Susan smiled as she turned to head back on the walkway.

"I know a bit about fires… dry is easier to carry anyway." Bruce said, returning her grin.

Susan returned in just under an hour to find Bruce standing in front of a pile of driftwood as tall as himself. He explained it was so plentiful he didn't know when to stop.

Another hour passed and they were back on the beach, a nice fire blazing. Sparks shot high into the air, mixing with the few stars just beginning to show themselves in the darkening twilight. No fog this evening, just a gently blowing breeze bringing in the scent of the sea. The two enjoyed a meal of fresh fish grilled beside the fire, bread and something new… an avocado. Bruce particularly enjoyed the creamy texture of the rough skinned, pear shaped food. They really couldn't decide if it was a fruit or vegetable; Susan said she'd been eating them since she was a kid and didn't know which it was. After their meal they sat closer on the blanket, his arm around her shoulders, watching the merger of sparks, stars and the lights of a few fishing boats on the water.

"I cannot imagine a more peaceful place… hard to think of the world at war right now", Susan finally said.

"Then don't think of the war", Bruce countered. He leaned in closer and kissed her. She softened and snuggled against him.

"You know, in the fire light your eyes are the same blue as that sky above the clouds I saw."

She smiled, pulled his head close and whispered, "Shhhhh…", as they kissed again, longer and slower this time.

The moon was rising behind them and the fire was glowing embers when Susan suggested they go in the house. The sand still held a bit of the day's warmth but the sea air was getting chilly. They picked up dishes and their blanket and walked away from the surf, now with foam glistening in the moonlight.

As they cleaned the dishes together, Bruce couldn't help but sneak a kiss every so often. He thought her lips were, well, perfect.

"Silly, we'll never get these done if you don't leave me alone", she playfully protested.

Bruce tuned the radio on the shelf to a station playing Glenn Miller's "Moonlight Serenade". He took Susan by the hand and they began to dance, moon beams filling the front room through the large window. Song followed song as the two moved together on the floor, looking into each other's eyes as the music played. Bruce guided her toward a bedroom. Susan hesitated and moved away, just a few inches.

"Bruce, you must know and feel I care for you so much. What you're doing, looking for your friends… I know it must all be so exciting and new. Maybe you've got other girls where you've already been, I don't know…. I hope not. I do know I don't want to be just another one… a girl you'll look up each time you're in San

Diego or something… I just can't. I need more time to think, to get to know you. Do you understand what I'm trying to say?"

"I think so. Truth is, and this will sound crazy I suppose. I've never been with a girl… never really even kissed one like I kissed you tonight. I don't know… I guess I figured it was just the next step. I do know I'm crazy about you… have been since I saw you in your work clothes the first time. Let's get some sleep, maybe things will be clearer in the morning."

Susan leaned in and kissed him again, saying, "I hoped you'd understand; now I could use one more kiss before I say good night."

They danced to more music, finally heading to their rooms as "Blue Birds over the White Cliffs of Dover" was ending. Bruce lay in bed for an hour, wide awake. His mind, again, was going a hundred miles an hour. He rose, quietly, and went into the living room. Looking in some drawers he found a pencil and a pad of writing paper. He began writing his article on Bobbie, Stan and their reunion.

The rising sun cast shadows in the living room when Susan found Bruce sleeping, his head resting on the table. Sheets of handwritten copy lay in a stack. She slipped into the kitchen and started some coffee. Returning to where he was still sleeping, she began reading his writing. Bruce stirred and opened his eyes to find Susan sitting on a couch, legs drawn up under her, focusing on what he'd written.

"Good morning", he said sleepily as he sat up, stretching and grimacing at the stiffness.

"Oh, hi… good morning. This is really good, Bruce. I finished the one about your friends and you three getting together. Now I'm reading about my job and how what we do is helping win the war. You capture things people feel, not just through the words they say, but how they say them."

"Thanks, Susan. Coming from you that means even more to me. If that's really coffee I smell, I'll grab a cup and be right back."

"Cream and sugar are on the counter. Would you mind bringing in the pot, I'd like a refill, too."

"Coming right up, Miss. Service with a smile", he said as he topped off her cup.

They sat together on the couch and chatted, telling each other of their own childhoods and dreams for the future. Bruce had never opened up like this with anyone else; he felt so at ease with Susan. She had a genuine laugh that was contagious and soon they were both wiping their eyes from giggling so much.

After a while, Susan announced it was time for breakfast, or lunch, or whatever meal was appropriate for whatever time it was. The clock in the kitchen showed nearly noon; lunch it would be. Sandwiches soon appeared and were wrapped up and stowed in the picnic basket, followed by pickles, apples and accompanied by a cooler filled with cold bottles of beer. Both soon were changed into swim suits and heading down the walkway to the dunes.

The afternoon was spent splashing in the surf and drying on the beach, highlighted by chasing each other around and kisses when one was caught. During one of his pursuits of Susan along the sand, Bruce stopped short and stared out to sea. There on the horizon were several ships; four smaller ones that looked like they meant business. They were sleek, low in the water and he could see the gun barrels on them; they were destroyers. The two others were much larger and reminded him of the *Chateau Thierry* that he had sailed on to Ireland. Susan came up behind him and put her arms around his neck.

"What is it", she asked him.

"I think, I feel like…. I know it's Bobbie. He's on one of those transports, heading out."

"Oh, Bruce."

Chapter 5
May 1942

"Bruce, while you're here, take a look at this. It just came in on the wire; my editors have already stopped the evening edition to do a special. How'd you like to help us on this?" Dave Rupert, Chief Editor of the San Diego Union, handed Bruce the teletype sheet.

"Coral Sea? That's down near New Zealand, isn't it? I remember that from school geography. Fifteen Jap ships sunk... doesn't list our losses. That would be great if it's true. Would it be possible to sink so many of theirs with none of our own lost? Sure doesn't sound like the Japs that kicked our butts all over Borneo and the Philippines."

"That's what I'm thinking. You know a guy at Navy Public Relations here, right? Call... see if you can get anything else from him, would you? Then hop down to the copy room and let my writers know what you find out. You might have to cancel those train tickets, or postpone your leaving a few days, huh?"

"I really don't think I can do that, Mr Rupert. I've got to get to Naples, Florida as soon as I can. My friend is supposed to be transferred out of there next week. I've been here in San Diego as long as... well, I need to go. I'll call Commander Mason and see what he'll tell me. But I've got a train to catch in two hours, sorry."

"Well, you might be leaving a great story behind… I understand. Say hi to that deskbound Bennett when you see him, OK?"

"Will do. I'll use the phone in the copy room to call Mason."

Susan met him at the station. After their goodbyes the night before, Bruce was a little surprised. They had spent the evening talking about their future together; Susan had declined his proposal of marriage and told him she'd reconsider when, and if, he showed up again. Bruce realized he'd probably overstepped again. Obviously, all the Hollywood movies didn't get that part right. Boy meets girl, boy has to leave, and they get engaged or…

"Bruce, I want you to know. Last night I didn't mean… well, I want you to know that I do love you. Come back to me and we'll do whatever you want to do. It's mostly that I worry about my dad…"

He hugged her tightly, wanting to swing her around in his own joy yet sensitive to her emotions.

"Susan, honey. I'll be back. The war is just getting started, read this afternoon's paper. We surprised the Japs in the Coral Sea. That's really about all I know, except that your dad's alright. The *HORNET* wasn't involved in the battle, though the Navy's not saying much else. I'm going to New York after Florida; I've got to convince Bennett to send me back here, somehow. I'll do it, too."

The overhead loudspeaker announced the imminent departure of his train to Los Angeles. From there he'd travel to St Louis, Cincinnati, Atlanta and down to Tampa where he'd catch the line to Naples. It was a four day journey with several train changes. He would have liked to take time to visit the camp at Manzanar, but it couldn't happen this trip. He might be able to use that story as part of the reason to return to California, however. Bennett had told him to "scoot back here to New York the minute you're done in Florida".

"That's my call, Susan. I have to go… tell Sam thanks from me and I look forward to having him drive me around next time. I'll write you and phone you whenever I can. I love you." One more lingering and passionate kiss and they were apart.

"I love you, too. Come back to me."

"That's a promise."

#

Being on the train gave Bruce time to think; the past week had been a whirlwind of events and news. The convoy he'd seen from the beach didn't include just Bobbie Milliken; Stan Larson was aboard one of the destroyers escorting the transports. Bruce had found out when he tried to contact his friend a few days ago. The news increased a sense of urgency in finding Jim Hartke in Florida before he, too, was sent somewhere overseas. He tried to relax as the train continued along the coast toward Los Angeles. A smile crossed his face as Del Mar passed by; this express didn't stop there. He remembered it all and the thought of Susan made it hard to concentrate on his plans for the next weeks.

Bruce went up to the second level of the dining car to have a cup of coffee and to watch the sun begin setting. Black coffee, with no sugar, was becoming a standard fare now that rationing had begun. He wondered what New York would be like with gasoline added to the list of harder to find items back east. A copy of the morning LA Times was on the next table; he reached over and picked it up. The sun had all but disappeared behind the low clouds moving in from the Pacific. Bruce read the earliest accounts of the Navy's fight in the Coral Sea. What he had learned from his friend, Dixon Mason, was quite different than the banner headlines of a tremendous American victory. "FIFTEEN JAP SHIPS SUNK" ran in large black type across the front; Bruce knew it wasn't even close to that. Two of our aircraft carriers had surprised a Japanese force intent on invading islands north of New Zealand. The Americans did sink a few of the Axis ships around Tulagi in the Solomon Islands to start the battle. Then Japanese aircraft carriers arrived in the area and each side lost a carrier, sunk by enemy planes. It was more a draw than an outright Allied victory, but it did turn back the invasion force headed to New Guinea.

Bruce spent a half hour perusing the Times, reading local news. There was a small article about more Japanese American citizens being sent east, away from the coast, to camps like Manzanar. Another was a commentary on the Navy's decision to allow blacks to enlist and serve alongside whites on fighting ships. Bruce made a mental note to ask Mason about that the next time they met. A change of trains at Los Angeles put him aboard the *Super Chief*, an express train that whisked across the west from southern California to Chicago, though he changed lines in St Louis. Bruce noticed one major difference on this trip, compared to his journey from Des Moines to San Diego the previous month. Nearly everyone on the train was in uniform; it seemed as though the entire country was in the military, or some organization that required one. He took to wearing his own, not wanting to stand out in the crowd.

#

Early May in southwest Florida is warm and the summer humidity is just beginning to set in. Bruce welcomed the scent of the Gulf, though it was a bit different than the Pacific in San Diego. He settled in his room at a small hotel on the beach and placed a call to Bennett in New York, letting his boss know he'd arrived.

"Really like what you wrote on San Diego, Bruce. Your story on the aircraft plant there paints a great picture of determination to win the war. Keep 'em coming. How long do you plan on being in Naples?"

"Just long enough to find Jimmy. I'll head to the base tomorrow, first thing. Right now I need a walk, not just up and down the aisles on a train. I'll send you a short story about the trip here. I've seen how things are changing across the country; uniforms everywhere in train stations of a half dozen cities. I did catch up on sleep. Once I'm done here, I'll be up to New York as soon as I can."

"Hey, bring me a few fresh oranges, will you? I spent time in Florida covering the Yankees' spring training in St Pete a few years ago and I love their oranges…"

"Sure… will do. I'll call again before I head back."

Bruce changed into the shorts and loose shirt Saul had suggested and headed to the beach. After an hour in the sun and sand, he felt refreshed… and hungry. His hotel didn't have dining but he was pointed to a small diner around the corner. He enjoyed fresh fish called black grouper, and the best fruit he'd ever eaten. When he returned to his room, Bruce knew he'd gotten a bit too much sun his first day in south Florida. Obviously he'd have to be more careful than in San Diego. He got to work and soon the article on his trip east was ready to send to The Daily News.

Next morning, before he headed to the small Army airfield, he asked the hotel desk to mail his packet to New York. The closest news wire service was in Fort Myers and he didn't have the time to go up there today. Bruce took a taxi through town out to the airfield, where the guards at the gate directed him, as usual, to the admin building. By now, Bruce could have guessed just where it would be. The clerk, a corporal, looked up Jimmy's billet and showed Bruce the way to the barracks on the base map. It was a short walk, some two hundred yards, and he enjoyed a breeze on what was going to be another humid day. He wished for shorts and light shirt over the long trousers with shirt and tie he was wearing. A few hesitant salutes and wondering looks came his way along the walk. War Correspondents, and their uniforms, were still too new to be taken for granted. Bruce walked into the barracks, a brand new structure that still smelled like fresh cut pine. He approached the first airman he found and asked about Jimmy Hartke.

"Sure, I know Jimmy… there's only a couple dozen of us here right now. He's overhauling one of the PT-19's we just got from Buckingham Field, up at Fort Myers. Jimmy's our lead mechanic for the planes… Go back out, take a right and you'll see a couple of big tents; the one on the left is the machine shop."

"Thanks", Bruce said as he turned to go. He found the tents and entered the one on the left. Inside he saw two men working under the front of a low winged, single engine plane.

"Jimmy?"

"Yeah, be with you in a second."

Bruce stood and watched the two work together, low mumbling voices cursing and encouraging some obscure engine part to fit in its place. Another minute or so and the job was finished by a triumphant "about time" by one of the two mechanics. Bruce smiled as they both crawled out from under the plane.

"Bruce Hollins, son of a gun... My folks wrote and told me you were coming down here."

Jimmy was wiping his hands on a towel as he spoke. He reached out a rather oil stained one and Bruce grabbed it. The smiles on both of them matched.

"Well, you know how it goes... saved the best for last, I guess. What are you doing under the hood of a plane, I thought you were a gunner for the Air Corps?"

"Yeah, well, somebody's got to do the maintenance on these birds. Gunnery training is up at Buckingham... here we're getting this place ready for pilot training, but no one seems to be in a big hurry right now. I've heard the first big bunch of trainees will be here in a couple of months. Shoot, they just got our barracks built two weeks ago. I finished my gunnery training but haven't been assigned to a squadron yet; working on engines fills the time and you know how much I love to do it. I still can't figure how the Air Corps decided to make me a gunner... I'd be a better Flight Engineer or simple mechanic."

"I'm sure your folks told you what I'm doing here... writing you up in the newspapers and all that?"

"They sent me a clipping of your article on Fred. So he's really all the way over in England?"

"Well, Ireland for right now... at least that's where I left him. I've been in San Diego the past month, looking up Stan and Bobbie.

They're both on ships heading out in the Pacific right now. And now I'm in sunny, hot Florida… this is my last stop. When I'm done here, it's back to New York; I'll find out what my editor wants me to write next when I get there. But for now it's about you and what you do… you know, winning the war all by yourself."

"Put me in a B-17 as a waist gunner and watch out Luftwaffe. In a way they got one thing right; it seems I can shoot ok. I aced gunnery training and that's not an easy thing to do. How long you got with me down here? We could go into town and have some fun… not much in Naples, too small. Fort Myers isn't that far, I've got my jalopy and it loves the high octane aviation gas… no rationing of that." Jimmy gave him a wink when he finished.

"That sounds great, when can you meet me? I'm at a small hotel, just off the pier in Naples."

"How about five o'clock this afternoon?"

"You'll be able to clear that with your sergeant, I suppose?"

"Hell, Bruce, I am the sergeant… been in the Air Corps since December. The stripes came when I finished Gunnery School last month. See you at the hotel, write down the name on this paper."

Bruce wrote the information and handed the paper back to Jimmy. A very hearty handshake and the two went their ways. Bruce walked back to the admin building where he had the clerk call into town for a cab. While waiting, Bruce interviewed him about the airfield. The corporal was only too willing to talk; he'd read several of the articles Bruce had written and was excited that one of the 'basketball boys' was right here at the airfield.

The cabbie dropped Bruce at the hotel. He entered the lobby and asked the desk clerk to put a call through to Susan West in San Diego. He went out on the hotel's back lanai overlooking the pier and the Gulf. The phone on the table rang once before he picked up. An operator said, "I have a Susan West on the phone, sir."

"Susan? Gosh it's good to hear your voice."

"Hi, Bruce. I just now got your letter posted in Albuquerque. Where are you calling from?"

"Naples, Florida... I arrived yesterday evening and went to the airfield this morning to find Jimmy. He and I are going to meet up tonight, again, after he's off duty. I wanted to call, say I miss you and find out how you and Sam are doing?"

"Oh... everything's fine here. It's only been a week, you know. My traveling man, that's what I think I'll call you. One end of the country to the other... how long will you be in Florida?"

"A few days, I suppose. After I visit with Jimmy I think I'll look up a friend of Saul's... the owner of Seven Seas. I hope to get a bit of fishing in, to relax, before I head back to New York."

The two chatted a few more minutes before hanging up. Bruce knew the call was expensive, long distance was more a luxury, but he didn't have much to spend his money on. Most everything else was on his account with the newspaper. He went to his room and found the list of friends and family Saul had given him. Then he rang the desk clerk and asked for a local line.

Bruce finished his phone calls in time to take a refreshing shower, change into civilian clothes and write letters to his parents and Susan. He posted them at the front desk and ordered a glass of iced tea with lemon. Sitting on the front veranda of the hotel, enjoying the cool shade and the salty scent in the air, Bruce heard a low rumbling noise down the street. It grew louder, not the abusive sound of a car simply in need of a muffler. This was a smoother, synchronized pounding in the chest, the heartbeat of a roadster well maintained. He stood, looking out in anticipation as Jimmy pulled up in a beautiful bright blue '32 Ford hotrod. Bruce laughed, shaking his head slowly as his friend parked and bounded up the sidewalk to the veranda.

"Hey, buddy, ready to go? The gas tank's full and I'm empty... something to eat and a couple of beers to wash it down sound good to you?"

They headed up the two lane highway toward Fort Myers, past houses on the beach side and wild looking swamps to the east. In the late afternoon Bruce watched flocks of big birds, most white and some a dull pink, settling into the swamps. Strange bushes grew out of the water, standing on roots that made them look like they could walk. Bruce pointed to one and looked at Jimmy.

"Mangroves… that's what they're called. They grow so thick you can't get in there. Snakes and alligators do, though."

Jimmy drove to a club he frequented in his off time. They both ordered a beer and a burger. Finding a quiet corner table wasn't easy, the jukebox was busy belting out tunes by Glenn Miller and Artie Shaw. Jimmy said he really liked Cab Calloway's music but it wasn't so popular this far south. Bruce took out his small notebook and a pencil and wrote short, simple notes as he listened to what had been going on in his friend's life over the past year.

Following graduation, Jimmy had worked hard helping Fred's father build hog sheds on his farm. He had gotten a contract with Hormel meats up in Minnesota to raise hundreds of the animals. Jimmy had built the ventilation system for the sheds. He'd thought about college, even applied and was accepted to the state university in Ames, but changed his mind. With the threat of war coming closer, he'd signed on with the Air Corps; he wanted to be a mechanic, but somehow had been assigned to Gunnery School after his boot camp in Texas. Despite his recognized ability with aircraft machine guns, he was now spending his time overhauling and doing maintenance on the training planes from Buckingham Field. He knew that soon he'd be heading to Europe, or the Pacific. The Air Corps was getting bigger fast and the need for qualified gunners would grow as well.

Jimmy was aware that his time here in Naples, a slower paced quiet spot, would come to an end soon. Rumors were that the gunners and mechanics would be on transports over to England as the new Eighth Air Force was building up strength to begin taking to the skies over Europe. His personal desire was to be assigned to fly in one of the big bombers rather than be stuck on a ship; Jimmy did not share Bruce's love of the water. He was working, even now, on trying to become a flight engineer; a gunner who also knew the mechanics of the big planes.

Bruce closed his notebook, satisfied he had enough personal information on his friend to write the article. Now he, too, could relax more; his work done for the day. He held up his glass of beer and toasted the success of the basketball team in their new endeavors. He felt a twinge of envy at the thought of his four team mates scattered around the globe while he would be stuck in New York pounding out words about the exploits of others.

The rest of their evening was spent drinking beer, shooting pool and talking with some of the local girls. Jimmy announced the end of the revelry; he had an early start next morning and needed to get back to the base. Bruce was ready to go as well; it had been a long day and he still had to start writing while ideas were fresh in his mind. It was a habit he knew was important.

As Jimmy drove back down to Naples the two made plans to see each other again in a few days. Bruce hopped out of the roadster at the hotel and watched his friend drive away, the powerful sound of the engine receding in the distance. It was nearly ten o'clock as he walked into the small lobby and the desk clerk motioned to him. He had a message from a G Gordon Bennett from New York. Bruce took the envelope and went to his room, thanking the clerk as he turned to go. Taking a slip of paper out of the envelope he began to read Bennett's message.

"When you're done in Naples, take an express up to New York. I've arranged for you to fly to England on an Army Air Corps bomber as press observer. The Navy has helped in getting your clearance for the flight. At this time, no one else has been told they can go. Don't forget the oranges."

Bruce chuckled as he put the note on the table in his room. Opening the window to let in the fresh salty gulf air, he pulled out his typewriter, rolled a sheet of paper in it and began to type. It was nearly three o'clock when he finished and went to bed.

The sun was shining through the window when Bruce awoke. Another hot and humid day was beginning. He showered, shaved and dressed to the scents of the flowers and the sounds of a gentle breeze in the palms. He thought of Susan and San Diego; how similar the sights and smells yet the difference in the humidity and temperature was noticeable. What he knew without a doubt was his preference of either over the cold of Iowa or New York.

He decided to take a walk along the beach first thing; he wasn't all that hungry and wanted to stretch his legs before the heat set in. The short block to the pier was shady and the cool air felt good on his skin. He thought about being a bit more careful with how much sun he got today. From the stairs at the pier that led to the beach, Bruce saw some young boys fishing; the lazy waves lapping at their feet in a slow, steady rhythm. One's pole bent and he began to run up the beach, along the surf line, laughing and struggling to land the fish. A bright silver flash came out of the water and landed in the sand. The boy jumped on it triumphantly, the others dashing behind to admire his catch. Bruce walked over, looking down at the tanned bodies of the boys and their treasure; a beautiful twelve inch long silver disk with a forked tail and yellow belly. The boy holding the fish smiled at Bruce and said the word, "Pompano".

Bruce was hooked as surely as the fish had been. He asked the boys if he could join them; they agreed on a price of one chocolate bar each for their help. Two of them started digging in the sand at the surf's edge frantically with their hands; one squealed with delight as he lifted out what looked like a rock or shell, about one inch long. He ran to Bruce and told him it was the bait he'd be using; it was called a sand flea. Bruce reached for it and the flea dropped to the sand. Faster than he thought possible, the thing had burrowed down, out of view. The disappointment on Bruce's face was not mirrored by the youth; he simply bent down and dug it back up. The boy was sure to put it on Bruce's hook himself and showed him how to drop the line a few feet ahead of where the waves broke. Bruce took his shoes off and waded in to his ankles, casting the bait out in front. In an instant, the line went taut and a fish began swimming hard up the beach; Bruce had to run to keep up with it or his line would surely break. He found himself laughing, just as the boy had been earlier.

The next hour was spent digging for sand fleas and catching the remarkably strong fish. Bruce was happy to pay the boys and added a bonus for ice cream all around. They responded by giving him enough of the "pomps" for a hearty meal, prepared at the restaurant across the street from his hotel. Lunch that day was fresh Pompano with a spicy, sweet sauce of mango and pineapple. He promised the cook it would receive a great review in his next newspaper article.

Bruce returned to his room at the hotel after the meal; a note was on the door. He unfolded it and found a phone number and name... Phil Steiner. He'd never heard the name before and the number was a local one. He returned to the lobby and had the clerk make the call, transferring it to the back lanai phone. Picking it up when it rang, Bruce found it was a cousin of Saul, his friend and tailor in San Diego.

"You're pretty easy to find, Bruce. I only had to call the newspaper in Fort Myers and they knew right where you're staying. I got a letter from my cousin; he mentioned you might like to do a bit of fishing? A couple friends and I are making a run to Key West day after tomorrow... wondering if you'd like to come along. Sure to be a good time and might be the last trip we make; fuel is getting harder to find with the rationing beginning to kick in and all."

"I'd love to tag along, Phil. I've got to rearrange a few things here, but that shouldn't be a problem at all. Where should I meet you and what time? Any suggestions on what I should be bringing along, too?"

"Tell you what, Bruce. Let me take care of the details and packing. Why don't we just pick you up early... say 5:00 am. We'll catch the tides right to get out of the harbor here in Naples and be on our way. I think we'll stay at the Keys for maybe three or four days of fishing… be back in a week, if that works. Saul even told me where to shop for your clothes and sent your size; it's the way he does these things."

"Really? I'm just beginning to get an idea of how surprising he can be. I'll be ready early. Phil, really, thanks for the call and the invite. I'm excited to get more fishing in down here. I just spent most of the morning catching pompano with a bunch of the local kids here on the beach."

"Fun, aren't they? I mean, both the kids and the fish; you probably were with a couple of my own nephews. They love to fish by the pier and pomps are good eating. I hope we can introduce you to some of the bigger fish we have… and a few new friends for you as well. See you when we pick you up."

He hung up the phone and had the desk clerk dial the airfield. Bruce was asked to wait a few minutes and poured himself a glass of iced tea. The phone soon rang and he was talking to the admin clerk at the base. Asking to speak with Sergeant Hartke, he was informed that Jimmy was up at Buckingham Field in Fort Myers and wouldn't be back to Naples for a few days. Bruce left a message for his friend to read on his return, explaining his sudden trip to Key West and saying he would call in a week. Hanging up, Bruce got the desk clerk again and dictated a short telegram to be sent to the Daily News that he planned on returning in ten days or two weeks. He then went to his room to finish the article on Jimmy.

#

Bruce was up early and ate a small breakfast with a single cup of coffee. He'd learned from the Atlantic crossing not to have too much in his stomach when going to sea. Right at five o'clock a car honked; Bruce went out and saw a new Cadillac convertible with three guys in it. He walked to the driver's door and met Phil Steiner.

"Good morning, Bruce. You ready for some time on the Gulf and fishing?", Phil said with a large smile.

"I sure am. I spent most of yesterday talking with some guys at the local bait shop and they said I'm in for some experience."

"We sure hope so. A friend of mine is going to join us in Key West, we'll actually be staying at his place. He loves to fish, have a good time and actually writes a little as well. I think you two will hit it off. Let's get you in the back with Steve... Steve Boss. The guy up front is Ed White. Steve, Ed... this is Bruce Hollins. He writes for a New York paper and is fast becoming quite a name."

Bruce shook hands with the other two and climbed in the back seat. Phil drove through the sleepy streets of Naples down to a canal connecting with the harbor. There they parked the car in a garage and unloaded suitcases out of the trunk. Phil explained that most of their gear was already on board; these were just their clothes for the week. The four walked across the street to a boat dock; below, in the early morning light, Bruce saw a beautiful white hulled boat with dark wood decking. It was over 40 feet long and had the most graceful look Bruce had ever seen on a boat. Phil explained that each would have a small stateroom; the galley was below deck along with the berthing area for the three crewmen.

The four fishermen climbed aboard and settled into their rooms. Bruce's had a small table and chair beside his bunk, which tilted up to reveal a clothes storage area beneath. He got busy unpacking the clothes Saul had told Phil to pick up; boat shoes, fishing shirts and pants, casual dining and even formal evening wear. The young man was completely astounded that his friend in San Diego would go to such extremes to outfit him on a simple fishing trip... or would it be more than just fishing? Twenty minutes later, Phil stuck his head in the stateroom.

"We're getting started; got all your gear stowed? Fresh coffee is on deck aft... it's where I like to sit and have a cup while we head out of the harbor."

"Thanks... I'm just trying to take all this in. I cannot believe I'm on this boat, heading to Key West with new friends I just met."

"Well, Bruce; sometimes things just happen. You're a friend of Saul, he's my cousin, we both like fishing and he asked me to do him a favor. Besides, I've read a few of your articles and I like what you write. I have a feeling that before this war's over, you'll see lots of places and have days far more exciting than this one. Wait and see..."

The boat got underway a few minutes after the four were seated with steaming mugs of coffee in their hands. One of the crew had handled the mooring lines while another piloted the boat, guiding it expertly through the harbor area, past several large homes, sprawling along the water, with boats like this one tied up at docks. As they cleared the final breakwater, the swells of the Gulf began to be felt and the boat lifted and dipped at a smooth, gentle pace. The pilot opened the throttle and the boat seemed to jump ahead; Bruce felt and heard the power of the engines beneath his feet. Phil said they would be in Key West, some hundred miles to the south, in about four hours. There Bruce would have lunch with Phil's friend before they all set out for their first afternoon of fishing.

Bruce and Phil spent the next hour in conversation; Phil talking and Bruce listening intently. He learned that his new friend had immigrated to America in 1932, right after Hitler had come to power in Germany. Phil's parents had the foresight to leave before the Nazi's persecution of the Jews became oppressive. Phil told Bruce he still suffered a deep sadness at his own inability to convince relatives to leave as life grew even harder in Europe. He, along with others who had escaped, were still working on getting Jews out from the horrors. His own story was one of opportunity and hard work. He had arrived, along with other family members, in New York and had connected with relatives living in California and Florida. Saul had been a tremendous help, sending for many to come and work with him in San Diego. Other cousins and uncles in Tampa and Fort Myers had also pitched in; Phil had come down to work in the construction industry and became very successful. A great part was due to the government's New Deal; Phil and his relatives had landed several large projects in the middle 1930's. They worked on everything from dams and irrigation to military bases for the Air Corps and Navy.

With the boat skimming over the emerald waters of the Gulf, Bruce was grateful for the cool air caused by their speed. Very little actual wind was blowing and the sun was scorching hot. Numerous islands of bright green were visible to the east as the boat cruised along. Phil said they were part of what was called The Ten Thousand Islands; an area south of Naples that curved around the southern end of Florida. He told Bruce of marvelous fishing and beaches that were nearly covered in the most beautiful sea shells. It seemed almost mystical to Bruce; his Midwest farm country background was awed at all the tropical beauty.

The hours of travel along the surface of the calm, blue green water lulled Bruce into a continuous sleepy haze. He napped in the shade on the after deck, rising every so often to get a glass of iced tea or water. He noted that Phil, Ed and Steve were enjoying stronger drink, in particular different concoctions consisting of liberal doses of rum. Soon the three were attempting what Bruce took to be renditions of various sea chanties on the order of "Blow the Man Down" and other favorites. Bruce smiled as he drifted into another light snooze. Ed gently shook him awake a bit later, pointing to one side of the boat as Bruce awoke. Getting up to look, he noticed a pair of large sea turtles heading toward a small island on that side. Phil explained that May begins the turtle nesting season in the Gulf and that they were quite tasty but his habit of killing them had stopped when the war began.

"There's enough of that going on around the world to satisfy anyone… I'll do no more than fish from now on."

Steve pointed ahead to a row of several islands that lay close together. Straining his eyes, Bruce could just make out what looked like a bridge connecting them. Ed told him he was right; the railroad connected Key West with mainland Florida. The track was like a necklace of pearls stretching a hundred miles south, each key anchoring sections of the line.   They began to see other fishing boats as the islands drew nearer. Bruce was told of the variety of fish around; snappers and grouper that liked the reefs and ship wrecks, the tuna and dorado that swam in the cooler Atlantic waters on the far side of the keys. Those were to be their prey this trip; black fin tuna with their vicious fight for a smaller fish, and the dorado, a beautiful blue, green and gold lightning bolt in the water that tasted just short of heaven. At least that's how Steve described them.

Key West rose up out of the water, buildings in white and pastel colors along the gulf front. A Navy fighter swooped down low from astern and flew past, the pilot playfully waving at them as he blazed by. The plane headed for the island just north of their destination.

"There's a Naval Air Station on Boca Chica, that key there." Ed pointed for Bruce to follow. He could see a small swarm of planes circling the island. A Navy destroyer came into view, also heading toward Key West. Obviously the military had a good presence in the area. Bruce also noted a large, fat blimp far out to sea, slowly making its way in the sky.

"There were two freighters sunk just last week not far from here by a German submarine. Several of the dead crewmen washed up on the beaches... it caused quite a stir for the locals to find they were on the edge of the shooting war." Phil went on to say that the Navy had increased patrols and, because of a shortage of long range planes like the PBY Catalina, blimps had been brought down to look further out into the Gulf. "Key West is only ninety miles from Cuba, Bruce, and the Germans have been having their own way in the Carribbean so far. We need to start convoying our merchant ships, like the British do in the North Atlantic. A single ship hasn't a chance against a Nazi U-boat."

"You know quite a lot about the situation down here, Phil. Is that from your work contracting with the Navy and Air Corps? I don't just write for a New York paper myself; I've been through training as a Navy War Correspondent, too."

"You don't say, Bruce. I have contacts inside Public Affairs and get to hear a bit about what's going on. My interest is also on the personal side; I have a son, about your age, that's in a Navy Construction Battalion training in California. He joined up a couple months ago when a call went out looking for guys with experience in operating heavy equipment like bulldozers. He thinks his unit will be working with the Navy and Marines out in the Pacific, building airfields and dock facilities. It's right up his alley; he's been doing it for me for the past three years. I'd love to do it too, except I'm a bit too old and I have the business to run here."

"I have two buddies out in the Pacific; I watched as they left San Diego a few weeks ago. I imagine they'll all be busy against the Japs; one's on a destroyer and the other is a Marine."

"Those are the two I read about... weren't you at the same high school? Wait, I remember... you three played basketball together, right?"

"Yeah, seems like a while ago now. Just last year we won the state title; only had the five of us on the team. We all graduated, the other four went into the service and I'm a writer. I had a seizure in a car accident just before school ended and I can't be in the military now. The other guy is an Air Corps mechanic and gunner in Fort Myers and Naples. He's why I'm down here."

"So your paper is having you find them and write their stories? I think that's a great idea; now that you've found them, what's next? You going to follow them around as this war gets going?"

"I don't really know. I'm supposed to head back up to New York when our trip here is over. My editor has a spot for me on a bomber flying across the Atlantic to England... I suppose I'll be able to find my buddy in the Army there. He was the first I wrote about; he's in the 34th Infantry Division."

"Well, I've an idea you won't stop in England. Americans need to know what's going on everywhere. I think your editor might get an idea to keep you going... you know, keep trailing your buddies and writing about what they're doing."

"That would be alright by me... I enjoy the travel and I've gotten to meet so many great people, like you and Saul. I especially want to get back to San Diego to thank him and see a girl."

"Girl, eh? Sounds a bit serious..."

The ship's pilot called for Phil; they were inside the breakwater and heading for a dock ahead. A car was pulled up and a man in a white jacket and trousers was waving to them. Bruce looked at the man intently, sure that he'd seen him somewhere before. Ed and Steve joined Bruce and Phil and the four walked up the plank from the boat to the dock. As some hand shaking and shoulder slapping started with the others, Phil introduced Bruce to his friend.

"Bruce Hollins, I'd like you to meet a good friend... Ernest Hemingway."

"Aaahhh, I don't know what to say..." Bruce stammered.

"How about 'Hello', it's the usual thing when you're being introduced.", said Hemingway. The other three laughed loud and long; the look on Bruce's face was priceless.

"H-h-hello....", he managed. "I never, really, in my wildest dreams..."

"Hey, I'm just a guy that likes to write; like Phil told me you do. I've never really worked for a newspaper... you'll have to tell me about it. Maybe if the fishing's slow."

The five piled into the car and went to a house the writer used to live in; now it was available for him, or friends, anytime... he actually lived in Cuba and just got in from China. He and his wife had been there for the past year; Ernest enjoyed spring and early summer in Key West and his farm outside of Havana. Fishing was what brought him to the islands.

"Phil, I'll have to stowaway on your boat this trip. I can't bring the *Pilar* into American waters since I had her outfitted in Cuba for fighting submarines, you know."

"That's fine... Ed and Steve can bunk together and you'll get their room."

"I'd be happy to share with someone if that works, too.", said Bruce.

Steve piped in, "Kid, you have no idea what you're talking about. The two of us snore so loud you'd never sleep. We'll be OK; won't be the first time."

The rest of the day and a good part of the night was spent talking.... when they weren't drinking. Bruce was the first to go... he lasted until midnight and two of the others laid him on a bed in a back room. A couple of Hemingway's cats curled up next to him and fell asleep as well.

Bruce woke up with the sun shining in the window. His head felt like it had been tumbled in a cement mixer. He found the kitchen and saw the others already gobbling down eggs, bacon and potatoes. Fighting the urge to throw up, he managed to hang on to a cup of coffee as he sat down.

"Hair of the dog?", piped Steve as he hovered a rum bottle over the cup.

"No... no thanks.", said Bruce.

The others erupted in laughter, then quieted down when they saw the grimace on Bruce's face.

"You'll have to learn to last a bit longer, if you want to be a writer. You missed whole chapters' worth of stories, Bruce." Hemingway was smiling, his eyes twinkling. "We'll be leaving shortly. How about you get some chow on the boat later?"

"That is the best idea I've heard this morning", mumbled Bruce.

#

The time flew by. Fishing was fun and the catch plentiful. Bruce's arms actually ached from fighting big fish like the marlin he landed the third day. It took him more than an hour to get the brute up to the boat; weighing more than a hundred pounds, the fish was nearly nine feet long with its rapier like front. He was looking forward to mailing the picture of his fish, with Hemingway alongside him, to his folks. He'd be sure to have them show it to his high school teacher, Mr Hopkins. He had to get a copy for Bennett, too.

During the days of fishing, Bruce spent as much time as he could with Hemingway, talking about their craft. He learned that his 1940 Quiet Deluxe typewriter was, in fact, the author's favorite model; that made both of them laugh. Bruce spoke of his being a War Correspondent; that he appreciated Hemingway's own writing about the Spanish Civil War and the importance of it. 'Papa' Hemingway was touched; he told Bruce he might just have to get into the current fracas as well.

When Phil deposited Bruce back at the hotel in Naples, he had material to write about for what he thought would be a lifetime. He was quickly brought back to earth, however, when the desk clerk handed him a note along with his room key. It was from Jimmy, dated a few days before. By now his friend had shipped out, heading to a transport up in Virginia bound for England and the Eighth Air Force. Bruce wasted no time in having the clerk help him book travel to New York; from a local out of Naples, through Tampa to Jacksonville to catch the *Champion*, which ran from Miami to New York. He'd be in his boss's office in three days.

Chapter 6
June 1942

The railroad trip to New York had provided Bruce time to write of his Florida exploits and to catch up on personal letters as well. At a stop outside Baltimore he resembled a postman as he carried all his envelopes and packages to the station's postal window. After mailing the pile of correspondence he placed a call to San Diego and spoke with Susan before she had to begin her overnight shift at Consolidated. She mentioned hearing from her father and, indeed, the *HORNET* was the ship that had launched the Doolittle Raid on Tokyo back in the spring. The news was already on the Associated Press newswire across the nation; just in time for the announcement of another victory in the Pacific as U S Naval forces had turned back a Japanese invasion of Midway Island, which would have posed a serious threat to Hawaii. Bruce scanned newspapers he bought, but didn't read anything about Stan's ship, the *LAFFEY* or Bobbie's Marine unit.

Bruce checked into a downtown New York hotel since his own apartment was being used by a co-worker. He reported to G Gordon Bennett the next morning at the offices of the Daily News. His boss was genuinely excited to hear of his meeting with Ernest Hemingway and appreciated the picture Bruce brought him of his fish and the author.

"Welcome back, Bruce. You'll be interested in opening your fan mail, I'm sure... there's about a dozen big postal sacks of it in the storeroom at the end of the hall… and I am NOT kidding! Oh, I might as well tell you this bit of news right up front. I've been contacted by a couple of friends of yours… Saul and Phil Steiner. Apparently they believe your stories are worth investing in. They both called to tell me they are bankrolling you."

"Come again, Mr Bennett? Bankrolling me for what?" Bruce was all attention at the moment.

"They want to cover any costs, beyond your salary, for you to follow up on all your team mates… travel, lodging, food, whatever. They've hired a lawyer here in New York to work with me about your expenses. We all want you to get your butt, and your typewriter, to England to look up your Army buddy and… uh, yeah, Jimmy. He should be arriving in a couple of weeks, too. Like I already arranged… you'll fly over on an Air Corps bomber; it leaves in a couple of days. Once you're there, find your friends, write about the war… same as you've been doing. When you're done in England, or if you hear news from the Pacific, you'll be heading there. Kind of shuttling between all the action spots they're involved in. Be glad you're not married." A deep blast of laughter erupted at that line.

"Be sure to stay in touch. Tomorrow you head to Mitchell Field on Long Island; you'll meet the crew of the bomber you'll be flying in. I know this is happening fast, but you have the chance to be the first reporter to fly over… these are the first bombers we'll have in England to attack Germany. Did you bring the oranges?"

"Huh? Oh, yeah, sure did. They're on your secretary's desk. Nice big juicy ones, too. And I also got a half dozen grapefruits for you."

"Good kid. Now go, get your scrawny self out to Mitchell Field in the morning. What you're writing is important, obviously, to more than just this newspaper."

Bruce left Bennett's office, his mind still whirling. He'd have to pack for another long trip; first, though he wanted to telephone his parents and Susan. He walked down the hall to his own desk, now cluttered with the detritus of a newspaper office; broken pencil stubs, half written notes of phone calls from the past weeks. Bruce spent a few minutes cleaning the top of the desk, shrugged and sat down to make his calls. He had the newpaper switchboard connect him with a long distance operator, then gave her the number for his home in Ames. After a few rings, his mother answered; he could hear the excitement in her voice as she spoke with the operator.

"Bruce! How are you? Where are you? Wait a minute, let me call for your father, he's home for lunch…" Silence for a minute, then his dad picked up the extension in the family den and he had them both on the line.

"Hey, son. How's my world traveler?"

"Fine, dad. I've got time to talk a bit but first let me tell you that I'll be leaving soon for England again. I don't know when I'll be able to talk with you… it may be quite a while. How are things at the bank?"

"Great, plenty going on to keep me busy. Seems like everybody's getting money to expand businesses and the farmers around here can't raise enough animals and crops to satisfy the demands. Frank Howard is building another hog barn, his third… he's running nearly 5,000 hogs a month through his operation for Hormel now. Folks are scrambling for building materials; State College landed a big government contract for expansion… they'll be training future Navy officers here… in the middle of the country! Can you believe that?"

"Well, dad, it's just like I've seen across the country. Factories are going up, ships are being built like never before… I don't see how the Germans and Japs can possibly keep up with us when we really get going. Did you get to see the article I wrote on the bombers being built in San Diego?"

"Sure, we get all your articles… Hopkins makes sure the Tribune prints everything you write. The whole town's proud of you, son. You heading to England to find Fred again? It was fun reading how you were able to get Stan and Bobbie together; people really like your stuff. You give us all a picture of life besides the statistics and bare facts we usually hear. Son, I'd best be getting back to the office; I'll let you talk with Mom. It's always great to hear your voice. I'm proud of you, Bruce."

His mom spent the next fifteen minutes filling him in on all the local news. The Ames' basketball team had won only a couple of games all season; that was expected after all five starters had graduated the year before. The moms were still getting together every Tuesday morning to pray and share what they'd heard from the boys. No news from Stan and Bobbie since they'd left San Diego. Jimmy's mom had just told the others about Bruce's visit with him in Naples and Fred's last letter was about life in an army camp in the farmlands of central England... he was dating an English girl, the daughter of a farmer. Fred was spending his spare time, what little he got, helping her father with their livestock. In exchange, he was getting fresh eggs and butter to share with his tent mates.

He also told her of Susan; how he'd met her in San Diego, was helped by her brother and that he looked forward to seeing her again somehow. Bruce and his mom both choked up when it was time to say goodbye. He had to take a minute to compose himself before he put through a call to Susan. The two enjoyed a full half hour on the phone together; she was now working in the public relations office at Consolidated Aircraft, handling other reporters and giving tours to military officers, both American and British. Numbers of the B-24's and PBY's they built were being sent to England for use in fighting the German submarines in the Atlantic. Just the day before she had escorted a Royal Air Force Group Captain as he inspected six new planes. She said he was very polite and loved his accent; Bruce found that amusing and promised to work on his own while he was in England. Their conversation took on a more intimate tone as the time drew near to ending the call; both expressed their love for one another and a desire to be together soon.   Before hanging up, Susan told him that Sam had been accepted for training as a War Correspondent with the Navy; he'd be starting his classes the next week with Commander Dixon, Bruce's friend.

"Susan, honey... I promise I'll post a letter to you as soon I get to England, though it'll probably take weeks before you get it. I love you and think of you every minute."

"Silly... how on earth will you be able to do your job if I'm all you think about? Just be safe and come back to me, OK? I love you, too, you know."

Bruce hung up and had one more call put through; this was a local one to the Air Corps base on Long Island. He wanted to confirm that he'd be arriving the next morning and get instructions on where to report. The clerk he was connected to gave him the information; Bruce practically mouthed the words along with the airman.

"Check in at the front gate and ask for Administration. It's the large building just across the parking area beyond the gate. Report to the clerk at the front desk for instructions."

The rest of his day was spent packing and buying the few items he'd need. A driver from the newspaper brought him over to Long Island where Bennett had arranged a hotel room for the night. He ate supper in the hotel dining room before heading up a few floors to his room, where he repacked his luggage and took time to clean his typewriter and make sure he had a good supply of ribbons and paper. He wrote a short thank you letter to Phil Steiner and another to Saul in San Diego. Sleep came surprisingly easy as he settled in for what might be his last good night's rest for some time.

Bruce was at the main gate of Mitchell Army Air Corps Field early the next morning. After showing his identification he was directed to the large Administration Building. The airman at the front desk of the Admin Office verified his identity and Bruce was soon met by a Captain Strothers who escorted him to the flight line off the main runway of the airfield. Parked there were a dozen new

B-17s; four engine bombers known as Flying Fortresses for the heavy armament they normally carried. On this flight, however, they had been stripped of their guns to save weight and extend their flying range. Strothers told Bruce that he would be flying in a bomber piloted by a Major Young, commander of the squadron. The Major would meet him here shortly; he was attending a final mission briefing at the moment. Bruce was introduced to the other officers of Young's plane, all Lieutenants; William Adams was copilot, bombardier Frank Herman and navigator David Preston. Lieutenant Adams helped Bruce stow his luggage aboard the bomber using the fuselage hatch just behind the waist gun position. Walking to the front of the plane, Bruce was shown how the officers entered the plane through a hatch underneath the nose by swinging their legs up and in, twisting their body as they went. It took Bruce three attempts, twice hitting a knee, before he succeeded. Once inside, he found a small table, wall mounted lamp and a great view out of the Plexiglas covered nose. From the seat up front, he could see a panoramic view of what was ahead. Adams explained that normally a bombsight was situated just ahead of the seat; this was the bombardier's station, the table was for the navigator. The pilot and copilot sat above and just behind this area, up on the flight deck. He led Bruce back and up a couple of steps to where the flight controls were located. Bruce noted the simple, functional look to everything; the only ornamentation at all being the winged "Boeing" label on each of the pilot controls. Adams continued the tour by pointing up to the top turret, where two .50 caliber machines were usually mounted. This is where his friend, Jimmy, would be stationed if he became a Flight Engineer. Behind the top turret was the bomb bay; a large area with racks on either side, a narrow walkway going back between them. This led to the radio room, followed by the waist gunners' station and the ball turret position in the floor. All the way back, through a small crawlspace was where the tail gunner was located. In all, the bomber carried ten machine guns to defend itself against enemy fighter planes.

Another officer joined them in the waist gunner area; gold oak leaves on his shoulders marked him as a Major. As Bruce turned to greet him, he was surprised to see the pilot from the Yankee Clipper that had brought him back from England months earlier. The Major smiled and shook his hand, saying "Bruce, I told you we might well meet up again. Now I'll get my chance to cross the ocean again, delivering one more passenger. Welcome aboard."

Major Young, Bruce and the Lieutenants all exited the plane and walked to a building between the hangar area and the Admin building. It was the first Officer's Club Bruce had been in. Decorated with insignia of squadrons that had been based at the field over the years, it had the atmosphere of a gentlemen's club; the smell of tobacco and leather permeated the air. The five of them sat and an enlisted man took their orders for lunch and drinks. Their conversation turned to the coming flight; Bruce had a hundred questions of what to expect. Their plane, along with the others in the squadron, would take off the next morning and fly to Presque Isle Airfield in Maine to refuel. Then they'd fly to Goose Bay, Labrador for another refuel stop. From there the long flight to Scotland, the most dangerous leg of the journey, would take them over the cold waters of the North Atlantic. Each plane was to navigate on their own, so there was a chance no other aircraft would be seen along the route. Bruce felt very reassured that his pilot, Major Young, had flown long distances many times before.

After lunch Bruce was escorted to a supply office and was issued a flight suit like the others on his plane. Sheepskin pants, boots, coat, mittens and even a cap made him feel like an arctic explorer. Major Young explained that, unlike the Yankee Clipper, these bombers were not pressurized, so the temperature inside the plane could get down to minus 40 degrees.

"Don't take your gloves off for any reason, Bruce. Fingers freeze quickly at high altitude in these planes. We'll have thermos bottles with hot coffee; be careful not to have too much. Adams will show you where 'to go' if you feel the urge… best to hold it if you can. You'll be in the top turret seat but feel free to visit the rest of us. The view from the nose is the best. I've also been ordered to review anything you write about our mission... don't worry on that one; editing is not my strong suit so I'll trust you to not say anything you shouldn't. Just wanted to make that clear."

"Thanks, Major. I'll do my best and I've learned about what and what not to write from the Navy and others. Do I need to learn how to use a parachute?"

"Well, I certainly don't think so... I trust my flying and the North Atlantic is so cold it wouldn't make too much difference. You've been over it on a ship, right?"

"Yes, in January. Seems like a lot longer than that though. I took a troop ship over with the first infantry to reach England, now I'm flying with some of the first Air Corps to head there... as excited as I am, somehow I think I should feel more honored or something. I mean, I appreciate it and all, but..."

"Bruce, you've seen more in five months than anybody I know; and this is just starting. Some years from now you'll look back in disbelief that you did all you'll do, I'm sure. For now, just look at it as a job to do one day after another."

"Thanks, Major. That helps... if I want to sleep on the trip, where is it safe to lie down?"

"The radio compartment would be the best, I suppose. Just aft of the bomb bay, you remember? There's an electric heater in there, too... make it a bit more comfortable. Put a few parachutes on the deck to lay on."

#

Their flights from Long Island to Presque and on to Labrador and Greenland had gone off without a hitch. All the planes landed within minutes of their expected arrivals. Major Young was pleased with his crews and the work of the navigators. Early in the morning, just as the sun was peeking above the eastern horizon, the first plane took off for the long haul over to Scotland. Bruce was looking out the top turret as they rumbled down the concrete airstrip and lifted

111

off, mere yards from the end of the runway as it met the sea. He heard Major Young on the intercom radio, "Well, that could be lengthened a bit. Never could make it with a full load of bombs. Next stop... Scotland."

Bruce stayed in his seat, enjoying the view of clouds and sea, for an hour. He stepped down, between the pilots and told the Major he'd be down with the navigator and bombardier. Turning and squeezing down the steps to the lower deck, he saw Dave Preston sitting at the small table, looking over maps and charts. Frank Herman was sitting on his seat in the nose, motioning for Bruce to come up front. Frank stood and let Bruce sit down. The view out of the plexiglas was beautiful; white caps in long lines across the surface of the bright blue water. It was hard to tell where the sea ended and the sky began. Dave came up and explained that the waves were very helpful in navigating the plane; they showed the wind direction and even held clues to the speed it was blowing. This made it easier for him to determine their own and to plot the correct course to follow. He pointed up to a small round window in the ceiling; it was for determining star positions at night for navigating in the dark. Bruce accepted a cup of coffee from Frank and the three talked about their homes, schools and sweethearts for a while. Bruce found it hard to jot down notes with the heavy gloves on, but was sure to keep them on. He could feel the cold on his face and each breath reminded him of winter in Iowa; and this was in the part of the plane with the most heat. The areas behind the bomb bays had almost no heat. Officers up front, enlisted in the back... rank has privilege.

Bruce began to feel sleepy; he said goodbye to the two Lieutenants and made his way back to the radio compartment. Turning on the heater, he spread six parachute packs on the floor and laid down. The thrum of the engines soon lolled him into a nice nap. A voice in his headphones woke him later; it was Major Young asking him to come forward to the flight deck. When he arrived, the Major pointed down to the water; Bruce could make out a couple of small spots on the surface. He went down to the nose compartment to look out the front; as he looked through the window, Frank told him they were lifeboats. A merchant ship must have been torpedoed by a German sub. Their orders prohibited any radio transmissions outside the intercom. The navigator had already made notes of the location in his log; all they could do was notify Air Sea Rescue when they arrived over the United Kingdom. It would probably be too late to save any lives. Bruce felt a tightening in his stomach as he recalled his own voyage and the drills he'd had on lifeboats and abandoning the ship.

Two hours passed with nothing but clouds and the ocean waves in view. Bruce was sitting next to the navigator's table when the copilot announced land was on the horizon ahead. Fishing boats began to appear on the water below and soon a few rocky islands dotted the sea surface. On and on the bomber flew, over a gray landscape that slowly became covered in green. Now a town with a small harbor and roads began to show up. Suddenly, out of the sun, a fighter swept by, wagging its wings in a friendly greeting. The red, white and blue roundels on the wings and fuselage identified it as a Royal Air Force plane. Bruce climbed up the steps to the flight deck and heard Major Young speaking to a ground station, confirming their own identity and receiving permission to continue to their destination in Scotland. Smiles broke out among the crew and a visible lifting of the stress of a long flight were noticeable.

The plane approached the airfield a half hour later, the intersecting runways below looking like a large 'X' on a map. Touching down with a smooth, gentle bump of the tires hitting pavement, cheers of excitement and relief filled the intercom. For all but two on board, it was the longest flight of their lives. A banner was hung on the front of a large hangar, "Welcome Yanks". Major Young taxied their plane, following a small car flying a large yellow flag. The car stopped in front of the banner; by the time their engines stopped and the crew, along with Bruce, had deplaned a small band marched out of the hangar and began playing military music. As a

Royal Air Force officer walked up and saluted Major Young, a second B-17 roared over the field on its own final approach to landing. Soon another appeared and as each landed and taxied over, the cheering and waving of those on the ground increased; all sense of control was gone as a crowd of civilians, RAF personnel and the few Americans shook hands, slapped shoulders, sang and cried. The band broke out in a rendition of "The Yanks Are Coming" adding to the celebratory cacaphony.

All twelve of the squadron's planes had made it to Prestwick, Scotland safely. Their pilots and crews gathered in a hangar the next morning for final instructions by Major Young for their flight to RAF Polebrook, the new home to the fledgling Eighth Air Force. Their arrival doubled the number of American bombers available in England to begin taking the fight to the enemy. It would still take weeks before they got into the fight. The enlisted gunners, mechanics and support staff were on troop ships in the Atlantic along with spare parts, ammunition, bombs, equipment and their precious machine guns.

Bruce spent most of the night banging out the story of their flight on his typewriter in a borrowed office at the airport. He was thankful for the few hours of sleep on the floor of the radio room aboard the plane and was looking forward to another nap on the flight to Polebrook. By first light he'd finished the article and arranged for it to be wired to New York using the Royal Air Force's communications office. As Bruce was walking back to the temporary quarters assigned to the air crews he was overtaken by an RAF sergeant.

"Excuse me, sir. Are you Mr Hollins?"

"Yes… Bruce Hollins. What can I do for you?"

"I'm Sergeant Bosworth, communications. I missed you in the comm office, sorry. I have a telephone message for you from a Roy Coffee, another Yank. He said he's also a newspaper man, following your 34th Division."

114

"Roy Coffee? How'd he know I was here… I suppose you wouldn't have a clue on that answer. Did he leave a number I can reach him at?"

"Yes, sir. It's with the message… you can use the telephone in comm to ring him up if you'd like."

"That would be great, thanks." Bruce turned and followed the sergeant as he unfolded Roy's message. It read, "Bruce, a nephew on flight with you. Have news you'd like to hear. Call when you get this. Roy C"

When he reached the communications office, Bruce asked Bosworth to put through the return call. In a couple of minutes, he was speaking with the reporter he sailed across the Atlantic with on the *Chatteau Thierry*. Bosworth told him it was a direct line to the 34th and was secure.

"Bruce… nice to know you made the hop across the pond in one piece. My nephew is on one of the other planes and called me last night when they landed."

"Roy, what news on the Red Bulls? Your note has got me interested."

"Yeah, hold on… got a note I wrote with the details… here it is. Fred Howard, that's your basketball team mate, right?"

"Yeah, we ran into each other on the ship."

"I remember… nice article by the way. My editor hinted he'd like more of that style in my dispatches." Roy laughed and continued, "I told him I'm too old to change and he probably couldn't afford you anyway. So, here's what I've got… your friend Fred is part of a new unit being formed… can't tell you just what they're up to, not over the phone at least. Let's just say you're younger and in better shape than me; I'm too long in the tooth to be going around getting shot at."

"Well, where is this new training and how would I possibly get to see Fred? You got any help with that?"

"As a matter of fact, I just might. The guy in charge is Captain William Darby. I've known him since before he studied at

115

West Point… this group he's putting together is mostly from the 34th; that's how Fred was picked for the training. They're at a place… let's see… Carrickfergus in Northern Ireland. It's along the coast, not that far from Prestwick. You know, I didn't give this a thought until my nephew called last night… it all fits in my mind. I don't know what connection you have with these Air Corps guys… just thought you might want to see your friend again."

"Yeah, I sure would. Thanks a bunch, Roy. I'll see what I can do about getting to this… Carrickfergus. Meanwhile, I'd better talk with Major Young, the squadron commander. Can you say hello to Frank Summers for me?"

"I would but Frank's down in London. He's covering the arrival of the fliers and plans for us to get into this war. You'll probably see him before me, especially if you don't go to Northern Ireland right away."

"OK… right. If I do, I'll give him your regards. It was sure nice to talk with you again; thanks for the info on Fred."

"You bet. Least I can do to help part of my fan club."

"Well, along that line… my pop is a real big fan of yours, Roy. He was more excited that I met you than anything. So long."

"See you down the road, Bruce."

Sergeant Bosworth helped Bruce with a map, showing Prestwick and Carrickfergus. The sergeant was from the area across the Firth of Clyde from Ireland and told Bruce his destination was actually quite close to Belfast. Bruce smiled at the thought he'd be returning to where he first landed with the 34th back in January. In five months he'd been across the Atlantic and the United States twice to get back here. He thanked Bosworth and headed back to his quarters. Looking up Major Young, Bruce told him of the phone call and unexpected news. The Major was more than a little surprised, but quite excited for Bruce.

"I guess news travels faster than I ever have. I don't have any orders beyond getting you here to Great Britain; I suppose

Scotland works as well as England. How do you propose to get to Northern Ireland?"

"An RAF sergeant has offered to help with my transportation; he thinks he can get me to this side of the water in a lorry; I think that's a bus. Then I can take a ferry over to Belfast, not far from Carrickfergus. I should be there day after tomorrow he thinks."

"We'll be leaving here tomorrow ourselves. If you can't make the connections, be here by 0830 and you can ride along with us to Polebrook. It's been fun seeing you again, Bruce. I look forward to reading what you thought of our flight. I suppose I'll have to wait to get a paper sent from America, though."

"No, sir. I had the RAF take pictures of what I typed up and wired over. A copy is to be delivered to you later this afternoon. Let me know what you think of it, please."

"I sure will." The two shook hands and Bruce went into his room to get some much needed sleep. He sat on the edge of his bunk, thinking about all that happened in the past month. He'd been in San Diego, on a beach with Susan, wanting life to slow down a little so he could enjoy more time with her. Here he was, half a world away, busier than he could ever imagine. He could write for years on what he'd already seen, if he had the time. Putting sleep aside, he pulled out some stationery and a pen and wrote a letter to his love, so far from him but right there in his heart.

#

The ferry slowed, drifting into the dock; two men caught the lines thrown and snubbed them down around the bollards on the pier. A gangplank was lowered and the passengers began to disembark. Bruce took his time, waiting until all the others had made it ashore. He walked past several fishing boats on the other side of the wharf, enjoying the fishy smell. He closed his eyes and took note of the odor and sounds; the same as back in January when he first landed in Belfast. Walking to a pub across the street from where he was standing, he tripped and nearly fell on the cobblestone street, its uneven surface a challenge; and he hadn't had a drink yet. He walked into the half-darkness, aware of a couple of older men sitting, hunched over their pints. Bruce asked the man behind the bar if the 34th Division was still in camp nearby. The man nodded and directed Bruce to the constable station down on the corner.

"They'll help you, Yank.", was all he said.

Bruce smiled, exited and headed the direction the man had pointed. When he got to the station, he walked inside and made the same inquiries. The police sergeant behind the counter was much more polite and asked Bruce his name and the business he had with the soldiers. He was genuinely interested that the young man before him was a war correspondent for an American newspaper. Bruce then asked the man if he could direct him to Carrickfergus; the sergeant's demeanor visibly changed in an instant.

"No... don't know a thing about such a place; and I wouldn't be asking anyone else about it either. If the blokes in the 34th clear you, that's fine and their business. I can't say more than that. I can get you a lift out to the Yank camp if you'd care to."

"That would be perfect, thanks. I didn't mean to... well, ask things I shouldn't. I'll wait until I get to the 34th to ask again."

"You do that, lad. Safer that way."

A few minutes later a cab pulled up and the sergeant pointed to it. Bruce thanked him, accepting the return smile as confirmation that all was right again. The cabbie was polite, opening the door for Bruce and putting his valise in the cab's boot. Fifteen minutes later, Bruce was dropped off at the gate leading to the 34th Division's camp; a familiar sight but more formidable with barbed wire strung to head height down along the road for a long way. The sentry asked for Bruce's ID and let him enter when he verified the picture to Bruce's face.

"Straight ahead, you have to check in at..."

"I know, the admin building.", said Bruce with a smile.

"What... you some kind of joker or something?", the sentry replied with a frown.

"Sorry… no offense. I've just heard that line a dozen times lately."

"Huh?", said the guard, as he waved Bruce through.

Once at the admin office, Bruce asked if he could see Captain Darby. The corporal behind the desk replied that it was Major Darby now and no, he wasn't on base at present. He directed Bruce to sit, pointing to a chair, and he'd have someone else speak with him. His bottom had barely touched down when two large soldiers with 'MP' armbands on, walked in and towered over him.

"Come with us, please.", said the one with three stripes on his sleeve. He didn't have a look on his face that allowed for anything but obedience. Bruce got back up and followed them down the hall and into a small office.

"What business do you have with Major Darby?"

"I'm a correspondent, writing for a New York newspaper. I actually sailed with the Red Bulls from there in January. I've come back to write on some of the men who have been assigned to a new unit commanded by Major Darby."

"Let me inform my superiors, see if they'll talk to you. Who were the other reporters on the ship when we arrived here?"

"Roy Coffee; he's still here… and Frank Summers… though he's in London now."

"Right. Wait here, I'll be back shortly."

Bruce waited with the other MP, who offered him a smoke as soon as the sergeant shut the door.

"You're the guy that wrote the great article on us when we got here, aren't you? Don't mind Sarge, he's all business and probably didn't bother to read it. You wrote about Fred, right?"

"That'd be me. Fred and I played basketball together before the war. I heard he's in a different unit now. I just want to find him and write another piece on his training."

"Well, that's not likely. No sir… Major Darby won't go for that, huh-uh."

The door opened and an officer stepped in, followed by the sergeant MP. The officer looked Bruce up and down, smiled and offered him a seat. Sitting in the other chair, he took off his cap and said, "I'm William Darby... you're Bruce Hollins, right?"

"Yes, sir. I got a call from..."

"Roy Coffey. He told me to expect you; though, to be honest, I thought it'd take a few more days for you to get here. You must have had help getting to the ferry on the other side?"

"The RAF let me hitch a ride down the coast. I'm not sure what to make of the reception I've gotten since the ferry arrived. Even the "bobby" in Belfast was wary of helping."

"That's good... good. The Brits take this stuff more seriously than a cop in Chicago would. Let me tell you a few things. Our army is not strong enough yet to take on the Wehrmacht anywhere; they've had time to build up defenses too tough for us to crack. At least... well, we can't fight a full scale knock down fight. So a decision was made a couple months ago to form a group like the British Commandos; small units that use a kind of hit and run approach. Maybe take out a single objective... anyway, it'll give our boys a chance to gain experience, learn a lot and also keep the Germans guessing where we might strike next... kind of keep them antsy. We'll be like bees at a picnic. Now what Roy Coffee and I've talked about is letting America know we're training our guys to do this... without giving away the farm. You know the Germans will get a hold of any information you write... well, we want them to be scared that we're training our own version of Superman in a way. You'd be in the training too, sort of... it seems to me that writing about something you're involved in makes for better reading. You interested?"

Bruce didn't know what to say; he had come here to interview Fred again and he was being handed the whole caboodle. All he could think to say was, "Major, what makes you think I could handle the training?"

"Look, you were a good athlete in high school, so I'm told… and not just basketball. You're comfortable outdoors, grew up in the country. Your buddy, Fred Howard, says you've never had another seizure… is that right?"

"I only had the one in the car accident…"

"So you probably don't have epilepsy or anything. We'll take that chance. What we'd like is a good writer that's not afraid of the dark and can run and hike his ass off getting to where the others are going… not combat, you'll not go on missions. That has to be… if you were ever captured, you'd likely be shot as a spy… Soldiers are covered by the Geneva Convention, sort of…. not civilians riding along. Every word you write goes through me… that's another concrete stipulation. Now, you want to be a part of this, or do I bring Corporal Howard in here for your fifteen minute interview with him before you go back to London or wherever?"

"Major, last summer I hit the lowest point in my life when I was told I couldn't join up… in any branch, because of my seizure. I'd like to accept your offer for two reasons; first, I know what I can write will help in the war effort. I've learned that from others that tell me the good my articles do. Second, I really feel I need to prove my physical abilities… not just to others, but more to myself."

"Good… and good reasons as well. I'll have someone show you where to bunk; we'll put you in Corporal Howard's section. Remember, run everything you write past me; I may or may not change things… we'll have to work that part out together. Welcome to the Rangers, Bruce."

#

Two weeks sped by like a Burlington Zephyr; the few hours devoted to sleep each night seemed to go fastest. Bruce had settled in to his new home quickly; not too difficult when you have very few possessions to begin with. A cot, footlocker and a small field desk with chair (normally reserved for officers, but his typewriter had to live someplace anyway). Probably the biggest advantage of his sharing a tent was for the others in it; they now numbered five

121

instead of the usual six. None of his cohabitants complained a bit, even when he was typing away at the strangest hours. Letters to Susan and his parents were handwritten. It was the newspaper articles that required the machine. In a telephone call Bennett said he liked the idea of doing a weekly overview, giving folks back home a taste of what the training was like for these elite light infantry. Naturally, none of the Rangers would think the term 'light' had anything to do with them.

A normal day began well before the sun was up. Hikes with full packs or multi-mile runs were followed by breakfast; then their work began. Hand to hand combat techniques, explosives training, communication, fitness conditioning, obstacle courses, practice in map orienteering and navigation… a Ranger was expected to master all of this. Bruce learned quickly that his friend Fred's personal favorite was the use of enemy weapons. He could field strip anything the Wehrmacht used as fast as the American ordinance he'd already qualified with.

The risks were high in Ranger training; not a day went by without strains, broken bones and the accidental death. Bruce witnessed firsthand a tragic example; a live grenade exploded after slipping out of the hand of a trainee during practice. Two young Americans died and three more were wounded by the shrapnel. Bruce was among the first to rush to their aid; he wrote about the carnage and blood in grisly detail, knowing Major Darby would edit out a majority of his work. The final article praised the Army medics in their treatment of the daily injuries that naturally happened in such intensive training.

Over the course of the six weeks that Bruce was a part of the Rangers, he personally benefitted from all the physical training. Losing the few pounds he'd gathered around his waist since high school, he cut a trim and muscled figure. He was never the tallest or most agile of the team; those traits actually belonged to Fred. The two had now become almost inseparable, challenging each other whenever the chance came up. On the obstacle course, a series of walls to scale, ropes to climb up or to swing on over pools of water and mud, or barbed wire entanglements to crawl under or through, Bruce kept losing to Fred by smaller and smaller margins. He could beat his friend now in a five mile run; his own smaller body seeming to glide along compared to Fred's own lumbering style. Though the two had been close friends on the team back in Iowa, here in Ireland they bonded like brothers. Nor was this bond limited to just Fred and Bruce; the writer had become a close member of the squad, always ready to take part rather than stand aside and observe.

Bruce also renewed acquaintances he'd made on the troop ship back in January. Sergeant Miller, the former cop from Des Moines, was here. He'd taught Bruce how to shoot rifles on the firing range months earlier. Miller now took the time to show him how to fire the M-1 Garand, the weapon that replaced the single shot rifle he'd practiced with earlier. He explained that this semi-automatic piece gave them a big advantage over other military units. While German, Italian and Japanese soldiers were armed with bolt action rifles that fired a few shots in a minute, the Garand fired a clip of eight as fast as you could pull the trigger. It also could be reloaded quickly, vastly increasing the firepower a unit carried; he called it fire superiority.

Bruce watched demonstrations of many other weapons; mortars, machine guns, small anti-tank guns and even the strange, rocket firing tube called the bazooka. One man put it up on his shoulder while a second loaded it from behind. With a loud "whoosh" the rocket roared out of the tube and could completely disable an armored car or small tank a hundred yards away. His only problem with learning about all the different weapons was that he couldn't share his knowledge through his articles. Major Darby made sure nothing was sent to the newspapers that would give away any real clues about the strength of the Rangers. He was able, however, to write all he wanted on the special qualities of the men themselves. Bruce always mentioned his subjects by name and included facts about their homes and what they did before the Army.

This personalizing is what made his writing so readable and loved by those back home.

He was not writing newspaper articles only, however. Every night, before he went to sleep, Bruce wrote a letter to Susan; or, at least, added to what he'd written the night before. For the first time since San Diego, he also received correspondence. Along with those letters recently sent by his parents and Susan, mail that had been forwarded would arrive. A letter from his old boss, Mr Hopkins, traveled from Ames to San Diego to New York and on to Ireland before reaching him. All that distance for less than a nickel.

It was now the middle of July and the Rangers' initial training was coming to a close. Bruce sat near Major Darby on a reviewing stand, along with selected officers and dignitaries, as the men he'd gotten to know so well, paraded by. Their measured cadence fairly shook the ground as they marched, each man in perfect step with the others. There was a ceremony as flags were presented to each company in the battalion; Major Darby was called down to the field to accept the colors for the entire unit. The 34th Division band was there to play appropriate martial music as well. After the graduation, Bruce joined his friends in celebrating their success in becoming Rangers; beer was provided and flowed liberally along with thick beef steaks and baked potatoes. Major Darby approached Bruce as he sat with Fred and the others from his tent.

"Bruce, can I have a minute?"

"Sure, Major… what is it?"

"All of us really appreciate the effort you've put forward the past weeks. Not only have you written about so many of us, telling America what we're doing here in preparation of bringing this fight to our enemies… you, personally, have taken the initiative to get into this training yourself. That's something special, very special. I want you, and everyone here, to know that I consider you a valuable member of our team… you've earned this along with all of us." Darby handed Bruce a Ranger patch; the gold trimmed, blue diamond with 'RANGERS' in it. The men at the table stood and applauded, the recognition spreading through the hall until all the newly formed battalion was on its feet clapping and cheering.

Chapter 7
July 1942

Bruce left Carrickfergus on a Tuesday and arrived at Polebrook on Friday. He again took the ferry across the Irish Sea to Liverpool just as he had in January. Instead of catching the clipper flight back to New York, this time he boarded a train heading to the airfield, located a bit more than 50 miles north of London. The usual 'check in at the main gate before the admin building' routine was followed by a tour of the base in a jeep, along with Frank Summers who came up from London to meet him. Bruce was amazed and impressed with the view of two dozen American B-17 bombers parked on their large concrete hardstands on the edges of the runway. Men were scurrying all over the planes, installing machine guns, working on engines, painting large yellow letters, three in all, along the fuselage sides. Each one had a different last letter.

"You're arriving at a perfect time, Bruce. The enlisted echelon arrived last week and trucks full of equipment, spare parts, guns and ammunition are coming every day. The push is on from London to get things organized here and to begin the last training before the first actual bombing mission using the Flying Fortresses. Just a few days ago, some of our boys flew RAF Boston bombers, smaller planes, on a raid over France. A couple were shot up by ground fire, but no one was injured; all the planes came back. The generals want to see what these 'heavies' can do... and soon."

"I'll have to look up my friend, Jim Hartke. He's a gunner and flight engineer in the 97ᵗʰ Group."

"Another of your team mates I take it? Roy called some time back and told me you'd found your friend in the 34ᵗʰ Division again. So what was the training like for the new Rangers he's part of? I wanted to ask you about that when you called from Liverpool, telling me you were on the way here... I know it's best not to talk on the phones."

"It was brutal... and thrilling. I've never felt better, physically... ever... and I learned more about weapons, radios... all kinds of things. I sure wouldn't want to be against them in a fight. I hope the Germans don't either."

"Well, at some point they'll get a chance to prove themselves. I've spent some time observing the British Commandos, same kind of group. Quick, quiet... get in, do the job and get out... that sort of fighting. Kind of like a boxing match... lots of small jabs before landing the haymaker, you know."

"Nice way to put it, Frank. You make things easy to see. I suppose it's the same with the bombing... start with the smaller missions, then turn up the heat when more bombers arrive."

"Exactly... say, I heard you flew over with Major Young? There's a few more officers here you'll want to meet. Let's head over to the Officer's Club and see who might be around."

Their driver turned the jeep down a short alley behind a hangar and headed back toward the main base buildings. In a few minutes they were in front of the "O Club".

"Colonel James Walsh heads up the 97ᵗʰ Group. Right now there's only a couple of the squadrons here... Major Young's and Major Paul Tibbetts'... though Tibbetts will be Deputy Group Commander... well, you'll meet them all in time I guess. Let's go in."

Frank and Bruce dismounted from the jeep and walked in to the club. A few officers were sitting around tables, conversing and drinking coffee. Major Young glanced up and, seeing Bruce, waved and walked over.

"Bruce... good to see you. How'd things go with finding your buddy in Ireland?"

"Hi Major... swell, I spent some time with him and a new group called Rangers, part of the 34th Infantry. I think you'll hear about them before too long."

"Well, without giving away secrets... hang around here and you'll see things start up, too. I don't think it'll be too long before we have ourselves a real shooting war."

"I heard the enlisted air crews are here now? I'd sure like to find out if another team mate of mine is with them."

"Staff Sergeant Hartke, isn't it? You never did tell me his name on our flight over, but I remember you mentioned having one in the Air Corps... and one of the newspapers we brought along had an article you wrote in it about Hartke down in Florida... Naples, right? We were at Sarasota but he joined the air crews just before they boarded transports in Virginia. I had one of my clerks do a little homework before the enlisted arrived. He's here... you can see him anytime you'd like."

"Wow... that's great. We didn't get much time together in Naples... other things sort of happened."

"Lots of things seem to be happening to you, Bruce."

"Amen.", piped in Frank and the three shared a laugh.

An hour later the three finished their visit and went separate ways; Frank and Bruce headed to the Admin Office while Major Young returned to his duties. Frank arranged transportation for himself back to London the next day while Bruce looked up his friend Jim. Directed to one of the barracks located a few city blocks away, Bruce said goodbye to his friend and fellow newspaperman. Sure that they would run into each again, the parting was easy. Bruce walked out and started up the street in the wonderful sunshine of an English summer afternoon. Within a block he was rained on, and again as he neared his destination. He thought about how he could see storms coming miles away in Iowa... not here.

Jim Hartke was laying on his bunk, reading an old issue of Life magazine when Bruce knocked and walked in. Smiles lit up both faces as they shook hands.

"About time you got here." quipped Bruce. "I had to spend over a month listening to Fred's yapping up in Ireland waiting for you. It only took me two days to make it across from New York."

"How the hell did you get here in two days... wait, did you get a flight on a clipper again?"

"No way; traveled in style once... that was enough. I roughed it out in something else... I think you'll like the B-17."

"Wait, hold on just a minute... you telling me you rode a Fortress over here while I got stuck on a puke bucket for two weeks?"

"Yep, that about sums it up. I flew with Major Young and his crew."

"My own squadron commander to boot... how do you like that?"

"I liked it quite nicely, thank you. Now... any idea what you're going to be doing around here now that you've arrived?"

"Matter of fact... tomorrow I start going over the plane I'll be engineer in. There are several that don't have regular crews. There's a bunch of us leftovers; we'll be assigned together and then will be playing catch up to qualify as a crew. Gossip is we'll be flying missions in a few weeks... that's not much time to get ready for some of us."

"Sounds like you'll be keeping plenty busy. Maybe in a few days I'll get myself down to London to have a look there and scoot back up before your first mission. I do want to spend some time here first, though; catch up on your transit... see how it compared to Fred's and mine in January."

"Got a spare bunk in the corner. Just three of us assigned in here; I'll go arrange it and have your gear brought over… it's in the admin office, right?"

"Yeah… two large bags and my typewriter case. Say, you know anyone that might figure how to give my machine a tune up? It's been quite a while and the keys are getting sticky… slowing me down."

"Sure. I'll have one of the guys in the machine shop look at it. I think one of them worked in a print shop back home… he'd probably be the one to check with first. When will you need it? I could see about borrowing one from a clerk here."

"Only if it'll take more than a day to get mine looked at. Thanks, Jim."

"First time you didn't call me Jimmie… what gives?"

"I figure by now you've earned a more adult name, I guess."

"Okay… Brucie." Jim almost succeeded in ducking before the pillow hit him as he sped out the door..

Bruce picked the pillow back up off the floor, sat down on the spare bunk and began reading the English paper he'd bought earlier that morning. The news was primarily about three subjects; the British and Germans were stalled in their fighting in Egypt at a place called El Alamein, German forces were driving the Russians back along the Don River toward Stalingrad and the trial of eight German saboteurs captured in New York and Florida was progressing in Washington. Bruce sighed at the thought of what a great assignment that would be for him to cover, though he appreciated what he was doing now. He'd always wanted to write about a court trial, full of intrigue and spies. The next hour passed as Bruce perused the English news; some minor labor unrest in the mines, relief work still going on in the areas of London hardest hit during 'The Blitz' two years earlier and other glimpses of daily life. He felt certain that the real stories going on were censored or not written of at all.

The door opened; Jim had returned. He stopped by to tell Bruce he could get his typewriter looked at the next day. Right now he had to help check out the electrical system on one of the newly arrived bombers; Bruce was welcome to tag along. The two grabbed a couple of bicycles outside the barracks door and pedaled their way past several B-17's sitting on their hardstands until they reached one with a few other Air Corps mechanics at work. The two ducked their way into the plane through the fuselage hatch and joined another sergeant in the radio room. Jim introduced him to Bruce.

"Vic, this is Bruce Hollins, a friend and newspaper reporter from New York. We went to school together before the war... Vic is from New York, too."

"Pleased to meet you, Bruce. What paper do you write for?"

"The Daily News... been there almost a year now, though the past several months I've been away from my desk."

"Yeah, lot of that going on around now. My family's always read The Times... so what brings you to England... I mean besides the war and all."

"Jim does... I'm writing about the fellas on our basketball team back in Iowa. He's here, that's one. Another is in Ireland in the infantry, two... then the other two are in the Pacific somewhere... one's a sailor, the other a Marine. I'm kind of following all of them around, writing on what they're doing. What part of New York are you from, Vic?"

"Me? I'm from upstate, near Saratoga Springs. I worked at the racetrack... horses. Learned how to operate and maintain the starting gate. It's electrical and so... here I am, another flight engineer and gunner that misses his new wife and waits for a letter telling me I'm a dad."

"Really? Congratulations. You want a boy or girl?"

"A girl I guess... I've got three brothers and never had a sister. I know my mom would love a granddaughter. Anyway, I think I'd like a girl first, then a couple of boys... might work out so my wife and I can get away from the kids later... you know, a built in babysitter." Vic poked Jim in the ribs and the three enjoyed the humor. Jim asked what the problem was with the bomber and the two got to work. Bruce took out his notebook and wrote a few lines about Vic to get the details down. He left them to their work and made his way back outside the aircraft to talk with the other mechanics. By the time Jim came out, electrical problem fixed in the top turret, Bruce had interviewed several other men and found that all of them came from different states and varied backgrounds. He thought about the scope of the war when just one bomber here in England was being worked on by young men from all over America for the single purpose of dropping bombs on another country.

"Bruce? You in there?" Jim was tapping him on the head.

"Huh? Oh, sorry, just thinking."

"Yep, it's high school all over... you really were the deep thinker. Good thing you didn't play golf. You'd stand at the tee for an hour thinking of where the ball might go. C'mon, let's get us some chow and a beer. Too bad I couldn't bring my hot rod over with me; we'd sure have a time here with it."

"What did you do with it when you left Naples? Sell it?"

"You kidding? I've got it in storage... took half a day to get it up on blocks and drain everything so it'll be ready to roll when the war's over. I'll find a way down to pick her up when I get back."

The two remounted the bicycles and headed for the mess hall. Potatoes, boiled cabbage and spam were on their trays as they sat down in the middle of several hundred other airmen, all talking loudly to be heard by the next guy.

"I wonder what this one's name was", Jim asked as he forked a chunk of spam toward his mouth.

"Probably came from Mr Howard's farm. My dad's last letter said he's raising more hogs now than there were in the whole state ten years ago."

"Well, my dad's raising more corn this year than ever before, too. I guess the war takes more of lots of things we're used to. One nice thing is my folks get the gasoline they need... with the farm and all they're pretty much exempt from the rationing; for now that is."

"I don't think the folks back home have any real idea of shortage yet. Can you imagine whole towns on bicycles?"

#

Bruce finished mailing letters to Susan and his folks, stepped out of the base post office and nearly collided with Major Young.

"Good morning, Bruce. I'm glad to see you… I was going to look you up later today. Have you got time to come over to my office this afternoon?"

"Sure thing, Major. How about in an hour?"

"That would be perfect, thanks."

When he returned to his barracks room, Bruce saw his typewriter case on the bunk. Opening it, the gleaming machine, keys shining, seemed to be smiling at him. It looked brand new, months of dirt and use seeming to have disappeared. He quickly rolled a sheet of paper in it and began to type… smoother than it had ever been. He'd have to find some way to thank whoever Jim had found to work on it. Meanwhile, he had an article to start on the mechanics of the 97th Group here at Polebrook. He settled in and had banged out several pages when he noticed the time; his hour was already over and he was due to meet with Major Young. He hurried to freshen up, grabbed a bike and was at the squadron's office in minutes. When he was ushered through the Major's door, he saw two other officers were already there.

"Come in, Bruce. I'd like you to meet General Armstrong, our Group Commander and Major Tibbetts, Deputy Commander. Have a seat."

Bruce shook hands with the two senior officers and sat down. An aide came in with coffee for all of them. General Anderson began the conversation.

"Mr Hollins… Bruce. First, nice article on your flight over here with the Major. I hope it went as well as you wrote. I understand you spent the past month or so training with the Army

Rangers up in Ireland? That couldn't have been easy… it tells me you're in fine physical shape and like to join in the action. I've met a few other reporters who'll have nothing to do with getting their hands dirty, so to speak. Now that you've had a long flight in a B-17, how'd you like another one?"

"Anytime you say, General. I really enjoyed the experience of flying, even without the comforts of the Yankee Clipper."

"General, the first time I met Bruce, he was a passenger on my last flight for Pan American in January, from Liverpool to New York." Major Young added.

The General nodded. "I see, well you certainly don't let moss grow under your feet. Bruce, we'd like you to take some training with us, the Air Corps, and have you tag along on a flight over France. We've flown a couple of sorties already, small numbers of light bombers… we'll be sending some heavies over in time. Interested?"

"I sure am, General… what sort of training am I looking at?"

"We can't take extra baggage up, Bruce. Operational personnel only, along with fuel and bombs. Think you could qualify as a gunner? You'll also have to learn the use of a parachute… not actually jumping with one, just how it works. I'm pretty sure I can get permission for you to ride along… if you're a working part of a crew. Never been done yet."

"There will be risks" added Major Tibbetts. "The Germans have a good air force themselves and will probably have fighters up there when we come over."

"Bruce, you'd be in my aircraft. You know my officers already… I'll have you meet the enlisted men. We'll have you riding along, not actually manning a gun. Sort of like the flight over; you can ride in the radio room. The gunnery training is really more of a formality… justification for your being on board. We'll start your training tomorrow."

Bruce could hardly wait to tell Jim of this new development. Though he wouldn't fly on the same aircraft as his friend, the idea of them both flying the same mission was exciting. The two spent the rest of the day going over the lessons Jim had learned from his own time at gunnery school.

"Aim like a shotgun, both eyes open, not like a rifle with one closed. Short bursts; you only have enough ammunition for about 30 seconds per gun. Don't try filling the sky with bullets, lead him like a duck and he'll fly right into your fire. Keep your head moving, scanning the sky... pay particular attention to the sun, they love to come out of the sun." Jim the teacher, Bruce the student, both would be rookies on their first mission.

Over the next ten days Bruce was introduced to Browning .50 caliber machine guns; how they worked, how to quickly fix a jam in the firing mechanism without losing a finger. He sat in a simulator, wooden dowels sticking out like gun barrels, as he practiced tracking an enemy fighter. He learned aircraft identification so he lessened the chance of shooting down a friendly escort in the confusion of aerial combat. Next was live fire from a stationary platform at a moving target rolling by on a track about 100 yards away. Then it was firing shotguns from the bed of a pickup truck careening around a course while clay pigeons were launched from the ground along their path. Finally he flew in a twin engine plane and practiced firing a Browning out of the fuselage at target sleeves towed by other aircraft. Following all the gunnery training, he was given a two hour course in parachutes. He thought it strange that he spent so much time learning to kill others and so little on saving his own life.

It was now the end of July; a large battle was brewing up along the western border of Egypt between the German Africa Korps and the British Eighth Army. Russia's army was being driven back to the city of Stalingrad, having lost oil fields along the way. In the Pacific, the Japanese were close to driving British and Australian troops out of New Guinea and most expected an invasion of Australia would happen soon. It was, some said, the lowest point in the war so far.

Bruce received a phone call from New York; Bennett really liked the final article he'd written on the Rangers' graduation and his first on the Air Corps at Polebrook. Both had sparked letters of encouragement received by the Daily News including one from President Roosevelt's wife. She had taken time to say his writing was lifting the spirits of the American public in a most positive way. Bruce was careful to say what his plans were for the near future, not mentioning the gunnery training and possible mission at all. He said he would like to see London before possibly returning to the United States later in August; he badly wanted to return to San Diego after seeing his folks again. Perhaps a vacation was possible? Bennett said it certainly was, provided Bruce wrote about the journey so others would know he wasn't a task master with his reporters.

Chapter 8
August 1942

The morning dawned clear with little wind. The air crews were assembled for their final briefing before the slightest hint of sunrise colored the eastern sky. Bruce was with the other official observers at the control tower, looking like a whipped puppy. General Anderson walked over to him.

"Bruce, it's a shame Headquarters won't approve you flying on this first mission. We just can't risk losing a civilian on the first one... depending on the success today, I'll push again for you to go along soon. General Eaker, commander of the Eighth Air Force, and I have already hashed this over. If today goes well, there's a good chance that you'll be going."

"Thanks, General, that means so much. It's tough watching from here, I'll admit. At least I'll be the first to interview them when they get back."

"Short flight today... they'll be back about four hours after takeoff. Would you like to spend the time with us listening on the radio?"

"That would be an honor, sir."

Colonel Tibbetts was in the lead plane; the second was co-piloted by General Eaker himself. In all, twelve planes took to the air to bomb a railroad marshaling yard in France... in broad daylight. The Royal Air Force had dismissed daylight bombing as far too dangerous, having lost heavily when they tried it earlier. They now concentrated their resources on night missions; individual planes forming what was called a Bomber Stream that flowed from

England over Europe to hit Germany and return. The missions suffered far fewer casualties but were not nearly as effective in the accuracy of the bombing. Their own surveys admitted that fewer than 5% of bombs even hit within 20 miles of their targets. But their commander, "Bomber" Harris, maintained his insistence on night raids, claiming it was easier to hit a city than a factory and that killing the employees in their beds was just as effective. He intended to destroy entire German cities to force a Nazi surrender. American Air Corps commanders believed that large numbers of B-17's and B-24's, flying in formation with a multitude of machine guns, could defend themselves and keep casualties to a minimum while delivering precision bombing in daylight. It was the higher moral road; to destroy factories, not civilians. The RAF predicted that only one or two of the dozen bombers would return from this first mission.

Bruce, along with the high ranking Air Corps officers, listened to the radio communication between the base and the planes in the air. Bruce could barely make out what was being said; others told him the mission was going well with no German aircraft visible. After the bombers unloaded on the railyard and turned back toward England, a few Luftwaffe fighters were seen, but few came close enough to attack. They appeared to be studying the American formation, more out of curiosity than anything more sinister. One enemy plane was possibly damaged and two American airmen were wounded.

Bruce was on the ground as the first bomber landed. He greeted Colonel Tibbetts and Major Young as they exited through the nose hatch to the concrete hardstand below. Jim Hartke waved to Bruce from the top turret, a huge grin on his face. All twelve B-17s returned, ten unscratched; the mission was a big success. Each airman received a shot of whiskey at the debriefing; some said it was to slow down their talking.

Two days later Bruce was wakened at 0400 hours by an orderly with a flashlight. The man also woke Jim. They were clean shaven and dressed and at their briefing by 0430 hours. This time no one told Bruce he wasn't going along. At the briefing they were told their mission was to bomb an airfield in France as part of a diversion for a planned raid by over 5,000 Canadian, British and American commandos. Bruce's heart skipped a beat at that statement, immediately thinking of his friend in the Rangers. Today he was to fly in the radio compartment but should feel free to visit the officers up front, remembering to not interrupt their duties.

Major Young shook Bruce's hand as the young man arrived at the aircraft.

"Now, put your glove back on and don't take it off until we're back... you'll need both to type the article tonight. Sergeant Hartke will be in the top turret, just ahead of the bomb bay, you remember. If the radio compartment gets too crowded, come on up front and there's a bit more room in the nose... better view, too. You probably won't be needed, but be ready to relieve a gunner if... you know."

"Okay, Major... and remember, third time's a charm... you've already flown me over the Atlantic twice, this is just a short one."

"Sure, but nobody had guns then. We surprised them two days ago... I'm not counting on them being fooled again."

The Flying Fortress was shaking a bit as Bruce settled in with the radio operator in his room. It was rather cramped with both of them in there, bulky sheepskin flying outfits and all. Sergeant Ely, the radio operator, helped Bruce put on a throat microphone and adjusted the headphones in his cap. Now he'd be in touch with everyone else on the plane. Bruce acknowledged when Major Young called off the crew radio check. Ely reminded him to unplug himself and plug in when and where he visited during the flight.

The plane started rolling down the runway, gaining momentum with the weight of bombs and fuel, faster and faster, rattling and shaking until, suddenly, they were up and the flight smoothed out. Bruce could hear and feel the landing gear rolling up under the wings. The plane banked; he looked out the small compartment window and saw the airfield dropping below them, a few other planes already in the air and circling into formation. Bruce sat back down, pulled his notebook from a coat pocket and tried to jot a few lines. He gave up when he couldn't feel the pencil through the bulky gloves, reminding himself to practice that if he was going to fly again.

A half hour later, over the English Channel, Major Young gave the order to check guns. Even in the roar and vibration of the plane Bruce could hear the sound and feel the hammering as each gun was fired for a second. It left him with an impression of immense power and protection. He requested permission to go into the nose; Major Young was agreeable and thanked him for asking. Bruce unplugged his radio cord; Sergeant Ely handed him a small oxygen bottle with mask to put on when they gained altitude. Bruce went forward, opening the hatch to the bomb bay. The sight of the 500 pound bombs hanging in their racks, jiggling slightly, startled him. Each was the size of a garbage can and made the bay seem much smaller than he remembered on the flight from America. He crossed the narrow catwalk and opened the forward hatch. Jim Hartke's legs were right in front of him, standing in the top turret, slowly revolving as Jim searched the air above them for enemy fighters. After giving a thumbs up to the pilots Bruce climbed down the few steps into the nose compartment. The navigator and bombardier both waved and showed him where to sit. He was able to stretch his legs out a bit more than in the radio room, his muscles seemed tighter than usual.

Bruce could see out of the clear nose where the bombardier's seat was located. He noticed a coastline approaching when the navigator tapped him on the shoulder. Turning, Bruce saw him point to the map… France. Bruce nodded and heard Major Young's voice in his headphones saying to go on oxygen. Bruce put on his mask and plugged in to an air fitting next to his seat. He was glad he'd shaved extra close this morning; the mask could rub a man's face almost raw in a short time if he had stubble.

A minute later he heard one of the waist gunners call out on the intercom.

"Bandits, three of them at six o'clock level. Look like 109s."

The voices became a cacophony of noise in his ears as others joined in.

"Top turret, we've got two more at 10 o'clock high, up in the sun...see 'em Jim?"

"Roger, on it"

Bruce felt the hammer fall again right above him as Jim opened up with his two .50 caliber guns. He unplugged his radio and oxygen, grabbed the small bottle and plugged it into his mask. Getting up, he climbed the steps and felt a rain of sizzling hot bullet casings from Jim's guns hitting his coat. He squeezed by his friend and opened the bomb bay hatch. There were the bombs, still jiggling, though the idea of a bullet hitting them suddenly scared him. Bruce opened the other hatch and landed hard on the floor, tripping on the bottom of the doorway. He got up, a thumbs up to the radio operator and slipped past him into the waist compartment. Both gunners were at their guns, back to back as they fired short bursts outward. As quickly as it started, it was over. All the guns went silent and no more chatter about bandits on the radio.

"Pilot to crew... looks like they're gone for now. Keep your eyes open... I'm sure it's not over. Any damage... report."

"Ball turret to pilot... a few holes in the right rear stabilizer... doesn't look too bad."

"Pilot to top turret... want to take a look?"

"Top turret... no sir, not at the moment. Right waist, what do you see from your position?"

"Right waist to pilot... can't see anything wrong, sir. Nothing leaking and no wires trailing."

"Roger."

The next twenty minutes were quiet; the hum of the four engines and the vibration of the plane lulled Bruce into a more relaxed state. He checked his oxygen, having connected to the plane's system in the waist. It was working fine, must be the letdown from the excitement before. He sat on the gunners' parachutes piled in the corner next to the radio room hatch.

"Pilot to crew... beginning bomb run... bombardier, she's yours to fly."

"Bombardier to pilot... roger... opening bomb bay doors... steady... bombs away."

The plane lurched upward, surprising Bruce. The weight of tons of bombs leaving the plane caused it. The Fortress began a slow banked turn to the left, away from the target and toward England.

"Ball turret to pilot... bandits at four o'clock... looks like six... 109s again."

"Roger... let 'em have it."

So began another round of fighting. Minutes went by, guns hammering, bullet casings flying through the air and landing on the deck. Suddenly the radio room hatch slammed hard against Bruce as he was sitting. A loud explosion filled the waist and smoke with flame shot out of the doorway. Bruce jumped up and looked through the smoke; Sergeant Ely was on the floor, his flying goggles shattered, suit torn and shredded. Bruce went into the compartment, radios were burning on his right. He picked up a fire extinguisher and put out the worst of the fires. There was a jagged hole the size of a basketball in the left bulkhead; Bruce could see the engine propellers on the wing through it. He stepped past Ely again and dragged him into the waist compartment. Taking off the goggles, he saw lots of blood and Ely opening his eyes; both were where they should be and focused on his own. Bruce got an oxygen bottle from a rack and hooked Ely up to it. Then he looked more closely at his shredded flying suit. It looked like the suit had absorbed most of the blast, saving the man's life. Bruce tried the intercom and got nothing but static. He motioned to both waist gunners, pointing to his ears and shrugging. Both indicated their radios weren't working either. He opened a first aid kit on the bulkhead; finding a bandage, he tore it open and held it over Ely's forehead, where most of the blood was coming from. The bleeding was already slowing and beginning to freeze from the altitude. Bruce propped up Ely's head to make him more comfortable and went to check on the fires again. They were out, but smoke was still coming from the equipment. Bruce went through the compartment and crossed the now empty bomb bay on the catwalk. When he opened the forward hatch, Jim was on the floor, laying in a pool of blood; the navigator was bandaging his head. Bruce looked up and saw the remains of the top turret cover, plexiglas pieces were everywhere.

Major Young and the copilot were fighting hard with the controls. Bruce could now discern a change in the vibration of the plane. It was coarser and seemed out of rhythm. He guessed one of the engines was no longer working. The bombardier was working at the navigator's table and handed Bruce a message, on paper, to give to the pilot. Young read it and nodded. Bruce stepped down into the nose compartment and looked out a window; they were over water and he could see tall white cliffs below and ahead... Dover, England.

Another twenty minutes and the plane landed, two flares were fired on final approach, indicating wounded aboard. An ambulance met them at their hardstand and within a short time Jim and Ely were on their way to the base hospital. Bruce joined Major Young and the rest of the crew in a truck, headed for their debriefing. The thought of a shot of whiskey was a nice one at the moment.

In the debriefing Bruce was asked to relive his actions during the flight in detail. The difficulties he had in remembering it all in sequence struck him as strange; he was a reporter, adept at gathering and laying out facts. The emotions he felt now had not been in him during the event. He had done all that needed doing, mostly by reflex and not by thought. At the end of the half hour session Bruce felt drained, physically and emotionally. Regardless, he knew he had to get to the base hospital to check on Jim and Sergeant Ely. Pedaling the bicycle across the air base, fresh air in his face, revived him. By the time he reached his destination Bruce felt more like himself. Entering the hospital, he was directed to the ward that both men would be in after they came out of surgery.

Bruce took a seat just outside the ward doors and began to read the day's newspaper lying on a table. United States Marines had landed in the Solomon Islands; their supporting supply ships and escorting Navy warships had been mauled by a Japanese task force. The Marines were now on Guadacanal but had limited food and ammunition. The article made it sound like the first American offensive in the Pacific may be headed for complete disaster. Bruce thought about his friends; Jim in surgery, possibly Fred was part of the Commando raid in France, Bobbie and Stan in the Pacific. He had seen all four in the past few months, pumped and excited about their futures in the coming conflict. Now they were in it and the thrill Bruce had also felt was turned to a cold, heavy dread.

A surgeon approached him through the doors to the ward. He was clothed all in white, his rubber gloves still on, blood splatters on his apron.

"Bruce Hollins? I'm Captain Prescott… we've finished with Sergeant Ely. He's in his bed, awake… you can see him now if you'd like."

"And Sergeant Hartke? Is he out of surgery, too?"

"Well, no. Captain Maki is still working on him… there's a chance, a small one, that he'll lose sight in one eye. He has several cuts and scratches that came after his goggles shattered. We'll know for sure in some days. I think it would be best if you visited him tomorrow. He'll be out from the anesthesia for quite a few hours yet."

"Thank you, Captain. I'll go in and see Ely…"

Bruce's visit with the radioman, who he had barely met before the flight, was brief. Ely was so grateful for Bruce's actions while Bruce tried to downplay his own part.

"You saved my life, Bruce. Getting me out of the radio room, bandaging my head, putting out the fires... hell, you saved all our lives."

"I just got in there first, was closest, that's all. The pilots worked much harder keeping the plane in the air. I almost felt in the way at times. Either of the gunners would have gotten you out."

"But you did it... I'll never thank you enough."

"Listen, I'll come back tomorrow and visit some more... by then Jim will be awake, too. I want to hear about your life so I can write some on it."

"Me? Nawwww... somebody ought to write about you, Bruce."

"See you tomorrow... you know, I don't even recall learning your first name. I've always heard it as Sergeant Ely."

"Hiram... my first name's Hiram. See you tomorrow."

"OK, Hiram... get some rest."

The next morning Bruce was back on the ward before breakfast was served to the patients. A nurse brought him a cup of strong, steaming coffee. Bruce smiled at her, asking her what had caused her to become an Army nurse.

"Oh... I finished nursing school back in November, weeks before Pearl Harbor. When I heard the news on the radio that Sunday, I knew what I'd do. I went down first thing Monday morning and signed up. I arrived here along with the last group two weeks ago. We've all been busy since... setting things up, getting ready... now the preparations are being tested... for real. Your friend, Sergeant Hartke, is in the far bed... down on the left."

"Thanks. Would you mind if I spoke with you a bit later? Maybe get some more background for an article I'd like to write?"

"Me? Sure, that'd be fine, I guess... nobody special though."

"I bet there's already a bunch of guys here that would disagree with you on that."

Bruce walked down to Jim's bed; half of his head was swathed in thick, clean bandages, the other half a collection of stitches over bruised, puffy flesh. His open eye was hard to see because of the swelling. Bruce tried to keep his own expression pleasant as he spoke to Jim.

"Hey, buddy. Sorry I couldn't get to you right away. I was back in the waist, keeping busy and out of the way."

"Bruce... Major Young was here earlier when I woke up. He told me what you did... putting out the fire and saving Hiram. If you hadn't been with us, we might all have gone down. Thanks."

"Well, you know me... can't write about dull things." Bruce smiled, trying to lighten the mood. "Do you remember much of what happened?"

"I remember a Jerrie fighter coming in, an ME109 I think... I hosed him pretty good with my guns, must have killed the pilot. The plane blew up right above us, it would have cut us in two if it hadn't... a big bright flash and I woke up here."

"Have you talked with your doctor yet?"

"Oh, yeah. We talked right after Major Young left... I'll know in a week or so if I'll ever see out of the left eye. Shit... I can't make out much with the right one. My face hurts like hell, that's about it. The Major said our bombs were right on the money, so that makes it better, I guess."

"Sure... Jim... you get more rest. It's what you need most. I'll wire your folks this morning and let them know you're ok. Why don't I check on you again this afternoon?"

"That'll be good, Bruce. Thanks for letting my parents know... send them my love..."

Bruce took his time leaving the hospital; meeting several of the staff and asking about names and hometowns, information he'd use in his article. Everyone he spoke with was surprised that a newspaper would be interested in them. Bruce stopped by the communications office, sending out wires to Jim's family and his own. Then he went to the barracks and began to write.

#

It was several days before Bruce received news that Fred Howard was alright. The Rangers had sent one company along with the Canadians and British Commandos on the Dieppe Raid; it was this raid Bruce's combat flight had been a diversion for. Over half of the Canadian infantry were casualties; killed, wounded or captured. The entire operation was a fiasco, with the exception of the part played by the Commandos and Rangers. They landed several miles away from the main beach and succeeded in neutralizing a strong German artillery position before re-embarking on their landing craft and returning to England. Fred had been part of the fifty Americans who had gone into the fight and returned.

Bruce continued to visit Jim twice each day. His friend's facial wounds were healing nicely, some of the smaller sutures were already removed, leaving behind small pink scars. His right eye was no longer as swollen, though it looked like he'd been in a prize fight with the shiner he sported. The trouble was the left eye and ear. At first the doctors missed a ruptured eardrum that went with the eye injury. The scarring on the eye would be permanent as well; Jim would never see much more than light and dark out of it and his hearing would be impaired, too. About the only good news the doctors had for him was that he was going home… alive.

Bruce would join him on his trip; they would be sailing on the *Queen Mary*, now converted to ferrying troops from America to England. Her return trips consisted of varied groups of passengers; children evacuated to Canada during The Blitz and Axis Prisoners of War also heading to prison camps in Canada. Her once gracious ballroom was now a makeshift hospital for transporting wounded back to the United States; a trickle of men that one day would become a flood.

Before they left, Bruce and Jim were both honored by Major Young at a dinner in the base mess hall. Jim was presented the

147

Purple Heart for his wounds and, though not an airman, Bruce was given an honorary Air Medal by the Major. Their departure found Bruce in Liverpool again, for his third time. As he helped Jim up the gangplank to the deck of the Queen Mary, Bruce turned to gaze on the shipyard docks, wondering if this was to be his last time here.

Chapter 9
September 1942

The *Queen Mary* quietly docked at night in New York; a stopover on her way to Halifax where she would be dropping off a thousand Italian prisoners of war from the fighting in North Africa. Dockside preparations had been made to disembark wounded American soldiers, airmen and merchant mariners who either needed stateside medical care or were being discharged for disabilities. James Hartke was among the latter. He and Bruce rode together on a bus filled with other GI's to Halloran General Hospital over on Staten Island. Bruce had already written an article on the wounded Americans during their voyage across the Atlantic, spending much of the seven days interviewing them. He'd also been allowed to meet with many of the Italian POWs that were destined for internment camps up in Canada. He was shocked at how happy these enemy soldiers were to be captured; to a man they had told him how much better they were treated and fed than compared to their time serving in Rommel's Afrika Korps.

Bruce made sure Jim was settled in at the hospital; his friend was scheduled to remain there for three days and then would be transferred home to Iowa. Bruce planned to make good use of the time to check in with his boss, deliver several articles he'd written on the ship, buy some gifts for his folks and have nice long telephone conversations with Susan. He had bounced around in Great Britain just enough to ensure his mail had not caught up with him, again.

He missed hearing her voice and was excited to have cut the distance between them in half. News received on the ship about the fighting in the Solomon Islands had shown that the Marines and Navy had their hands full with the Japanese. Bruce wanted, somehow, to get over there to cover the action and to find, again, Bobbie and Stan. He now realized that this was not an insurmountable task; with the cooperation he was getting from the military he would be able to make this trip... with a nice stop in San Diego to catch up with Susan.

The hospital was kind to provide him a bed to sleep in for what remained of the night. Early the next morning Bruce woke, showered and had a bite of breakfast with his two cups of fresh coffee before catching a cab for the Daily News. He hadn't thought of phoning Bennett before coming over; he was confident the paper would know of the arrival of the *Queen Mary*. When his editor opened the office door, a look of surprise was on his face.

"Bruce... what the devil? You're not supposed to be here until tomorrow. What'd you do, swim the last hundred miles to get here ahead of the ship? We've got a surprise welcome back party planned for the afternoon... anybody see you get up here? We can hide you in my file cabinet until then, I suppose."

A loud laugh blast brought a smile to Bruce's face; he'd almost come to miss Bennett's signature sound... almost.

"Hmmm... maybe nobody's supposed to know her schedule? At least no one except the hospital and their transportation service. We got in just past midnight; I was a bit surprised at the lack of a reception at the dock. Must be for security from the subs out on the seaboard."

"Well, you look great, Bruce. Lost a bit of weight and your handshake grip nearly broke my hand. I guess that Ranger training toughened you up... think maybe they'd take me? I could stand to shed a few... hell, more than a few, pounds myself." Bennett patted his 'more than ample' middle. "So tell me, how was the trip over?

I swear I don't know anyone that's been back and forth, twice, in this short a space of time."

"Quiet, nice and quiet. No escort, let alone a German u-boat, can keep up with the *Queen Mary*, so we sailed like the wind. I got to meet a bunch of Italian POWs, too. Here, I wrote some stories I think you'll like. I'll be here in New York a few days... if it's okay with you, I'll go with my buddy, Jim, to his folks' home in Iowa. I'd like to visit my own parents there, too. But I really want to talk to you about my getting to the fight in Guadalcanal... if that's where Bobbie Miliken is. I can find out where he is when I stop in San Diego on the way. There's even a chance I'll locate Stan Larson on his ship, too."

"That the only reason you'll go by way of San Diego instead of, say, San Francisco?" Bennett winked as he said it. "Is there still a certain young lady that interests a correspondent I know?"

"Yes there is... in fact, I'm going to leave, grab an empty desk, pick up a phone and call her in about five seconds. I'll even pay for this call."

Both men laughed, though Bruce's own was drowned out by the foghorn of his boss.

As stated, Bruce wasted no time in getting an operator to put through a long distance call to Susan. Three hours' time difference meant he should be waking her up. He did... though it was one of her boarders first. A minute later his voice was in her ear.

"Bruce? Oh, what a wonderful way to wake up... where are you?"

"I'm in New York, darling. I arrived here late last night... took a ship across from England. I don't suppose you've gotten the letter yet I wrote the day we sailed?"

"No, the last one is from Ireland... Carrick... something. I'm not entirely sure how to pronounce it."

"Carrickfergus... well, you'll be getting a few more I'm sure. Obviously the mail takes a while."

"Why are you in New York? Everything all right?"

"Sort of… I'm here with Jim Hartke, my Air Corps buddy."

"He's the one you wrote about in the article on your bombing mission. I take it his wounds didn't heal well?"

"Right… he can't see much at all out of one eye and an ear isn't good either. I'm going to go with him to Iowa. Gives me a chance to see my parents, too. How are you doing, honey… and have you heard from Sam?"

"Oh, he's doing well. He left last week for Hawaii… he's trying to get to dad's ship. Commander Mason has been a great help to him."

"And how are you, Susan? How are you doing… missing me tons, I hope."

"Of course I am, silly. I dream of you every night, at least when I'm not woken up by the real thing like today. Work is actually fun; I get to guide all sorts of visitors around the factory and don't have to work those ungodly long night shifts. I went up to the beach house at Del Mar last weekend… I couldn't stay because I missed you so much. Our time there together was so special to me that without you… well, anyway, I came right back. An evening with a fire on the beach will have to wait until we're together again. Any ideas about that?"

"As a matter of fact… yes. I've just told Bennett I'm heading out to the Pacific to find Bobbie and Stan again. I think I'll even add Sam and your father to the list, too. But first… seeing you is my 'top priority'. I should be in San Diego by mid-month… that will give me time to visit Mom and Dad and make sure Jim gets home alright."

The next several minutes were filled with "I love you" and "can't wait to hold you" and other endearments. Bruce and Susan took time saying their goodbyes; when they were finished, Bruce placed another call through to his parents. He told them about everything, his father joining in on the extension. Bruce spoke of the bombing mission, seeing the radioman and Jim. He talked about Fred and the Rangers, being sure to leave out any details compromising the unit. He was able to speak evenly, with a strong clear voice until he mentioned sailing back across the Atlantic and Jim's condition. His mother whispered a soft, "Oh, my Lord". That's when Bruce broke down, crying for the first time. His parents gave him time to get his voice back. They would meet the train in Des Moines, along with Sidney and Clara Hartke. He asked her what he could pick up to give his dad as a gift and if there was anything she'd like from New York. She quickly replied that his father needed a new briefcase and that she'd be "tickled pink" just to be able to hug her baby again. When they said goodbye, his mom mentioned having "a million things to do to get the party planned".

"Mom, really... it's not necessary. I'm sure Jim would appreciate just some time of peace and quiet with his folks."

"Now you just get him here, dear... Clara and I will take care of things when you arrive. Bye"

After making one more call and leaving a message for Phil Steiner, Bruce fairly snuck out of the building, swearing to secrecy the only two employees he met along the way. It was a sunny, warm late summer day in New York City and he enjoyed a couple of hours, looking for a nice briefcase and picking his mom up some Chanel No 5 perfume at a Fifth Avenue shop. He checked into a hotel near the newspaper office before putting down a couple of Coney Island dogs, with mustard, and a Coke from a street vendor. Taking a cab back to the hospital on Staten Island, to visit Jim and retrieve his luggage, occupied the rest of the afternoon. When he returned to his hotel room, Bruce put through another call to Phil in Fort Myers.

"Bruce, good to hear from you. All of us down here have been enjoying your articles. I've even got one copy you can frame; Papa Hemingway sent one up from Cuba and wrote a note on it for you. I'll send it along to Bennett's office. I got your message and it's all taken care of... the car will be delivered up in Iowa before you get there... two days from now to be exact. A friend of mine owns a shipping company. When I told him whose car it is, he said he'll be proud to get it there at no cost, it's the least he can do for someone like your friend. That was some writing you did, describing that mission… I felt like I was right there in the plane myself. You back for a while or are you heading out again?"

"I'm hoping to get out to the front in the Pacific… Guadalcanal if I can arrange it. I want to visit a few ships, too. After all, I got my training from the Navy."

"Well, Bruce, you've sure done the Army and Air Corps proud as well. Keep up the great work and be safe. Maybe think twice about another flight in a bomber over enemy territory?"

"Thanks, Phil. I'll do my best to remember that… any news about your son in the Seabees? I've read a bit about that group, going to build airfields on islands."

"Yes. My son completed his training last month. He telephoned to say he was boarding a ship out of San Francisco… that was three weeks ago."

"Hey, if I run into him I'll be sure and let you know. My newspaper articles seem to be a lot faster at getting news around than a letter… and thank your friend, really, he's doing much more than I anticipated."

"Sure… will do. Goodbye Bruce."

Feeling better than he had in a long time, Bruce fell asleep almost immediately. He awoke the next morning relaxed and refreshed. Calling room service, he ordered breakfast and copies of the Daily News and the New York Times. When they arrived, Bruce enjoyed a leisurely two hours perusing the papers. He read about the fighting in the Pacific and the arrival of the first Seabee contingent on Guadalcanal; he thought Phil's son might be in that unit. His own articles on the Atlantic crossing of the American wounded and the Italian POWs were in the Daily News and the Times carried the one on the wounded as well. It still thrilled, and humbled, him to see his own words printed in a paper with the prestige and following of the Times. By mid-morning he was finished with his reading and got dressed. He walked through the lobby to the street and hailed a cab for the ride back to visit Jim.

As he entered Jim's ward at Halloran General, applause and cheers broke out from the GI's in the beds. Bruce was visibly embarrassed by their reaction; he addressed them and let them know he believed it was his duty to report their own bravery. Their actions are what deserved an ovation. Jim had become the most popular man on the ward, second most now that Bruce had arrived. He said that all morning, guys wanted to hear stories of their times together growing up, going to school and winning the state championship. The hospital administrator stopped by and asked Bruce to autograph a copy of the front page of the Daily News; he was going to frame it and display it in the lobby of the facility. Bruce consented and spent the next hour visiting his friend and shaking hands with the patients that would stop by Jim's bed. He was in fine spirits as his cab dropped him off at the Daily News offices that afternoon. When the elevator door opened on the fourth floor, where Bennett's office was located, the hallway was filled with his co-workers... all clapping and whistling and loudly welcoming him home. The two he had sworn to secrecy yesterday, nodded and winked as he walked by; they hadn't said a word about his early arrival the day before. Bennett had high praise for his 'star reporter' and encouraged the rest of the staff to follow Bruce's example of tenacity and honest character.

#

"Hey, Bruce... you sure you don't mind traveling with me home? I mean, with all the attention you can get in New York, why don't you want to just stick around and soak it up?"

"Jim, some guys live for the attention I guess. I've seen how Hemingway lights up when he comes in a room and everyone goes nuts... that's just not me. I don't know... maybe I haven't gotten it long enough. The other day at the hospital about knocked me down. That's never happened before, all the hoopla and hand shaking. Remember how Ames went crazy after the championship game? We all thought we were heroes or something... now I've met a few real heroes and, well... the ones I've met hardly get a cup of coffee or anything. I want America to know that the real heroes we have are the everyday folks. Somewhere I read once that heroes are 'ordinary people doing extraordinary things'. That's what I want to write about."

"Bruce, I think someday you might wake up and see that your writing is pretty extraordinary... that's what I think. Anyway... I called my folks. They're going to meet us at the train station in Des Moines, along with yours. That'll be all the welcome crowd I need... be good to be home. Thanks for being with me... I think it would have been pretty lonely otherwise."

"Well, did you talk with your dad about helping out on the farm?"

"Nope, don't think so... not that many acres. I'm thinking of asking Fred's dad for a job... he's got his hands full trying to supply Hormel with hogs. He told my dad to talk with me about it... I'd like to go back to college at State, maybe do evening classes while I work days. I'll figure it out... one thing's sure though. There's going to be a need for guys around Ames to keep all the girls busy with the war on." Jim grinned and elbowed Bruce in the side. "First thing I'll do is get my butt down to Naples and pick up the car. Getting gas on the way back might not be easy, but I'll figure out a way."

They were crossing Ohio as they spoke. Chicago was several hours away and the sky was getting dark. They walked to the dining car and enjoyed a meal before heading to their stateroom in the sleeper. A good night's rest and Iowa in the morning.

The train pulled into the station a short time after a rain; the sky was filled with clouds, threatening more. A fresh scented wind blew strong, the banners tied to the sides of the four buses flapped noisily. Jim climbed down the car's steps and looked up.

"What the hell..."

The cheering started immediately. Ames high school cheerleaders began the chant... "Jim, Jim he's our man..." The school band started the familiar fight song as Clara Hartke stepped up and gave him a welcoming hug, her husband Sid hanging back. Bruce looked over at his own parents and gave them both thumbs up. Pandemonium ensued for the next quarter hour as everyone wanted to greet the returning airman... and Bruce. As the rush quieted down and people began to board the buses for the ride back to Ames, Bruce heard, and felt, a familiar rumble. Jim turned his head, the good ear picking up the sound as well. He looked at Bruce, who simply smiled back. The blue jalopy nosed out from behind a bus, their basketball coach at the wheel. Jim saw it, wiped his good eye and broke down. Bruce put his arm around his friend's shoulder.

"See what I mean about all the attention?"

Bruce spent most of his time over the next several days visiting the parents of his team mates, sharing the stories of his time with each of their sons. Frank and Mabel Howard welcomed Jim and Bruce as they arrived in the blue hot rod, engine growling and tires kicking gravel up the drive. Frank stood with his fists pumping up in the air at the sound of the engine; he'd always been more of a kid than any of the boys. As soon as they stopped the car, he had the hood up and was eagerly checking out the engine. Mabel wore the easy smile of a woman content with her life; being the spouse of a successful farmer and the mother of two kids, one an Army Ranger, suited her just fine.

"In the kitchen, you two... coffee's on and a fresh baked apple pie with cheddar cheese on top... I recall that's how you all liked it."

It was a race; Frank actually beat the two younger men to the door and held it open for them, bowing low and laughing. Fred's sister, Francine, was in the kitchen serving up slabs of pie. Frankie, as the boys called her, was a year younger than Fred. She had graduated in June and was enrolled as a freshman at State College. She said hello to Bruce and her gaze lingered a bit on Jim. The group sat at the familiar Howard kitchen table, large and round with plenty of room for the five of them.

"Mom, dad... how about after we finish, you and Bruce talk... I'd like to get a ride in Jim's car before I have to leave for school... classes this afternoon." She looked at Jim as she said the last bit.

"I guess that will be fine, if Jim doesn't mind having Fred's baby sister in the car." quipped her dad.

"Oh, dad. I'm hardly a baby anymore."

"I don't mind at all, Mr Howard. I could even give Frankie a ride to campus. I'd like her to show me where I need to go to enroll myself; night classes as soon as I can start."

"Good move, Jim. Getting back in school will be good for you. You'll have a head start on all the other boys when they come home. I do want to talk to you later about a job with me... no rush. Take some time to unwind first."

"Thanks, sir." Jim finished the last bite of his pie, swallowed the coffee. He and Frankie stood up; he waited while she got her books.

"Be back for you, Bruce... maybe three or four hours?"

"Sure, Jim... take your time. I've got the whole afternoon... I want to talk to Mr Howard about his hog operation myself."

Frank and Mabel had an enjoyable time learning about Bruce and Fred's times together. The surprise of running into each other on the transport in January, the time they spent in Ireland before Bruce came back to the states. Then the reunion in Carrickfergus and training with the Rangers. Bruce brought them up to date with the news of Fred's action at Dieppe and safe return to Ireland.

"So what do you think is next, Bruce? Any inkling at all about what might be in store for him?" Frank Howard had a curious, concerned look on his face.

"Can't really say, sir. I'm not at all given information on the future of things... especially with the Rangers. Talk is that we won't be going across the English Channel to France for quite some time... maybe a couple of years. Even southern France is not probable; we're not at war with the Vichy government there. Best guess I've heard, and it's just a guess, is Africa. Maybe helping out the British Eighth Army in the east by Egypt or a landing in the west behind Rommel's Afrika Korps. I'm sure the Rangers will be it from the start, or even before. The training they...we... got is for the kind of fighting that is ahead of a major landing."

Mabel was speaking while working her napkin in her hands. "Meantime... we have the Japanese. I feel so worried for Stan and Bobbie... the Larson's and Milliken's are very nervous about their boys. Neither family has heard anything from them since they left Hawaii in late July. I don't suppose you'll be heading out to find them again, will you Bruce?"

"Yes, ma'am... that's exactly what I hope to do. I'm only home here for a week or so. I want to get enough information from you and the Larsons and Millikens so I can write about what impact the war is having on my friends' families and the rest here at home... then I'm off to San Diego to try and get to the Pacific... where those two are."

"Anything you want to know about the local impact... I'm sure you'll learn from your own dad... along with the rest of us. His bank has made a big difference in how we've all built up our businesses." Mr Howard began telling Bruce how he shifted from raising a handful of hogs, along with chickens and milk cows back in 1940, to an operation raising thousands of hogs for the meat industry, chiefly Hormel up in Austin, Minnesota.

"C'mon Bruce, I'll show you." The two men walked outside the farm house. Bruce saw the familiar barn where the few animals he remembered had been kept. But beyond the barn, in the distance, stood five large, new, white buildings; much longer than but not as tall as the barn, they were neatly arranged in a rank, newly planted trees in a ring around them, partially shielding them from view.

"Each of those has 1,000 hogs inside. It's kind of a finishing operation. We also have another site up north a few miles for the farrowing. Here the hogs are penned up and fed until they get to the weight Hormel wants before slaughter. When a barn is ready, all the hogs are loaded on trucks and shipped up to the processing plant. We figure that one barn... well, each can handle three groups a year... each will produce near to 650,000 pounds of hogs a year... a bit under half that weight in cut meat, so... about 320,000 pounds or 160 tons of pork per barn each year. That, son, is a hell of lot of squeal with the tail off. And it all, every bit of it, goes to the military and, through lend-lease, to our friends the British and Russians."

"I had no idea... that staggers the imagination. All that increase in two years?"

"Yep... and I'm hardly the only one. Iowa stands to lead the nation in hogs this year, I'd bet. Bill Larson still contracts with me for feed, just like before. Only now... I'm his only customer. I'm not even exactly sure how many tons of feed... others keep track of those numbers now. We even contract out the pig shit... there's tons of that to be sure. Farmers use it, spray it on their fields now for fertilizer. You'll know when, if you're downwind."

They walked back in the house, Mabel met them with a glass of iced tea for each. The three sat down on the shade porch and enjoyed the afternoon breeze. Bruce was sniffing the air.

"Not today, Bruce... wind's from the wrong direction." Frank said with a chuckle.

The remainder of their visit was about local news; the school was not much changed, except that the senior class was short several of the boys that had already enlisted before graduating. It was an issue that had strong feelings on both sides; some parents felt it their patriotic duty and others believed that an education first was the best policy. The shadows grew longer in the yard as they talked about rationing of gas not being so bad in a rural setting where farmers got what they needed and most shared with friends. Scrap drives were held periodically in Ames and groups stopped by once in a while for donations. Frank said one bunch of scouts came and cleaned out his wooded area, hauling three generations worth of rusting farm machinery away. Mabel saved all her cooking fat drippings along with aluminum pots and pans; she preferred cast iron anyway.

The sound of Jim's car came on the breeze. The three stood, stretched from their sitting so long and walked to meet him, and Frankie. Jim got out, walked around the front of the car and opened the door for their daughter. Frank smiled and Mabel raised her eyebrows.

"Sir, there's a football game this Saturday at State College. Would you mind if I took Frankie to it?"

Frank looked at Mabel; she nodded.

"Sure, Jim... that would be fine. Why don't you come over in the morning and we can talk a bit about that job."

Their conversation was more lighthearted bantering as Jim barreled down the county road toward Bruce's home in Ames. Bruce started it by imitating Jim's talk of filling the absence of men in the area with all the girls. Jim said that was fine and a fellow has the right to change his mind; besides, life might be good dating the boss's daughter. Bruce just smiled and told his friend to keep his eyes on the road when he drove Frankie to class.

That evening Bruce sat down with his father to talk. Earl quietly closed the door to his study, looking at his son while crossing over to his desk. He opened a bottom drawer, withdrawing two glasses and a bottle.

"A little brandy doesn't hurt... especially after a good dinner." Earl poured each small glass half full of the brown liquid and handed one to Bruce.

"To your writing and travels... a clear head for one and safety for the other."

Although Bruce drank beer and even had a few mixed drinks over the past year, he wasn't prepared for the warm smoothness of the brandy as he took his first sip.

"Not bad, not bad at all... time in the bottle doesn't seem to diminish it at all..." his father said, a satisfied smile on his face.

"Mmmm... a guy could get used to this." Bruce countered.

"Don't even think of it... a bit now and then, on special occasions only. Too much of a good thing is the way to perdition."

Earl smiled and set his glass down. "Now, what would you like to talk about, son?"

"I spent quite a bit of time with the Howards today, dad... they're doing really well with the war on... I can't believe how big his hog operation is now. You know I haven't spent much time in the States since December... what's your take on business in Iowa. I want to send my boss an article on home life here and I think some information on the money situation is important."

"Sounds like you've come a long way in the past year. When you left for New York, I was convinced you were destined to write obituaries and local news for a long time... Roy Coffee wrote and said you were maturing as a writer; I'd say it goes for insight along with the writing itself. Beyond the writing, son, you've seen and experienced things most would consider nightmarish; would never want to be a part of. For that courage... and that is what it is... I toast you again. Hmmm, let me gather some thoughts before I start."

Earl sat back, reached for his favorite pipe, packed the bowl slowly and carefully before he struck a match. Putting the flame to the tobacco, he puffed a few times before a full, blue cloud of pleasant smelling smoke drifted up.

"The bank here in Ames, at least our bank, has seen a tremendous increase in business, lending and investing, over the past year and a half. It really began before war was declared... before the Japs hit Pearl Harbor. Roosevelt started the country on a war footing long before the shooting started... for us. Neutrality Act, Lend-Lease, the Arsenal of Democracy... all the things you hear take money, and lots of it. What Frank Howard has done is a great example of the potential in getting behind this war. I think, though, you'll see a different attitude and result when you get with Jim's folks... Sidney and Clara don't see the growth as necessarily a good thing. They've had opportunity... well, I've presented them with chances to expand their own farm... crop farming is just as important as hogs. Sid doesn't want it... I think he doesn't have that personal initiative to succeed. Some folks are just content to stay where they are. That's fine... but I think their son see's it a bit different and that will cost them their farm down the road. No one to come along behind and take over. It may be up to Jim to take care of his folks some day because of it."

"But what about other things... beyond the farms here?"

"Right... well, State College is really growing, too. They've got lots of money from Washington, doing research on several things... some are very hush hush. New buildings are going up... a new agricultural research facility. Some say it'll be bigger than the University over at Iowa City. I'm sure they're getting their share as well. Bill Larson, Stan's father, has bought several new trucks... just to supply feed to Frank's hogs. I've had to hire six new employees this year to keep up with the flow of money through the bank... most is ag business... which figures for our part of the state. I also hear that manufacturing is way up over in the Quad Cities... Burlington, Davenport... you know. Can you imagine how many railroad engines and cars will be needed to fight the war in Europe? They're also building tanks, armored cars and what not for the Army directly. Bruce, I don't think you can capture all the growth in one article."

"Sounds like you're right. I'll start with what I get while I'm here... I plan on writing it on the train west. I'm sure I can add more along the way."

"West? How soon are you leaving? Mother and I really enjoy you being here, you know... What's the rush to go west... wait, forget I said that." He smiled, less like a father and more like a friend. "Susan... when do we get to meet her?"

"I'm not sure yet. We talk as often as we can and I write her nearly every day... but we've only spent a few weeks really... together. I mean, she wants to take more time before we commit to anything."

"Sounds like a smart girl; what are her parents like?"

"Her dad's in the Navy... a Chief Petty Officer on the carrier *HORNET*... the one that launched the raid on Tokyo. Her mom died a few years ago… Susan lives in her parent's house with a couple of co-workers and Sam, her brother, has his own place; but he's also a War Correspondent for the Navy. Susan said he's on his way to the Pacific, probably get there before I can. That's all I know about her family."

"How does she feel about you wanting to go to war? Some girls, I'm sure, aren't too excited about their men leaving."

"Oh, she understands my job. I know she'd like it better if we could be together… so would I. But for now I've got to travel to do my job. I would have said it's not really dangerous… before I flew with Jim. I'm sure she'll want to talk a while about that when we get together again."

"And she should, son. So… when do you leave?"

"I do want to talk with the Hartkés, Larsons and the Millikens before I go… probably beginning of the week. I'll take the same train as last time; I want to see about visiting a relocation camp in California before I head to the Pacific."

"Ah, the Jap camps; I've been reading about them. I suppose it's important for the west coast defense… but quite a few of us think the country is making a big mistake in having those camps. A bunch of folks they're locking up are American citizens… smacks of what the Germans are doing with their concentration camps, depriving people of their liberties."

"From what I've read…well, I'll maybe be a better judge after I've visited one, Dad."

"Point taken… don't mean to sound too critical, really. It's just that with the war on, some politicians take things a bit too far with security… and other things."

A knock at the door and his mother came in. She sighed when she saw the bottle and glasses, but didn't say anything… it wasn't necessary.

"Oh, Louise, Bruce and I only had one… man to man."

"Now Earl, did I say a word? I just wanted to get in on any conversation… especially if anything is being said about a certain young lady in San Diego…"

Bruce answered. "Sit down, mom… we were just getting to that. I'll tell you all about Susan…"

The three talked until after midnight. Bruce noticed the eyelids getting heavier on his folks and suggested they continue the next evening. His mom got up, kissed him and went to bed. His dad said he had a few minutes of work to do; Bruce said goodnight and went up to his room. He stayed awake for an hour thinking about home, friends and the coming trip back to San Diego.

Bruce dropped his dad at the bank after breakfast; he wanted to borrow the family car to visit the Hartke farm. Driving out the familiar road, he enjoyed the smell of the gravel dust and the drying field corn. Tractors were disking in harvested sweet corn remains along the way and apples were fat and almost ready for picking near several of the farm houses. The Hartke place came up; it was more run down and the outbuildings were in need of painting. Bruce parked the car in the shade alongside the house, got out and bounded up the porch steps. Even these were loose and sagging. He didn't see Jim's car and wondered if his friend was still home. Sid Hartke came to the door as Bruce knocked. He was not quite as tall as Jim, thinning hair on top and a bulging stomach behind his overalls.

"Morning, Bruce. Jim's at the College… registering for classes. We just finished breakfast, you can have some coffee if you want."

"That would be great, thanks Mr Hartke. Good morning, Mrs Hartke" he said, coming into the kitchen.

"Good morning, Bruce. Sorry Jim's not here; take anything in your coffee?"

"No, ma'am… just black, thanks. Actually, it's you and Mr Hartke I'd like to visit with, if you have the time."

"Sure… why don't we sit down in here? It's still nice and cool inside."

The three sat and Bruce asked about farming, Jim being home and the war. Sid said he hoped to get around to fixing the place up and, maybe, getting a bit more land to farm. He was glad Jim was home and wished his son would show more interest in helping him farm. All the boy seemed to want to do was work on machines and make them go faster. He, himself, had been glad to get the land from his folks, had been working the same acres his whole life.

"Now, Sid, the boy's not cut out for farming, you know that…" said Clara.

"He ought to be, came from us you know. Farming is good, working the land. I don't know… I guess he's just different."

Bruce squirmed a bit in discomfort. He hadn't wanted to hear the same things he remembered from high school. He hoped the war would have changed Mr Hartke somehow, made him less… depressing. The talk turned, at his urging, to the positive signs of growth in the area. Bruce mentioned some of the things he'd learned from his dad about the college and the new ag research center. None of it seemed to affect Sid at all. Clara shrugged and apologized as her husband actually got up and left the kitchen to "go see about getting some work done" as he put it.

Bruce gave her a hug and said his own goodbyes. As he got in the car, he saw that Mr Hartke hadn't even made it to the barn in his shuffling walk, hands in his pockets… like a man already defeated.

Bruce picked up his mom at home and the two went to the bank to meet Earl for lunch. They walked to the café around the corner and took a booth. After ordering a sandwich and soup, Bruce spoke up.

"You were right, dad. Mr Hartke just doesn't want to improve much, the way I see it. He was against anything nice or good we talked about."

"Clara has a lot to say when we get together for tea", his mom replied. "She's very worried about Sidney. His health is not good, he's like a broken man."

"Well, Jim's not interested in helping on their place; he's told me that himself. I see him working for Mr Howard and making a start on his own. That has to make his dad feel even worse." Bruce added, "I'm going to talk to him… maybe he can get Mr Howard to help. The Hartke place is close by; maybe he could use the land for hogs somehow."

"Maybe… perhaps he could at that." said his dad.

After eating and walking back to the bank, Bruce and his mom headed home. He dropped her at the house and drove up to Jewell to visit the Millikens. As he drove through the fields of corn, Bruce was aware of all the pheasants flying across the road, their unique "awk…awk…awk" making him wish he'd remembered a shotgun. Pheasant and dumplings sounded good, even on a full stomach.

Edith Milliken, Bobbie's mother, was home. His father, Bob Senior, was at a construction site a few miles out of town. His business as a carpenter had become too much for one man. Over the course of the spring and summer, Bob had launched out and started working as a general contractor. Now he had more than a dozen different jobs going on at the same time, spread out all over the county. He had acquired a knack of coordinating the work; concrete, plumbing, electrical and finished carpentry that was putting up houses, barns and even much of the new ag center at the college.

Bruce told Edith of his time in San Diego finding her son and Stan. She laughed at his story of getting the two together for a photo; tears were in her eyes as he told of seeing the transport ships out to sea from the Del Mar house.

"So, Bruce, your mother HAS hinted that there's a girl in your life now?"

"Yes, ma'am. She lives in California… San Diego. I'll be seeing her again soon. I'm leaving for the west coast in a few days.

I want to head into the Pacific and hook up with Bobbie and Stan Larson. I've already written twice about Fred Howard and Jim Hartke's back home now."

"I know... we wanted to make it down for you two in Des Moines; it's just too busy now with all Bob's work. You know, it's not just the men that are busy either. I've been working with the local Red Cross, sewing, knitting and working the canteen at the college for the officer candidate cadets in training there. It's all work but so much fun. It feels good to contribute a little with you boys doing so much... and your mother, goodness sakes alive... she is even more involved. Why, she's in charge of all the entertainment for the cadets... she's practically a one person USO show. By the way, I got a letter from Bobbie yesterday; would you like to hear it?"

"I'd like to very much, yes, thanks."

Edith read the letter; it was from Guadalcanal. Bobbie had landed in early August, along with the rest of the Eighth Marines. They had taken the Jap airfield and were still holding it. The food was okay and he was fine... all the things a good soldier writes home about. Bruce knew it was probably very different but didn't want to alarm anybody. He'd wait to get there and see for himself.

"I'm glad he's doing well; the Navy has had a real fight with the Japs out on the water. I guess the land war's going better."

"I do hope so. I was dreadfully worried when he joined the Marines, but he does look dashing in his dress uniform."

"You know, Mrs Milliken... I think I'll swing by the feed store in Ellsworth and see if I can catch Mr Larson there. I'm trying to get together information for an article I'm writing on the economy and building boom. That's part of why I came up... I was hoping Mr Milliken would be home. I should have phoned first, I'm sorry for not doing that."

"That's perfectly alright, Bruce. It was so good to see you. I suppose I'll run into Jimmy Hartke soon; it's too bad about his wounds. I do hope he'll get better. Can I have Bob Senior write you about what he's been doing the past several months? It may take some time, but I know he'd like to do it."

"That will be fine, ma'am. Jim says his ear is already not ringing quite so much and the doctors think his eyesight problem is permanent... but maybe by the end of the war they'll have it figured out."

"Yes... hope is something we always have. Nice seeing you Bruce... say hello to your mom and dad."

"I will... goodbye."

He started the car and drove the five miles east to Ellsworth. The feed store was right alongside the railroad tracks running through town. Bruce noticed the additional storage buildings that had been added. Piles of sacks of feed filled each of the four garage size sheds.

"That's ALL for Frank Howard's hogs?" he said as he pulled up.

#

His mom had spent much of the day preparing his favorite dinner... where she got the pheasants for the dumplings, she wouldn't say. His dad joked it might have been anyone that provided them, except himself. He'd been much too busy at the bank to go hunting this season. Bruce ate two full helpings with a relish that pleased his mother and made his dad's eyes pop.

"Did the Rangers hollow out one leg while you trained with them? You didn't eat that much when you had basketball five nights a week."

"Well, dad, I haven't had home cooking five nights a week lately either."

After dinner, Bruce and his folks sat on the front porch in the cool evening air, just a hint of the coming frosty nights. Earl smoked his pipe while the three talked about the future. Louise asked if Bruce thought he might be back home soon. He told them, again, of his desire to get to the Pacific front to find Bobbie and Stan. He really had no idea how long that might take.

"You know, mom and dad, I've had the chance to speak with hundreds of guys like me, at least nearly the same age, from all over the country. They talk about their folks, their schooling... all that sort of thing. What I've gotten as I listen to them is just how lucky I am to have such swell parents. You two supported me in sports and I've had a really great home to live in. Most of the guys I've talked with can't say this. I want you both to know how much I love you... awwww, mom."

Louise was already dabbing at her eyes with a hankie. His dad reached out a hand and shook Bruce's. The three stood and hugged each other. Louise managed to say, "Okay, dominoes in the closet... how about one game of 'chickie-foot'?"

The rest of the evening was spent at the kitchen table, each trying his or her best to beat the others in several rounds of their favorite game.

#

Bruce settled in to his seat on the upper deck of the observation car; his typewriter was on a small table in front of his chair. As the train left the Des Moines station and picked up speed, the rhythmic "clack, clack...clack, clack" of the wheels on the track and the gentle swaying reminded him of why he so enjoyed traveling on a train. It seemed to him the three ways of travel he'd used over the months since the war began all had their unique qualities, yet one similarity... the swaying motion. The synchronized whining buzz of aircraft engines, the churning wake of a propeller on a ship were alright, but the sound of a railcar's wheels was like music. A metronome couldn't sound out a better beat to type a news article by.

He began his newest work, on the war's impact to Midwestern life, before the sight of the Iowa capitol dome disappeared over the horizon. He would have the time he needed on the train to organize and write; hopefully Mr Milliken's letter would meet him in San Diego shortly after his own arrival. He wanted to include those comments on the building frenzy sweeping the Ames

170

area in his article. He was glad for the chance to see all of his friends' parents. More than anything, though, was his joy in spending time with his own folks. Bruce knew that once he arrived in southern California, he would find little time to finish writing before another project came up. There was something about the military presence there that caused news to happen. All the work he anticipated didn't begin to equal the time he wanted to spend with Susan. He hoped she might take some time from work to go with him on a trip to the Owen's Valley, to visit the relocation camp and to continue on for a few days in Yosemite, a hundred miles further north. He remembered a book about the beauty of the place, written years ago by John Muir, the naturalist who helped it become a National Park. Bruce actually wrote an article about his dream of visiting it one day; Mr Hansen had used it in the school's paper. He could think of no one else to share in his first view of Half Dome and the beauty of Tuolumne Meadows than Susan.

That evening the sun had set when a porter informed him his sleeping berth was ready. He had made good progress so far on his work; the notes were now organized, as were his thoughts. A night's sleep and, with no distractions, he might get the whole thing typed in the morning. Then he could see what interesting passengers and crew he might find to talk with... he'd written about his flights from and to England; then there was the one he wrote about his first sea voyage on the troopship. Now he might pen something on train travel across the United States.

#

San Diego looked the same as his first time coming into the station there; the same camouflage netting over Consolidated's factory, the same hustle and bustle of the people on the streets. If anything, he noticed there were even more military uniforms on pedestrians crossing Broadway, and Saul's Seven Seas was more crowded than he imagined possible. Bruce had to stop there on his way to the US Grant Hotel, where he would, again, be staying.

Saul was so glad to see his young friend, and to hear just a few quick stories about his time in Naples. Bruce made plans to visit Saul at his home on Point Loma for dinner; he'd be sure to bring Susan along with him. When Bruce checked in to the hotel, he asked about the former clerk Bernice, who had been so eager to 'help' him last trip. He smiled when told she had married a sailor and was no longer working there. He was shown to the same room he had months earlier; life seemed to be on hold when he opened the door to the familiar living area. The table where he had typed his articles then was still in front of the same chair; almost as if he'd never spent all that time in Florida, Ireland and England.

Bruce unbuttoned his coat and waited a few minutes until he knew Susan was off work to phone her. A roommate told him she hadn't arrived yet but would have her return his call. Moments after he'd hung up the phone there was a knock at his door. He opened it and was surprised to see his love standing there.

"I couldn't wait to see you, so I walked over from work. I had to make sure you're really in one piece. May I come in and freshen up in your bathroom before you take me to dinner?" she declared with a kiss and a smile.

"Wouldn't have it any other way... come in." He closed the door and gave her a much longer kiss. He held her at arms' length and admired her.

"You know, silly, I really haven't had much time to change since you last saw me."

"I know... I just want to look at you. I've seen you when I close my eyes, but sometimes I wonder if you're really as beautiful as what I see."

"Well?"

"More beautiful in real life. My own imagination doesn't do you justice. You are stunning."

"Thanks... now let me go freshen up before I melt." she said, blushing. "You know... you're looking even more dashing in that uniform. Your time with the Rangers was good for you."

A few minutes later Susan emerged from the bathroom with makeup on, her hair brushed out and hanging over her shoulders. Bruce noticed the same shade of lipstick she wore the first time he saw her dressed up. Her hair was longer, by a few inches and was that same golden blonde color he loved.

"You're still staring, you know." Susan said, her eyes laughing at him.

"I cannot help myself. I'm sure it sounds corny, but I could look at you all night long... just look at you."

"That's so sweet... thanks. But I could use a bite to eat; you mind looking at me over a table in a restaurant?"

"Anywhere you'd like... "

"Ooooh, an offer like that I can't refuse. How about we walk down to The Harborside? They have a wonderful selection of fresh seafood, right off the boats. It's my dad's favorite... he and my mom used to go there."

"But of course, lead the way... my lady." Bruce bowed and held the door open, sweeping his arm out toward the hallway, doing his best impression of Errol Flynn. Both laughed as they walked to the elevator. The sidewalks were still full of people as they left the hotel lobby. He held her hand as the two walked closely side by side; he could feel himself relax.

Over a dinner of succulent scallops and fresh albacore tuna, Bruce and Susan caught up on all the past months' happenings they hadn't already discussed by phone. Bruce suggested the possibility of a train trip to Yosemite Valley for a few days; she loved the idea and would look at getting time off in the morning. Susan talked of her brother and his arrival in Hawaii.

"The day after your last call from home, I got a letter from him. It was dated two weeks ago, almost three now. He wrote from a Marine camp on the island of Hawaii. The unit he's with is getting ready to head to Guadalcanal to reinforce the First Marines on the island. He made it sound like they'd be leaving shortly, though he couldn't give a date, of course. I've also received letters from Dad on the *HORNET*. He writes that he's fine, the ship's fine... nice weather... you know, all those things he thinks I want to hear. I'm sure it's not all fine... the newspapers are pretty clear that we're not gaining much against the Japs."

"It's not just the Japs, honey. The Germans are still fighting for Stalingrad against the Russians, the British have their hands full with Rommel... about the only real damage we're doing to anybody, it seems, is from the air in England. The Royal Air Force is starting to firebomb whole cities instead of just hitting the factories. This war is getting to a level the world has never seen."

Susan looked down at her lap as she quietly spoke.

"Any chance of you staying here in California for more than a few weeks?"

"Susan, you know I want to spend all my time with you... and I mean ALL my time. But I HAVE to go and to write; it's more than the job to me. All the guys I've met... the dangers they face... how can I do less? When we win this thing... and I believe we will, then we'll have all the time we want to be together."

"IF we win... Bruce. My father and brother... all the family I have, is out there. Now you're going, too? I've never felt more alone than the day you got on the train to Florida... and then Sam shipped out. Every time I look at a newspaper, I don't just think of you and something you've written. I think of turning a page and reading about the *HORNET* being sunk with all hands or some Japanese submarine sinking a transport with my brother on board. What will I do if it happens?"

"For starters, you could go to my parents' home... I mean it. They are going to flip over you when you meet someday. Honest."

Susan's face went white as she looked over Bruce's shoulder. A man at the next table was reading an evening special edition of the Times. The headline, in large bold print, read JAPS SINK US CARRIER IN SOLOMONS.

"Oh, my God... no". Susan's eyes pleaded with Bruce as he bought a newspaper from a boy selling them in the restaurant. He

174

quickly scanned down the article. Several lines into the story he found the name of the carrier... *USS WASP*.

"It's not your dad's ship, Susan... I'm sure he's alright. The article doesn't mention the *HORNET* at all." He took her hands on the table, looked into her tear filled eyes. "This is why I've got to go..."

"When can we leave for Yosemite... is the day after tomorrow too soon? I've got to get away for some time. I want to spend every moment of it with you, Bruce."

"I'll make a couple of calls in the morning. Can I meet you for lunch at the diner across from Consolidated?"

"Twelve thirty... don't get your hopes up for a hamburger. Tomorrow is "Meatless Thursday". She wiped her eyes and continued. "In the meantime, I'd like a dish of ice cream... no, an ice cream cone we can eat while we walk along the Promenade at the waterfront. You'll like the tuna boats; there are dozens tied up along the wharf."

The moon was up, casting a wide, bright path across San Diego Bay as they walked past the boats. The sounds of hulls creaking lightly in the gentle swells and the smells of fish, diesel fuel and salt water made Bruce think of going to sea again. He thought of ships fighting; blasting and bombing each other to oblivion. Nope, he thought, rail travel is much nicer.

#

"Thanks, Saul. I'm sorry we have to back out on dinner; it's just that we'd like to have some time alone before I head out again. Susan and I leave tomorrow morning for Yosemite... I got us reservations at the Lodge there for a few nights. On our way back, we're going to try and visit the relocation camp at Manzanar, up near Lone Pine... in the Owens Valley."

"Don't worry about it, Bruce. I'm not going anywhere, especially as busy as we are now. My wife will love cooking a dinner, whenever you and Susan can make it. How do you plan on getting from Yosemite to Lone Pine? That country's kind of sparse up there... no trains and not much except a small road."

"You sound like you've been there, Saul."

"Oh, I do get around."

"Well, something will turn up... we can always take the train back down to Los Angeles and go over through San Bernardino."

"That'd be your best bet. Now you sound like you've been there." Saul chuckled and wished them the best on their short trip.

Bruce met Susan for lunch; she could hardly sit still in the diner as they talked about plans for their trip.

"Really, you'd think they wanted to get rid of me. I asked my boss for a few days off and he asked if that's all I wanted. I did mention you taking me along to the relocation camp and all... I think he's giving me the time off as much for you as for me. I keep forgetting what a celebrity you are."

Their train left early the next morning, before sunrise. They sat in the dining car, coffee and breakfast, as the train made its way up the coast to Los Angeles. Susan napped with her head on his shoulder part of the way north as the city turned to country and the foothills of the higher mountains slowly climbed, giving way from desert scrub to pines. Bruce noticed on a map that they were now about even with Lone Pine, separated by fifty or so miles of rugged high country. He thought about how long it might take to hike that country, wondered if there were any lakes or streams full of trout up there. It looked so beautiful... he put it on his mental list 'of places to see when the war is over'.

The train arrived at the Yosemite Lodge the next morning, their night spent in separate berths in the sleeping car. A small bus, from the Lodge, picked them up and brought them through a grove of huge Sequoia trees, tall as New York skyscrapers. Both of them were stunned by the size of the trees; pictures could never capture their majesty. A herd of deer grazed on the Lodge lawn while a bellhop unloaded their luggage. The clerk was very pleasant as he helped Bruce check in.

"Yes, Mr Hollins... everything is all set. Here's your key; the bellhop will bring you and your luggage to your room. Anything we can do or help with, just ask, sir."

The bellhop led them up several flights of stairs to their room on the top floor. Opening the door, Bruce and Susan looked in.

"But, this is a suite... I booked us for two separate rooms?"

"Well, sir, the suite has two bedrooms. Mr Price left explicit instructions that this is to be your room, sir."

"Mr Price... Saul Price?"

"I'm not sure of the gentleman's first name, sir. I am only the bellhop."

They walked in and found a note on the table, along with a huge fruit basket. "Enjoy your time together, away from everybody else. Saul"

The phone rang. Susan answered it, saying a few words before she hung up.

"Bruce, I cannot wait to meet this friend of yours. That was the front desk; a Park Ranger will be here in half an hour for our horse ride through the Sequoia grove. If we don't think we have proper clothes, we're to visit the store downstairs."

"What?

#

Their time in Yosemite was more inspirational than either could have imagined. Guided tours by Park Rangers included the best the Valley had to offer; panoramic views of the most beautiful landscapes they had ever seen. Hikes to the edge of streams that ended in torrents of water cascading down a thousand feet to the valley below. Another horseback ride to the bases of those same waterfalls completed their visit to the park. When Bruce checked with the front desk about their return train reservations, he was told that arrangements were in place for Susan and himself to be taken to the eastern entrance of the park. There a car was waiting for them to drive down to the Owens Valley at Lone Pine and on to Manzanar; the officer in charge of security at the camp was expecting them.

Bruce could think of no way to repay the kindness shown to them by his friend Saul.

A ride through high country to the eastern gate passed Tuolumne Meadows, the area Bruce had especially wanted to see. When they reached the entrance gate a Park Ranger met them, car keys in hand. The vehicle was a 1938 Plymouth convertible; Bruce and Susan put their luggage in the back seat after thanking the Ranger and the Lodge driver. Getting directions to Lone Pine from the gate attendant, Bruce started the car and away they went. The drive to Lone Pine took the rest of the day; they spent the night in a small motel along the highway running down the middle of town. Both were impressed with the amount of activity for such a small place. The motel clerk explained that Lone Pine was a site used by most of the Hollywood producers for making very popular western movies and serials. The unique topography and rock formations, along with the clear weather, made for ideal conditions.

Their visit to Manzanar was the following day. Bruce checked in at the main gate and was escorted to the security office. Set against a backdrop of magnificent snowcapped peaks, even in late September, the camp was surrounded by guard towers and miles of barbed wire. Several dozen long, low black tarpaper covered barracks were arranged in rows with chow halls and other administrative buildings interspersed. It looked more like a prison than a simple relocation camp. Bruce was introduced to a few members of the 'town council', a group of Nisei elders overseeing more domestic affairs in the compound. He also spoke with several younger men, close to his own age. To a man all of them wanted to join the military and do their duty; most had been denied permission, although they were in good health and American citizens. Bruce found it hard to reconcile their denials with the needs of the armed forces he continually read about. Their visit took almost four hours, after which they were invited to dine with the internees. A delightful dinner of fish and vegetables, most caught and grown by the people themselves. After eating, the two departed; free to leave the camp and drive away, unlike the other citizens behind the fences.

The two spoke of little else than their own bewilderment at what they had seen for the first hours on the road. Neither could understand how such kind and patriotic people could be put away, out here in a wilderness, because of their language and culture. Bruce knew that what he wrote might rankle some of his readers, but felt strongly that he should, at least, help the young men in their quest to serve America.

#

As Bruce pulled up in front of Susan's house and shut off the car, she asked him to come in for a few minutes. He carried her suitcase up the sidewalk and in the front door. They both recounted stories of their time away to her roommates, who were getting ready for their night shifts at Consolidated Aircraft. The few days away had been filled with wonder, excitement, shock and surprise. When the girls left to catch their bus for work, Susan and Bruce sat in the living room, together on the couch.

"Honey, I don't want this to end... ever. Being with you these few days has been the best thing to happen to me. I know I love you and that love gets stronger every time we're together. There's no stopping it, in my book."

"Bruce, what are you saying?"

"Susan", he said, getting on his knee, "Will you marry me?"

She looked at the small box he was holding. Tears welled up in her eyes as she stammered... "Y-Y-Yes, silly... of course I will. Yes."

Bruce stood as she opened the box, revealing a lovely diamond ring.

"I don't suppose Saul Price arranged for this, too..." Susan said through her smile.

"No, honey, he didn't... this part is all on my own."

They kissed… again and again. Bruce slipped the ring on her finger; it fit perfectly. She lifted her hand, looked at it in the window's moonlight and kissed him again.

"It's lovely, like I've always imagined it should look. You know you'll still have to ask my father, of course."

"That's part of the plan, dear. Your brother, too… I hope to see them both soon. I've been in touch with Commander Mason, he's in Pearl Harbor now. Seems he's moving up fast in this war. Anyway, before we left I got his number and put through a call… lucky I caught him in his office before our train left. He's helping arrange travel for me to Guadalcanal… I can see your dad, Sam, Bobbie and Stan easily from there… I think."

"Yeah… lucky." Susan replied. "What if I'd said 'No'?"

"Then I wouldn't be leaving so soon. My air travel to Pearl is scheduled for three days from now. I would've cancelled that flight and gone later. But Susan, dear, I didn't want to leave without us at least being engaged. I'll marry you tomorrow if you want, you know that… or we can wait until I get back… or until the war ends. That part is not as important as knowing you love me enough to say 'Yes'."

"Bruce, I do love you. I've known, inside, that I would say 'Yes' since you left for Florida. I do want to marry you… but I want my dad and Sam at the wedding, too. Is that fair?"

"Absolutely… I understand. I suppose I could talk to Commander Mason about getting you on my transport, too… but I don't like the idea of you being the only good looking girl in the middle of a hundred thousand sailors and Marines."

"Oh, I'm sure you could handle a mere hundred thousand, Bruce."

When Bruce returned to the hotel he immediately telephoned Saul Price. He needed to thank his friend and make arrangements for the car to get home, wherever that was.

"Bruce… I hope you had a good time on your little getaway."

"Thanks, Saul. Susan and I had the best time, far beyond what we thought it would be like. I can't thank you enough."

"You already are thanking me, Bruce. The words and feelings you put into your writing makes me believe each of us has a part in this war... and I'm not alone in my belief. You capture something greater than the fighting... you get into the 'why' of this thing. The least I can do is make your time something special... well, more special."

"How do I get the car back to you, Saul?"

"If you have time, why don't you pick me up after work Thursday at Seven Seas; do you have time for dinner with Susan and us... my wife and I?"

"Sure, we were going to dinner together... I'll let Susan know we'll pick her up."

"Fine... say 4:30 Thursday?"

"Great... Saul, thanks again for a great time."

"You are more than welcome, my friend."

Bruce spent Wednesday on a balcony of the hotel, overlooking San Diego Bay. The warm sunshine and cool ocean breeze made for easy writing. He completed his article on Manzanar and arranged for a San Diego Union newspaper employee to stop by and pick it up at the hotel lobby. It was great that the paper had offered to help him again on this trip; they would wire the article to Bennett in New York for publication. He also phoned Susan's office at Consolidated to let her know about tomorrow evening's dinner with Saul and his wife. She was not in; Bruce left the message with a receptionist. He headed down to his room to shower and get ready to pick Susan up for dinner and to see a bit more of San Diego. Having a car available was an added bonus.

The two drove out to Ocean Beach, on the far side of Point Loma. There they ate while watching the sun set over the Pacific. Both shared their thoughts as the sun disappeared over the horizon.

"I can't help but think of my dad on the carrier, Bruce. He's seeing the same sun, much higher up in the sky. Sam, too, wherever he is… on his way to Guadalcanal. I hope he doesn't get seasick."

"That would be rough, alright. I wonder what Stan thinks of being on a destroyer. I remember seeing one lean far over in a sharp turn in the Atlantic, chasing a sub… or a whale… we never did find out for sure. Those smaller ships are much worse on a guy's stomach, so I hear. Maybe I'll find out soon…"

"Day after tomorrow… our last evening together will be at Saul's home. Where does he live, anyway?"

"Somewhere up, behind us on Point Loma. I've got the address, how about we drive past it tonight on our way back to the city? That way we'll know right where it is tomorrow?"

"That's fine… day after tomorrow… then you'll all three be gone. I'll be praying that you can get together with dad and Sam somehow… along with Stan and Bobbie while you're gone. Promise you'll come back to me… I need you to say it… need to hear it."

Bruce took both her hands in his and looked deep into her eyes. "I promise… I'll be back… no matter what… I'll be back. Let's go walk on the beach before we leave."

The next afternoon Bruce drove to the Seven Seas, a few blocks down Broadway from the hotel. He parked behind the building and went in the back door. One thing he needed to purchase was a sea bag, the large duffel that sailors stowed all their gear in. It would hold much more than his suitcases and was easier to carry. He met Saul in the manager's office and the two drove to pick Susan up from work. Saul greeted her warmly and told the two to get in the back seat while he drove.

"Last night together for a time… get comfortable. We'll be at my place in a few minutes."

"Actually, Saul, we drove past your house last evening, on our way from Ocean Beach back to town." Susan said.

"That so? And the car let you go past... I'll have a word with this one... my other would drive itself into the garage. This one is Marge's... my wife."

"And she was okay with letting us use it for days?" piped in Bruce.

"Her idea... who do you think had time to put together your trip... me? Her father was an Admiral... she knows how to get things done."

"No kidding... maybe I could use her help later, when I get to the Pacific?"

"I'm sure, Bruce, that Marge would say "just ask"... she's got a heart of gold... that one."

"She sounds wonderful and amazing. I can't wait to meet her." Susan added.

"You'll get your chance... this is our place now... The one up ahead."

Bruce and Susan looked out the front window of the Plymouth; there in front of them was the driveway from the night before, curving up to a large house... a huge house. It overlooked both San Diego and the Pacific. It sat directly on the spine of Point Loma with a clear view to the east and west.

"We had it built when the kids were home; now the two of us kind of rattle around in it, bumping into each other once in a while." Saul smiled and parked the car. The front door of the house opened and two large black dogs, more like small bears, loped out and toward them.

"Newfoundland's... this one's George and the other's Grace... a favorite radio show of ours."

Marge met them in the foyer as they entered; she was a bit shorter than Saul and had beautiful silver hair. Graceful and lean, she was a kind of opposite to Saul, with his balding head and rather paunchy, rumpled look. She shook Bruce's hand firmly and gave Susan a warm welcome hug.

"Dinner will be ready shortly... Saul, dear, bring them out back. I've got cocktails waiting on the deck. It's a marvelous sunset."

"Is there anything I can do to help, Mrs Price?" asked Susan.

"No, no. Everything's fine... you go, get a drink... and the name is Marge." she replied with a smile.

Saul guided his guests through the house to the back deck, overlooking the ocean. Lights from ships and boats could be seen miles out to sea. The glow of Ocean Beach was below, to the right a mile or so, behind the trees.

"This view takes my breath away... I imagine it's wonderfully different during the day?"

"Susan, this view has been enjoyed by Marge's family for a long time. Her grandfather, also an Admiral, bought the land before the Spanish American War. Her father had a smaller house built just below here; a fine view of San Diego but not the ocean. With this new war...well, Marge and I are considering letting the government have it. There are plans for a new military cemetery up here on the Point. Great place and view for all those boys to enjoy, don't you think? We're thinking of moving to Florida... nearer our kids and other family. Besides, tailoring is becoming a lost art... most clothes now are made to fit. I'm getting a bit too tired to keep going in every day; Marge agrees it's time to retire so I can lose to her in tennis... can you see me playing tennis?" Saul patted his stomach and made a face; both of his guests laughed heartily.

"Ahhh... she made Manhattan's... my favorite." Saul continued as he served up the drinks.

Marge walked in at that moment. Bruce lifted his glass and toasted, saying "To our friends and hosts... Marge and Saul. May you find happiness and peace everywhere you go."

"Not likely the peace with all the grandchildren..." added Saul.

"That was nice, thank you Bruce. Pay no attention to man who will soon be behind the curtain. I love my grandchildren... and so does he, spoils them rotten as you can imagine. What I want to know is if there's any water in the falls at Yosemite now…"

The evening began and ended with talk of their trip. Marge said she always enjoyed hearing, first hand, of others' adventures. She loved to live through the eyes of travelers. It was going on midnight when Saul announced an end to the festivities.

"Our war correspondent has a long trip tomorrow and Susan, I'm sure, will be heading to work after seeing him off. Myself, well… I believe I have a coat and two pairs of pants to alter for an overbearing Marine Colonel in the morning. I'll call a cab… which will give us a few minutes for a final drink."

When the taxi arrived, Marge and Saul walked Bruce and Susan to the street. Hugs all around and handshakes, followed by farewell waves from inside the cab.

Early the next morning, Bruce picked up Susan in another taxi. They rode to the ferry crossing to Coronado Island and took it to the Naval Air Station there. A short walk led them to the front gate, guarded by four serious Marines. Bruce showed his identification and got permission for Susan to join him. Another longer walk and they were at the seaplane boarding area. Bruce noticed that the plane was a model similar to the Clipper he'd flown in from England to Long Island. He remembered Major Young saying most had been taken over for military use.

"Well, dear, this is it… God, that sounds so cliché. I love you, Susan. I'll keep my promise to come back… and in one piece. You keep writing me, even if I don't get the letters. I'll try sending notes back with Sam's pieces for the San Diego Union when we get together; mine go straight to New York."

"Give dad and Sam my love… and don't do anything silly… silly. I love you and can't wait to marry you. If you can, call me from Hawaii before you leave there, alright?"

The first kiss lacked something; they tried it again. By the fourth or fifth, they both seemed somewhat satisfied. One more for the road and Bruce was walking toward the large plane. He turned to wave and, instead ran back for one more.

"There. Now I can go… I love you, Susan."

"Me too… darling." She tried, but the tears came anyway.

Bruce headed to the hatch at the top of the gangway. Once inside, he immediately noticed the difference; this plane was gray… inside and out. No white linens, leather overstuffed couches. Just several rows of slightly padded, gray seats. The white coated waiters and stewards were replaced by young sailors in dungarees and boondockers, white 'dixie cup' hats tipped jauntily on their heads.

Bruce sat, opened up one of the papers he'd bought earlier at the hotel and began to read. England's Royal Air Force hit Munich in Germany using their firebombing technique. Bruce wondered how the Nazis felt having their symbolic city torched. He remembered reading somewhere that most Japanese houses were made of paper; they would make a fine fire one day, he hoped.

Chapter 10
October 1942

"Say... that article you wrote on the Nisei guys at Manzanar wanting to get into the war sure was timely, Bruce."

"Really? What have you heard that makes you think that, Dix?"

Bruce and Commander Mason were meeting for lunch at the Officers' Club at Pearl Harbor. Mason's office was helping Bruce arrange transportation to Tulagi, an island near Guadalcanal in the Solomons. He would not be able to fly there; no civilians were landing at Henderson Field on 'The Canal' as the Japanese were shelling the airfield regularly. Intelligence was predicting a major Jap offensive to retake the island soon. Tulagi was Bruce's only choice; he'd have to get himself over to the fighting once he arrived. He had already confirmed that Bobbie Milliken was still there fighting and Stan's ship, the *LAFFEY* was operating in the waters surrounding the Solomons.

"Well, a communique from Washington this morning said a new Army unit... a battalion of Japanese Americans was being activated any day now. It'll not be assigned to the Pacific in any case... they'll be sent to Europe to fight the Germans."

"Makes the most sense, I suppose. I know the Army has already been assigning some of the men from the camps to a language school up in Minnesota. They'll be sure to stand out in

Minneapolis; I can't recall ever seeing Japanese in Iowa when I was growing up."

"Let's have lunch… I'll go over your travel itinerary while we eat. You'll be heading out this afternoon… not too much time to dilly dally."

Commander Mason briefed Bruce and gave him his voucher and other papers he'd need. His flight from the seaplane base on Ford Island would take him south and west, refueling once at a Navy base just over halfway to the Solomons. He'd be on Tulagi in a couple of days; much faster than a ten day voyage on a ship. Mason had several suggestions for how to get to Guadalcanal once he arrived. After their meal, the two shook hands and parted ways for another time.

"Bruce, it's always good to see you. Hopefully, I'll have a command on the water next time we meet up… and I'm sure we will again. Meanwhile, I'd seriously consider the advice you said Susan gave you… no more bombing missions!"

"Well, that's one I'll probably never have a chance to do again, anyway. Dix, thanks for everything… good luck on a new command. Each time I see you, you've been promoted…"

"I certainly hope that string of luck holds up… I'd love to hear you say 'Captain Mason' next time. Good luck, Bruce. Keep writing… it's working."

Bruce tried putting phone calls through to San Diego and even Ames. The circuits to the mainland were all busy; he was told the wait could be several hours. He wrote quick notes to Susan and his parents, telling them of his departure from Hawaii. The Admin Office clerk called for a driver to bring Bruce to the seaplane base at Ford Island. His flight took off of the smooth waters right on time; Bruce could see the work progressing on the sunken battleships still in the mud from the attack last December. He'd been told they would be joining the fleet sometime in 1943 and would certainly exact revenge on the enemy. Bruce had noticed an air of confidence among the Navy and Marine personnel he'd met over the past several days. Since the victory at Midway in June, there was a more determined and positive attitude about winning the war. New ships were already on their way... cruisers and destroyers first, soon battleships and new carriers would be arriving.

A steward on the plane had a copy of the Honolulu morning paper and asked Bruce if he'd care to read it. The Germans and Russians were still fighting hard in the city of Stalingrad. There was more information about the sinking of the US carrier *WASP* the week before. Bruce remembered his dinner with Susan when she had read the headlines in the restaurant. Putting down the paper, he daydreamed about her until he fell asleep; the hum of the aircraft engines lulling him into an afternoon nap. He was awakened by a steward serving dinner; ham slices, boiled potatoes and a wedge of apple pie. He thought of what Bobbie might be eating in the jungles of Guadalcanal and then reminded himself he'd soon be finding out. Bruce had no real idea which of his friends he could arrange to visit first, not that it much mattered. He was glad for the chance to, perhaps, see both soon. After dinner the interior lights were dimmed and several other passengers did their best to get comfortable and fall asleep. Bruce picked up the newspaper, asked for a second cup of coffee and went page by page through the entire edition. He even filled out the crossword puzzle, his first in more than a year. He made his way up to the flight deck and asked the engineer if he could interview the pilots at their convenience. He was ushered in and spent an enjoyable hour getting to know them and sharing his own experiences in a Boeing 314, particularly the last flight from Liverpool with now Major Young as pilot. Neither of these two had heard of his friend, which didn't really surprise Bruce. They had both received their training in the Navy and had never worked for a civilian airline. Finishing his interview of them, Bruce asked if he could use the radio room to type an article; the noise from there wouldn't carry into the passenger area. He finished the overnight leg of the flight banging away on his trusted Royal Quiet Deluxe.

Bruce was the first to find out their destination change. The radio operator clued him in before bringing the transmitted message to the pilots. They would not be landing at Tulagi; rather, the plane was diverted to Espiritu Santo, an island further from Guadalcanal. Apparently the Japanese had launched a major attack on an area overlooking Henderson Field, called the Matanikau River. There may be several days delay before getting to Tulagi. Bruce was disappointed but knew better than to voice it. When the plane landed in the harbor and taxied to the seaplane ramp, Bruce noticed a Navy destroyer tied up at a pier nearby. He hoped he might get some information on the whereabouts of the *LAFFEY* from someone aboard. His sea bag would be brought to the Admin Building while he walked the half mile to the moored ship. He was met on the quarterdeck of the destroyer by the ship's Public Affairs Officer (PAO), who was willing to help him find information he was looking for. This ship was part of the squadron *LAFFEY* was assigned to until a short time ago. They had both been part of the antisubmarine screening force for the *USS WASP* when the carrier was sunk. The *LAFFEY* had actually been at Espiritu Santo a week earlier, dropping off survivors of the carrier that had been fished out of the water following the sinking. Now the destroyer was headed for Noumea in New Caledonia. The best news he shared with Bruce was the possibility of a plane flying to the Navy base there; supply planes flew regularly between the two sites.

After leaving the destroyer, Bruce hurried to the Admin Building. Enlisting the help of the base PAO, he made arrangements to hitch a ride on a cargo flight leaving the next day for Noumea. Hopefully his information from the destroyer was correct and the *LAFFEY* was still in port there. There was a good chance he'd be seeing his friend, Stan Larson, in a day... two at most. He asked the PAO if he could also look into the whereabouts of another Navy trained war correspondent, Sam West... Susan's brother. The Lieutenant said he would try and get back to Bruce with any information he could round up.

Bruce gathered his sea bag and typewriter case and headed to the Officers Club. He'd been assigned a bunk in the berthing area behind the Club. There was no one in the bar and only two officers eating in the dining room. Bruce walked through the door to the berthing area and found a bunk. Putting his bag and case at the foot end he took off his shoes and laid down. In a moment he was asleep.

Sunrise the next morning found Bruce walking along a beach, admiring a cool breeze and the gentle lapping of waves on the sand. As the light grew brighter he noticed, along the edge of the palm trees, three soldiers in a machine gun emplacement grinning at him. Bruce walked over and asked what the joke was.

"Well, sir, we've been tracking you for at least fifteen minutes, wondering what rank you were. No gold on the sleeves but an officer's uniform had us a bit curious, you see. With the island on alert, we wanted to make sure you're not the first of a thousand Japs coming ashore. Then we noticed your insignia. We never figured a War Correspondent would be out strolling so early, I guess."

"So what are your names, where you from? If I'm going to mention the vigilance of three outstanding GI's like yourselves, I'd best get the information right... America needs to know every inch of our soil is safe... even a few square yards of beach with coconuts and crabs on an island I can hardly pronounce..." Bruce squatted down, shook hands with the three and got the information he wanted. All were nineteen years old, came from different states and none of their backgrounds were remotely alike. This was just what he loved to find; it was so American to him.

After his encounter with the front line, Bruce headed over to the club for breakfast. Coffee, real eggs, spam and more coffee greeted him there. After his meal, he walked back to the Admin Building to see about the departure of his flight to Noumea. The clerk handed him a note from the PAO along with his travel permit for the flight. It would leave before noon, arriving in New Caledonia several hours later. The note contained information on Sam; he was with the Eighth Marine Regiment, Bobbie Milliken's unit, on Guadalcanal. Now he knew where to find both of them after he'd located Stan Larson. He asked the clerk for some paper and a couple of envelopes. Sitting at an empty desk, Bruce penned letters to Susan and his folks. He let them know things were fine, being careful not to mention his location or travel plans. He handed the unsealed envelopes back to the clerk; they'd have to go past a censor before getting off the island.

The plane sitting on the runway was a new one to Bruce. A crewman explained it was a C-47, two engine cargo plane that was also used to carry paratroops or just about anything else that would fit inside. Bruce had seen a few that looked like it at the airport in Long Island when he landed in the Yankee Clipper from Liverpool. The crewman nodded and said the C-47 was its military designation; it was known as the DC-3 in the civilian world. The man had been a mechanic for an airline out of Chicago before the war and was familiar with the plane. That's how he ended up servicing them for the Army. Bruce would be one of three passengers along with a load of supplies for the base at Noumea. The other two people were both military officers; one Navy and the other Army. Bruce stowed his gear on board and sat down on his typewriter case in the shade under the wing, watching the ground crew fuel the plane and check flaps and other mechanical parts. The late morning sun was already scorching hot; surprisingly, it was cool here in the shade, a nice breeze blowing along the runway from the beach a few hundred yards away.

His two fellow passengers showed up a short time later, the Army captain was a newly assigned doctor heading to the hospital on New Caledonia. The Navy lieutenant commander had a locked briefcase shackled to his wrist. Bruce knew not to ask about it. He politely shook hands with both and introduced himself. The doctor cocked his head a bit and asked if Bruce wrote the newspaper articles he'd read so often. The other was also interested to meet the young man who 'captured the hearts of the country in this war with his pen'.

The three were told to take their seats along the side of the aircraft, just behind the cockpit. They were joined by two enlisted crewmen, both in coveralls with no visible rank showing. One said there was an icebox with bottles of beer and Coke along so they could help themselves if anyone got thirsty during the flight. Bruce smiled at how different each flight he took was; from white linen and champagne to grab yourself a beer.

The plane slowly taxied along to the end of the runway, then throttled up and began rumbling down the strip, lifting smoothly into the air well before the end. None of this was visible to the passengers who sat facing the large crates of supplies. They didn't even see the two fighters that took off and flew above and around them as escorts. The doctor tried to start a conversation but gave up after a few minutes; the noise made shouting necessary and he'd need his voice when they landed. Bruce wished he had a book or newspaper to read. He settled back and worked over his notes about people he'd met so far on this trip.

The plane landed nearly six hours later; each man walking stiffly and quickly to the building they hoped contained a bathroom. It was a long, warm flight; the beer and Cokes demanded attention. Afterward they returned to the plane to gather their gear and said goodbye before setting off for their separate destinations. Bruce inquired about the location of the *USS LAFFEY*. He was directed to a group of sailors unloading some of the supplies on the plane.

"That's a shore party from the *LAFFEY*, sir. I'm sure you can hitch a ride with them to the ship." The clerk went back to his work; Bruce headed out to the group. He introduced himself to a First Class Petty Officer and was told to "hop in the cab of the truck; I'll be driving it back as soon as we get this stuff loaded."

Bruce put his sea bag in with the supplies and climbed in the truck. A few minutes later, the First Class got in and started the engine. He reached over, shook Bruce's hand and said, "I'm

Thompson, storekeeper. Can I ask what your business is with the *LAFFEY*, sir?"

"Bruce Hollins, correspondent. I'm looking for Stan Larson... gunner's mate on the ship. I'm..."

"Hollins? You're the guy what wrote that article Stan carries with him? Since he got onboard he tells everyone about being in the papers. I don't know him much, but I've heard his story. You two played ball together in school, right?"

"Right... won the state championship in Iowa last year. I've been tracking down the other guys on the team... one's a Marine on Guadalcanal. I'll be heading there after I talk with Stan. I hope to be here several days, if I can talk my way aboard."

"Getting on shouldn't be your problem... getting off might be, unless you only want to talk with him for a few minutes. We're scheduled to shove off as soon as we get this shit aboard." Thompson cocked his thumb toward the back as he spoke.

The truck pulled alongside the destroyer; Bruce looked at the large gun mounts, each with a single barrel sticking out. Other guns were located along the sides and in the superstructure of the ship. It looked long, low and sleek in the water... like it was already moving. Small white numbers, '459', were painted on the bow. Each man of the shore party grabbed a box and headed up the gangway to the quarterdeck. Thompson gave orders to men on the ship to lower a net from a small crane above the main deck. The net came down behind the truck and Thompson began loading crates and boxes in it. The other men returned and helped him until the truck was unloaded. Bruce walked up and reported to the Officer of the Deck, a lieutenant (junior grade). A call was made to the bridge and a full lieutenant came down to meet him.

"Mr Hollins? The Captain sends his compliments; he'd like to meet you in his cabin, if you'll follow me, sir."

Bruce was told to leave his gear on the deck. He followed the lieutenant up a very steep ladder to the bridge and into the Captain's cabin. A lieutenant commander met him and shook hands.

"Bruce, welcome aboard. I'm Commander Wall, skipper of the *LAFFEY*. As soon as I heard your name, I knew why you're here. I've already sent for Gunner's Mate Larson. I'm afraid you're interview will have to be short... unless you'd care to join us for a few extra days? We're just leaving... should be back in a week. Heading down 'The Slot' to take position guarding the beaches on Guadalcanal."

"Guadalcanal? That's exactly where I need to go after I see Larson, Skipper. I'd love the chance to see what a new destroyer is like. I was on a troopship over to England just after Pearl Harbor... loved watching the escorts cutting through the water."

"I don't see a problem with you coming along. We could see action... you never know in these waters. We seem to have the upper hand while the sun's up... when it's dark the Japs come down between the islands, bringing reinforcements. That's what we call 'The Slot'... their convoys are called 'The Tokyo Express'.

There was a knock at the door and Stan Larson announced himself. Commander Wall said to Bruce, "Feel free to use my cabin for a bit. I'll have your gear stowed with another officer. We'll be underway soon."

"Thank you Skipper. I'll keep my time with Stan short for now. I'm sure he's got duties associated with getting underway; I don't want to keep him from that."

"I appreciate that Bruce. Let me know when you're done here; I'll be on the bridge."

Bruce and Stan spent a short half hour reconnecting and catching up from their last meeting in San Diego. Bruce filled him in on Jim and the mission they flew together. He also told what he knew of Fred and Bobbie. Stan was hoping he'd have a chance to see his Marine friend, but knew the likelihood was pretty remote. He was glad that Sam and Bobbie might get to see each other again. Stan had been promoted to Gunners Mate Third Class and was in charge of one of the 20mm anti-aircraft guns on the ship. His crew of four other men included three loaders and a gunner. They had plenty of experience firing the twin barreled Bofors during the fight that claimed the *USS WASP*. Stan said it was unforgettable; pulling the wounded sailors out of the water after the battle. He'd never forget how many he saw floating face down in their preservers as well.

The word was passed for underway stations; time was up for the two friends. Bruce went to the bridge and reported to Commander Wall; he was promptly invited to observe the ship leaving the harbor from the Captain's chair on the port wing, just outside the bridge hatch. It was the perfect place to watch all the activity as lines were cast loose and brought back on board the ship. The destroyer slowly backed away from the pier and swung out into the harbor, her prow pointing directly at the entrance about a mile away. Bruce felt the engine vibration quicken through the deck as the ship moved a bit faster forward. In a short time *LAFFEY* had cleared the final buoy marking the channel; she fairly leapt forward as the skipper ordered "Full ahead, make 35 knots".

A tap on the shoulder got Bruce's attention. A tall sailor with two chevrons under an eagle on his sleeve indicated a Second Class Petty Officer was there.

"Mr Hollins, sir. Yeoman Second Hansen... I'll take you to your quarters now, sir."

"Thanks, Yeoman. This ship is sure fast."

"Yes, sir. The new Benson class, like the *LAFFEY*, can do a full 5 knots faster than the older tin cans. Wait until you feel her turn, sir... you'll think we're going to tip over. But she's fine... can handle any but the roughest waters."

Bruce followed Hansen down a passage through a hatch marked 'Officer Country' and into a cabin. There were two bunks stacked in one corner, a double locker and a small table with one chair. Not much else would actually fit in the room.

"You'll be here with Lieutenant Sims, sir. He's the exec... Executive Officer of the ship. If there's anything you need, my office is just beyond the hatch we came through. Skipper says you've got the run of the place… feel free to explore. By now, most everyone on board knows you're here. If anyone tells you to do something, please consider doing it. Situations can change quickly out here… if you hear us go to battle stations, please make your way here, this is where we will look for you."

"Thanks, Yeoman. I'll do my best to not get in the way and follow orders."

Bruce began putting away his own things in the standing locker, and the horizontal one beneath his bunk. There was plenty of space for all his clothing and the typewriter case fit in the bottom of the locker. He was just finishing when the door opened and the lieutenant he'd met on the quarterdeck came in.

"Hi, Bruce. My name's Mike… Mike Sims. I guess we'll be cozy as roommates for a time, eh?"

Bruce extended his hand. "Hi Mike… thanks for letting me bunk here."

"No choice, really. My cabin has the extra rack for the rare times we have visitors or inspectors aboard. I'm pretty used to it… hasn't been long since our sea trials and we were full up on inspectors then, I'll tell you. Have you been assigned your battle stations position?"

"Yeah, I'm supposed to stay here… though, honestly, I'd rather be just about anywhere else."

"I know, Bruce… you know, things get pretty dicey at times. I don't think our good Yeoman will have time himself to look for you. Just be sure to stay out of the way… better yet, be useful if you can. I read about your flight over France… I have no doubts of your abilities."

"Thanks, Mike. That means a lot… I think if trouble shows up, I'll be at Stan's gun position."

"Good to know, I'll be sure to remember that."

The two chatted about life before the war for a few minutes when a knock at the door announced dinner in the wardroom. Bruce was invited to join the ship's officers for the meal. He followed

197

Mike in to a room barely large enough to hold the table set for twelve men. Several officers were already seated; Mike made introductions and, before the Skipper joined them, told Bruce there would be a test of all the names and jobs later. Laughter greeted Commander Wall as he came in to the wardroom. Everyone stood until he seated himself.

Two white coated stewards, one black and one Pilipino, served the officers. A delicious clam chowder was followed by fresh vegetables, broiled fish and steamed clams. A surprise birthday cake was served for desert, along with ice cream. The youngest officer, Ensign Walthrop, was all of twenty years old today. He was a Naval Reserve officer, fresh out of school and served as the Deck Division head. His men took care of just about everything topside that needed cleaning, polishing or painting.

After dinner Bruce found Stan and the two friends sat together on the forecastle, or foc'sle as it was called, at the very front of the ship. Listening to the sound of the water being sliced by the bow as the ship sped along was exhilarating. The stars were unbelievably bright and there was no moon.

"Good night for the Japs to try slipping down The Slot to unload more men. They like the dark… and the Navy used to think they couldn't see at night because of their slant eyes. What a riot… they see just fine, better than we do. Trouble is, we just started practicing night firing… our admirals always planned for a daytime battle."

"How do you see what you're shooting at in this darkness?" asked Bruce.

"Hell, Bruce, you just shoot at whatever's shooting at you. Gun flashes light up the sky… there's tracers from the smaller guns and the fires and explosions from hits… well, it doesn't stay dark long when it begins. I've only been in the one engagement, but that's enough for me. Most of us wouldn't mind sitting out the war in a nice quiet corner of this here ocean. That is, if we had a choice."

Stan pointed out into the inky night. Bruce could barely discern the pale wakes of other ships, but couldn't even see silhouettes of them.

"We're up front with two other destroyers... there and there." He pointed and Bruce began to see, faintly, black shapes against the horizon. "There must be cruisers behind us, we don't usually go in alone. I think there's something building... you, my friend, are going to be a witness to a sea battle, mark my words."

The two rose from their perch on the foc'sle and made their way back towards the starboard side forward 20mm mount... Stan's duty station. At that moment a claxon made a clamoring noise and the ship gained speed as she turned, hard, to port.

"Battle stations... battle stations... this is no drill. Prepare for surface action. Gunners to their guns."

"Here, put this on... and this." Stan handed Bruce a life preserver and a helmet. "You can be a loader tonight, if you'd like. I don't know how much our mount will be used... have to wait and see."

Bruce quickly nodded to the other three loaders as the gunner took his seat. Stan stood slightly behind and directed the men, sound powered phones on his head. The 20mm ammunition came in a sort of stack of seven shells, all locked in a curved slide that joined them at the base. Each loader held one and, as the gun fired, placed it on top of the one being fired. It was fast work and the stacks weighed more than Bruce imagined. For now, though, all was quiet.

Stan shouted, "Bridge reports a Jap cruiser off our starboard bow, range 3,000 yards and closing. Get ready." At the same moment, the two five inch guns forward of them began firing... a steady boom every five to ten seconds as they alternated their fire. The darkness lit up with the first gun... Stan was right. Bruce's eyes took a few seconds to adjust to the sudden brightness. Then he saw the enemy ship; it looked twice the size of their own. A flash from her side and a second later a geyser of water shot up less than 30 yards away. Several more flashes and the sound of the first Jap gun echoed across the water. Geysers were erupting all around them, water soaking their clothes as the LAFFEY quickly closed the distance. Bruce heard a new noise, sort of a 'whooooosh'… another loader told him it was the destroyer firing torpedoes at the Jap cruiser. The ship shuddered as a Jap shell hit somewhere and the smell of hot metal and burned gunpowder filled Bruce's nostrils.

"We're going along her starboard side… make ready. Commence firing, rake her bridge and decks. C'mon you sons a'bitches, let 'er have it."

The Bofors was jumping as the shell stacks began dropping in. Bruce could see, just beyond the muzzle flashes, their own shells hitting the Jap cruiser as the two ships slipped past each other. In one bright blaze of light, Bruce saw a shell explode as it hit a Jap sailor looking at him. He was so close, Bruce could have yelled at the man and been heard. He didn't have time to turn away, just keep putting new stacks in the loader. Stan's gun must have fired hundreds of shells all along the side of the cruiser as the two ships passed. They were so close the enemy's guns could not depress down to fire on the destroyer effectively… but the LAFFEY's own 5 inchers and the 20mm mounts were blazing away, doing considerable damage and killing any of the Jap sailors who were exposed at all.

It was over in, at most, four or five minutes. Their ship had passed the cruiser and seemed to be all alone. Suddenly, looming out of the darkness, Bruce saw, or felt, the presence of a black mountain approaching. Stan was frantically yelling into his phone…"Bridge, forward 20mil… Jap battleship dead ahead… yes, dammit, I said battleship."

The ship immediately heeled over to port and Bruce did, indeed, feel like they would tip over. They passed within 20 feet of the battleship's bow and steamed along the starboard side, just like the cruiser, only closer… much closer.

"Commence firing… fire like hell."

The Bofors jumped again and all the loaders did their jobs as fast as they could. The shells striking along the Jap bridge front and side could be felt by the American gunners. Glass and chunks of Japanese steel were raining down on the yanks. They could hear the screams of the enemy sailors and saw bodies, and parts of bodies, flying through the air. Again, their position, so close alongside, prevented the bigger ship from firing back... for a time. As the *LAFFEY* sped on her way, Jap battleship disappearing behind her, the after turret of the enemy ship fired. Shells the weight of a small automobile hit nearby, throwing gigantic columns of water into the air. One hit the destroyer amidships; the whole gun crew were thrown into the air by the impact. Bruce hit his shoulder hard on a handrail coming down. His left arm went completely numb... useless.

The destroyer came to a halt as more Japanese shells roared overhead and hit the water just beyond her. Bruce could feel the deck shudder; sounds of creaking steel filled his ears. An immense explosion hurled him up and out into the blackness. He hit the water, staying on the surface because of the life preserver. Turning, he saw the *LAFFEY* tilting at both ends, her back was broken and she was sinking... fast. He made out a few more heads bobbing in the water nearby and shouted... "Stan!!!".

Throughout the night Bruce called for his friend; in the occasional light of the distant naval battle still raging, he saw others trying to swim or climb on pieces of floating wreckage from the ship. His left arm was still mostly numb, but he was able to propel himself slowly through the water. Bruce caught sight of a life raft, apparently empty, about fifty yards away. Ever so slowly he managed to draw himself closer to it, finally getting hold of a trailing line in the water attached to the raft. Despite the warm temperature of the water, his teeth were chattering and his body shaking uncontrollably as he crabbed himself over the side and into the net bottom. Alone in the dark, Bruce fell into a fitful, exhausted sleep. He awoke to a glowing eastern sky; his shoulder painful but no longer numb. Sitting up on one side of the raft he looked out over the calm surface; no land was visible, though at this height he was only able to see a few miles. He called his friend's name again and again; no answer could be heard.

Later in the morning, as the sun shone hot with no cooling breeze, Bruce spotted movement on the horizon. He was unable to gauge the size of the object, but it seemed to be getting bigger, slowly. It was several minutes before he recognized it as a ship! He knew there was nothing in the raft and then remembered the line dragging in the water. Pulling it in, he realized there was some weight at the end. As he brought it in he could see, partially intact, the remains of a package. Lifting it out of the water revealed part of a survival kit; he opened it as fast as he could, keeping his eyes on the distant ship. Inside was a can of dye, two flares but no gun to fire them, and a small mirror! Bruce took the mirror and began to flash the sun, hoping he was aiming it toward the ship accurately enough to be seen. In a minute he noticed the ship begin to turn a bit in his direction. It worked; the ship was coming his way! He fell back in the raft again, laughing despite the pain in his shoulder.

Bruce watched as the ship approached; he was balanced on his knees, waving his right arm as it pulled close. Nothing he could think of looked better than the American flag fluttering at its mast. A cargo net was hanging down into the water from the railing on the main deck; Bruce grabbed it and, with one hand, slowly climbed. A sailor, seeing his other arm hanging, climbed down and helped him up.

"Welcome aboard the *USS DUNCAN*... the ship's doctor will see you in a minute. What ship are you from? Have some fresh water, here..."

Bruce drank and immediately threw up a lot of salty water. He had no idea he'd swallowed so much.

"I'm from the *LAFFEY*... a destroyer. It was blown up last night. I'm a correspondent, newspaper man."

The chief petty officer looking at him chuckled. "It's sure you're not a sailor, son. No one in the Navy would say IT was blown up. We always say SHE..."

Over the loudspeaker came the announcement, "Men in the water, port side ahead. Prepare to bring more aboard."

Two men gently helped Bruce to his feet and brought him back aft to the fantail. A canopy had been stretched over the deck; Bruce was thankful for the shade. A doctor came and examined his shoulder. He said it was badly bruised and his collarbone was probably broken. He'd have to wait for an x-ray until they got to shore. In the meantime he had a corpsman wrap Bruce's left arm tight to his chest to immobilize it. Clean dry dungarees were brought for him to wear, along with dry socks and shoes. The chief he'd met earlier passed by.

"At least you're looking more like a sailor, son."

"Thanks, chief... I'll take that as a compliment."

Bruce ate some bread and water offered by a steward. He waited anxiously as more men were brought to the fantail; one or two at a time. It was nearly an hour later that a familiar voice was heard calling his name. Stan came up to him, half his face black with oil and a good part of his hair singed off. He slumped on the deck next to Bruce...

"What'd I tell you about seeing a little action last night?"

"Stan, I only remember what you said about finding a quiet corner on this here ocean. I tried to find you last night, called your name a long time."

"It's strange, Bruce. I remember seeing you... actually SEEING you blown out of the gun mount. I went straight up and came down in an oily, fiery mess. I tried to dive down... had to take my life jacket off to swim through the flames. I was lucky... got out and in to clean water, but lost my preserver. A dead seaman saved my life I guess... he floated by, head missing. I took his... and put it on. There's no way I'd have made it this long without one."

203

The search continued through the early afternoon. Another destroyer could be seen slowly moving through the area looking for survivors. While the sun was lower in the sky, but still several hours to sunset, the two ships turned and headed toward safer waters. With the coming darkness, the threat of the Imperial Japanese Navy increased. All of those rescued were brought back to Noumea. There the wounded were tended to, rosters of the survivors created and interviews of the night's events conducted. Preliminary reports indicated fewer than 75 of the ship's complement of just over 200 had been found; plus one correspondent. The search would resume the next day. Bruce's shoulder was x-rayed and showed a cracked collarbone and no breaks. His doctor was the new Army captain he'd met on the C-47 flight the day before.

"Mr Hollins. I'd say you've seen more in the past 36 hours than most experience in a year."

"Captain, I'll be happy to keep a slower pace from now on. I still need to get to Guadalcanal… and I need a new typewriter. Mine went down with the ship."

"Well, Bruce… you're not going to be able to type very fast for several days, to say the least. Settle in here a bit; we've got an office you can use during your stay."

"Thanks… I'd like a pad of paper and pen right away. I need to write notes… replace the ones I lost and about last night's battle. It has been a long day, but I can't sleep with all of it still in my head."

"Sure, I'll see you get a pad and pen. There's a quiet veranda we take our breaks on… coffee or whatever you'd like there, too. Down the hall, turn right and on until the double doors."

Bruce headed to the veranda. On the way he ran into a Red Cross volunteer handing out stationery; he picked out several pieces with envelopes. When he reached the outdoor area, he asked for a cup of coffee and a glass of water. He located a quiet table in the shade, sat down and began writing letters to Susan, his folks and to Saul Price. When he finished the personal correspondence, he began rewriting notes associated with the past days of travel and his recent naval activities. The writing took him past the supper hour; he picked up a sandwich and a Coke from the USO canteen in the hospital and returned to his ward bed. He didn't feel at all tired until after he ate, realizing it was the first food he'd had since the piece of bread on the *DUNCAN*. Despite the noise of other patients on the ward, Bruce got his first full night's sleep in days.

In the morning, after a breakfast of powdered eggs, spam and bread, Bruce located an office with an extra desk and typewriter in the supplies requisition area. He set to work, slowly, typing with one hand. It took most of the morning for him to type up a firsthand account of the battle. He was sure some of it would be censored; he hoped it would not reduce the impact of his description on his audience. Bruce walked the article draft to the Public Affairs Office; fortunately the PAO was a naval officer. Bruce introduced himself and handed the lieutenant his writing. Enjoying an offered cup of 'Joe', he realized this was the first time his writing was being edited in his presence. Even Majors Darby and Young had done their work away from him. The lieutenant glanced at Bruce every so often, his red pen poised and then returned to the desk.

"I don't see anything that needs to be removed, or even rewritten, except your mention of another ship's name. Your discretion is a credit to you, Bruce. I'm not surprised at the following you've worked hard for. I've had the chance to read a few of your pieces reprinted in The Navy Times as well as other service papers… you have a gift for writing… I'm sure you've been told that before. I'll see that this gets as high a priority as I can in wiring it to New York."

"Thanks, lieutenant… and thanks for the good marks. Sometimes I struggle to think what folks back home would like to read. I know quite a bit of what I read in the papers is a lot different."

"That's what makes your pieces so likeable, Bruce. You put a personal touch in them that others don't. I feel like I know the gun crew you were helping that night, because of the way you describe them. Don't change your writing, please."

Bruce left the PAO's office and was walking through the hospital lobby when he spotted Stan. He'd not seen his friend since their medical exams after the rescue.

"Stan, hey buddy... what gives? Why the long face?"

"I just came from the docks; the two tin cans sent out to search the area have come back... they only found seven more guys. It was easy to see that... except for you and me, all the rest of my team are dead or missing. One of the rescue crew told me they saw lots of our guys in the water... wearing life jackets that were all shot to hell, barely afloat. It looked like the Japs machine gunned them in the water. Their story is spreading all over the base."

"What? That can't be true... even the Japs wouldn't do that. What do you think, Stan?"

"Well, we've heard rumors about the way our Army guys were treated in the Philippines after their surrender last spring. Stories about the Japs bayoneting our wounded that couldn't keep on a march. Then there's the picture of the Japs beheading one of Doolittle's pilots that got captured."

"I'll have to check with the base Public Affairs Officer for the official line. You're looking better after the haircut... how are your burns?"

"The burns weren't bad actually... it's the damned oil that got everywhere. The corpsmen are still cleaning it out of my ears. How about that shoulder of yours? Is that sling for good measure or did you break something?"

"Bruised, sore and a cracked collarbone... no breaks. Lucky I guess."

"Yeah, lucky... well, we'd better make any visiting quick... I've been told to get ready to ship out in a few days. San Francisco and home for two weeks! Then back to the west coast to pick up a new assignment... probably another tin can."

"That's great, Stan! You'll be able to see your folks and hook up with Jim back there. Two weeks... is that once you get home or from San Francisco?"

"Don't know… guess I'll find out. You going back, too… or heading on to find Bobbie and Susan's brother…"

"Sam. No, I can't go back to the states right now. It took quite a bit to get me out here as it is. I'm so close… been working with the Supply Office to try and make room for me among all the stuff they're sending the Marines on Guadalcanal."

"Well, good luck with that… hey, let's go get a cup of joe at the canteen. I could use one and we can talk."

"Stan, that's a great idea. I have a copy of my article on the fight… I'd like you to read it, let me know what you think. I didn't feel right about waiting to get all the gun crew's personal information… I'm not sure it'd be a good idea to mention them by name, in case they got captured."

"Smart thinking… but I'm pretty sure Tojo would've knocked them off in any event. The things those rescue boys told me…"

"Sorry I brought it up. Let's have that coffee."

At that moment, a Navy officer approached. Stan saluted, which made Bruce turn around.

"Excuse me… are you Bruce Hollins? I'm Lieutenant Commander Aaron Steiner, I think you know my dad, Phil Steiner, of Naples."

"Sure… wow! Phil told me you'd joined the Seabees… he didn't say you were a Commander! I'm Bruce, this is Stan Larson, a good friend of mine… one of the fellas I'm writing about, from the basketball team."

"Pleased to meet you, Stan." Aaron reached out his hand.

"Ahhh… I really don't know if I should shake your hand or salute again. Ah, what the hell…" Stan took the hand and shook it.

"You know, Bruce, the officer part wasn't my idea at all. I signed on to run heavy equipment… bulldozers and such, you know. Anyway, I got to Port Hueneme, in California, and there were orders for me… as a Lieutenant Commander. I think Uncle Saul's wife, Marge, had more than a little to do with it."

"So like her, I'll bet you're right, Aaron. Anyway, it's great to meet you… we're on our way for some coffee… care to join us?"

"Sure, yeah. I was going to Supply to requisition transport for some gear. We're heading to Henderson Field to take over construction of the runways there…"

"Henderson… on Guadalcanal? You wouldn't, by chance, have room for one more body… without even a typewriter I might add. I don't take up much room anymore."

"Sure, Bruce… I can arrange that, no sweat."

"Friends in high places", added Stan, as they walked into the canteen.

#

The freighter came alongside the pier, deck hands tossing and catching small lines attached to the larger hawsers that held the ship tight for unloading. Bruce watched from an upper deck as the ship's crane lifted a bulldozer out of the hold and swung it up and over to set it on the dock. No sooner had it touched down than four Seabees had the lines securing it removed; one climbed up into the driver's seat, started the diesel engine and drove it away, to the cheers of everyone around, including several Marines

Henderson Field was not yet firmly in American hands; the Japanese Navy still came by often, lobbing big shells inland. Their bombers also flew over, but not as frequently now that more Navy Hellcat fighters were around. Marine and Navy aviators flew together to fight off the enemy air attacks. Though heavy fighting still could be heard in the distance, beyond the high ground surrounding Henderson… there was a feeling that the tide had turned.

Another bulldozer touched down and was driven off the pier, followed by a truck with cement mixer in tow. Bruce climbed down a ladder to the main deck and approached Aaron Steiner.

"Thanks again for the lift, Commander. I'm sure we'll run into each other again… Guadalcanal isn't all that big."

"Right, Bruce. I'll send greetings along to dad; he'll be glad to know we're both alright. Say, was Supply able to get you a typewriter?"

"Yeah, but this thing is a leftover from the last war, I think. It'll do... I'll just write shorter articles."

"Well, keep your head down... maybe you shouldn't tell too many Marines about your Navy fight... some are pretty superstitious and may not cater to someone who has trouble following so close behind."

"Oh, good advice! I'll let 'em read about it later."

The two friends shook hands and parted. Bruce was thinking about Stan as he left the large ship. His friend should already be nearing San Francisco for his well-earned leave back home. Bruce had sent along letters for his own folks and one for Stan to mail Susan when he got to the California. Now he had to find Bobbie and Sam; shouldn't be too hard. He'd go to the PAO and check up on Sam... that should lead him right to both; easier than finding a single Marine on this island.

In less than an hour Bruce was standing with Sam and Bobbie. Both of his friends were watching the Seabees beginning to work on the expanded airfield. They weren't alone; the work had attracted hundreds of Marines and soldiers as spectators. Suddenly, pilots were running to parked Wildcat fighters while flight crews met them and got the planes started. The air raid warning siren began to wail and Bruce could begin to hear the low pitched sound of larger plane engines in the far distance.

"Here come the bastards... go get 'em Navy." Another voice rose with a challenging "After 'em, you Marine aviators." Bruce called to Bobbie and Sam.

"Maybe we should head to a shelter?"

His two buddies just smiled and shook their heads. They turned to watch the developing air fight as the Wildcats swooped up from the field directly at the Betty bombers. Before a single bomb fell, two Bettys were plunging into the jungle on fire. The whistle and whump of bombs mingled with the roar of straining aircraft engines and the chattering of machine guns. Two more Bettys fell towards the sea and another, one engine on fire, was being chased by two Wildcats.

"That piece of crap won't get far." said Bobbie.

"Right you are, chum." added Sam.

Bruce was surprised at the calm demeanor of his two friends in the face of bombs falling and aircraft tearing the sky apart with guns. They were both calmly smoking their Chesterfields during the whole ordeal. Bruce was clearly more concerned with their, and his own, safety. But they simply would not be fazed by it. Finally Bobbie spoke to Bruce.

"Y'know fella... once you've been in the jungle for a few nights, this sort of thing is more entertaining than dangerous. After all, none of them was shooting at us!"

The enemy bombers departed, followed closely by the snarling Wildcats. Sam and Bobbie turned to Bruce.

"Good to see you. We were wondering when you might show up." Both grabbed Bruce and hugged him tightly.

"Bobbie and I heard from a friend you were with the Seabees coming in. The jungle telegraph is usually right. Here you are... we didn't plan this shindig, but the Jap attack came at the perfect time, I'd say." The two enjoyed a good laugh at Bruce's expense. He couldn't do anything but join in.

"Bruce, I've already cleared it with my Lieutenant... you'll come with us, just like Sam is. We're up on that ridge... over there, the bald one." Bobbie was pointing to a spot above and beyond the airfield. "The Japs are hitting us all the time, so be sure to keep your head down. It can get pretty dicey at times."

"I'll testify to that." Sam added, showing Bruce two bullet holes in his Marine dungarees. "I've had to dress like the natives since my own outfit rotted clean off. It's no sweat to get clothes from supply here... they love it when you mention their names in the newspapers back home... in fact, you taught me that. Hey, what news of Susan? I haven't gotten one letter from her in the month I've been in this hell hole."

"First off, you'll have to learn a bit more respect for your soon to be new brother-in-law..."

"What!?! How much did she have to drink to agree to that?"

"Stone sober, she was when she said yes, as a matter of fact. She's doing well at Consolidated. She misses you and your dad all the time though... and she loves getting letters, lots of letters. Apparently your dad and I are leading in that department."

"Not much to write about here, Bruce... except Japs, foot long centipedes, mud... that sort of thing."

"Don't forget the leeches... tell him about the leeches." said Bobbie.

"Oh, yeah, the leeches..." Sam shuddered and leered at Bruce.

"C'mon, you two. We gotta get going back to the outfit." Bobbie had already picked up his pack and rifle. Bruce swung his nearly empty, borrowed sea bag over his shoulder and the three headed across Henderson Field toward the heights beyond.

#

The week had been one of nearly sleepless nights filled with intermittent flares lighting up the darkness, random mortar fire all along the dug in lines of Marines and Japanese banzai attacks. Groups of the enemy would sneak close to the American positions and rise up, yelling and screaming as they charged. Machine guns, artillery, grenades and fierce hand-to-hand fighting would erupt into an intense hurricane of death for a short time. The quiet afterward was nearly as unnerving.

For the first few days Bruce declined to carry a weapon, believing in his non-combatant role. As he was shaving one morning, using his helmet as a wash basin, a Jap stepped from behind a tree nearby, raised his rifle and fired. Nothing happened; the gun misfired. Sam, standing a few feet away, pulled his own .45 caliber handgun out and shot the enemy soldier in the head.

211

"You okay, Bruce? This is why I carry one... and you will, too. I know we're not to fight and that's fine... doesn't mean we can't defend ourselves. This place has no rules... well, maybe one. Live to go home."

Bruce stared at his friend, said nothing. He went into their tent and came back with a webbed belt on, holstered .45 at his hip; carrying it with him until he left the island. He managed to finish his shave, nicking himself a few times in the process. Heat and humidity he could handle; it wasn't much worse than Naples in late May. The mosquitoes gave you a fever and you expected that would come. He could even kill the foot long centipedes without it turning his stomach over now. He had seen the leeches, but hadn't found one attached... yet. But the Japs, sneaking through their lines, popping up, then disappearing to shoot at you from another angle; that was hardest to take. He knew it was a process to endure; degrees of insects and rodents. He thought of the English soldiers and airmen he'd met, so 'proper' in their ways of fighting. Bruce wondered if they'd be the same here, in the jungle, against this enemy.

Several days later Sam and Bruce were invited to view the results of a larger engagement along a river near the coast. It had been the usual cacophony of mortars and machine gun fire, punctuated by the brightness of flares in the sky. When they arrived at the beach where the river met the sea, the two were shocked. Even Sam, with his longer time on the island, had never seen this magnitude; hundreds and hundreds of dead Japanese soldiers filled every space on the sand. The gentle waves were, even now, lining them up in neat rows as if for an inspection. Marines that had fought them the night before, wandered around or just sat with vacant, dull eyes. Sam pulled two cigarettes from his pocket and handed one to Bruce. He broke his own in half and shoved a piece in each nostril. Bruce did likewise the moment he caught a whiff of the smell. The whole scene was like a macabre painting of hell.

When they returned to their tent, Bruce sat down at his antiquated typewriter. His hands paused over the keys. Turning around, he saw Sam, head down, sobbing on his bunk. Bruce got up, sat next to his friend and joined him. Neither would write of their experience on the beach... let others do that.

The days passed in heat and humidity. The nights continued their terror, though the number of banzai attacks slowly decreased. Bruce and Sam took occasional trips back to Henderson Field with its symbols of civilization. Beer, not cold, and a hamburger could be gotten there. Each time they returned their pockets would be stuffed with goodies for the Marines they lived with. On one of their forays to the rear, Bruce ran into Aaron Steiner.

"Commander, good to see you."

"Hello, Bruce. I've been meaning to get out to your position... I have something for you. It arrived a few days ago; sorry I haven't sent it out. We've been a bit busy. The airfield is nearly completed, as far as our crew is concerned. The army will be relieving the Marines soon, so I hear. Looks like your friends will finally get a break. Come on, I'll give you the package."

"Package?" Bruce's mind filled with an image of a cake from Susan in a box, or some homemade cookies from his mom."

"Yeah, it came from my dad by way of Uncle Saul. Apparently Marge got it out here... that woman is amazing."

"Tell me about it... better yet, let me tell you one day." Bruce managed a smile; a rare occurrence lately.

They were walking toward the Seabees compound. Bruce could see the top of the Quonset huts among the coconut palms. They were like large cans cut in half lengthwise and laid on the ground. Some were storerooms, others offices, most were living quarters.

"Here we are... my office and home." Aaron handed Bruce a wooden box, securely containing... something.

Inside was a typewriter case just like his old one. A note was attached.

"Bruce, I hear you're in need of this. I'd be more careful on the water, especially when you're not fishing. Papa H"

"Hemingway sent you a typewriter? Now I wonder how he knew…" Aaron was smiling and winked at Bruce as he said it.

"That just beats all… in the middle of a war on an island in the Pacific…" Bruce was shaking his head in disbelief. "You know, Aaron, we ARE going to win this war. If this is possible, we can't lose."

"I believe you, Bruce… I really do."

That night the staccato sound resumed, but not that of a Nambu or Browning machine gun… Bruce was back at work with a Royal Quiet Deluxe. As he typed he looked out of the tent. From this new location on the high ground he could see out over the ocean; Ironbottom Sound was spread out in front of him. He saw a storm brewing over the tropical waters far in the distance. It looked like a lot of lightning; then he realized it was a naval battle, a big one, he was watching.

The next morning's scuttlebutt around their camp was that, indeed, a large number of warships had engaged out to sea. Both sides had lost heavily, including American aircraft carriers. Bruce and Sam decided to head down to Henderson Field again to find out what had happened. They would also be able to dispatch their latest writings. Bobbie joined the two correspondents on their walk to the airfield. When they arrived, the scene was one of destruction and activity that reminded Bruce of an ant hill having been stepped on. Burned hulks of destroyed aircraft lined one side of the pock marked runway. Seabees were already in their bulldozers, graders and trucks scurrying around, filling bomb craters and moving the wrecked planes to a giant pile at the far corner.

"What the hell happened here last night? I can't believe we didn't hear or see any of this going on from where we're positioned." Bobbie was shaking his head as the three friends made their way to the Public Affairs Office. Bruce introduced himself to the Marine clerk at the desk, asking for details of the last night's attack.

"The Japs pulled one over on us alright... the 'Tokyo Express' poured more of their infantry onto the island a few nights ago. We expected something, but not with their air force and navy joining in all together. I'll let you talk with the Lieutenant, he's the one that knows exactly what info we can give out..."

A Lieutenant Wilson came over and ushered the three into his office further down the hall in the Quonset. They sat and Bruce introduced his two companions, asking for information on the night's fighting.

"Japanese air strikes started at dusk; fighters strafed the field, destroying several of our planes on the ground. Then two of their battleships began pounding the airfield from miles off the coast. At the same time, just before dark... a Japanese task force struck our own, including carriers, off the Santa Cruz Islands. We damaged several of their carriers, but not before they sunk one of ours and damaged the other. *ENTERPRISE* will be out of action for some time for repairs... and the *HORNET* is gone, sunk this morning by Jap torpedoes while under tow by the *NORTHAMPTON*, a cruiser. There was little loss of life as everyone was evacuated during the night. I'll have more details I'm sure as they come in... that's what I know right now."

"Thanks, Lieutenant. I'll be back later to check up on any new information." He was thinking of Susan; how she'd react to the news that her father's ship had been sunk. He told the other two to grab some sandwiches, one for him as well, while he ran a quick errand. Heading back into the Quonset, he asked Lieutenant Wilson if he could wire something short to his editor in New York. The PAO told him he'd have to limit the length of such a transmission and that it couldn't contain information about the battle. Bruce agreed and wrote a quick note to G Gordon Bennett at The Daily News. It read, "Special attention Susan West. Sam and I okay. Not sure on Dad, looking into it. Bruce"

Studying the note, Lieutenant Wilson said, "I see nothing in it that refers to any activities of the armed forces at present...

approved for transmission." After initialing it, he handed the note back to Bruce with a smile. Bruce gave the note to the Marine clerk who promised to send it as soon as possible.

Finding his two friends at the mess hall, Bruce ate a spam and cheese sandwich and washed it down with a lukewarm Coke. Grabbing a few more to stuff in pockets, they headed back up to the lines. As they reached their tent intense firing erupted yards to the front, about where the platoon's foxholes and dugouts were located. Bobbie yelled at Bruce and Sam to stay in the tent as he ran toward the sounds of combat. Bruce took one look at Sam and they both followed their Marine buddy.

Nearing the edge of the jungle, they could see it all. Japanese soldiers by the hundreds were hurling themselves against the barbed wire entanglements while the Americans hurled grenades, fired rifles and machine guns and taunted them to 'come and get it'. One Marine stood up, firing a shotgun as fast as he could pump it, hitting several of the enemy until he spun around, shotgun flying in the air. Bruce could see the tangled mess that had been his throat, blood soaking his dungaree top.

Sam had run into a trench ahead of them and began helping to load a Browning water cooled .30 caliber machine gun. The loader had been wounded and Sam fed belts of ammunition into it as fast as he could; the gunner was helping, teaching him to go faster. The bodies at the fence line began to pile up two and three high. The Japanese faded back into the jungle, their high pitched screaming quieting as they left. Seven Marines had been injured along with the one killed. At least fifty dead Jap soldiers lay in the field before them, more were moaning and trying to crawl away. One raised to his knees, hatred filling his face. He primed a grenade and was about to throw it when he was cut in two by a Browning gunner. Bruce turned away, sickened by the sight, as Sam bounded up like a crazed puppy looking for another bone.

"Do you think they'll come again? Now I've got the hang of loading that thing just in time for them to leave. I wish they'd come back; I owe them that for my dad..." He looked at Bruce and burst into tears. "He's dead... I know it... we'll find out in a couple of days, but I already know it... He was in the engine room and would never leave it... that was his job... his life."

Bruce tried to console his future brother-in-law but Sam just walked away toward the tents. He watched his friend go and began helping the hospital corpsman bandage and tend to the wounded. An hour later Bruce returned to the tent; Sam was laying on his bunk, facing the tent wall.

"I'm going home, Bruce. As much as I wanted to come out here and write about all the action and excitement... it's not something I can do. I can kill them without feeling bad at all... what does that make me? Not a journalist... I'm going home. I need to see all that's left of my family... I miss Susan."

"So do I Sam. How can you feel so sure about your dad? I mean... reports are of very light casualties. There's a thousand men on that ship... why do you think he's dead?"

"I know my dad... his job was to be in charge of a section in the engine control room. As long as that ship was floating... towed or under its own power, he'd never leave his station. If the *HORNET* was torpedoed, like Lieutenant Wilson said... dad was right down where he was supposed to be... he's dead and I'm going home."

"I'll help you arrange travel back to San Diego tomorrow... I'm sure Aaron Steiner can help, if the Navy can't. C'mon, I'll help you pack."

A few hours later, having made the trek up to their camp and back, Bruce and Sam said farewell alongside a C-47 aircraft on Henderson Field. Commander Steiner had been able to secure a seat on the plane which was evacuating several of his Seabees that had been wounded in the Japanese shelling of the runway in the previous few days. In the past the enemy air force bombers and naval gunships had arrived with clockwork precision. Lately the tactics had changed; now the sporadic attacks came with little warning and were proving more effective. The plane's engines were running and a few minutes remained before it would take off.

"Bruce, I'll be sure to deliver your letters to Susan the moment we get to San Diego. I plan on calling her from Hawaii to let her know I'm on the way… I won't tell her about dad until we're together. Besides, with no confirmation it's only my opinion anyway."

"I think that's best, Sam. I'm sure you'll get there before any Navy Department telegram anyway… IF he's dead. I'll keep checking from here and will get news to you and Susan as soon as I hear anything. Good luck… I'll be seeing you on the beach along Point Loma before long."

The two shook hands and Sam climbed the few steps into the cargo plane. All the wounded had been loaded and the plane began to taxi to the far end of the runway. Bruce watched as it made its turn and began revving up the engines for takeoff. At that moment the air raid siren began to wail; airmen were running to the fighters sitting nearby. The C-47 had started its own way down the strip and had barely gotten in the air when the first Japanese Zero fighter appeared, strafing the pilots and crews getting the American planes ready. The Zero spotted the larger plane just getting airborne and pounced on it, guns blazing. The C-47 didn't have a chance; it veered to the left, struggling to gain altitude when it abruptly nosed up and came down in the jungle beyond the airfield. A huge fireball erupted from where it crashed. Bruce stood, eyes transfixed at the sight of the oily black mushroom cloud coming up out of the dense growth.

"NOOOOO!" Bruce began to sprint to the crash scene when a Marine air mechanic grabbed him and threw him to the ground, moments before the spurts of sand from the Zero's machine gun bullets spattered them both. Bruce rolled hard, losing his glasses in the fall. The Marine grabbed his own knee, blood already flowing between his fingers and yelled for Bruce to get to cover in the nearby trench. Instead, the reporter grabbed the airman and threw the larger

218

man over his shoulder, running to the trench, some thirty yards away. When they landed in the bottom, Bruce tore off the sleeve of his shirt, reached for a wrench laying close by and fashioned a tourniquet around the man's thigh, staunching the flow of blood. The two lay there and prayed for the air attack to subside as bombs began falling all around them.

During a lull in the bombing a helmeted head peered over the edge of the slit trench; a red cross on it identified the owner as a Navy hospital corpsman.

"You guys alright down here?" he asked as he rolled in and alongside the two.

"No... he's been wounded in the left knee... lost a bit of blood but I've got a tourniquet on it for now." Bruce pointed to the Marine. "He saved my life when the Zero started strafing us."

"Wait a minute, man. You saved my ass too, you know. I'm still wondering how the hell you picked me up and carried me to this trench. Your name Clark Kent or something... you sure are as strong as Superman... especially for a reporter."

"How do you know who I am?"

"C'mon... since you got here... we've all been wanting to meet you. Now I've got the lead in bragging over the other guys in my unit. Name's Flynn... Tom Flynn... Portland, Oregon." He reached out and shook Bruce's hand. The corpsman had given him a shot of morphine, which was already taking effect. His speech slurred into non-coherence as he slumped back down on the trench bottom. At that the Jap Navy took over and for the next half hour their world became gut wrenching, ear pounding explosions, lifting them off the ground with the percussive waves as the shells arrived in groups of three, each weighing the same as a small automobile.

When the explosions stopped Bruce looked over at his new Marine friend, lying in the dirt dazed and drugged. A moment later another corpsman stopped by, wondering if they were alright. Bruce quickly explained Flynn's condition as he climbed out of the slit trench and headed to the downed aircraft Sam had been in before the attack. Others were also running in the same direction, the cloud of smoke from the crash still marking the location. When he arrived, several Marines and sailors were digging through the wreckage without finding anyone alive. Bruce pitched in and tore away the chucks of dirt, coconut trees and fuselage that lay about. He found most of a torso and a leg before he staggered aside to vomit. Another man took his place and Bruce stood, speechless, watching. He saw where the bodies were being brought and hurried over. He spotted the blond hair and clothes of his fiancé's brother. He knew that now he would have to bring the news of Sam's death to Susan, along with the possibility that her father had also been killed. Bruce knelt and said a tearful prayer for his friend and fellow correspondent before returning to the airfield in search of Aaron Steiner.

#

The plane touched down, tires chirping as they hit the asphalt runway. Bruce knew Susan would meet him at the terminal; he'd told a 'white lie' when they talked during his layover in Honolulu. She didn't fully understand why his boss wanted him back stateside, especially when it took so much to get him out to the Pacific to begin with.

"I suppose it's one of a myriad of things I'll never really get about the military. Anyway, the important thing is that you'll be here in a couple of days. With the mail as slow as it is at times... well, I don't suppose you have news of Sam and Dad? I haven't gotten letters from them in quite a while... it makes me nervous, you know."

"I've got to go. There's a bunch of guys wanting to use the phone. See you soon... I love you."

"I love you, too, Bruce. Goodbye."

Now, as the aircraft taxied to the gate, Bruce felt a lump in his stomach the size of Gibraltar. He was wrong in lying to her, but didn't want to say anything without being able to hold her as he said it. Now there were only a few more minutes to prepare; his mouth was already dry as cotton. He saw her through the window, standing alone. The plane stopped and Bruce walked down the stairway wheeled up to the aircraft's hatch. As he approached Susan, his eyes met hers. She had a steeled, angry look about her that Bruce had never experienced.

"You rat... I should have heard this from you... but no, I get a telegram... taped to my front door when I got home from work. You... you should have told me, Bruce."

At that, she went limp. Bruce caught her, holding her up while he put his own sea bag down. She put her head in the crook of his neck and wept, great heaves of grief that somehow reminded him of the huge Japanese shells rocking him in the trench.

Bruce whispered in her ear, "I couldn't tell you about Sam until I could hold you, like this. I knew how hard it would be on you, darling. I love you and I've cried a thousand tears for your brother."

"My brother? What are you talking about... my father is dead, not... no, NO... NOOO!" She beat on him with hard fists until she didn't have any more strength. Bruce gently sat her down in a chair next to a water cooler, got his handkerchief wet and began to wipe her face and neck. She looked up at him with a blank stare, her mind somewhere deep within where Bruce couldn't get to quite yet. He stood her up and walked her out of the terminal; other passengers quietly opening a way for them through the crowd of travelers. He hailed a taxi and gave the driver Susan's address, hoping that at least one of her boarders would be home to help him with her.

Later that evening, Bruce had a chance to call his parents from Susan's house. A boarder had been home; her boyfriend was a Navy doctor and he had him come over to give Susan a sedative to help her sleep... a long, deep sleep.

"Son, I'm so glad you're safe and this news is terrible... a horror. Is there anything we can do to help? I know we've not met Susan, but that's not important at a time like this..."

"Thanks, dad. I don't know just what's going to happen… not tomorrow morning when she wakes up, or the day after or next week. I'll be sure to keep you posted. Please let mom know and tell her to call me here when she gets home from the USO?"

"Absolutely, Bruce. Remember, anything at all that you need… well, you just ask."

Bruce finished his conversation when there was a knock at the door. He opened it to find Saul and Marge Price standing there. They had heard the news of Susan's family from Aaron, by way of Phil Steiner. Marge had lost no time finding out when Bruce had landed.

"How is she?" Marge asked when Bruce opened the door.

"Resting… beyond that I don't really know."

Marge, ever a mixture of compassion and command, began; "Well, Bruce… Saul and I would like you and Susan to come to our house for a few weeks. We both think it will be better for her if she has a new surrounding while she grieves. I simply cannot think of how hard it would be in her father's house and all. I know it will be a difficult decision for you, but we feel it's the right one. The two of us have already booked transportation to Florida to visit family for a month. We've got two nieces who will cook and clean for you while you're staying on Point Loma. Take some time to let Susan miss her men before she has to go through all their things. She's certainly suffered enough of a shock…"

"Why don't you two come in? I'm expecting a phone call from my own mother any moment… I'd really like to hear what she might suggest."

"Certainly, Bruce. That's wisdom."

Saul and Marge made themselves comfortable in Susan's small living room as Bruce made some tea. When the phone rang, he nearly upset the tray as he rushed to answer it. It was his mom; they spoke for several minutes before he appeared in the doorway from the kitchen.

"I'll take her advice, and yours, as confirmation. My mother thanks you both more than she can say... when would you like us to come over?"

Marge stood up.

"Right now. You're already packed... I spotted the sea bag when I came in. I'll pack up a few things for Susan. You can come back and get more when she wants you to. Anything you or she needs in the meantime... well, you just let our nieces know and that will be that."

Bruce looked at Saul, who shrugged.

"You can't stop the Navy.... any more than the Japanese can."

Chapter 11
November 1942

"Bruce, darling... will you please stop pacing around like some tiger in a cage. Really, it's not going to get the train here any faster."

Susan was not as annoyed as she appeared to be; it was actually fun seeing a part of him she didn't know yet. His parents were arriving on the *San Diegan* from Los Angeles in a few minutes and he was a bundle of nervous energy.

The past weeks had been hard on both of them. Looking ahead to a life without her father and brother was something Susan had never contemplated. The reality of their deaths was still somewhat untouchable. Bruce had been by her side from the moment she woke up at the Price's home on Point Loma. She had not been able to return to her own house until a few days ago. Bruce had been the one to go and pick up things she wanted; he had also taken time to look after Sam's small place in the Hillcrest neighborhood. Finding a renter there had not been a problem; with the war on, housing was at a premium.

The train glided into the station, nearly silent, and came to a gentle stop. Passengers began pouring out of the cars; most were in uniforms of the Navy or Marines. The passenger trains along the southern coast of California had become some of the busiest in the nation since the war began. Bruce stood on his tiptoes to try and see his parents among the throng. He glanced at Susan and smiled.

"I should have guessed my dad would wait until everyone else was off the train. He hates crowds... I wonder what he's thinking with the whole population of Ames here on one platform. Wait... there they are!"

Susan looked to where he was pointing. A couple were walking, hand in hand, alongside the train. She noticed the trim figure of the man in a nice suit, snap brim sitting square on his head. Her first thought was knowing what Bruce would like in twenty or so years. His mother was looking everywhere, trying to soak in all the newness of the place, not missing one detail. Susan smiled, seeing Bruce as a perfect combination of the two.

"Mom... Dad... welcome to San Diego. This is Susan." Bruce was surprised he didn't start crying with the emotions he felt saying these few words.

"Susan... let me get a good look at you." Earl stood holding her shoulders at arm's length. He smiled, eyes twinkling as he said, "And what, exactly, do you see in this son of mine?"

"Earl.... really!" Louise butted in, giving Susan a warm, welcoming hug. "These Hollins men... so analytical, just like their jobs. I've been beside myself waiting to meet you, Susan."

Louise took Susan's hand as Bruce and Earl led the way out of the station. The warm sunshine caused Earl to look up and take off his hat. Holding his face upward, he let out a long sigh and said, "A man could get used to this. It's just starting to feel like winter back home."

"Oh, it'll get colder tonight. Winter is coming here, too." Susan noted. "I often need a jacket this time of year."

"You come to Iowa in winter... you'd better have a parka handy", returned Earl with a grin, "and don't forget galoshes."

The four walked across Broadway to the taxi stop. A driver approached as Bruce nodded to him. He stowed the bags in the trunk and opened the doors; Bruce sat up front while Louise and Earl sandwiched Susan in the back seat.

As the cab drove out to the Point, Susan pointed out several places along the way. She told them about her job at Consolidated, where she'd return after their visit. Susan had been given six weeks leave of absence for her loss. They went past the Marine Corps base with groups of new recruits marching around, looking like square blocks gliding across the parade ground. Next to it was the Navy's boot camp area, also covered with young men marching. Earl commented that the entire state of Iowa seemed to be in ranks of khaki and blue. He had never seen so many people in one area before. The taxi climbed the heights of Point Loma to the top, offering a panoramic view of the harbor, with North Island and the city spread out below.

"Here we are", said Bruce as the cab stopped.

Louise and Earl got out, transfixed by the view. One of the new aircraft carriers was docked at North Island and three destroyers were making their way through the harbor toward the open sea. To their right, beyond the end of the point with the lighthouse, were anchored several other ships; a battleship, two cruisers and a handful of smaller warships.

"Since the attack on Pearl Harbor, the Navy's been careful not to keep all the ships in one place, moving them around a bit before they head out to the central Pacific", explained Bruce. "San Diego was the main base before the fleet was moved to Hawaii a few years before the attack. Now a good part comes back for provisioning and repairs. I'll take Dad past the shipyards in a day or so; that sight will make your head spin."

Susan led the way up and into the house. Saul's nieces met them at the door; Eunice would cook for them and Bernice kept the place tidy and in order. They walked through the house and out onto the back, overlooking the Pacific. Bruce's folks were smitten by the view, just as Susan and he had been on their first visit.

"Yes, indeed... a man could get used to this." Earl commented.

Eunice came out and asked Susan if they would like cocktails before dinner out here on the balcony; she had prepared a meal of Mexican beans and rice with a fresh garden salad, a fruit cup for dessert. Susan smiled, thanking her for the reminder that it was 'Meatless Thursday'. The four sat and enjoyed a bottle of California white wine in anticipation of a light dinner.

"Susan... I know we've said it in letters and on the phone... we can't say how much we feel your loss. We hope our visit is not too soon for you." Earl's words were sincere. Susan felt like they had been right here, along with Bruce, during her ordeal.

"Actually, dad... it was Susan's idea that you come out." Bruce broke in. He nodded to Susan, who continued.

"Not just mine... Bruce and I both wanted you to be here now. You know we love each other... Bruce has been absolutely wonderful to me... and for me. It's very difficult for me to say that... just like I'm returning to work soon... he has a job to do as well. Bruce will be heading back east shortly after you return to Iowa. His editor in New York wants him to go to North Africa to follow up on Fred... the Army Rangers are over there."

Bruce continued, "So... we wanted you here now because... well, with me leaving again... well... ummm."

"I think what he's trying to tell you is that we're getting married and couldn't bear to do that without you here." Susan spoke with the confidence that showed Bruce and his folks she was sure of their decision and the future.

"That's wonderful..." chirped Louise as she rose to give her future daughter-in-law a hug.

"Congratulations!" joined Earl as he stood to shake Bruce's hand. His smile grew as Susan wrapped him up in a hug after Louise's.

"Now I won't have to wonder how to address you... Mom and Dad sound great right now."

"A toast to the soon to be bride and groom!" Earl raised his glass as he said it, joined by the other three. "When is the happy day?"

Bruce explained, with face already blushing, "We thought a simple ceremony the morning of the day you leave to go back home. Your train is an overnight... so it leaves late in the evening. That way..."

"Always thinking, that son of mine..." replied his dad with a wink.

"Oh, Earl!" exclaimed Louise, slapping him on the arm.

Dinner that evening was the best Susan had enjoyed in a month.

#

The next day Bruce and Susan took his parents on a tour of San Diego in Saul's convertible, the same car they had driven back from Yosemite. They drove as far out on the Point as they could, before reaching the Army road blocks protecting the defensive guns and ammunition storage area. Doubling back brought them, again, past the two huge training centers and on through downtown San Diego. Bruce pointed out Saul's Seven Seas and the Grant Hotel he had stayed in as they traveled down Broadway. They drove down to National City with the shipyards; busy bee hives of activity. The prows of new ships pointed forward in a row that seemed to go on forever. They stopped at Susan's house for a quick lunch, compliments of her boarders, before heading toward Balboa Park. The Navy hospital there was undergoing expansion, as was most of the city. As they left the hospital area, Bruce stopped the car suddenly and jumped out, to the surprise of the passengers.

"Stan...Stan Larson!" Bruce shouted at a sailor walking along a sidewalk. The man turned, surprise written all over his face.

"Bruce! What the...". He paused when he saw Bruce's folks in the car. Walking up to the convertible, Stan said "Howdy Mr Hollins... Mrs Hollins. What a surprise seeing you two here."

"Good afternoon Stan. You're looking wonderfully fit and well... your mother will be glad to know we saw you on our visit. I'll be sure to tell her just how good you look."

"Thank you, ma'am. You must be Susan? I'd know you from the description Bruce gave while we were together... except he didn't do you quite enough justice."

"Why thank you, Stan. Bruce has talked a lot about you, too."

"How's your brother, Sam? I haven't seen him in San Diego since I got back. I suppose he's busy at the newspaper?"

Susan's expression changed in an instant. Bruce took Stan's arm and motioned him aside.

"Sam was killed while we were in Guadalcanal together. Jap Zeroes shot down the plane he was taking back here... happened a month ago. Bobbie is still there, I think... though I've read the Army is relieving the Marines now."

"Gosh, Susan, I'm so sorry... I had no idea. I really liked Sam."

"Thanks, Stan... I'm sure he liked you, too. I found out about his death the same day I heard about my father. I'm better now... it still hurts, all the same."

"And it should, dear." said Louise. "You've been through an awful shock... one I'm not certain I could have handled at all. Your strength is a wonderful encouragement to me." She leaned over and gave Susan a warm hug.

"Stan... how long are you in San Diego? Susan and I are getting married in a week... wondering if you could be there? I suppose a guy needs a 'best man' and I don't know anyone better... at least not here in San Diego."

"Nicely put, pard. As it happens, I'm an instructor at the Gunnery School on Point Loma now... so being there should be no problem."

"Hey, that's great. Can we give you lift to the Point? We're heading that way and have room, if you don't mind sitting with the women?"

"Mind? Me? Girls? Don't forget, friend, I'm a sailor."

The drive through Balboa Park and on to Point Loma was filled with laughter as Stan related story after story of his time in the Navy. He was even able to lighten up the time he and Bruce spent together, fighting against the Japanese ships. Everyone in the car had a taste of 'sea stories' by the time they dropped him off at the Gunnery School with a promise of dinner together soon.

#

The week together flew by, full of walks on the beach and hours spent talking of the past and the future. Bruce learned things about his parents he'd never known, or at least paid attention to earlier. Susan loved his parents; their easy manners and humor reminded her of where Bruce came from. Several times they reassured her that, at any time, if she grew tired of San Diego she was welcome in Ames. There would always be a room for her, as Louise put it.

Bruce and his father enjoyed a day together; Susan had arranged a tour for Earl through the aircraft factory. It was, he said later, the most amazing place he'd ever been in. Watching truckloads of parts go in one end of a building and finished airplanes coming out the other was one thing. To see how they were assembled as they rolled through was quite another. He especially enjoyed seeing all the women working, doing jobs that were for men only a year earlier.

The two had lunch together at El Indio's, where the owner asked Bruce about their friend Saul, el sastre (the tailor). Earl enjoyed hearing Bruce tell of his first encounter with Saul and the many ways he and Phil Steiner had helped him. Earl told his son that he, himself, was quietly involved with a group from up in Minneapolis that was helping Jews escape from the Nazi's and that he'd be most interested in meeting Saul and Phil someday. Bruce was flabbergasted at the news and promised to make such a meeting happen.

"I know Mom's involved with the USO in Ames and the college and all that… but you working on the Jewish situation in Europe?"

"Bruce, I own a bank… even if it's a small bank. Many of the great financiers in the world are Jewish. At first I didn't know anything that was going on… through my own ignorance and the lack of information in the press. Once I heard it first hand from some who have relocated in the Midwest… well, I realized it's my problem, too. We all have a part… Stan's fighting an enemy, so is Bobbie. James Hartke was, too, until he was wounded. You're fighting to make folks aware of what's going on… maybe that's the most important part. Many of us at home are fighting, too… sacrificing things we like and want so the fighting men will have what they need. I guess I look at my own involvement as a sort of fight that I can do… helping arrange for the money to buy freedom or transportation for someone… that sort of thing. I know it feels better than financing a new hog barn or feed mill. Enough, I'll get off my soap box and quit politicking… aren't we supposed to be picking up your marriage license?"

"Oh… gosh, I almost forgot! Thanks, dad. Don't tell Susan, please…"

"Secret's safe with me, son."

The next morning Bruce and Susan, along with Earl, Louise and Stan went to a small chapel at the San Diego Mission for their wedding ceremony. Meeting them there was Susan's friend and coworker Janet, a welder at Consolidated. Janet was a few inches shorter than Susan with auburn hair that shone red in the sunlight. The sparkle in her green eyes when she laughed so mesmerized Stan that he, a sailor, was almost unable to speak. Susan and Bruce joked that there just might be one less sailor roaming the streets of San Diego before long.

The ceremony lasted ten minutes. Stan and Janet signed the license as witnesses; Bruce and Susan were man and wife. His parents wore, perhaps, the biggest smiles. The entire party went to an early dinner on the waterfront before Earl and Louise caught their train back to Ames. Stan and Janet bade the new couple a bon voyage and disappeared, hand in hand, down Broadway toward the city's night life. Bruce and Susan looked at each other and laughed; the grand expectation most newlyweds had of a joyous and noisy sendoff was not at all on their minds. They retreated back to their rooms at the Price's home and began moving Bruce's things into Susan's room... playfully. Eunice and Bernice had been given several days off earlier, with their joyful consent and best wishes. Before they left, Saul's nieces had decorated the living area of the house with bird of paradise and other tropical flowers. Glasses and a bottle of champagne soon appeared, in Bruce's hands, as Susan relaxed on the rear balcony. A full moon shone brightly overhead creating a surreal atmosphere of light and dark. The waves on the beach far below were like silvery spider's silk. Bruce turned on a radio and the sounds of Glenn Miller's "Moonlight Serenade" completed the scene. Pouring two glasses of the bubbly, Bruce was interrupted by Susan's whispered "Let's dance..." in his ear.

It had been a short six months since their first meeting in a car outside the main gate of a Navy base. In that period their love had grown until, at moments, restraint was very difficult. Now their feelings for each other reached a crescendo of passion that began with a dance and settled into a leisurely stroll along a beach to the sounds of those gossamer silken threads lightly stroking the sand at the water's edge.

"I suppose we really should have had at least one glass of that champagne, darling. It'll go flat before we're back up at the house, you know."

"Susan, no champagne can touch the past hours. I don't need bubbles to float away... I already feel light as a feather... just being with you makes all the world's mess go away."

"Mmmm… say things like that every day, promise? Write them to me from wherever you go… they give me a thrill. On second thought, don't write them… no need to excite the censors."

"Why, Mrs Hollins, you made an outright joke… and you've only been a member of the family for twelve hours. Let's go check that champagne…"

#

As all honeymoons do, theirs ended far too quickly. Susan reported back to work a few days before Bruce had to leave for New York. Their time together had taken them to depths of feeling neither had experienced before. Neither wanted it to end. Susan came home from her first day back at Consolidated to announce she had quit her job and intended to go with Bruce on the train.

"What about the house, Susan? Who's going to take care of things here in San Diego?" Bruce was thrilled at the prospect of them being together; if she decided to sell both her dad's and Sam's homes, he was more than agreeable.

"Oh, I took care of that at lunch. Dad's friend, the one with the beach house in Del Mar, said he'd be glad to manage renting both places 'for the duration'. He's already started putting Dad's things in storage. We're free to go where we want… he'll make arrangements for the money to be available to us."

"That's wonderful… but I don't have a place in New York for us to live and you can imagine how hard that might be to get…"

"Who said anything about New York? I'm done, I think, with big cities. I stopped after work and bought a couple of things… see?" Susan opened a large shopping bag and took out a parka and galoshes. "The clerk had to look pretty hard to find these boot things."

"Oh, no…. wait until I tell Dad what you called them! But I know they'll be delighted to have you with them… at least until we find our own place somewhere."

"Anywhere, darling… as long as it's with you."

#

Bruce and Susan boarded the train on their way to Iowa three days later. Thanking Eunice and Bernice was a happy, and tearful, event. The two young ladies had become like extended family all around. Saul and Marge phoned that same morning to extend their congratulations on the marriage and to say that they had "taken care of" the travel arrangements to Iowa and for Bruce's trip on to New York. A final telephone call to Ames caught Earl home for lunch with Louise. They were both excited to hear that their two children would be with them in a few days.

Their trip would take them on a longer, more scenic route, thanks to the Price's. Traveling up the coast of California and over the Sierra Mountains near Yosemite, they saw the best of the west. Changing trains was well worth any minor inconvenience compared to the beauty of the Rockies, Yellowstone and a short stop at the new park of Mount Rushmore, completed only a year earlier. They arrived in Des Moines thoroughly refreshed, with a new found love of the American countryside. Earl and Louise were there to meet them at the train station, along with Jim Hartke and his fiancé Frankie Howard, sister of Fred, who Bruce hoped to find in North Africa soon. Susan came out of the train dressed in her parka and galoshes, to the astonishment of Earl. He proceeded to grab her and swing her around, as Bruce was want to do. The six made their way to Ames to find the Hollins' house decorated by the neighbors with a banner welcoming the newlyweds. The next afternoon Frank and Mabel Howard hosted an indoor summer picnic despite the blowing snow outside. Pork chops and potato salad were served on a tablecloth spread on the straw covered floor of a barn. Susan was enthralled by her welcome and said to Earl, "A girl could get used to this."

Three days later it was time for Bruce to leave for New York and, after a short stay there, to Algiers in North Africa. There he would locate the 1st Ranger Battalion and Fred Howard. Earl, Louise and Susan accompanied him to the train station. His parents said their goodbyes in the main depot while Susan walked with him to the train.

"You've got everything? Make sure you phone me as soon as you get to the paper's office. I love you…"

"I know… I love you, too. Susan, you'll be fine here with Mom and Dad. Be sure to ask them if you need anything. I'll be fine, too… and I'll write as soon as I get an address over there."

The conductor called for the final boarding; Bruce and Susan shared one last embrace before he hopped up the steps into the car. She waved until the train was out of sight.

#

"Married? You got yourself hitched in California? I think that's great… well, for most people. Never seemed to work quite right for me." The eruption of a laugh brought Bruce back to earth faster than the familiar creaky chair with no bottom support in the editor's office.

"So when do I shove off for Africa, boss? I can hardly believe I'm actually excited about getting back to a front, eating Army chow and all."

"Yeah, well… I've known other writers who couldn't live without it either, Bruce. I don't know what it is. Me… I can hardly stand the sight of an under cooked steak, or the sound of a car back firing. Anyway, you're out to Mitchell Field again, on Long Island. The Air Corps came through with a place on a transport for you. You'll be flying with officers of a new group assigned to the Mediterranean Theater. I think you know at least one of them… the group commander is a Colonel William Young."

"Colonel Young? Well, he's done alright… he was the Major that flew the B-17 last time I went to England. It'll be good to see him again… when do I leave?"

"Tomorrow morning… first thing. You've got time to call Susan… with no time for second thoughts about going." Another blast of laughter; Bruce smiled.

"One of these times in your office... let's take time for a game of cribbage or something... OK, boss?"

"If you think the war will slow down long enough, sure thing. Bruce... take care, really. You're a hell of a writer... don't lose your edge. The public has been missing your articles. Not that I'm putting pressure on you, but the war is calling."

"Got it; I understand. I think you can expect something on the wire about the time I arrive. Crossing the Atlantic on a plane full of Air Corps officers ought to give me something to write."

"That's my boy... go get 'em."

Bruce found an empty office with a phone and called Susan. In a way he was glad Bennett had mentioned second thoughts and the public wanting his writing. Hearing her voice made him miss her all the more. A part inside him wanted to go back to Iowa and get a job there. A larger part was telling him he had a duty in this war, like his friends and even his own father. He told Susan he'd be leaving the next morning. Then they spent half an hour dreaming together about the future before both knew it was time to hang up. He hitched a ride on one of the paper delivery trucks carrying the afternoon edition out to Long Island, being sure to grab a copy when he was dropped off at Mitchell Field. Showing his identification at the gate, he said he knew where the Admin Building was... with a knowing smile.

Bruce enquired where he might find Colonel Young. He was told to have a seat while the clerk checked. In a minute the clerk informed him that the Colonel was in the Officer's Club at dinner. Bruce thanked him and picked up his sea bag and typewriter case, telling the clerk he knew where the 'O Club' was. He walked the quarter mile, enjoying the opportunity to stretch his legs. Over a month without active exercise had tightened him up a bit; he'd be sure to remedy that in the weeks ahead. Even his shoulder felt better carrying the weight of his gear.

Colonel Young spotted Bruce when he walked in the room. He got up and strode briskly over to his favorite war correspondent.

"Bruce Hollins... I heard you might show up for this flight, though you hadn't arrived as of yesterday morning. Bennett said you usually get somewhere just in the 'nick of time'. I guess he's right... how are you?"

"I'm fine, Colonel. Congratulations on the promotion... group commander. A long way from jockeying tourists across the ocean... even well-heeled ones."

Young laughed and slapped Bruce on the back. "Come and join us. We've eaten... just enjoying one last drink before heading to quarters... though one more last drink might not be a bad idea."

The Colonel introduced Bruce to several officers at the table. Most were pilots but some were now of higher rank and helped command squadrons. They were the core of a new air force assigned to the bombing of Italy and other targets in the Mediterranean. All were enthusiastic about meeting him, had read his articles, loved what he wrote and so on. Bruce was honestly embarrassed by the attention. He took the opportunity to thank them all for the job they were doing and explained that he felt honored to be able to write about men like them.

"And this guy wonders why he's so popular everywhere he goes... no boasting of his own accomplishments like other writers I've met." was what a captain responded when Bruce was finished. He was welcomed by all and paid attention to names and home towns of each he spoke with over the course of the evening. It was well past midnight when the group broke up, each heading to his own quarters. Colonel Young called and arranged a room for Bruce. Reveille was at 0500 and takeoff at 0700.

This flight was much different from his second flight with the Colonel. The aircraft was pressurized, had comfortable seats and their flight took them from New York to the Bahamas and on across the middle Atlantic to Africa by way of the Canary Islands. Bruce managed his time well; a long nap, interviews and plenty of time to bang out the article on his machine. When they landed in Oran, Algiers he was ready for the Air Corps to wire it to Bennett in New

York. Bruce figured getting it to Bennett that quickly would buy him a few days to find Fred before writing more.

Apparently it wouldn't take too long to locate the Rangers; the first soldier Bruce came across after leaving the air base was part of the 34th Division. The familiar Red Bull patch caught his eye immediately. He and Bruce discussed the quickest way to get to the division's camp. The GI was happy to accompany Bruce. In less than two hours Bruce was in Colonel Darby's office in an ancient fort outside the city.

"Bruce… good to see you. Did you come here to train with us a bit more? Looking just a bit thicker around the middle there. What brings you to Algiers besides, I assume, another Iowa farm boy under my command?"

"Right you are, sir. Congratulations, by the way, on your promotion to Lieutenant Colonel… I noticed it on your door."

"Thanks, though the credit goes to the Battalion itself. The boys did a hell of a good job during the Torch landings. The attack we were part of was pretty well screwed up… pardon my French. But the Rangers did everything we were assigned and opened the way for reinforcements to arrive. A few of our guys were wounded by the Vichy French defenders… including Fred Howard. I'm putting him in for a decoration and promotion for the part he played in our success."

"Fred's hurt? How badly, if I might ask?"

"Oh, he's coming along fine at the aid station. No real need to send him to the Division Hospital, actually. I was over there earlier this morning… had no idea you were about to show up. I'll have a driver give you a lift there when we're done talking. So what are your plans… and do they include the Rangers?"

"Well, since being with you in Ireland this summer, I've been to Guadalcanal and had a destroyer sunk under me during a fight with the Japanese Navy. Now I'm here to see what's happening against the Germans and Italians. Don't know how long I'll stay or exactly who all I'll be staying with."

"You know you're always welcome with the Rangers. Many of us have read of your exploits in the Army Times here. Why don't we set you up with Howard's platoon? You can get the details on his action from the other boys. Fred won't say much about what he did, even to me… Why don't you head over to see him?"

"Thanks, Colonel… I'd like to… could I trouble your driver to drop my things off with Fred's platoon?"

"Not a problem, Bruce." Colonel Darby called for an orderly and told him exactly what he wanted. Bruce was in a jeep heading to the Battalion aid station in a few minutes. When he arrived, a medic pointed out where Fred was. Bruce walked up to the bed; his friend was sleeping. Both arms were in casts up to the shoulders and one leg was heavily bandaged. There were numerous small cuts and bruises on his face as well. Bruce sat down next to him and began going over notes from his flight; items he'd not included in the article to Bennett. A few minutes later Fred opened his eyes and looked over.

"Bruce? How did you know I'm here?"

"Just got through talking with Colonel Darby, Fred… how are you feeling?"

"Ahhh, not so bad. My leg hurts worse than the arms… they mostly itch from the casts. Drives me just about crazy. What gives? Last I read, you were writing from the Pacific with Bobbie… did you hook up with Stan while you were there?"

Bruce brought his friend up to date on his own travels and encounters with their friends. Fred's eyes were wide open as he described the naval fight with Stan and the Jap attacks on Guadalcanal. He laughed a bit at Bruce's description of Stan's hair after the sinking of the *LAFFEY*, though he knew it was a serious matter.

"And to top it off, you go and get married… not enough adventure being a war reporter, I suppose. Sounds like you've been through more shit than any one of us. So how are Sid and my sister getting along? That was another surprise… but a nice one. I think the two will be happy together."

"They sure seem to be. Sid's helping your dad in the business as well as studying hard at college. I think they'll do fine… I'm glad they're close for Susan, too. Now, how did you happen to get here in this shape? It looks like a pretty big truck hit you."

"Aww, I was just doing my job… you know. Part of my squad was pinned down by a couple of Frenchies in a pillbox… machine gun and all. I'm just glad it wasn't a damn German MG-42… that would have cut me in half. A buddy says I slipped as I tossed a grenade in… didn't quite get out of the way fast enough. Anyhow, a couple of bullets in the leg and pieces of shrapnel all over. Doc says I'll be good to go in a few weeks. What will you do while I'm in here?"

"Not sure… I'll write about you and your buddies… that's for sure. Then I might hook back up with the Air Corps group I flew over here with. They're a new unit… I suspect they'll be flying against the Italians soon. Maybe I can hitch another ride on a Flying Fortress…"

"If anyone can… my bet's on you, buddy. Gosh, it's sure good to see you again."

Just then a doctor came up to check on Fred's wounds. He smiled when Bruce introduced himself.

"I'm Doctor Standish. Glad to meet you, Bruce. I don't want to sound like another admirer, but you write what I like to read. Keep it up."

"Thanks, Doc. So how's my friend doing, really?"

"Well, there's always infection to be concerned with… but I think he'll do fine. It's time for some medication to make him sleep. He's got to rest… much as he doesn't like to."

"That'd be Fred. I've got to go see to my own lodging. Fred, I'll be staying awhile with your platoon, Colonel Darby's orders."

"Great… don't believe everything they tell you… they like to make more of this than what's real."

Bruce left and got directions to Fred's outfit. He walked to where the platoon's tents were located and checked in with the lead Sergeant, a man he knew from the training in Ireland. Bruce was billeted in Fred's tent and soon had the whole story from his squad mates about the fight. It certainly was more than Fred had told him; apparently a "couple of Frenchies" was actually more than a dozen and Fred had taken them all out with his Thompson and three grenades; most of the fight had happened after he was wounded. It had opened the way for many of the Rangers to get to their objectives successfully. Bruce spent most of the next day writing, when he wasn't visiting Fred; sitting and watching him sleep.

Bruce returned to his tent after another time chatting with Fred to find a note on his bunk from Colonel Young, inviting him to a tour of the new air base. Bruce hurried to the Battalion's admin office to contact the Colonel with a reply that he would certainly enjoy the opportunity. Arrangements were made for him to be picked up the next morning. That afternoon and evening Bruce finished another article on soldiers stationed in North Africa. His tent mates were treated to a pre-release reading of the article, after which they made Bruce an honorary member of their squad, for what it was worth. A good time followed with warm beer that magically appeared at the end of the reading.

Bruce arrived at the Air Corps base and was ushered into Colonel Young's office. Present were several of the same men he had flown over from New York with. A briefing on the first mission by the group against fascist Italy was presented by the Air Operations Officer. Sixty B-25 Mitchell medium bombers were sent to attack railroad marshaling yards at Milan in northwest Italy. Though not capable of carrying as heavy a bomb load as the B-17's these planes had proven their ability to strike the enemy hard, beginning with the Doolittle Raid on Tokyo the previous spring. Then they had launched form the deck of the *USS HORNET*; Bruce recalled the event and mentioned his father-in-law had been on the ship when it later sank off Guadalcanal. Colonel Young said he had invited Bruce to the briefing because of their flight together against occupied France. The planes were due to land at the base in just under an hour, returning from what was an historic mission; the first direct aerial attack on another Axis country. Now only Germany itself had not felt the destruction of American bombers. Colonel Young intimated that before many weeks were past, that milestone would also be achieved.

The group of officers, and Bruce, then moved up to the field's control tower to watch the returning aircraft. Thirty minutes later the first of the B-25's roared over the runway, circled and touched down. One after another followed, a few firing flares to indicate they had wounded airmen onboard. Of the sixty that departed before dawn that morning, fifty seven returned. Three had been shot down by an estimated 50 enemy fighters that defended the Milan airspace. Later Bruce learned that 11 enemy fighters had been destroyed during the mission.

Bruce thanked Colonel Young for the chance to see the end of the flight and to interview several crewmen about it. He also mentioned his own desire to return to the air on another B-17 mission in the future. Colonel Young said he would see what could be done about that. He knew about a group of correspondents training in England to fly on the first mission to Germany. Bruce returned to the Rangers encampment late that night after a victory celebration by the air crews.

Chapter 12
December 1942

Bruce woke to an excited discussion between members of the squad. News was that the French naval fleet based at Toulon in France had been scuttled to prevent it being captured by the Germans as the Nazi's took over the southern region of the country from the Vichy Government. The Allies had hoped that the French Navy would, somehow, sail the ships and join the English and American fleets against the Nazis. It was still a victory, of sorts, since Hitler would not get his hands on any of the large French warships. Bruce hurried to the Officer's Club to try and find a copy of the day's newspaper.

He was encouraged by what he read; the allies were beating their enemies almost everywhere. The fighting in Tunisia, just east of Algiers, was progressing at a slow grinding pace against German forces. Guadalcanal was now all but captured from the Japanese and the Marines had turned it over to the Army. Bruce knew he'd have to find out where Bobbie was, if no longer on the island. The U S Navy had won several victories despite a setback at a place called Tassaforonga in the Solomons. Russian armies had nearly encircled German forces at Stalingrad; millions of men were fighting in that one battle alone. The scope and scale of the war staggered him; he felt rather small and insignificant for a moment, wishing he was somewhere near the fighting. Then he thought of his good friend, lying wounded nearby, and realized he was in the right place for now. If he couldn't write about the fighting, he could certainly write about those doing the fighting.

Bruce knocked on Colonel Darby's door and was told to enter. He found his friend standing over his desk, studying a map.

"Colonel... excuse the interruption... I was wondering if it might be arranged for me to accompany a patrol out against the enemy, sir."

"Bruce... I told you before, reporters are not allowed as combatants. There's no way I could guarantee your safety and you would not be allowed to carry a weapon."

"Colonel Darby... on Guadalcanal I carried a .45 caliber for my own protection... and used it more than once. I feel confident in my ability to keep up and not get in the way. Sir, I feel stagnant here... waiting for Fred to get better so I can what... watch him go and fight again? I'm no soldier, but I believe my duty is to let America know what we're doing here."

"Let me think about it... I'll get back to you. That's all, Bruce."

It turned out he didn't have long to wait. A few hours later, as he was typing on his bunk, a corporal came in with several wrapped bundles.

"Mr Hollins? Colonel's compliments... says you should be ready by 2100 hours... uhhh, 9 o'clock tonight. Sergeant Willis will stop by for you." The corporal turned and walked out, leaving the bundles on another bunk. Bruce opened the first; new army dungarees. The others contained web gear; belt and shoulder harness, canteen and helmet. There were also new boots and... a holster containing a .45 pistol with spare magazines.

Bruce was dressed and ready by 8:30 that evening. He'd written a letter to Susan, 'just in case', and left it with one of his tent mates. The man took it and said he'd be sure to get it delivered... that it wasn't the first one. Sergeant Charles Willis came at precisely 9 o'clock and announced he was called 'Chuck', nothing else, and was from a small town in West Virginia; so small he didn't need to say the name of it. Bruce liked the man at once, which was probably the last thing Willis wanted. He also said he was the oldest man in the Rangers and had been a soldier longer than Bruce had probably been alive.

The two left the tent into the pitch dark night. Willis told Bruce to stay close to him… 'closer'n a damned tick on a coon hound's ass' to be more precise. They were going out to capture some 'Nazi sumbitches or Eyetie shitkickers' and hoped to be back by morning. Bruce nearly laughed at the expressions, but thought better of it. They were joined by another twelve men, all armed with Thompson submachine guns and pouches of grenades over their shoulders. One man, Lowell Ball, helped Bruce smear black greasepaint on his face. 'Low Ball' was the son of a Baptist preacher from Georgia, loved to hunt deer at night with dogs and had three girlfriends back home that didn't know about each other. Low Ball asked Bruce if he needed his glasses to see; if not, it would be better if he put them away. Bruce put them in his pocket; he couldn't see more than two feet in the dark with or without them anyway.

The squad headed out by truck for about 10 miles, dismounted and began to walk single file, each man about fifteen feet from the one ahead. How they managed to see each other baffled Bruce; he was almost in Chuck's back pocket and still could hardly make him out. They'd gone about four miles when Bruce saw a man ahead kneel down and motion to stop. He was surprised how well he could see now that his eyes had adjusted. He and Chuck went to the front and found out the Italian outposts were right beyond a slight rise ahead. Crawling now, Bruce joined several other Rangers in crossing the short distance silently, as he'd been taught in Ireland. Two of the men ahead disappeared; there was a muffled cry of surprise and the two came back dragging an unconscious Italian soldier.

Chuck told them to hold him here while the squad moved on. In a matter of twenty minutes or so, five more enemy were in their hands. The squad returned along a different route to the rendezvous point with the truck, loaded their captives in, stacked like cordwood in the middle of the truck and sat on the benches along the sides. They were back to base by three o'clock in the morning. Not a shot had been fired, no grenades thrown, nobody killed or injured. Several maps and a code book had been taken along with the prisoners. Colonel Darby was very pleased by the operation and thanked Bruce for joining along.

"Of course, you know you can't write a single word about this, Bruce." Darby looked at him with a very serious expression. "Just kidding!" His face broke into a smile. "Hell, the Jerries are out doing the same thing; you probably passed one of their patrols along the way. I just want you to pass what you write through me, like before."

"Thanks, Colonel. I have to admit that even without guns blazing or bombs going off, I was as scared as I've ever been."

"Yep… most of the fear comes from the expectation… not the action. By the way, you recall today is December 7th… we've been at war for one year."

Returning to his quarters with the squad, Bruce lay on his bunk and contemplated the past year. Twelve months ago he'd been writing small articles and obituaries for an obscure New York paper. It amazed him that since the attack on Pearl Harbor he had traveled to Great Britain twice, crossed the United States more than once, been in the South Pacific and was now in North Africa. He was married to a wonderful girl he'd not known a year ago, seen many men die, been on a ship that sunk and flown on a bombing mission over France. Now he could add going on a night raid against the Germans and Italians in the deserts of Algeria. He closed his eyes and fell into a sleep, wondering how many other beds he'd had so far… or would have in the future.

PART TWO

Chapter 1
January 1945

"Five…. four…. three…. two…. one…. Happy New Year!"

Bruce kissed Susan and hugged her tight against himself, just like he'd wanted to a million times in the past two years. He was so glad to be home again in Iowa. It seemed a lifetime had passed since he had physically held her in his arms. An Alberta Clipper was blowing hard outside, temperatures well below freezing and snow piling up. There was snow where he'd been up until the week before as well. But the drifts around the village of Bastogne, in Luxembourg, had been tinged with blood, turning them into streaks of pink. Bruce was riding north with the tanks of Patton's Third Army on their drive to break through the German lines and relieve the paratroopers of the 101st Airborne Division. That's when the message reached him from his editor, G Gordon Bennett of the New York Daily News, telling him of the fire and arrangements for his travel back to Iowa. Bruce's friend, Jim Hartke, lost both of his parents when their farm house went up in flames. Jim was in the Eighth Air Force earlier in the war and had been wounded during a bombing mission that Bruce flew along on. It took five days for Bruce to return to New York and catch a flight halfway across the United States. He'd arrived mere hours after the funeral. After all the traveling he'd done in the first year of the war, Bruce had chosen to follow the 34th Division and the Rangers in their fighting from North Africa through Sicily and into Italy. When the invasion of

France took place in June of last year, he elected to cover the American advance through that country as well.

Jim and his wife, Frankie, were at the Des Moines airport to meet him, along with Susan. When Bruce offered his condolences to his friend on the loss of his parents, he was reminded of the lack of a strong positive relationship between father and son. He spoke of missing his mother but never mentioned his dad. Frankie had taken the leadership in making arrangements for the funeral while Jim organized the care of the farm animals left after the fire.

Frankie's brother Fred was now in the Second Rangers; he was a big part of the reason Bruce had been in Europe. The Rangers were fighting in the Hurtgen Forest when the Germans launched their attack through the Ardennes known as the Battle of the Bulge. About the time Fred was wounded and evacuated to England, Bruce was offered the chance to ride along with Patton's tankers toward Bastogne.

"Darling, you're squeezing me a bit too tightly, not that I'm complaining." Susan looked at him with loving eyes and continued, "You know... you've got that faraway look again. Thinking of Fred, dear?"

"Yeah... it's just not fair, somehow... he's the one that should be here for his sister. Being wounded and stuck in the hospital, while his family grieves."

"Bruce, we're all grieving... not just for the Hartkes, darling. The whole country is sad and tired... we've all suffered loss. Sure, we're beating the Nazi's, finally... you need to stick around awhile and listen to what's happening here, too. Not all the news is from the front. Now, let's get back to the New Year celebration... I'm one that's hoping and praying it's the best year we've seen. It's starting out well, with you finally home."

"You're right, Susan... all the traveling... seeing so much death and destruction has gotten to me. I think I'll tell Bennett I'm here for a month... I wonder how he'll take that... you know, there's a story right here I can write. Jim was wounded, now he's back in

Ames finishing college, married… working, too. Yeah… Jim's just what this war's coming to. When we win… and we will… there's going to be a million Jim Hartkes around the states. Guys that have seen horrible things, suffered… now they're expected to just get back to normal?"

"It's not only the men, Bruce. Several million women have been pushed and pulled out of their formerly normal lives, too. When you met me, remember how surprised you were at the job I had? Now all the men come home and what… Rosie the Riveter is expected to just give up her job and start having babies? I'm pretty sure that won't be an easy pill to swallow for everyone, though I won't mind. You could spend a long time writing about the changes you've missed out on right here at home while you've been gone. I think you're the best at what you do, not just because we're married… and you've seen too much of the horrible side of this war. Maybe you should look to what changes are coming when the fighting stops."

With this new found idea, Bruce started right in the next morning. He telephoned the Daily News and spoke with his editor, outlining his desire. It took a bit of convincing, but Bennett eventually saw the benefit of a look toward the future and the end of the war. He gave his blessing and told Bruce to try to hold his stay to a month, if possible. There was still a lot of war to cover and he needed his "star reporter" out there. Bruce then called Saul Price in San Diego and Phil Steiner and explained to them his idea. Both immediately grasped the significance of such articles and even suggested good ideas for Bruce to consider, such as the growing population of Jews coming from Europe being settled in a part of Minneapolis, just a few hours north of Ames. They reminded Bruce that his own father was also involved in helping the Jewish refugees.

Bruce telephoned Jim and Frankie; both would be home that evening. He made a date with them, including Susan, to talk about his idea and begin the interviews. His mind was afire with the thought of another article on his closest friend from the basketball team. Bruce also placed a call to Captain Dixon Mason, Director of Navy Public Relations in San Diego, asking him to get any update on Bobbie Milliken and Stan Larson in the Pacific.

Driving to Jim's home brought Bruce and Susan past the Hartke farm. The charred remains of their house stood black and sooty against the new fallen snow. Only a small part of the rickety porch remained erect, the rest having fallen in a great heap.

"Figures that the weakest part of the whole place would be the only part left." Bruce mused as they drove by. "I remember almost falling through the boards on that porch many times over the years... and Mrs. Hartke standing in the doorway with warm cookies and cool lemonade for us kids, too."

Susan was in a melancholy mood herself; the funeral brought back memories of her own father and brother. It sometimes felt an eternity since they had been killed by the Japanese near Guadalcanal and she had heard of both deaths on the same day. When she arrived in Ames shortly afterward, Susan took a job at the bank owned by Bruce's father. She enjoyed the time spent with them, becoming part of a new family, but knew she needed a place for Bruce and herself. Now she and Bruce were living in their own home in town, near his parents but not in the same house. Susan used some of her father's life insurance money to buy a nice three-bedroom place that she was still busy turning into their home. The third bedroom would be Bruce's office until it, too, was needed for an expanding family; it was her hope, and his, that this month would leave behind much more than a closet full of his civilian clothes.

Jim answered the door and welcomed them in. Their house was a new one built on land near the hog operation Jim helped oversee while not in class. Frankie's dad insisted that they live in their own place and had it placed on the opposite side of the barns, about a half mile away. He would joke with people that it was so they could "enjoy fresh air no matter which way the wind was blowing".

Frankie was wearing a blouse that hinted at a secret they'd not told anyone about. Susan spotted the little bulge immediately and squealed with delight as she ran and hugged her best friend.

"Just over three months along and beginning to show a little", Frankie said to Bruce.

"That's great!! Ours will have a playmate when he... or she arrives..." He looked at Susan who was blushing. "But we're only still trying... no news yet. I mean I just got home and..." Susan hit him on the arm and told him to be quiet. Jim grinned at Bruce, who was digging a hole deeper with every word.

The four sat and their conversation began, after the usual coffee and cakes. Before he was interviewed, Jim wanted to hear Bruce's update on his own adventures. It had been quite a while since the two had been together. What Jim had learned of his friend had been through Susan's visits or Bruce's articles.

"Two years is a lot to cover but I'll give it a whirl. I was in Algeria, North Africa with Fred, then flew another bombing mission as an observer... this time over Italy. That was in November of 1942. Spent more time covering the battles that drove the Germans out of Africa... stayed with the Rangers through Sicily and into Italy in 1943. When Fred was transferred to the new Second Rangers, he went back to England for training... good thing, too. His old unit was pretty well wiped out in the Anzio breakout... Cisterna was the name of the place... that was a year ago this month. Anyway, Fred was safe at that point... training for the Normandy Landings in France. I was still in Italy, covering the Red Bulls... the 34th Infantry, and was in Rome the day it fell... that was June 5th, the day before Normandy itself. I got to France and met up with the Rangers again in the drive across France last summer... was covering the fighting near Aachen in Germany when Patton asked me to come for a 'joy ride', as he put it."

"Wait... wait a minute... you're saying General George Patton asked YOU to come along to Bastogne?" Jim was amazed as he said it.

"Yep... that's one piece of paper I've managed to hold on to." Bruce took a folded scrap of paper out of his wallet and showed it to his friend. The scribbling was not easy to read but Jim was able to make it out.

"So I was with Captain Abrams' unit when I got the message from Bennett to come home... I heard later it was the next day that the tankers hooked up with the paratroopers. And now... here I am."

"You make it seem so simple... so easy. I've gotten dozens of letters from Fred these two years. Time didn't seem to go quite so fast for him."

"I know Frankie... I'm just brushing over the whole time. There were days that flew past and ones that seemed to last an eternity. My only regret is that I've not been able to get back out to the Pacific to check up on Bobbie and Stan. A whole lot of fighting has been going on over there, too. I'm crashing the ladies' tea time tomorrow morning at mom's to find out what they know of those two."

"I'm sure they'll know more than what I can tell you, Bruce. Let's see... Bobbie is a Sergeant now and last I heard was on an island... Puvuvu, something like that... for training. Stan left the gunnery school in San Diego and was hoping to get on a new ship, I think. It's been about a year now. I know his mom doesn't get many letters from him, but you know how he is. Bobbie has only written a couple of letters since he was in a battle on Pelielu... I've read a bit about that place. It was really bad."

Jim broke in. "Those damned Jap bastards... they're not fighters, they're butchers. What they did to guys..." He looked at Frankie who frowned. "Well, anyway, nothing we do to them is enough in my book."

"At least we're gaining the upper hand in this thing." Susan added. "It seems that the Russians, the British and our own guys are pushing forward... slowly and with great loss, but we are winning..."

"Yeah, and then Hitler gave us the Bulge." broke in Jim.

"But Jim... the word there is that he's shot his bolt. There's not much left for him to fight us with now. It was his last throw of the dice and he crapped out. The Russians are pounding the German Army to pieces while we bomb their cities off the map. And what our Air Force is just starting to do to Japan... well, their cities are made of paper for crying out loud. They'll burn the whole chain of islands. Japan is a hollow shell... but they still won't surrender. There's just no understanding them. Anyway, that's not what I'd like to talk about... there's enough news on the war in all the papers already. I'd like to ask you both some questions about life here now and how your college classes are going. You're almost finished, right?"

"Sure am; this is my last set of classes and I'll graduate in June. It's not been easy, I'll tell you. Between the studying, working on the farm here, the fire and now getting ready for the baby... let's say it'll be good when I'm done."

"He really is enjoying the school, at least that's what he tells me", added Frankie. "Jim's helping to tutor other guys that are back from Europe, too. There must be ten or twelve that get together a couple of times a week to study and help each other. It would be nice if the school itself pitched in but I guess that's asking too much. Jim is getting good grades and even though he's only a year or two older than most of the others in his classes, several of his professors ask him to lead groups and things."

"Well, I'm sure the time you spent in the Air Corps taught you things the college can't. Just the experience of being overseas would change your perspective. So, Jim... what's the biggest challenge for you right now? I'd like to write about what others will face when they come home... the war will be over soon, we all feel that. What can be done, in your opinion, to make it easier to shift back into civilian life?"

The next couple of hours were filled with questions and answers, from both Jim and Frankie, on the change coming for those in the service. The insights they provided gave Bruce a good start on the next article he'd write. Before he and Susan left their friends, he arranged to meet with Jim's study group. He also made notes to speak with administrators at the college about their needs for the future when the soldiers, sailors, airmen and Marines would be coming home.

The next morning found Bruce and Susan at his parent's home as part of the weekly tea. It started with heavy hearts over the missing Clara Hartke. Her cup was placed upside down on its saucer and all promised it would remain on the table as long as they met together. The ladies were all excited that the two had joined them and were eager to share news about their sons.

Edith Milliken spoke about Bobbie's promotion to Sergeant and his horrible time on Pelielu; now he was back on Puvuvu, resting and getting ready for more action. She said his letters were always bright and cheerful but she read about the fighting in the newspapers and realized just how bad his reality was. Her biggest fear was how he would be when he came home. Edith volunteered one day each week at a small hospital up in Webster City, meeting and talking with wounded soldiers. She had come to know how the fighting affected the minds of these young men.

Olive Larson spoke next. Her son, Stan, was still in the Navy. He and Bruce had survived the awful night battle near Guadalcanal Island when the small destroyer they were on fought against the huge Japanese battleship. Bruce was fascinated to learn that Stan was now on the new *USS LAFFEY*, another destroyer that was named for the one that had sunk. He was sure Stan had somehow arranged to get transferred to her. Olive said it was built and launched a year ago on the east coast and had been part of the invasion at Normandy in France. The latest letter she'd gotten from her son said the ship was now heading for the Pacific through the Panama Canal. He hoped they would spend some time in Hawaii but was pretty sure they'd be heading to the western Pacific, maybe the Philippine Islands. Stan was now a Chief Gunner's Mate and in charge of several anti-aircraft guns on the ship. Susan saw Bruce's face light up when Olive was talking; she knew the night with Stan in and after their battle had been his most challenging time of the war. She wondered just how long she'd be able to keep him home before he'd be heading back to the Pacific War.

Last to share was Mabel Howard, Fred's mother. She had received a letter from him just the day before. He was back in England, recovering from his wound, safely away from the fighting near Germany. Still in the Rangers, Fred's job now would be as an instructor, teaching the new men what to expect when they reached the front. Fred had also been promoted to Staff Sergeant and used his experience in North Africa, Sicily, Italy and France to offer sound advice to others. He had been wounded three separate times and was highly decorated. Mabel said it was hoped that he would receive a commission as an officer before the war ended and that Fred planned on staying in the Army.

The time with the ladies went by far too quickly; they had so many questions about Bruce's own time spent with each of their sons. He was sure to focus on the positives that happened during those times; there was no need to frighten them with the whole truth of combat. He spoke of the great care he and Stan had received after being rescued from the ocean near Guadalcanal. Bobbie's tight friendship to his platoon mates was what Bruce spoke of most about the Marines; he hardly mentioned the difficulty of wresting the island from the Japs at all.

His personal feelings of concern, which he didn't share with the ladies, were for Bobbie and Stan out in the Pacific. The war in Europe was definitely winding down and Fred was in an enviable position far from the front lines. The Navy and Marines still had more than a thousand miles to go before they reached the main islands of Japan and the enemy's determination to increase the cost of each of those miles to the United States was stiffening. Bruce was intent on getting back out there to find his friends again and to be a witness to the end of that theater of fighting. He would have to wait a bit; he had several people to interview yet about the college and he wasn't in a particular hurry to be away from Susan either.

It was a week later when Susan interrupted his writing to say that Bennett, from the Daily News, was on the phone. Bruce groaned as he got up from the desk and walked into the living room to take the call.

"Bruce! Great to hear your voice… those first two articles are outstanding! They'll be on the street the next two issues. No doubt in my mind that people will be glad to start looking at what things can be like when this crap finally winds up. Did you hear that Boeing has stopped making B-17's? Yeah, they're already starting one production line on a new passenger plane for after the war. You'd think, from listening to business owners here in New York that the whole thing is nearly done. The fight against the Japs is so far away… now that Europe is almost ours. There's even talk now that the Russians are more of an enemy than the damn Germans! Can you believe that?"

"I've heard comments along those lines here in Iowa as well. We might still be fighting the Japanese a year from now the way they're defending each place we hit. I'm sure Boeing won't stop producing the B-29's soon. Those monsters are hardly even in the fight yet; though the first few missions have flattened large chunks of Jap cities. They just might be the ticket to victory, though we still need the boots on the ground over there."

"You're right, as usual… say, are you getting any closer to being able to head out to the west coast and on to the Pacific yourself? This idea of writing on the home front, especially of the boys coming home, is great… but I'm thinking we need more stuff on the Navy and Marines to get people behind the fight again."

"I really want to thank you for arranging for my return. I'm not sure Jim needed my support as much as I needed my time here with Susan after being away so long. You know, boss… I've gotten kind of used to home cooking and a warm bed each night."

Bennett's response to that could be heard by Susan, without the help of the telephone. She knew, even as she frowned toward him, that hers was a losing fight. Bruce had to go away again... and far too soon to suit her. Then she thought of all the other wives and sweethearts, missing their men. She startled Bruce by taking the telephone receiver from him.

"Mr Bennett, this is Susan... Bruce will be finished here and ready to get on a plane to San Diego in four days... no sooner but no later either. I'll see to it. Have the tickets ready... yes, I said tickets... plural. I'll be flying with him to San Diego. Yes, it would be nice for the paper to pay my way, too. No, I'm not saying you HAVE to, but it would be nice. Here's Bruce..."

"OK, tiger, call her off. Two tickets... I'll have my secretary phone with the details tomorrow morning. Tell Susan she can replace me when I retire."

"Actually, boss... I'm thinking she'll start her own paper when the war's over with me as lead writer."

"You wouldn't... you couldn't... well, you could, but I know you wouldn't."

"Nope, just kidding. I'll send the final columns from San Diego. I've still got more interviewing and now a deadline to boot. Talk to you again, soon."

As he hung up the phone, Bruce turned to Susan with a look of amazement on his face.

"If I didn't know better, I'd say Saul's wife Marge was just on the phone, talking to a certain newspaper editor in New York."

"Well, we do phone each other nearly every week, dear. Marge has been a tremendous help and encouragement to me."

The next morning's Des Moines newspaper headlined the American landings on Luzon, one of the many islands in the Philippines. Though General MacArthur's army was already fighting on Leyte and Mindoro, the island of Luzon was critical to capture the country; the capital, Manila, as well as military bases like Clark Field, Bataan and Subic Bay were all there. The paper also mentioned an increase in Japanese Kamikaze attacks. Months ago, at Leyte, the thought was the planes were not deliberately aimed at our ships by suicidal pilots. Now we knew better; young Japanese airmen, barely trained in flying, were willing to crash into our ships for their Emperor. One man, in one plane, could do massive damage when the attack did not include a desire to escape and fly again.

Susan surprised Bruce with a marvelous dinner that evening, including a real steak! She had scrimped on ration stamps and, with the help of a local farmer who happened to have a steer die recently, put together a feast they shared with his parents. Earl and Louise arrived at six to cocktails with fruit and a cheese plate. Bruce quietly spoke of their pending flight to the west coast.

Susan would be staying with Saul and Marge Price at their home on Pt Loma while she took care of the last details of her father's estate. She always thought life could be difficult but had no idea how hard death could be on those left behind. It had taken more than two years to settle accounts and satisfy all the loose ends of his life; though part of it was also because of her brother's death, too. The end result was a large amount of money from the sales of several properties he had owned, along with insurance policies. She and Bruce would not really even have to work if he didn't actually enjoy what he did. Susan was hoping the Prices could offer her advice and introduce her to someone who might help with investment of their monies. To be sure, Bruce was also making good money from the Daily News. His salary alone would provide for the children they hoped to have one day.

Earl and Louise were more than pleased to watch the Ames house while their son and daughter-in-law were away. Bruce slipped his father a list of projects that he and Susan had talked about having done in the future on the place. Earl slyly looked it over and nodded to his son. He was aware that Bruce had been depositing sufficient funds into an account at the bank to cover the work. He would make sure the work was done and done well. Bobbie

Milliken's father would be the perfect choice as a general contractor to oversee the work.

After dinner the four sat and talked in the living room; Susan learned many stories of Bruce's youth she'd not heard before. She also shared some of her own, most about fun at the beach in Del Mar; the same beach she and Bruce had grown so fond of. She spoke of her dream to buy a small house in Del Mar for their own family to enjoy in the future. Because of the conversation, coupled with the wine, Susan and Bruce were both feeling warm and cozy inside when his parents bid them goodnight.

"Forget the dishes, darling... I think it might be much more fun to spend the time in a different room", she whispered in his ear as she led him down the hallway. He blinked, smiled and picked her up, carrying her the rest of the way... both laughing.

Early dawn brightened up their bedroom, finding the two with arms and legs intertwined in a sort of human knot. Slowly untangling themselves, they spent the next hour continuing what had begun the night before. Afterward, Bruce went into the kitchen to make coffee. He returned some time later, having cleaned up the dishes from dinner. Susan was sleeping lightly as he set the coffee next to her on a nightstand. He bent and kissed her ear as she woke and stretched. He had never felt more in love than at that moment; realizing this memory would be exactly what he'd remember when he was in the fighting again.

They were finishing breakfast when the phone rang with a long distance call from New York. Bruce jotted down the travel information that Bennett's secretary gave him. The flight, in three days, would leave from Des Moines and connect in Denver, Prescott, Las Vegas and arrive in San Diego the next day. A hotel reservation in Las Vegas was included and meal vouchers would be at the airline office in Des Moines. Bruce's first thought was how nice it would be when Boeing gets longer range aircraft into the hands of the airlines. The B-17 he flew out of England could have carried a load of passengers non-stop to San Diego from Des

Moines. He thanked her for calling and told Susan about the arrangements; she was excited about a layover in Las Vegas.

"We might get a chance to visit one of the casinos while we're there; at least dinner in a nice restaurant. What fun!"

Bruce began to think about the trip differently. He remembered working almost the entire train ride the first time he traveled west. Now he'd have Susan to talk to; he'd still have to finish two articles when they arrived in San Diego, but the thought of writing on Saul's veranda overlooking the ocean on Point Loma was a grand one. He would have to pick up new War Correspondent uniforms as well; his old Navy ones went down on the destroyer and he disposed of what he'd been wearing in Europe. He honestly didn't want Susan to even see what he'd worked in over there.

The remaining time he had in Ames was spent making contact with a few final people for his articles, saying his goodbyes to friends and making sure to spend as much time as possible with his folks. They would drive the two to the Des Moines airfield of course and say farewell there. The hours sped by with the anticipation of travel and, for Bruce, of returning to his friends in the Pacific. At the airport there were tears when it came time to say goodbye. After the last hug between Earl and Susan, he smiled and reminded her to remember her galoshes when she returned. It lightened the mood at the perfect time as the loudspeaker announced the boarding call for their flight.

#

The plane bounced twice, not too hard, and rolled smoothly to a stop near the terminal. A sign proclaiming, "Welcome to Las Vegas", covered a good portion of one hangar nearby. Looking out the window, Susan shielded her eyes from the overly bright sunshine reflecting off the light colored desert sand and the concrete of the runway. When the flight attendant opened the door, a blast of hot air cruised through the plane, hurrying the departure of the passengers. The runway was so hot Bruce could feel the heat through the bottoms of his shoes. They walked into the terminal and were greeted by a cool, moist atmosphere. He'd never been in an air-conditioned building this big before and was impressed with the effect. Susan's skirt was wrinkled and her hair was in need of some attention. She pointed to a women's lounge and headed off in that direction. Bruce asked an employee for the information desk and was led to it by the airline's version of a red cap.

"Mr Hollins? Yes, sir... I have it right here. Arriving from... Des Moines? Are you the New York reporter? Flying from Des Moines? Pardon my surprise, sir."

"That's okay... we all have to start somewhere. That's where I grew up. Can you get us transportation to the El Rancho Vegas? That's where we're spending the night..."

"Absolutely, sir. I don't suppose you know John Wayne, do you? He's from Iowa, too... at least that's what I've heard."

"He is.... Winterset. A smaller town south of where I come from. No, we've never met. I guess the dozen or so of us from Iowa don't get together much."

"What?!?... Oh, I get it... good one Mr Hollins. I'll get your cab right away, sir."

Susan was coming out of the lounge, looking combed with fresh makeup and the wrinkles smoothed down. She sidled up to Bruce and said, in a sultry voice... "Hey, good lookin', you got the time?"

"Yep, it's quarter to five." Bruce gave her a wink as he looked at his watch. They both giggled as they walked to the taxi area. A chauffeur, dressed in a suit and tie in this heat, approached and asked if he was Mr Bruce Hollins.

"That's me. How can I help you?"

"Funny, sir. I'm your driver... the El Rancho sent me over to collect you, Mrs Hollins and your luggage, sir. Follow me."

Susan's jaw dropped. She looked at Bruce and started laughing at the same expression on his face. Neither expected anything remotely like this in an airport so far from home. The driver opened the door of a large limousine; Susan immediately noticed the miniature stocked bar in the front of their seating compartment.

"When we come back, you tell Bennett to have one of these take us from San Diego to Ames, dear.", Bruce said as he looked over the bottles. "Oh, for crying out loud, there's even a small refrigerator full of beer and wine here!"

"Darling, I can see you've got a lot to learn about being a celebrity. Oh, it's a rough life, but someone's got to live it." Susan poked her nose up high and did her best "Hollywood Actress" look. They were still laughing when the driver returned, stowed the luggage and drove away.

When the car pulled up to the El Rancho, Bruce noticed the manager and lots of other people gathered at the entrance. "I wonder who they're expecting? Maybe we'll get to see John Wayne after all", Bruce joked.

The chauffeur opened their door, and the hotel manager took Susan's hand to help her out of the vehicle. She smiled and said "Thank you" to which he grinned, revealing perfect teeth to match his dark tan.

"Welcome, Mr and Mrs Hollins, to the El Rancho Vegas. On behalf of the entire staff, we hope your stay here is a most pleasant one."

"I haven't even been inside and it's better than anything I've had before", was all Bruce could muster as a response.

"We've taken the liberty of reserving a table for you and Mrs Hollins for dinner and the show this evening, sir. Seating is at eight o'clock; if you need anything, please ask any one of us."

"Is it formal? I didn't travel with a tuxedo and..."

"Oh no, sir... our guests seldom wear formal attire for just dinner and the show. Any suit and tie will suffice, I assure you. And your wife would be stunning in practically anything, if I might be so bold..."

"You might, you might indeed", quipped Susan with another smile. "Can we be shown our room now; I'd like to freshen up… I feel a fright with all the travel."

"Naturally, ma'am. Please follow me." The manager snapped his finger and the luggage was picked up by a young man who immediately followed behind the group.

Bruce turned to give the chauffeur a tip, which was politely turned down with a smile. "No need, Mr Hollins. That's all been taken care of quite adequately. Thank you just the same… and I really, really like what you write." The man had taken off his hat to say this with all sincerity. Bruce was humbled as he smiled and nodded to the driver.

The room was actually three; a bedroom, a living room and a huge bathroom with shower and a large tub. All three rooms had separate balconies looking out over the large swimming pool area. The entire suite was, like the rest of the place, in a western theme.

Bruce looked at Susan when they were alone and said, "Now I know we're going to meet John Wayne tonight!"

A short nap together and time to shower and dress led them to the dinner hour. Joining the line of people waiting to enter the dining room, called "The Opera", Bruce and Susan were competing to see just what celebrities were there. Suddenly, Susan saw a familiar face from the movie screen stroll across the lobby up to Bruce, wrap him in an embrace and kiss him!

"Bruce… Bruce Hollins. They said you were here. I just love the things you write and couldn't wait to meet you personally." With that, she was gone, disappearing into the dining room.

"If John Wayne greets you like that, I'm leaving", Susan said.

"Say, just who was that, anyway?"

"On no, mister. Even if I remember her name, I'm not telling you."

Just then a Rancho employee approached and explained that there was no need for them to stand in line. Their table was ready and he would show them to it. That was when several of the others in line began to applaud, the accolade quickly taken up by all of the people in the lobby.

"Welcome back to the United States... husband of mine." Susan said with a smile.

#

The dinner and show were marvelous, even though they hadn't met John Wayne. Their departure was quieter, if only because of the early take off for San Diego. When they arrived at the airfield next to the huge Consolidated plant, Susan let go a sigh at the familiarity of the view.

"Over two years... the time has slipped by... wonderful, sad thoughts and memories of my home town. Bruce, I want you to know that I may decide to stay awhile after you leave for the Pacific; at least through to warmer weather."

"That's just fine, dear. Mom and Dad won't mind, I'm sure. Saul and Marge, especially Marge, will love hosting you, too."

"I'm glad you mentioned the Prices... can we make a stop on our way to The Seven Seas? I know you want to get measured up for the new uniforms right away."

"Sure", Bruce replied with a smile. "I could use a good El Indio lunch myself about now."

They managed to get through the airport without attracting attention, easier since no one was there to pick them up. A short taxi ride, with a stop at the café, and they were at Saul's store. Bruce marveled at how the place seemed to hold even more of an assortment of items for anyone in the military. He asked an employee if Saul was in; a few moments later and the two friends were face to face.

"Bruce... Susan, welcome. We knew you'd stop by when you got in. Say, is that my favorite lunch I smell... mmmm... it'll have to wait until we get you measured up, I suppose."

"Not a chance... we brought our own along, too." Susan held up a second paper bag, wonderful spicy aromas wafting around them.

They passed a half hour talking between bites of enchiladas with rice and beans. Saul quickly measured Bruce from head to toe, frowning making little sounds every so often. He'd give Susan a wink and saved his scowl for Bruce.

"Young man, have you been watching what you eat? If you're not careful, these inches will add up to another size bigger."

"What... I just got back from Europe a few weeks ago... I can't have gained that much so quickly!"

Susan was the first to laugh, followed by Saul. Finally, Bruce realized he'd been taken by the two. Saul told him he'd actually stayed the same size since his first measurement so long ago. The uniforms would be ready in a day or so; they would only require a minimum of tailoring. Saul phoned Marge to say that the three of them would be home shortly. They left the store and walked through the nearly empty parking lot to his car; the familiar pale yellow convertible. As he drove, Saul pointed out changes to the city along the way; the war had caused quite a building boom for San Diego. Other changes had come as well.

"You know, gas rationing really has not been a problem for us Bruce. It's getting easier to fill up lately. The difficulty is getting new tires; I've been looking for a set for some time now. I shouldn't complain... Marge and I don't drive that far anyway, I'm sure they'll last a bit longer. Here we are."

The house hadn't changed at all; walking through to the back veranda brought back a flood of memories for Bruce and Susan. The view of the waves breaking on the beach far below them reminded the two of their first married night together. They smiled; holding hands they turned to see Marge bringing out a tray with glasses and Saul holding a bottle of chilled champagne.

#

"Captain Mason will see you now, Mr Hollins." The Yeoman was quite polite as she opened the door for him, and was the nicest looking sailor Bruce had ever met. He'd seen Navy and Army nurses, some WACs and a few WAAFs; but here the halls seemed filled with trim, tanned girls in Navy blue.

"Bruce! Great to see you again. Yeoman Rand, would you please get us some coffee?"

"Aye, aye, sir." She smiled at Bruce as she left through the door.

"So, you're ready to head to the deep blue again? I've been trying since the last time we saw each other. It seems I'm destined to remain a "PR" guy instead of a battleship captain. You know the truth; since I'm also in charge of Naval Intelligence here in San Diego, I'm considered indispensable and I really don't think anyone would relish my risk of being captured if I was commanding something on the front lines."

Dixon came around his desk and shook Bruce's hand. He handed him a manila folder. "Sergeant Milliken is finishing up training for the First Marine Division's next assignment; they'll be loaded on transports soon. I don't have to tell you that all this is classified, right? Didn't think so... anyway, with MacArthur's soldiers involved in the Philippines, Nimitz wants to use the Marines to take an island halfway to Tokyo from our air bases in the Marianas... you remember last summer we took back Guam with Saipan and Tinian? We've turned them into giant airfields. Well, the Air Force has been losing B-29s that can't make it back from missions when they're damaged or low on fuel. So we're heading to a place called Iwo Jima... we'll make it a sort of emergency landing area for the bombers. Once that's done, plans call for an invasion of Okinawa; the first of Japan's homeland islands we'll take. That's where the First Division will be heading."

"Last time I was here, we could barely hold Guadalcanal and the Japanese Navy still outnumbered us on the water. I read about the Navy's growth while I was in Italy and France, but..."

"Bruce, you wouldn't believe how American manufacturing has worked a miracle, a real miracle. You remember when, during Guadalcanal, we only had the *ENTERPRISE* as an active aircraft carrier... the rest were either sunk or damaged and being repaired? I mean, we only had three total in the Pacific. Well, now we have two dozen fleet carriers... the big ones! The Japs have managed to build one while we've put out over twenty! It staggers the imagination how many ships we're building. We're sending more fighting men into action each month than they have in their army, for crying out loud."

"What I hear you saying is that, before long, we'll so outnumber the Japs that they'll have to quit?"

"Quit... I wish. Their view of the Emperor as a god makes it impossible for them to just quit. He'd have to order a surrender and I don't think the military leaders will let him... especially their army. The Japanese Navy is a paper force at best; they have practically no fuel for their battleships or aircraft. We're chewing them up out there, but now with the kamikaze... you now that word means "divine wind" in Japanese? Well, you get the picture. No, they won't give up until we kill their last soldier somewhere in Tokyo. One of the changes being incorporated right now is the protection of all those new aircraft carriers and the troop transports... the suicide attacks on our ships have a terrible potential. Our destroyers are taking the lead in providing anti-aircraft cover for the big ships. Miles away they're using radar to identify enemy aircraft approaching and shooting down as many as they can. That makes them the first line of defense and the toll is horrible.

Having said that, your other friend Chief Stan Larson is in charge of several of those AA guns on the *USS LAFFEY*; kind of ironic he was assigned to the new destroyer by that name. I'd love to claim credit for helping with that assignment, but it all happened just by chance. The *LAFFEY* arrived in the Philippines the end of November of 1944, a few months ago. It's been working as part of amphibious operations in various landings, the latest at Luzon. Now that I know you've arrived back here; I'll start checking to see about arranging transportation for you out to the western Pacific; probably Guam. That would be closest to hooking up with the transport with Sergeant Milliken is in and I'll find out if the *LAFFEY* might be part of the Okinawa operation. It'll probably take a week or two to get it all worked out; your first flight will be Pearl Harbor from here."

"Dix, that would be absolutely perfect... as always, your help is top notch. I can never thank you enough."

"Bruce, the writing you do has probably resulted in more enlistments for the Navy and Marines that any advertising we could ever achieve. That alone would be enough... but what you're doing is important for the whole nation. Oh, one other thing... you ever meet Ernie Pyle, another writer very much like yourself? He's been in Africa, Italy and France..."

"Sure, I've met him a few times. We were covering different units, but some of the same fighting. I remember he served a short time in the Navy during the First War."

"Right you are... much older than you; more like your father's age. Anyway, he's out in the Pacific, too. You might run into him; it's uncanny how much you write alike. Ernie's not as popular with the Navy as you are, though. He's seems to prefer the foxhole guys of the Army in Europe."

"Well, I certainly developed great respect for them as well the past two years. But there's still something extra special about sailors and Marines."

Chapter 2
February 1945

All of the preparations had been completed for Bruce's return to the Pacific Theater. His latest articles looking to the future of men returning to their homes when the fighting was over, were a topic of conversation from coast to coast. A new GI Bill, begun the previous summer, was authorizing millions of dollars for tuition at colleges for the returnees. Susan and Bruce were now able to get away for a final few days before he'd be on a plane to Pearl Harbor. They chose to spend their time together at the beach house in Del Mar where they had gotten to know one another early on.

They walked hand in hand the few blocks from the train station, each with a suitcase. They had managed to escape being recognized on the ride up from San Diego and enjoyed the quiet of another afternoon, this one was unseasonably warm, near the beach. As they turned the final corner and saw the familiar cottage, Susan could no longer contain her own excitement.

"Darling, remember when you picked me up and carried me over the threshold of our home in Ames? Do you think you have the strength to do that again now?"

"What? I don't understand... you want me to carry you in?"

"Well, I know it's not exactly tradition... except for newlyweds. I just thought that since we own this place now..."

"You bought this place? Is that what's been going on with you meeting your father's friend and all? I thought he was helping with the last hurdles on Sam's and your dad's places."

"He has… and he's been an absolute dear. Then last week he asked if we might like to buy this… he's being assigned to the East Coast and plans to retire from the Navy there when the war ends. He gave us a very good deal; Saul said it would be foolish to pass it up."

Bruce put his suitcase on the front walk, took hers and set it down as well. He let out a quiet grunt as he scooped her up in his arms, which resulted in a punch from Susan. Laughing, the two entered their new beach home, with the beautiful walkway out to the sand and the setting sun.

Inside there were fresh flowers in the living room, mostly orange and blue bird of paradise blooms and the wonderful scent of gardenia blossoms floating on water in a bowl. Sam found a bottle of champagne in the refrigerator and a note from Marge Price. Susan cried with joy at the love of their friends. They hurried to get changed into more comfortable beach wear and then raced down the path to the water, only pausing to take in one quick look from the highest point above the sand. Then it became a dash to see who would reach the surf curling onto the beach. The two spent the next hours enjoying the sun, sand and waves. Neither paid attention to the colder, winter water.

After showering off the sandy, salty aftermath of their fun the two were dancing in the living room to music from the radio. They held each other tightly, Susan's head against his chest. Both were remembering their first time here, dancing like this; each wrestling with desire for the other. Now there was no hesitation, no inhibitions. They danced down the short hallway that lead to their bedroom and made love as the setting sun filled the room with gold and rose light.

The following days were filled with time together. They prepared meals side by side, took long walks through the beach community; mostly they enjoyed the beach at their own new cottage. Too quickly the time came for them to pack their bags and return to San Diego. Bruce would be leaving in the morning; Susan would stay with Saul and Marge before moving into the Del Mar house by herself. They bought a newspaper to read on the hour ride back to the city; it was the first they'd seen in nearly a week. The feature article was about the fighting for the capital city of Manilla in the Philippines which the American army had first entered two days earlier. Bruce read of evidence that the Japanese had killed many civilians and were using groups of them as shields in front of their lines in an effort to slow down our attacks. His mind raced back to the scenes he'd witnessed on Guadalcanal of Marines that had been viciously dismembered when the Japanese captured them. He realized the nature of the fighting he was heading to had only grown more fierce in the time of his absence.

#

"Goodbye, darling. I'll try calling you when I arrive in Pearl Harbor. I'm sure it'll be easier than the last time I was there."

"Bruce... I love you. I wish you didn't have to go; I hate being apart. I know what you're doing is important... to me and to everyone. I'll be waiting for your call."

He chuckled as he reminded her it would be very early in the morning when he landed. Then he saw 'the look' forming; he held her and promised he'd use the first phone he found, whatever the time was. She smiled and they shared a long, lingering kiss goodbye. Bruce turned and waved several times as he walked to the large seaplane, his mind already returning to the first time he'd seen a Clipper in the water at Liverpool. That flight had been a couple of weeks short of three years ago. He marveled at all the places he'd been and things he'd seen in that time. The entire world had changed.

"Sir, Mr Hollins? I'll show you to your seat if you'll follow me."

The seaman, in his familiar dungarees, smiled in recognition of Bruce's name. Bruce noticed how young the sailor looked and suddenly felt much older himself. He settled down in the comfortable seat and watched other passengers board. He was introduced to several Navy officers and a Marine Colonel. A group of four older men in civilian attire entered; one smiled at Bruce and extended his hand in greeting.

"Bruce Hollins, the steward said this was you. It's a pleasure to meet you... my name is James Anderson; I work for the Justice Department. Looks like this will be an interesting trip... plenty of guys to visit with."

"Pleased to meet you James. I was thinking the very same thing..."

A minute later the engines increased their tempo and a slight shudder was felt in the aircraft. It slowly began to move through the water. Bruce looked out the window next to him and caught one last glimpse of Susan standing on the pier, waving goodbye. He waved back, unsure if she saw him, and choked back his own tears.

The hours of the flight passed quickly as Bruce spent time getting to know all of the others on the plane, including the flight crew. The Navy pilot, a Lieutenant, had been a Pan American employee before the war, like his friend Bill Young. Bruce thought of Major Young, now in the Army Air Corps, and wondered how he was doing. He'd met so many...

His conversation with James Anderson was a highlight. Anderson was part of a team that would be working with the Army and Navy, investigating war crimes that would result in trials after the fighting ended. At least that was the plan; the same thing was being started in Europe by other members of the Justice Department. The plan was to hold leaders, both military and civilian, personally responsible for the war. The idea staggered Bruce in its enormity. James told him this had never been done before; actually no one really knew if it could be done. He and the three others with him were flying on to Australia to meet with lawyers and investigators from England, France and other allied countries to try and put together a plan on how to accomplish it.

The plane touched down in the darkness; besides the uncomfortable feeling in his ears from the altitude change, the only indicator for Bruce was the initial thump and deceleration as the plane's bottom contacted the surface of the bay. Soon the plane had maneuvered up to the wharf and the passengers were allowed to exit. Bruce said goodbye to those he'd had a chance to meet, which was nearly everyone on board. Then he asked about the location of a phone to place a call back to San Diego. He was directed to the ever present Admin Building, which was open at all hours. His knowing smile brought one in return from the Clipper's crewman.

Susan was awake when the phone rang, it being just after midnight. The two spoke for a few short minutes, reassuring each other with their mutual love. Both sighed when they hung up; an event unrealized by either. They had agreed to talk again when Bruce found out his pending departure schedule for the front lines, far across several thousand miles of ocean. As he approached the Admin Office's front desk again, he noticed a headline on the early morning edition of the Honolulu paper; it reported news that the last pocket of German resistance west of the Rhine River had been eliminated by French troops. The war in Europe was definitely winding down, with nearly all the fighting now confined within the Nazi borders. He went on to read of the continued fighting in Manila and the repatriation of a camp of American and other Allied civilians near the center of the city. His first thought was of the opportunity for James Anderson to interview the newly released prisoners; the paper had mentioned they were to be evacuated to Australia soon.

Bruce was offered a ride to his hotel room by a couple of MP's that were heading to the King's Alley district downtown, an area known for late night carousing sailors and Marines. He accepted and thanked the two with a cup of coffee in the hotel dining area, now just opening for early breakfast. Bruce ate heartily,

274

checked into his room and sprawled on the bed, asleep before his second shoe hit the floor.

A knock at the door woke him several hours later, the sun high in the blue Hawaiian sky. A Navy courier stood with a packet in his hand, asking for identification. Bruce showed the petty officer his correspondent card and the man handed him the packet, thanking him for his skill at writing. Bruce phoned room service for coffee and a sandwich before he sat, opening the packet. His travel papers were all there, along with a briefing on the situation in the Mariana Islands, his initial destination. His food and coffee arrived at the same time the phone started to ring. Bruce quickly handed the delivery boy a dollar and hurried to the telephone.

"Hello... this is Bruce Hollins, operator. Yes, I'll wait... Saul!!! What a surprise... how are you? I just spoke with Susan when I got here. Oh, don't mention it... no, it's the least I can do for you... really, you've been great with Susan and me. Are they the right size? Phil said he'd arrange to have them mounted, too. Already on? That's great! OK, hey... say hi to Marge and tell her the Navy is still here at Pearl... right, I'll call in a few hours. I just got my travel papers... it'll take a bit to go through them all. Talk to you soon. Bye."

Bruce was glad the set of tires he'd bought through Phil Steiner had arrived and been mounted on Saul's car. Susan may have surprised him with the new beach house, but every so often he felt capable of pulling off one as well. Bruce was pleased he could help Saul, even with just new tires on a car. He spent the remainder of the afternoon reading Captain Mason's briefing and going over his travel itinerary. He'd be flying to Midway Island, scene of that great naval victory that turned the tide against the Japanese nearly three years ago. Then it was on to Guam; he'd have to arrange travel from there to either the *USS LAFFEY* to see Stan or wherever Bobbie was on his transport. Either way, Bruce felt sure the letter he'd be carrying from Mason would get him a ride.

275

After taking time to make sure all of his papers were in order, Bruce had the hotel operator place a call to the Navy's transportation office and verified his departure time on a plane to Guam. He was already listed as a passenger on a plane leaving the next day and was expected to arrive in Guam two days later. The officer helping him had been a classmate of Dixon Mason at the Naval Academy and was glad to be of service. He explained that transportation to a particular ship from Guam or other islands would be totally dependent on the ship's exact location and there was no way to determine that ahead of time from Pearl Harbor. He'd simply have to rely on the assistance of others at the forward location when he arrived. Bruce thanked him and asked the operator to place a long distance call to Susan in San Diego.

"Bruce, dear... Saul said you'd be calling so I've been sitting on the veranda enjoying the sunshine waiting. That was a wonderful thing you did for him, you know... he was completely taken aback when he saw the tow truck show up to get his car. The driver was quick to explain; Saul was wondering if his car was being confiscated or something... Phil did call Marge earlier and told her what was going on. She played along wonderfully... had both of us fooled completely!"

"I'm glad that worked out. I had called Phil several days ago, asking where his son, Aaron, is now. He's on Guam, building airfields! There's a great chance I'll meet up with him again in just a few days. Anyway, Phil asked if there was anything I needed and I thought about Saul and his mentioning new car tires... I asked Phil and, presto, it's taken care of. The guy is pretty amazing, huh?"

"I look forward to meeting him someday. Saul mentioned you got your papers? When do you leave Honolulu? You know, if there's time... Marge says she could have me there pronto."

"No time, honey. I leave tomorrow at first light and I'll be in Guam two days later. I probably won't have a chance to phone you until I get there. The plane will stop at Midway Island for fuel only, then we're across the ocean."

276

"Oh, pooh. I was hoping for a little excitement, too. Oh well, I'll have to settle with fixing up the Del Mar place while you're away. I'll call Mom and Dad and let them know I've heard from you; I know they'll be worried."

"Thanks… I'll be sure to write them a letter tonight as well and have it mailed before I board the plane. Thanks for thinking of the call; I'm not really good at staying in touch like I should. I'm sure Mom let you know about that."

"She did, in a nice way. All of us like to know how our men are getting along… and don't you forget that includes me."

"I'll try to remember that, especially since you packed all that wonderful writing paper and envelopes for me. Thanks, honey."

Their conversation lasted a few more minutes, full of more personal feelings and promises to be fulfilled when they were together again. They lingered over the goodbye and finally hung up. Bruce sat and stared at the phone for a while…

#

The flying boat settled down once more on the smooth, glassy surface of the bay and motored up to the ramp of the seaplane base. When the door opened, the hot, damp air reminded Bruce that he was, again in the tropics. Somehow Hawaii never felt as humid as the islands like Guadalcanal or Espiritu Santo. Now Guam could be added to his list of tropical paradises that had somehow shown him an uglier face than in travel brochures. As he exited onto the wharf where the plane had moored, Bruce heard the sound of a hundred or more aircraft engines… big ones. He squinted and shielded his eyes against the bright sun as a silver B-29, bigger than any plane he'd ever seen, cleared the end of a runway and flew out over the water a quarter mile or so away. A minute later and another followed, then another, until he had watched a couple of dozen wing away into the bright sunshine, reflective flashes showing their direction.

"Goin' to the Jap's back yard.", said the Navy deck hand standing near him. "A friend of mine... in the Air Corps. He told me today was the first big show. Those planes are loaded with incendiaries... gonna burn the shit out of the Japs tonight. Where you headed?"

"Base Admin; name's Bruce Hollins. What's yours?"

"Bruce Hollins... the newspaper writer? No kidding? Sorry about the swearing, sir... we kind of get carried away with our manners out here. My name's Williams, Seaman William Williams... I know... sounds like a stutter. My friends call be Bill Bill for short."

"I like it... mind if I mention you later? Where you from, Bill Bill?"

"North Dakota... little town of Grand Forks, across the river from Minnesota. You're from Iowa, right? I played basketball in high school, remember reading about your team winning the state title. Sort of a David and Goliath thing."

"That it was. Which way to Admin, Bill Bill?"

"Sorry, sir. Straight across the ramp there and third building on the right. Can't miss it."

"I've seen enough to recognize one, I'm sure. Thanks..."

Bruce hefted his bag on to a shoulder and headed the way Seaman Williams had pointed. Ten minutes later he was setting it down in front of the duty Yeoman. He asked about a room assignment while he arranged further transportation. The Yeoman placed a phone call and told Bruce to wait a few minutes; a jeep would be by to give him a ride. Bruce walked over and studied a map on the wall of the eastern Pacific, showing lines and markings that had been added and erased as the Americans advanced. He noted that the island of Iwo Jima was right on the edge of a new line; wondering if Bobbie Milliken was near there.

A horn honked outside and the Yeoman was hooking his thumb in that direction as Bruce looked over. Picking up his bag, he went outside into the bright sunshine again. A Navy sedan, painted battleship gray, was parked with Aaron Steiner standing alongside.

"Hey, Bruce. Long time no see… how are you?" Aaron came over, grabbed the seabag and stowed it in the trunk.

"Aaron! What a surprise. I just told my wife I was looking forward to running into you and here you are. I'm not sure what to make of you Steiner guys… always surprising me."

"Well, my dad got a message through to me that you'd be arriving and I know a few folks in Admin. You'll be staying with the Seabee's if you don't mind. Not exactly the Ritz but it beats a tent on Guadalcanal."

"I'm sure it does. Commander now, is that what I see there?"

"Yeah, I'm just finishing here on Guam. My boys are building the bases on Saipan and Tinian; the Air Corps are already using the runways while we finish putting the individual hardstands in. You won't believe the size of the airfields; the one here is small in comparison. We'll be flying a thousand bombers at a crack to Japan in a matter of weeks. This morning was the first really big raid… I've got us seats for their return tonight. If you didn't sleep on the flight in, you might want some chow and a bed for a few hours first. They won't be back until early morning."

"That would be perfect. Say, is there a phone I can use to call San Diego around here?"

"Not really… I'll fix you up with a way to get a message home to let them know you're here. Some things take a little longer… personal telephone calls is one of them."

"Sure, I understand. Can you imagine the looks we'd have gotten for asking back in the Solomon's a few years ago?"

Hours later, refreshed with food, sleep and a shower, Bruce stood with Aaron Steiner and a group of Air Force officers in the control tower above the airbase on Guam. Blinking lights could barely be discerned amid the stars shining in the clear night air. The radio was filled with voices of pilots as the planes returned from their long journey… well over a thousand miles each way to the main islands of Japan and back. Bruce looked for the arching flares that were familiar to him from his time in England with the Eighth Air Force. They would indicate wounded airmen aboard or mechanical trouble, depending on their color. He didn't see a single one and inquired whether they were still used or not.

"Oh, yes, we still use them. But this raid caught the Japs by surprise." The voice was an Air Force Captain, there to answer questions. "We're trying a new tactic; coming in low and fast, something they won't expect with heavy bombers like these. We haven't been getting accurate bombing results from high altitude and General LeMay wants to try this. His second in command, Brigadier General Young, is on the lead plane. You can talk with him after his debrief is over... maybe an hour or so."

"Young... that wouldn't be Bill Young by chance?"

"Yes it is; you know him?"

"Sure do. It's funny how I keep running into people I know all around this big war. I flew with him... Major Young then... on a mission from England early on. Now he's here, too."

"And the timing of these raids couldn't be better. With Iwo Jima, we'll be able to build a fighter base within range of the P-51 to escort the '29s there and back. It will also be the site of an emergency landing strip for the bombers that can't make it all the way back to here. Right now they ditch in the drink and we try to find them with subs and long range PBY aircraft." Aaron joined in. "My next job is the field construction on Iwo; as soon as the Marines are done, or nearly done... we'll be there with our heavy equipment starting to work."

The Air Force Captain nodded his head in agreement. "Shouldn't take more than a week or so now. I saw a great picture of our flag going up on the top of the volcano... Mt, uh, Som'bitchee or something like that. It's being cleared for release today... should be in all the papers stateside tomorrow."

Bruce wasn't so sure; estimates of how long the enemy could hold an island had been far too optimistic in the past. He wondered, again, if Bobbie might be on Iwo.

"Anyway, Bruce...how'd you like to go up to Tinian and see what we're building up there? It's nearly done and I'll bet it's the biggest airport you've ever seen."

"You know, Aaron, I'll take you up on that trip. There's a few things I need to square away here about travel and the whereabouts of a ship. You remember Stan... he was with me at Guadalcanal when our ship went down?"

"Sure... he's a gunner, right?"

"Right... good memory. Anyway, he's a chief gunner now on a destroyer somewhere between here and the Philippines. I'd like to find it and find out how to get on board; it's another thing I need to do here."

"No sweat. I'll be here on Guam for at least another week; might be you'll be able to get your information in time to fly out with me. Otherwise we can arrange seating for you on another day... we have planes heading there most every day."

"Great! Now I'd like to see about joining General Young if your invitation still holds, Captain?"

"Absolutely, if you'll follow me; we'll see if he's finished with his debrief yet."

A half mile walk over fresh concrete and asphalt led Bruce and the Captain to another building with the insignia of the new Twentieth Air Force. Technically the 20th didn't exist for another month or so; it would be made up of the 21st Bomber Command, based on Tinian and Saipan and other units, including those on Guam. The building was fully enclosed and wonderfully air conditioned, which was a relief after their walk over the hot concrete and hotter asphalt. Bruce was directed into General Young's office, where he was greeted with a handshake and friendly smile.

"Bruce Hollins! How the hell are you? It's been far too long, Bruce."

"Hello, General. It seems the tides of war have brought us together again. I was surprised, and pleased, to know you were here. Congratulations on your promotion… a long way from piloting the Clipper to Long Island."

"Sometimes I wish for that simpler life, Bruce. But we've still got a job to finish before we get to do the fun things again. What brings you to Guam?"

"More of the same. I'm looking to find my two team mates out here again. Haven't seen either of them in more than two years. Europe is just about wrapped up and this is where the story is."

"From what I remember… if you hadn't been writing from the Solomon's in the summer of 1942, none of us would know where here is. Hey… you flew with me over France and Italy. How would you like to get in a B-29 with us and see Japan from the air?"

"You think that's possible?"

"Sure… restrictions have loosened up a bit now. Let's see, I have to get the Deputy Commander's permission. Wait, that's me! How about it?"

"I'd certainly have something to write about, wouldn't I? When can you arrange it? I'll be here about a week, then I'm heading up to Tinian with a Seabee commander friend of mine."

"Perfect. Check with me at North Field on Tinian; that's where my headquarters is located. We'll figure out a nice mission to go along on then, Bruce. It's been great seeing you; sorry I don't have more time right now. We've still got plenty of paper to write ourselves about this morning's bombing. We plastered the dockyards around Yokohama; fires were total when the observation planes took pictures half an hour after we hit them."

"I know a former Air Corps top turret gunner that would love to hear an eye witness report of that. You remember Sergeant Hartke? He's back in Iowa after losing part of his eyesight and hearing on that early raid I was along on."

"Of course I remember him; one of the best Flight Engineers I've flown with. When you come up to Tinian we'll have dinner and talk about the past few years, okay? I'd like that, Bruce."

"So would I General… so would I."

Chapter 3
March 1945

The B-29 seemed a century ahead of the B-17 to Bruce. Instead of suiting up in a bulky, layered ensemble topped by heavy sheepskin coat, pants, gloves, hat, boots and an oxygen mask; he entered the plane in a pair of coveralls. He remarked how much he felt like a mechanic and General Young laughed.

"We've come a long way in just a couple of years, to be sure. This Super Fortress, as it's called, is pressurized so there's no need for the clothing, oxygen… and no frost bitten fingers or noses. Of course, there's always the possibility of an emergency; being hit by the enemy or mechanical problems… they don't happen often at all and we have the gear with us just in case. This baby also flies faster, higher, farther and with a bigger bomb load… much bigger. The gun defenses are controlled by computer gunsights and we carry 20 mm cannon in addition to the usual .50 caliber machine guns we had on the B-17."

Bruce placed himself on a seat just behind the Flight Engineer. The cockpit was roomy enough for four of them with both pilots. As the crew went through their flight check lists, Bruce made sure his camera was working and loaded with film. He was going to try and get some pictures of their mission. They would be flying from Tinian to a target outside Tokyo and then back to their base. The mission was scheduled to last twelve hours; Bruce could hardly believe the plane could fly that long without refueling. It was a beautiful aircraft to look at; long and sleek with the large "Boeing" tail that reminded him so much of the older Fortresses. The wings, though, were longer and narrow; the design of them was more like that of a B-24 Liberator, the other heavy bomber being used in Europe. The B-29 was designed with this Pacific war in mind; the range necessary between island bases and the Japanese homeland required a plane such as this.

The engines were starting, sending vibrations through the ship that soon settled into a rhythmic hum, loud but not overpowering like the older planes. They were soon moving slowly down the runway to the take off point. General Young and his copilot spoke on the radio with the control tower and Bruce could see a long line of other bombers stretching back behind them as he looked out of a rounded "blister" window. There seemed to be no end of the planes preparing to go on this mission.

Taking off in the afternoon, the flotilla of bombers would be over their target in the dark of night; several pathfinder aircraft had already departed. Their job would be to lay a pattern of incendiary bombs across the city below, making an 'X' that would identify the target. The following planes were to lay their own giant loads of bombs from the center of the mark towards the outside; spreading the fires below into a giant firestorm, with hurricane strength winds that would destroy the city. Such was the plan; it had been tried a few times with increasing success. General Young confided to Bruce that Tokyo itself would be a target when they had perfected the technique. Bruce frankly shuddered at the picture he imagined; an entire city wiped out by one or two of these huge missions. The Japanese would have to surrender to prevent the destruction of their entire nation from the air.

Bruce was excited to be given the opportunity to fly on another mission with the Air Force. Word had reached him that he'd be able to meet up with the *USS LAFFEY* and his friend, Stan Larson, in a couple more weeks. His other team mate, Bobbie Milliken, was still far out to sea on a slow transport and Bruce would have to wait a bit longer to meet up with him. The offer to fly from General Young came at the perfect time.

He took photos of all the crew on the bomber; moving about the plane and making his way to each position including the bomb bays. The racks of incendiaries looked neat and organized; it was hard to fathom the destruction they would bring in a few hours. He met the gunners, all comfortable in coveralls at their stations. When he returned to the cockpit the Flight Engineer offered him a cup of fresh coffee. Bruce thought of his first mission with Jim Hartke and Major Young. Coffee in a thermos bottle that was lukewarm; here it was a steaming mug right out of the pot! He held the cup of java up for General Young to see and remarked the service was nearly as nice as on the Clipper from Liverpool to Long Island. The General smiled and gave him an OK sign back. Bruce settled back in his seat and enjoyed the hot drink. The droning of the bomber lulled him to sleep despite the coffee.

Bruce awoke to darkness outside the plane; small lights illuminated the Engineer's desk and the instrument panels for the pilots. Looking out the window he noticed other planes in their slow motions of gentle up and down movement. The light of the moon reflected on the aluminum skins, making them look a bit other worldly, like a flock of birds without flapping wings.

Over the intercom Bruce heard the Navigator's voice tell of their approach to the coastline of Japan. General Young motioned for Bruce to come up between the pilots' seats and pointed ahead and to the right. There in the moonlight was Mount Fuji; Bruce recognized its beautiful profile from travel magazines he'd seen in high school. The snow covered peak glowed white against the star studded sky.

General Young had the radio operator transmit a course change that would direct them to the target. Bruce sensed an increased attentiveness in the officers and was sure the gunners were also focused at their stations. He quietly took in everything, comparing it in his own mind to the other missions. His first thought was the absence of enemy fighters and lack of anti-aircraft fire from the ground. Then he felt the bomber losing elevation as the formation dropped down to their bombing altitude. Ahead, through the windows in the nose, Bruce could make out a glowing line on the earth. Quickly it turned into a giant 'X' shape and he knew they were a minute away from incinerating a city. He heard the Bombardier calmly say "Bombs away" and the plane jumped only slightly upward at the loss of tons of weight. Bruce watched out the side window as other planes disgorged their own loads; hundreds of light colored canisters fluttering out of the belly of each craft. Their own plane banked slightly and began to gain altitude for the return flight back to Tinian. He turned to the window on the opposite bulkhead and, looking down, began to see small pinpoints of light that soon grew and spread over his entire view.

"If we flew directly over the city on our return, you'd feel the heat and it would force us up several hundred feet in the updraft. In a few minutes it will look like a giant charcoal pit… waiting for someone to throw some steaks on." Chuck Bates, the Engineer wasn't grinning as he said this. His face was a serious one; he knew what was happening on the ground. Chuck had flown a few photographic missions; pictures were taken the day after each raid to examine the effectiveness of high explosive to incendiary mixes in the bombloads, bombing altitudes, wind direction and speed and so on. This was fast becoming war science; the elimination of an enemy city from a list of targets. Bruce guessed the list would be getting shorter quickly.

On and on the planes flew; it seemed the return flight took longer. This was due to a desire to arrive safely back at their island home coupled with the anxiety of continued hours of monitoring engine performance, fuel use and keeping alert for possible enemy fighters. A slight irritability seemed to creep into conversations as everyone grew tired. Bruce noted the concern in General Young's voice as another of the bombers reported engine problems. It was exactly the reason Marines were fighting to take Iwo Jima, the small island halfway between Tinian and Tokyo. The coordinates of the B-29 that had to ditch in the ocean were forwarded to the air and sea rescue network; a long range rescue plane and a Navy submarine would do their best to locate and rescue the bomber crew. Hopefully a successful mission would result... before a Japanese boat got to the downed plane.

The engines on their own craft were humming with the same constant rhythm Bruce had heard for the past nine hours. He settled back in his seat and began to write down his own thoughts and reactions to the mission he'd been witness to. He honestly struggled with the mental picture of a city snuffed out in a sea of flames; that image of a bed of coals glowing red with the intense heat. He remembered the dozens of quiet and friendly Japanese from California he'd met at Manzanar, that internment camp near the base of Mt Whitney. Their faces were superimposed over the glowing coals, seeming to melt like wax and then curl and char like old photos tossed on a fire. He knew he, too, was tired and in need of a good night's sleep; but could he sleep after seeing a city destroyed?

A few hours later the plane slowed and stopped, brakes squealing as the big ship came to rest. Bruce joined the General and his crew in the debrief session and in the customary shot of whiskey to relax and loosen tongues. The Air Force was quite interested in any photos Bruce had shot and offered to develop his film and make prints for him. General Young nodded and Bruce handed a specialist his camera. The debrief lasted about an hour; longer than most because of the General's participation. After a nice hot shower and change of clothes, Bruce met with Commander Steiner for dinner at the Air Force Officer's Club. Bruce asked many questions about the construction of the airfields on Tinian and Saipan and Steiner was ready with answers for him; a few times Aaron was careful to remind Bruce of classified information. When dinner and

288

their conversation were over Bruce returned to the Navy Admin Office to see about borrowing a typewriter. The Yeoman smiled and went into an adjoining office, returning with a Royal Quiet Deluxe in a traveling case.

"Compliments of the Commander, Mr Hollins. He said you may well be stopping by this evening. I'll tell you, sir... I'd love to get my fingers on one of these. Did you know it's the model Ernest Hemingway uses?"

"You don't say? Huh... I guess that puts me in the 'majors', doesn't it? Kind of like pitching for the Yankees instead of Toledo... When you see Commander Steiner, please extend my sincere thanks. Oh, and Yeoman... ask the Commander about our fishing friend in Key West."

The Yeoman nodded; a quizzical expression on his face. Bruce smiled, thanked him again and headed to his quarters. Soon the click-clacking increased in tempo until the sound mimicked a machine gun. By morning Bruce had pounded out articles covering the Air Force bombers, the air bases, traveling across the Pacific, running into friends in remote places, the destruction of a city in one raid and the beauty of Mt Fuji on a bright moonlit night. He felt mentally drained and his fingers were cramping when he got up from his desk. An empty thermos of coffee stared at him, a reminder that he had to visit the bathroom quickly.

Bruce freshened up and headed out to have copies made of his work and to get them transmitted to New York; he was sure Bennett was anxiously awaiting something from him. It had been two weeks since his last submission from Hawaii before his journey here. While he waited for a clerk to finish, Bruce took out paper and pen and wrote letters to Susan, his parents and to Captain Mason. The clerk returned with the copies and transmission receipt and accepted the letters for posting. Bruce headed to the Officer's Club for a late breakfast and more coffee. On the way, he stopped by the Admin Office to inquire about meeting with the Transportation

Officer after his meal. The Yeoman was again behind his desk and greeted Bruce with a big smile.

"Mr Hollins... good morning, sir. I spoke with Commander Steiner this morning and he told me about Key West and a certain friend. You got me good last night, sir, feigning ignorance about the typewriter. If you ever happen to get an extra one of those... well, I am a fan of them."

"I'll be sure to keep that in mind, Yeoman. The one I have at home was a gift from the Commander and his father, replacing one I lost on a sunken destroyer in the Solomon Islands back in late 1942."

"Well, I certainly hope this one brings you more luck, Mr Hollins."

Bruce arranged for an appointment in an hour and left for breakfast, which would now be better termed an early lunch. He ate while talking with several young Navy rescue pilots and a navigator. They were quick to talk to Bruce about their mission this afternoon; they were on standby while the Air Force was finally going to Tokyo itself...

After his meal, Bruce walked back over to Admin and was soon speaking with the Transportation Officer. Lieutenant Baker had managed a travel agency in Chicago before the war; a great fit for his present job. He explained to Bruce how he would have to get to the *LAFFEY* and Stan Larson. First was a flight to Ulithi Atoll, the main anchorage for the Navy now. Assuming the ship was still there, it was just three days earlier, Bruce would have no problem getting out to her and on board. There was a chance, however, that she was not there and Bruce would have to arrange a flight back here to Tinian... a considerably more difficult feat. Then Lieutenant Baker dropped a bombshell on Bruce.

"You didn't get this from me; I'm only the Transportation Officer. The *LAFFEY* and her squadron mates are scheduled to be off Okinawa the beginning of April. They're to be part of the invasion close support group and will be screening the battleships and carriers, too. I happen to have a brother on another destroyer in the same squadron…"

Bruce was more than surprised; he remembered that Bobbie was part of the force that would be landing on Okinawa. Mason had mentioned that back in San Diego! So if he could get himself out there, he'd be close to both. Now he had a few weeks to wait, not much longer than he'd been counting on. He telephoned General Young's office from Lieutenant Baker's and asked his friend if it might be possible to hitch another ride on tomorrow's post mission photo flight. The General was hesitant; there was no assurance that the Japanese would not pursue that plane, given the target for tonight. When Bruce persisted, stating he was quite aware of the danger, Young relented. He'd arrange for the correspondent to be aboard the plane as an observer. He would actually be taking off tonight, as the photographic flights arrived over the target in daylight. Bruce hadn't slept since his time in the aircraft on the bombing mission, but didn't mention that to the General. He had about five hours until take off; if he slept in his coveralls near the briefing room…

The sun was rising over the 'Land of the Rising Sun'. Bruce thought about the irony of the statement in view of their situation now. Japan had not just seemed invincible a few years ago; she had been damned near just that. Her armies were marching around in China and her navy was on a par with the United States. It was not that the country was really a 'paper tiger' but that America's industrial potential had risen out of the Great Depression into the most formidable force the world had ever known. Production of aircraft, ships, weapons and equipment to supply the millions of our men and women who answered Uncle Sam's call was humming along now at a rate unimagined in 1940.

Bruce had time to think long on this subject; their flight had already taken somewhere near five hours. In another, they would arrive over the capital city of Tokyo; the site of the fire bombing attack the night before. What looked like brown fog already could be seen, nearly blocking out distant Mt Fuji. How different it looked compared to a couple of nights ago, bathed in bright moonlight. He wondered just how the city would appear. He'd seen photographs of other burned out targets, but felt confident looking at the real thing out a window would be different. At the higher altitude they were maintaining, details would be difficult to make out; that was the job of the cameras mounted on the underside of the plane. As they approached the coast, rising sun at their back, Bruce noted the increased attention of the crew as they straightened in their seats and focused on the instrument panels in front of them.

Again there was no anti-aircraft fire nor did enemy fighters come up to attack them; Bruce was reminded of their mission briefing that single planes were rarely challenged. He looked out the side window and raised the binoculars to his eyes. One of the pilots had provided them to him at takeoff. He could make out boats on the bay below them and some buildings along the water's edge through the smoke. Suddenly the city opened up below the aircraft, spreading out nearly as far as he could see. With the help of the field glasses, Bruce saw a grayish wasteland, some remains of buildings sticking up here and there. They appeared like skeletons rising from the ashen ground. One green, living patch of city revealed the Imperial Palace area; declared off limits to bombing. The rest of the capital lay there before him like a lumpy, charred blanket. Despite the plane's pressurized construction, Bruce smelled the burned landscape; the scent ascending thousands of feet into the air. He was appalled and transfixed at the sight of square miles of smoking desert. There were no streets, no parks, no way to tell which section of the city he was looking at. How many people had been incinerated in the fires? His mind reeled at the thought. How could a nation suffer attacks like this and not surrender? He slumped back in his seat, quietly reflecting on what he'd just witnessed. He would have to write about this day; but how to capture the overnight death of an entire city?

Hours later Bruce, along with the crew, were sitting in the debriefing room. No one joked or exulted over the mission's success. Every man had a quiet, contemplative expression. There was not much to report. They had seen no enemy fighters, had nothing go wrong mechanically with the ship. It had been a routine twelve-hour flight; except for what they had seen halfway through. Bruce personally felt like he had, somehow, violated an almost sacred thing... like bursting in on a funeral to snap photographs of the corpse. Accepting the ration of whiskey, normally reserved for actual bombing missions, Bruce welcomed the numbing sensation it provided. He was driven back to his quarters where he showered and laid on his bed, visions of Japanese faces melting and dripping in the fires filling his mind. He finally slept... and awoke nearly sixteen hours later.

The next morning Bruce was writing letters to his parents, Susan and the Price's when he heard the sound of bombers returning. He imagined another Japanese city name being struck from a list with a wide, red brush stroke. He felt he had to get away from Tinian. As he walked to the Admin Office to make another appointment with Lieutenant Baker, Bruce overheard two Air Force personnel talking about the American Army's crossing of the Rhine River at a place called the Remagen Bridge. Apparently the Germans had neglected to blow one bridge over the river, or the demolition had not been successful. Regardless, American armor and infantry units were now on the German side of the river. This was a real game changer and would allow rapid penetration of the Nazi's defenses. Bruce's spirit was lifted at the news; once the war in Europe ended, overwhelming force could be brought to bear on Japan and they would have to surrender.

Lieutenant Baker was in his office and Bruce was directed in right away. Baker repeated the news from Remagen and the two talked about if for several minutes before Bruce came to the point of his visit.

"Lieutenant, how might it be possible for me to connect with the *LAFFEY* later and get to the Marines on the transports heading to Okinawa? Wouldn't I be able to get to the destroyer after I've landed on the island?"

"Bruce, I know you were on Guadalcanal, but honestly… making a landing against the Japanese now, side by side with the Marines… well, sir, that would be downright foolhardy. Why not wait a few weeks, visit the *LAFFEY* and then meet up with the Marines on Okinawa?"

"I've just returned from my second bomber flight over Japan… I've faced combat in North Africa, Italy and France. I've had a ship sunk out from under my feet. Nothing the Japs can do will frighten me more than I've already been. Now… is it possible to get aboard the right transport?"

"Well… I know there are over 40 attack transports and nearly 70 LSTs in the flotilla carrying the Marines. Can you give me until tomorrow to find the right one and arrange a means for you to get to her?"

"That would be perfect; take an extra day if need be. I'd just like to leave Tinian as soon as I can."

"Alright. I've got you at the Temporary Officer Quarters in the Seabee complex… is that correct?"

Bruce nodded with a smile. Lieutenant Baker nodded back and immediately began paging through a printed roster, picking up his telephone to make calls. On the way back to his quarters, Bruce dropped in the Officer's Club; he asked the officer in charge there if he could have a bottle of Johnny Walker delivered to the Transportation Office. He was assured it would be in Lieutenant Baker's hands within an hour. He dropped his letters off at the front desk of the officer quarters, realizing he'd neglected to do so on his way out. He used the desk phone to call Aaron Steiner and arrange for lunch with him. Aaron was delighted and asked Bruce to swing by his office on the way.

When the two met an hour later, Aaron invited Bruce to pick up the telephone on his desk.

"Long distance operator... can I be of service, sir?"

Bruce nearly cried with delight. He and Susan were soon jabbering to each other and had to learn a new kind of verbal dance. Because of the delay in sending and receiving, what Bruce said was not heard by Susan for nearly 30 seconds and so on. They soon got the rhythm down and were having a less disjointed time talking to each other. Aaron held up five fingers indicating minutes and stepped out of the office.

"I can't believe I'm hearing your voice, darling. Are you well... getting enough sleep?" Susan said through her tears of joy.

"I'm OK and sleep is hit or miss. I've met with several people I know and have done some flying. You can read about it in the papers; don't think I should talk on the phone about it."

They spoke of the beach house, Saul and Marge and Bruce's folks, who were arriving for a visit the next week. When Bruce asked why his parents were coming out so soon, Susan teared up and gushed...

"Because I want your mother here when our baby is born and she insisted on coming out now. Your dad will be going back in a week by himself."

"Our baby? We're having a baby?" Bruce was laughing, crying, shouting in disbelief... all at once.

The door opened and Aaron rushed in.

"Everything OK? I heard a lot of shouting and didn't know..."

"Fine, fine... I'm going to be a father!"

"Well, I'll be darned... I'm almost afraid to call my own wife now.", said Aaron, joining in the celebration.

#

It was a week since Bruce had left Tinian; the distance being nearly 1,500 miles to Okinawa in a direct route. Lieutenant Baker had found a supply ship that would meet up with the invasion flotilla four days before the landings were to be made. Barring any delays, Bruce would have that much time to meet Bobbie Milliken and acquaint himself with the platoon before joining them in the landings. The supply ship was not fast, like a destroyer; they still had more days sailing to catch up with the attack transports. Already, though, naval vessels were visible; ocean going tugs, other supply ships and oilers were on their way from various points to rendezvous with the main fleet. Occasionally a PBY aircraft would fly overhead, patrolling the seas from the sky, looking for submarines. Thankfully the seas were calm, as the ship was not deep hulled and rolled like a cork on the water. He'd spent the first day at sea on his knees in the 'head' and the second in his bunk. By day three, with a completely empty stomach, he felt much better and slowly had become accustomed to the wallowing motion.

Today he had gone around interviewing several of the crew and was treated to a nice breakfast of powdered eggs, toast, canned pork and apple pie. He felt much better, despite the full belly. All on board were in good spirits now that other ships were in view; they knew the fleet was close ahead and that meant protection from enemy attack. When he was on the bridge, Bruce was taken aside by the ship's Captain.

"I've received word that we'll meet up with the transports near the Kerama Islands, just a bit south and west of Okinawa. It's to be the main anchorage for the fleet during operations here. Your transport should be present and we'll send you over on a tug as soon as we are in visual contact. Glad to see you're feeling better, Bruce; had me worried for a day or so. It's been a long time since I've had a passenger… a sick one at that."

"Thanks, Skipper. I'm fine now; the cook made me a great breakfast this morning and I'm feeling on top of the world. That's good news about the transports; I'll be glad when I can meet up with the Marines."

"Well, better you than me, I'd say. I'm still not sure why anyone would WANT to go ashore against something like that. I've heard nightmares about the landings on Iwo Jima. Our guys were slaughtered on the beaches there... no cover and the Japs had the entire area pre-sighted for their artillery. It was rough going."

"Then I hope the Navy and Marines learned a valuable lesson there."

"Could be. Come out on the bridge wing with me, Bruce."

The two stepped through a hatch and onto a small platform with railing just outside the bridge. This is where the Captain usually sat when the ship was docking or in close proximity to other vessels.

"Listen carefully, Bruce. What do you hear?"

Bruce cocked his ear, tilting his head away from the wind. He could hear a faint rumbling... like the sound of a summer thunderstorm far beyond the horizon back in Iowa.

"That, my boy, is the sound of the Navy at work. Battleships letting go broadsides of 16" shells that weigh as much as a small car. Cruisers and destroyers getting in close to pinpoint enemy bunkers and hitting them with smaller guns, 8" and 5". But what am I doing? You were on a destroyer in Ironbottom Sound, right? Took on a battleship alone in the dead of night; that's what you wrote in the papers? You write a hell of a good story, that you do. Truth or fiction?"

"All true. I was with a friend, a gunner's mate, on the first *LAFFEY* the night she went down. We raked the bridge on a battleship pretty well; heard later the Japanese task force commander was killed. I wasn't doing all that much; I'd only been on the ship a few hours. I wonder how the crew of the new *LAFFEY* will feel when I show up in a couple of weeks; I hope they don't think I'm a 'Jonah'. I plan on going out to her after I make the landing on Okinawa and spend a few days with the Marines there."

"Well, Bruce... you're either the bravest young man I've met... or the most insane." The Captain laughed and slapped him on the shoulder. "Come on... let's see if Cookie has any of that pie left to go with a cup of java. I could use one of each about now."

The two descended down the ladder to the main deck and headed to the galley. While devouring a huge slab of warm apple pie, the Captain was given a message by one of the crew. He looked it over and handed it to Bruce.

"It seems we're right on schedule to drop you with a tug late tomorrow afternoon. We made better time with the calm water; have to say we're all glad to have had you on board. Every one of the boys on my ship reads your articles; lifts their spirits and gives them motivation to press on. Life on a supply ship is not glamorous; in fact, it's damn boring. Anybody would rather go face to face with a Jap battleship... except me, of course. Had my chance in the last war against the Kaiser's subs in the Atlantic. Much warmer out here and calmer, too."

"I'll be sure to write one about what you're doing, Captain. Without your help, none of the islands could be won. You bring the equipment and supplies we need after the beaches are secured."

"Thanks... it's that sincere attitude that makes your writing so nice to read."

#

Bruce's transfer from the supply ship to the attack transport by way of an ocean going tug went smoothly enough. The transport's skipper was surprised and somewhat amused that a correspondent would go to such lengths to have the chance to storm an enemy beach. Bobbie Milliken was standing on the quarterdeck when Bruce climbed aboard from the tug. His smile spoke volumes of how much he'd missed his friend. Bruce was welcomed by the platoon; several new faces greeted him among the few familiar ones from Guadalcanal. After stowing his gear, Bruce and Bobbie had a visit, alone on the fantail of the transport.

"After you left for the States, all hell broke loose. The Japs had landed an entire division, some 7,000 men, on the north end of the island. They wanted the high ground around the airfield bad... right where we were. I tell you, Bruce, what you saw was nothing, nothing compared to what we did to them. Blew 'em to shit with

298

our artillery before they even hit our wire. Then, while they were cutting their way through, we detonated barrels of gas that we'd buried... set 'em off with white phosphorus grenades. Incinerated the yellow bastards by the score; and still they kept coming... screaming and yelling. Their officers with swords up in the air. It was total lunacy. We swept 'em off the ridge like flies in a cow barn." Bobbie was shaking his head, eyes moist with the memories.

"After that we were told the Army was taking over; we were being relieved. We ended up in Melbourne, Australia... heaven on earth to us. Almost no men; they were all fighting the Germans or on New Guinea against the Japs. The girls were everywhere, and the beer and ale was sweet. Lots of adventures, I'll tell you. A couple of months and we went to Cape Glouchester in New Britain... that was December of '43. Fought on, mostly against the jungle and rain until spring of '44. The heat and humidity there ate your uniform first and then it ate you. All of us had sores that didn't heal and got sicker than dogs. They told us we won a victory and shipped us to a shit hole called Puvuvu to rest and refit. Had to build our own base there before training for Peleliu, a coral island they said had to be taken so MacArthur could get to the Philippines. I know I'm going to heaven, Bruce, because I've sure as shit been to hell. My platoon went in... supposed to take three days... with 19 guys. About six or seven were from Guadalcanal. After almost a month there we came out with four of us... I was the only one not wounded bad enough to be evacuated. Now I'm the platoon sergeant; managed to get a few guys back from the hospital... but most of us are new. Next is Okinawa and why you'd want to go in with us is beyond be, brother. I don't think any of us will last an hour. Did they tell you we'll be in the first wave to hit the beach?"

"They told me. I wanted to be with someone I know... and that would be you."

"Well, we've got a couple of days to get you some gear. I've still got your .45; haven't used it much. It'll be easier without it on my hip anyway I suppose. You're not planning on toting the

299

typewriter along, are you?" Bobbie smiled, an uneasy expression on his face.

"You know Bruce, a lot of the fellas really like what you write. Some of us think it might be a little too much of the flag waving, you know. We've seen a different war than most, I suppose. Mine has been close up; when you get a Jap in your foxhole that wants to kill you... well, you stick your fingers in his eyes, bite his ears off, break his nose with your forehead, whatever it takes to kill him first. The little shits don't give up; they lay on the ground, wounded and wait for you to get close... then blow themselves up with a grenade, hoping to get you, too." He paused, started to cry, embarrassed...

"Now you know why I don't write home much. What the hell do I write to my mom? 'Dear Mom, I bit a Jap in the neck and held tight while he bled to death, because I couldn't reach my rifle to shoot the bastard?' If I do get home, which I cannot imagine, how am I going to go to a normal job, or out on a date to the movies? Nope... probably be best if I just meet my end out here somewhere."

Bruce was shocked into silence by the depth of depressive feelings Bobbie shared. His happy-go-lucky basketball team mate and friend was gone from the world, replaced by a conflicted, killing machine. Bruce knew if Bobbie did make it, and he prayed he would, his friend would need a long period of help to feel normal again. He vowed to himself to see to it Bobbie got the help he needed, and others like his friend. For now, with no words to say, Bruce just hugged Bobbie while the Marine cried and shook with emotion. After several minutes, Bobbie wiped his eyes, looking to make sure no one had seen them.

"Wow... haven't done that since the night on the ridge above Henderson Field. Sorry, Bruce; didn't mean to go nuts on you."

"Never apologize, Bobbie. Never apologize to me or to anyone about your life. Not your choice. Someday, something special will happen to you to make up for this."

"Yeah? I'd like some ice cream; that'd be special right now."

"Well... let's go see if we can get you some. It'll be a start."

The two found a quiet place on the ship's mess decks, normally reserved for the crew; Bruce introduced his friend to the mess chief and was graciously admitted. Two dishes of vanilla ice cream, complete with chocolate sauce, were brought out and placed in front of them. Bobbie could not believe his eyes.

"Haven't had ice cream since we left Puvuvu on this bucket. If my platoon found out they have it here, a way would be found to steal it. So tell me about your life the past two years or more since we parted."

Bruce filled him in on events since Guadalcanal, including the whereabouts of Stan, their sailor friend. Bobbie expressed thanks for Bruce visiting his folks each time he was in Iowa, and was very pleased to hear about Jim Hartke and Fred Howard's sister, Frankie, and their marriage and baby on the way. Bobbie was excited to hear about Susan, Bruce's marriage and their baby as well.

"I suppose if I do make it back, I'll have some catching up to do. How's Fred doing? You said he's in England, but what's he doing there?"

"Well, last I knew he's up for a battlefield promotion to Lieutenant and plans on staying in the Army Rangers after the war. He's an instructor after getting three Purple Hearts and other decorations."

"I knew he'd do well. Fred was the leader of our team, too. Remember how he'd always threaten to kick our butts if we didn't practice hard? Seems to have paid off for all of us, especially him."

"Fred's doing OK; at least he was the last time I saw him. You and Stan are the two I've not seen in quite a while. Stan was at my wedding... stood up for me as best man there. Haven't seen him since; got one letter from him when he was still a gunnery instructor in San Diego, but that was more than a year ago. His mom said his ship was built on the east coast and he was part of the Normandy landings last June. Since then the ship's gone through the Panama Canal and was in the Philippines for the landings there. Now it's supposed to be part of the covering force for the battleships blasting Okinawa for our assault. I plan to get to the *LAFFEY* shortly after we go ashore. I don't really know what I'll do after that; I'd like to stick around out here until the end of the fighting. If I headed back to Europe now, it'll probably be over before I get there. Besides, it'll be nice being with a Marine and a sailor again." Bruce smiled at Bobbie.

"Have you heard anything about the destroyers around the Philippines or the Marianas when we invaded there? The Jap kamikazes liked to target the radar picket ships, mostly destroyers and other small escorts. That's the scuttlebutt we hear; those boys get pasted. You wait... once we get ashore, they'll come out in droves. I'd almost rather be on the beach than stuck on a ship with a bunch of those suicidal nuts overhead."

A sailor approached the two and picked up the empty ice cream bowls, not offering any refill. He told Bruce the ship's captain would like to see him in his cabin. Bruce told Bobbie he'd see him later and followed the sailor through the galley and up to the deck just below the bridge. Captain Sommers invited Bruce to come in when the sailor knocked and announced their arrival.

"Bruce, it's a pleasure to meet you. I trust you've had some time to visit your Marine friend. He's the one you were with on Guadalcanal, right? I remember reading about your time there. Awful what the fighting is like for these young guys. They should be back home, hopping up cars and racing on Main Street. Instead they're thousands of miles away, fighting the Japs and the jungle because a country isn't satisfied with what they have."

"And what about you, Captain? What would you be doing if the war hadn't started?"

"Me? Oh, I'd be doing this, only on some smaller rust bucket, I guess. I'm regular Navy... graduated from Annapolis in 1920, just after the last war. I've done my time on the old four stacker destroyers, was a gunnery officer on a cruiser and now I'm temporarily in command of five of these attack transports. There were too many officers for the ships that were still afloat after Pearl... rather than wait for a new cruiser to be built, they offered me this command, which included yard time while they were designed. Amazing how fast they came together; we've been in two assaults so far... Tarawa and Saipan. Now Okinawa, this is called 'Operation Iceberg', and I imagine next will either be Japan itself or Taiwan."

"You really think the Japanese will hold out after we take Okinawa?"

"I can't imagine them doing anything else; they sure don't look like they want to give up. I suppose it's OK to share this with you; got the word yesterday. Iwo... you heard we secured it middle of the month... anyway, casualties there were higher for us than the Japs. It's the first time that's happened. It's possible the Japs will let us land unopposed and wait to hit us when we're more strung out somewhere on the island... it's a big damn island. Of course, we'd prefer to slaughter them all right away... but they've had this place forever; part of their homeland, really. We have no real idea where their main defensive line is. We do know you'll be going in soon. We're moving the timetable up a couple of days to try and surprise the Japs a little. Fact is... the bombardment group claims they're running out of targets. Can you beat that?"

"In that case, Captain, I'd better be getting back to the platoon I'm going in with. I'd like to meet all of them... and I have to get some more gear before we land. Just how do we get to the beach?"

"Good question. Let's take a walk and I'll show you... make a good story, I'd think."

Captain Sommers gave Bruce a tour of the transport, specifically a *HASKELL* class ship, and how the LCVP'S (Landing Craft Vehicle Personnel) were lowered over the side before the men climbed down the cargo nets and boarded the landing craft. Each transport carried 23 LCVP's and two larger landing craft, primarily for shuttling supplies ashore during and after the landings. The transport herself carried 1,500 fully supplied Marines. Most of the ship's guns were for anti-aircraft use, 20mm and 40mm rapid fire types that Bruce recognized as similar to those on the old *LAFFEY*. Bruce also recognized the LCVP as the Higgin's Boat that was famous from the D-Day invasion of France.

The tour ended when Captain Sommers was called to the bridge. He excused himself and directed Bruce to where the Marines were quartered. At the bottom of a ladder he found himself surrounded by the men in green. The berthing area was much different from the old transport he'd been on crossing the Atlantic with the 34th Division to Ireland a month after Pearl Harbor. That voyage seemed like ages ago to him now. He found Bobbie and his platoon and settled in to meet the others.

Chapter 4
April 1945

Bruce tilted his helmet back a little and lifted his head to peer over the gunwale of the landing craft. He saw other LCVPs spread out on either side of the one he was in, all straining forward, churning wakes of foam behind. Ahead of them was a maelstrom of smoke and flame where he supposed the beach was. The noise was deafening; explosions, shells whistling and whining overhead and American aircraft heading in to attack targets. He thought how all soldiers and Marines must believe the same thing on their first beach landing... "How in hell could anything survive the devastation ahead?". The Navy had been pounding the island for days from the sea and air. Bobbie tugged at his sleeve and Bruce stepped back down into the boat.

"We're close enough now for their machine gun fire... not safe up there." Bruce could hardly hear his friend shouting in his ear. He nodded and forced a tight smile. His stomach was completely cramped up and Bruce fought back against the urge to vomit. He found himself cursing the Navy and their glorious send-off breakfast; Bruce remembered the rookies gobbling up the bacon and eggs while the veterans ate slowly and carefully. Now several of the 'first timers' were throwing up on the deck, making it slippery. Normally the stench would have made him sick as well, but the smell of the Navy's bombardment was overpowering.

The boat's coxswain held up three fingers... thirty seconds until the ramp lowered. Men around him tightened their belts and straps, adjusted helmets, checked their weapons, prayed and looked frightened. Bobbie yelled again in his ear.

"Stay with me, hold tight... keep your eyes on my back."

An enemy shell landed close by, showering the men with salt water, sand and pieces of dead fish. Bruce felt the flat bottom of the landing craft scrape and they shuddered to a sudden stop. The ramp lowered and the men ahead began running out into the foamy surf. Bruce held on to Bobbie's belt as they, too, ran down the ramp into knee deep water. He could hear a couple of Japanese Nambu machine guns firing from up ahead, but the beach was clear and the squad advanced some twenty yards, off the sand and into brush without suffering any casualties.

Bobbie halted his men and ordered them to find cover. He and Bruce jumped in a shell crater along with the radioman. Bobbie was on the radio in an instant, connecting with his superiors. Bruce watched as the landing craft backed off the beach and, turning around, headed back to the fleet offshore. A minute later more of the Higgins boats were beaching, ramps dropping as another wave of Marines was deposited on the sand. Soon there were hundreds of men finding cover in the brush; Bruce could see, through gaps in the smoke, more long lines of landing craft heading in. He wondered why the Japanese weren't firing at them; even the few machine guns he'd heard earlier were silent now.

Bobbie stood and ordered his men to gather around. He'd received orders to move inland until they contacted the enemy; how far that might be nobody could guess. Bruce helped by picking up a container of ammunition for a machine gun, getting a smile and nod from one of the gunners. The squad moved out and walked for close to half a mile before a Nambu started firing from their front.

"We stop here", Bobbie shouted. "Set up the machine gun twenty yards to the right... I want two men to a hole, make them five yards apart along a line here."

306

Bruce looked to their left and saw the next squad come up and begin to do the same. It had all been too easy...

#

The landings had been virtually unopposed; the same held true for the Army down on the south end of the island. Contact with the Japanese hadn't happened until the troops were well inland and established on the beaches. Supplies were now pouring in and the offensive to take Okinawa could begin in earnest. Bruce was relieved at the ease of the assault; Bobbie told him not to hold his breath.

"These Japs are sneaky, Bruce. They have a reason to everything they do. They're not licked yet... you wait. Their planes will come out against the Navy soon and they've had years to fortify this island. You weren't with us when we landed on Guadalcanal... it was kind of like this, too. Quiet at first, then... WHAM! Anyway, we've got orders to move east, across the middle of the island. First Division, that's us, gets to take the northern half, along with the 6th Marines. The Army will take the southern half; at least that's the plan. Word's coming down that this will be over in weeks. I remember when they said Peleliu would be over in three days and that took a month. Maybe now would be a good time to go see Stan. You could fill up on that good Navy chow and then come back for the finish here."

"That's a good idea, Bobbie. This might be a time to go. I know it's been quiet to now, even though only a handful of days ago we were still on the transport. I'm sure the *LAFFEY* is around somewhere. While I'm gone, you keep your head down. This war is just about won, believe it or not. I've seen what our bombers are doing to the Jap's cities and I'm convinced they can't hold out much longer. They might surrender before I get back."

"Yeah, yeah... I've been hearing that since I was in boot camp. It just seems like every time somebody guesses how long they'll fight; the bastards hold on ten times longer. I'll do my part to stay alive; maybe you should tell the Japs to stop shooting at me."

307

"You know I would if I could... Let's go see about finding Stan."

The two headed to company headquarters to get Bruce started on his way back to the beach and on to his friend on the destroyer. Bruce had to drop his dispatches and a Navy ship would be a better place to do that as well. His days on Okinawa had been relatively uneventful, by Marine standards. The men were glad of it, but knew that there was still fighting ahead. As long as there were Japanese soldiers alive on the island, there would be a struggle. Company HQ sent him to Battalion and from there he was escorted to the beach and hopped a ride out to an attack transport where he could make arrangements to get aboard the *LAFFEY*. He and Bobbie had said goodbye on the beach and Bruce told his friend to look for him around the end of April. The transport Bruce boarded was on its own way to the main anchorage in the Kerama Islands. Bruce was given a bunk in a stateroom usually used by the officers of troops being transported. He had sent out his early dispatches, covering the landings and his time with Bobbie and the Marines on the way to Okinawa. Now he finished writing of his time since they went ashore. It was hard to believe that it had already been five days since the assault.

A sailor stuck his head in the stateroom and announced that the captain would like to see Bruce on the bridge. He followed the young man through the maze of passageways, up ladders and on to the weather deck. Up one more ladder and through the hatch leading to the bridge and he was introduced to the ship's skipper, who was extending his hand.

"Commander Stanton. Glad to meet you, Bruce. Wondering if you'd care to join us in the wardroom for dinner at 1800? We'll be getting underway shortly after we eat, but there will be time to get to know the other officers first. Captain Sommers, our squadron commander, also sends his greetings and is looking forward to seeing you at the anchorage when we arrive day after tomorrow."

"Thank you, Commander. I'd enjoy meeting the officers at dinner. Would you mind if I have breakfast on the mess decks with the enlisted men in the morning? I'd like to have a chance to speak to some of them, too."

"By all means... make yourself comfortable. I think you'll find the crew will be very interested in meeting you. I'm sure you find a welcome most places you go, Bruce."

"Commander, I'm always humbled by the reception I get... and thanks again for the invite to the wardroom. I look forward to the meal and the company."

Bruce took leave of the skipper and returned to his own quarters. Finishing up his work an hour later, he stopped by the ship's office and left his package with the Yeoman there, being assured it would be going out as soon as the ship arrived at the Kerama anchorage. Walking out to the fantail of the ship, Bruce saw what looked like smoke on the horizon, to the northeast of the island. He could faintly hear the sound of gunfire from the same direction. It must be some ships firing at Japanese positions, he thought... probably supporting the advance of Bobbie and the Marines.

The ship's claxon began ringing, followed by the announcement 'General Quarters... General Quarters... all hands man your battle stations'. Bruce was sure to get out of the way as sailors hurried about, donning life jackets and helmets, uncovering the 20mm and 40mm anti-aircraft guns and bringing ammunition to the gun mounts from the ready lockers.

Bruce looked up, shielding his eyes from the bright sun. He could see contrails from planes making crazy patterns on the blue background. The sound of aircraft engines straining could be heard and, occasionally, the chattering of machine guns. A plane began a lazy, circling dive toward the sea. It was painted a dove gray and had two dark blue planes following it, guns blazing. The plane caught fire and Bruce looked hard for a parachute, seeing none. The plane suddenly looped up and dived straight for a ship about a mile from where Bruce was standing. As it burst into a ball of bright yellow, the aircraft slammed into the stern of a small warship; Bruce thought the ship was a destroyer or one of similar size. A fireball erupted from the stricken vessel, followed quickly by several more immense explosions. In seconds the ship was eclipsed by smoke and fire; Bruce could no longer see it. When the smoke cleared in less than one minute, all that remained was debris floating on the surface; the ship had sunk that quickly. He overheard one gunner saying the Jap plane must have hit the depth charge racks on the destroyer.

Bruce was shaken by the intensity of the action. Several more Japanese planes were blown out of the sky by Navy fighters or the guns on the ships below. He saw one American plane auger into the sea, a white parachute following it. Immediately a transport nearby launched a small boat to rescue the aviator. As quickly as it had started the fight was over. In a few minutes the call to stand down from general quarters was heard over the loudspeaker. Bruce hurried back to the bridge to find out from Commander Stanton what was going on.

"Kamikazes. They came from the direction of Formosa... but we can't be sure. Our radar never picked them up until they were already over the picket ships. That destroyer that went down was on her way to join the pickets herself. We've been wondering when they'd begin to show up here. It looks like your time on a destroyer might be a pretty hot one, Bruce. Maybe you should reconsider and head back to the Marines on Okinawa."

"No, sir... but my friend was right. As long as there's a single Jap around, there's danger. I watched as that pilot intentionally crashed into the ship... he could have parachuted safely... I watched one of our guys do it. How can he do that? Commit suicide like that... doesn't life mean anything to them?"

"Well... I can't really answer that. It's not the way we fight, or have ever fought. But when you consider that one man just blew up an entire ship... in their minds it seems worth the cost."

Dinner in the wardroom was full of talk about the afternoon's action. There was certain relief that the ship would soon be underway toward what was considered a safer place. Though the anchorage was still within range of Japanese planes, there was significantly more air cover for the fleet. Dozens of aircraft carriers, large and small, were there along with two Army air strips on nearby islands. The officers knew that the number of guns on board their own transport were not sufficient to drive off a concerted enemy attack from the air; and they were a damned big target. Hopefully a Jap pilot would realize they were empty, not carrying thousands of soldiers at the moment. It would be their only salvation if the attacks increased and the ship didn't leave the area.

Bruce was toasted by the officers for his own contribution to the war effort; he was a bit embarrassed by the attention and steered the conversation away from himself and back toward the fighting.

"So what's next, after Okinawa?", he asked the group.

An excited discussion began, each offering his own idea of what was the best strategic move. Some would take Formosa, others suggested China or Korea. A majority agreed that the main islands of Japan would be the next target. They had read reports of the progress of the fire-bombing of the major cities. American submarines were sinking large fishing boats and small inter-island freighters now that larger targets had disappeared.

After the meal and conversation, Bruce was invited to join the wardroom any time he'd like to in the future. He walked with the officer in charge of the deck hands to the bow of the ship and observed preparations to get underway. The anchors, each weighing five tons, were noisily raised by the windlasses, reminding Bruce of huge fishing reels set on their sides. The anchor chain was made up of links nearly the size of a man; two men with fire hoses leaned over the side rails to wash the chain and anchors as they lifted out of the water. Once they were finished, Bruce could feel the increased vibration in the ship as the engines picked up speed and the transport began to slide through the water. He stood at the rail, looking through the darkness toward Okinawa and could make out where the fighting was going on by the lines of fire snaking across the land. Explosions, large and small, were mixed with tracers to produce a picture like he'd never seen before. He said a quiet goodbye to his Marine friends and started back to his stateroom.

He was intercepted by another message from Commander Stanton, summoning him back to the bridge. When he arrived, the mood of everyone at work there was light and spirited. Stanton walked over to Bruce, shook his hand and began to tell him of a dispatch they'd received as the ship was getting underway.

"That action we had this afternoon was just the tip of the iceberg today, Bruce. Several of our big flattops caught the Japs trying to make a run for the island from the north, up where your Marines are. Don't worry… they didn't even get close. Our aircraft blew them out of the water; even their biggest battleship, *YAMATO*, was sunk. The dispatch said she took something like twelve torpedoes and seven bomb hits to go down… biggest battleship ever built. We got her sister, the *MUSHASHI*, last fall in the Philippines. This may well be the death of the last of the Jap navy."

Bruce felt a rush of exhilaration at the thought that, perhaps, now the enemy would finally surrender. He expressed this to Commander Stanton and was cautioned by the skipper.

"Bruce, I've known Japanese officers before the war; I sailed there several times. I think they'll hold out longer than anybody can imagine. They still have a huge army in China and hold lots of areas like Korea and Indochina… they figure America will get tired of the fight and settle for some sort of peace that will leave them with what they're holding on to. I don't agree we'll let that happen… I think America will bring everything we've got in Europe here when Hitler gives up and that's sure to happen soon. There won't be much left of Japan after we're done with her. Anyway, for now, we have a lot less to worry about with their navy on the ocean floor."

Smiles and cheerful faces were evident on Bruce's walk back to his stateroom; the word had spread throughout the ship about the *YAMATO*. He sat, pulled his small table over and began to write a letter to Susan.

The next morning found Bruce on the mess deck, surrounded by enlisted men of the crew. Laughter and jokes were the order of the day at breakfast; news of the destruction of *YAMATO*'s escorts had been received, putting the finishing touches on a day of American victory. Bruce enjoyed meeting guys from all over the states, including one seaman who had graduated from Ames High School like himself. The seaman recounted the shot Bruce made to clinch the state title four years earlier, which brought compliments and words of surprise. Most people assumed Bruce was much older than his true age; his rise to prominence in journalism had been so dramatic and sudden that few suspected how young he was.

A Chief Petty Officer put a close to the morning's reverie by reminding the younger enlisted men that they still had jobs to do, despite yesterday's good news. Bruce was then invited to coffee in the Chief's Mess, where he was, again, treated to a wonderful hour of meeting more of the crew. These were the glue that held all things military together; senior non-coms in all the various branches were the sinew that made things work well. Bruce thoroughly enjoyed talking and listening to these experienced veterans. He accompanied the ship's Chief Quartermaster to the signal shack, one deck above the bridge, and had a great time learning about all the different flags still used for signaling, the blinker lights for night and peering at other ships with the big eyes, the largest set of binoculars he'd ever looked through. Altogether, his stay on this transport was becoming the most educational time he'd had yet on a naval vessel. The Chief Engineman came up and reminded Bruce of his own promise to show the reporter the ship's engine room. The two went down several decks, deep into the bottom of the ship where he was shown fuel tanks, boilers, shafts and all the other machinery necessary to make the ship move. It was all so complex and huge, yet the chief was able to explain it in a way that Bruce felt he actually understood the mechanics involved. The chief said one thing that stuck with Bruce; all ships were primarily the same. Though each had different shapes, sizes and functions they all needed engines, fuel storage, weapons systems and the locations for control and information. A tug had its pilot house and a battleship its bridge. Both were the same; one was simply much larger. This basic knowledge gave Bruce an understanding he'd not realized before.

The day passed quickly, Bruce's head filling up with nautical terms, names and hometowns. His supper with the officers in the wardroom, his second, was a time of him asking questions to the delight of the officers. They applauded his quick grasp of naval fundamentals and quizzed him on what he'd learned. The evening ended with him becoming an honorary crewmember of the ship, to everyone's enjoyment.

Bruce slept well that night; his stomach filled, mind exercised and body tired from countless ladders, passageways and ducking his head through hatches. He showered early and grabbed some coffee on his way to the bridge. He didn't want to miss the view of the fleet anchorage as the transport pulled into it. A half hour later he was joined by the skipper and invited to sit on the flying bridge... in the captain's own seat while the ship maneuvered to its own assigned place. Bruce saw every type of ship imaginable; fleet tugs, destroyers, repair ships, cruisers, transports, battleships and even several aircraft carriers, just returned from their sinking of the *YAMATO* and her escorts.

As the transport passed several destroyers anchored in one area, Commander Stanton paused, peered intently through his binoculars, and pointed to the first in the row.

"There's the *LAFFEY*, Bruce. First in line of the four there... I'll contact her as soon as we're anchored. Your welcome to go over to her in my barge if you'd like."

"Thanks, Commander. I'd appreciate that very much... and please pass the word to the crew how much I've enjoyed their hospitality and friendship."

"I will… and I hope to see you again one day. You're a fine writer, Bruce. I have no doubts the world will continue to hear from you. You're welcome on any ship of mine any day."

A few hours later, the captain's barge pulled alongside a ladder on the *LAFFEY*. Bruce climbed up and aboard, being sure to stand and face the colors before asking permission to come aboard; it was one of the formalities he'd learned during his day of naval schooling.

"Welcome aboard, Mr Hollins. The Captain knows you're coming; he's asked that you join him in his cabin. Seaman Worth will show you the way."

"Thank you Lieutenant. I'm looking forward to meeting him and my friend, Chief Larson."

"I believe Chief Larson is with Commander Becton. At any rate, I know he's onboard and we can call for him if needed."

Bruce followed Seaman Worth up the starboard side of the main deck to a ladder which went up one level. The Captain's cabin was just forward, almost directly below the bridge. Bruce looked back, along the length of the destroyer; many more anti-aircraft guns were mounted than on the old *LAFFEY* he had sailed on. The 5" guns were also different; two guns to a mount instead of one and three mounts rather than four, making six guns versus four. She was a fine, trim ship and Bruce was sure she was faster than the older *LAFFEY*.

A knock on the door and Bruce was invited inside. Standing there was Stan, in his chief's uniform, and Commander Becton. The Commander walked over and shook Bruce's hand, backed away and made room for the two friends to come together. Smiles and slaps on the back accompanied the hug they shared. It was more than two years now since they had been together and both wanted to talk. Commander Becton laughed and excused himself, saying he had about an hour's worth of work to do. Bruce noticed two empty coffee cups and a full pot on the small table between two chairs in the cabin. Both thanked the captain and sat down.

"You go first.", said Bruce.

"Okay... let's see. You got married, I've sailed practically around the world and here we are. How's that?"

"You know, for a guy that's known for never shutting up, you've changed a lot."

"Ahh, what a friend. First, thanks for visiting my folks, especially mom. She'll never get as many letters from me as she'd like; even if I wrote every day. When you got married to Susan and left San Diego, I didn't see any real need to stick around myself. Susan's friend, Janet, and I dated for a few weeks... but that didn't work out for either of us. I decided to transfer from teaching; there were plenty of others to take my place. Anyway, I heard they were building a new destroyer on the east coast... it was being renamed *LAFFEY* in honor of the old one. So I applied and, PRESTO, I got orders for Maine and the yard where she was being built. After sea trials and all, we got in on the Normandy landings... did quite a bit of shore bombardment, that sort of thing. I've never seen anything like it with all the ships, planes and all. We had one good chase after some German E-boats; you know, those small, fast suckers that carry torpedoes but they got away... and then we came back to the States, turned around after some work on our bridge design, and headed through the Panama Canal to the Pacific. Made it to the Philippines just in time for the Luzon landings and now we're here at Okinawa. Lots of miles, not many smiles... no time for liberty ports. We've been all business and our skipper, Commander Becton, is a straight shooter. He demands our best and gives us his in return. I tell you Bruce, I almost pity the Jap pilots that try to take us on. Our gunners are some of the best there are and we're all good at damage control. We have to be; these picket positions are almost suicide themselves. One small ship out there to give warning of approaching Japs... well, most of them just want to hit ANY ship, large or small. The first one is better than the last, because nobody has shot at them yet, you see?"

"I saw one destroyer, on its way to a picket position, get hit day before yesterday. I swear it went down in less than a minute."

"Yeah... we heard. Lucky Jap bastard crashed right into the depth charges. That's a hell of a lot of explosives in those cans. I'm sure it tore the stern right off that ship. Our ship is a new one; we have release mechanisms that'll roll the depth charges right over, lickety-split, if we get in a jam with a bunch of kamikazes. So, now I can catch my breath, have a cup of this joe and listen to your story."

Bruce caught his friend up on their time apart from his side. He related stories on Fred, Jim and Bobbie and his visit to Iowa. Stan was interested in hearing about changes at the college.

"I hope to go back to school, but I'll still be in the Navy. I plan on staying in and becoming an officer... kind of like Fred, I guess. Glad to hear of his success and hope I'm as lucky. I want to study rockets and missiles; they're going to replace guns on a lot of ships in the future and I'd like to learn about them."

"That's great, Stan. I'll see what I can find out about where you might study when the war ends. I'm sure there will be plenty of opportunity when the shooting stops."

"If it stops, you mean, Bruce. All the ships in the world can't conquer a country like Japan. We're going to have to occupy every one of their islands and hold guns to their heads to get them to stop. Or get their zany emperor to tell them to quit... good luck with that. I think they're all nuts."

Stan suggested they take a walk around the *LAFFEY* so he could show his friend some of the areas he was responsible for. The two climbed ladders, opened ammunition ready lockers, visited the main gun control room and other points of interest. Bruce took it all in with an earnest zeal; it reminded him of his day on the transport and all he had learned there. He surprised Stan with his own knowledge of terms and an ability to navigate his way around the ship. It was much smaller than the transport, but Bruce remembered the important lesson that all ships are similar in design. They ended up on the bridge, nearly empty except for a seaman on watch and a

317

Quartermaster going over charts of the area they would be responsible for as a picket beginning in less than a week. They were assigned a potentially hot corner north of Okinawa along the path most kamikazes had used to date.

The days passed quickly. Bruce had ample opportunity to help out and learned how to splice lines, tie knots, clean and lubricate the 20mm guns (his favorite), swab a deck (not his favorite), send messages with a blinker light and tried to understand a sextant to find their position. He was amazed that sailors still used the sun and stars to sail by. He remembered his time in the B-17 out of England when the plane's navigator had shown him the small, clear bubble window that was used to plot a position by stars at night. His last instruction was on how to handle one of the ship's fire hoses; a job that was not easy for a single person. He learned the difference between fog and stream nozzles, water and foam systems and how to back up another team in fighting a fire. He was having fun while learning the importance of self-sufficiency at sea; a ship only had herself to depend on in battle.

Stan and Bruce arranged a day ashore, requisitioning some new proximity fuses for the 5" ammunition, to visit the base exchange and savor a couple of beers. It was a rare chance to walk on dry land for Stan, who said he'd been at sea over five hundred days of the past six hundred. While there, Bruce literally ran into Ernie Pyle, another correspondent who focused on the army. Both had been in North Africa and Italy at the same time and had met briefly once before. Ernie was much older and also wrote in a homey, get to know the soldier, style of prose. He invited Bruce to join him in a few days as he was going to visit Ie Shima, a small island nearby where the Army was clearing out the last of the Japanese defenders. Bruce explained his own assignment; Ernie had once been in the Navy himself, but didn't care to cover that branch of the service now. They parted company with the promise to meet up again in Japan and share a toast of sake and champagne.

Soon it was time for the *LAFFEY* to head out to sea; she would be part of the screening force for several battleships. The big guns on the 'battle wagons' were needed to help break through a Japanese stronghold on the island. The Shuri line was the main defensive position on the southern end of Okinawa. The Marines, in the past week, had taken the northern part of the island and were reinforcing the army, who had now stalled in front of this line. For the next two days, *LAFFEY* and several other destroyers were protecting the big ships, alerting the Navy's Combat Air Patrol (CAP) of incoming Japanese planes. Kamikazes were targeting the destroyers, though some of the battleships were being hit as well. In one day, no less than three destroyers and four destroyer escorts had been hit. The sky seemed to be full of enemy planes, all intent on crashing into the ships. Bruce was constantly by Stan's side, helping how and when he could. No Jap planes threatened them directly, but in the distance, fierce battles could be seen involving one or two ships and many aircraft. The second evening out, a destroyer limped by, riding so low in the water it seemed she might submerge like a submarine. She was being helped by a minelayer and two tugs; one of the tugs steamed alongside and was using her pumps to stay ahead of the water gushing into the destroyer through holes ripped in her sides.

Bruce was called to Commander Becton's cabin; when he entered, Becton came straight to the point.

"Bruce, I've just been ordered to run over to Kerama Retto and pick up a fighter – director team (FIDO) from another destroyer, the *CASSIN YOUNG*. This means we'll be heading out from there to a forward picket position. I'm sure you realize what that entails; you've been hearing from my officers and men what's happening to our ships out there. Since I can't guarantee your personal safety, I'm offering you the chance to go aboard the *CASSIN YOUNG* and return with her to the anchorage. You have to make the decision; I'm not ordering you off my ship…"

319

"Captain, thanks for explaining things. I'd really rather stay aboard the *LAFFEY*, if it's all the same to you. Stan, Chief Larson, and I survived quite a night together once before... I can't think of any place I'd rather be right now."

"Good... how would feel about helping our Doctor? If things get dicey, and I think they will, he's going to need some level headed assistants. I think you'll fit the bill quite nicely. I've read some of your writing... you've seen quite a bit in this war. I was particularly impressed with you saving that radioman in the bomber and what you did on Guadalcanal."

"I was simply in the place to help, Captain. I'll go let the Doctor know he can count on me for whatever he needs, sir."

"You know, it's too bad you're not here as a Naval officer... you'd make a good one."

"Thanks, Skipper."

As Bruce left to find the ship's Doctor, he felt the destroyer almost leap as her speed increased and a hard turn to port had him walking with one foot on the deck and the other on the bulkhead. This is something I'll have to get used to... he thought as he headed to the sick bay. He found the right office next to the officers' wardroom. When he knocked, a voice told him to come in. He opened the door to find an officer seated at a small desk in a corner of the room.

"You must be Bruce Hollins... I'm Matt Darnell, ship's doctor."

"Hi Matt, pleased to meet you. How did you know who I am?"

"Well, seeing as I heard you were aboard, and you're the only person wearing a correspondent's uniform... lucky guess I suppose."

"Ha... joke's on me. The Captain suggested I'd be useful helping you if we run into trouble. What can I do when that time comes?"

"If it does… get here and there will be plenty to do. We use the wardroom next door for operating and it takes a bit of work to set it up. This will be your battle station when the claxon goes off… you'll know."

The two spent some time over a cup of coffee getting to know one another and what Bruce could expect to help with. Matt was a Reserve Officer from Knoxville and two years out of medical school. This was his first assignment; he'd been with the *LAFFEY* since just after Normandy the year before.

After their visit, Bruce headed back topside and watched as the *CASSIN YOUNG* came up and several men were transferred aboard. This was the FIDO team, specialists in radar and communications; they would make the ship into eyes and ears for the rest of the fleet when she reached the picket station tomorrow. Bruce could see the increasing tension on the faces of crewmen. The seriousness of what was ahead caused all to be quieter, more determined. The usual banter and joking stopped as the team came on the ship. Commander Becton was there to greet them and soon Bruce was called to the wardroom where he met Lieutenants Molpus and Porlier, the two FIDO officers. Both seemed too young to be commissioned, but Bruce knew he was still the youngest in the room. They exchanged pleasantries before Bruce was ushered out of the wardroom, knowing the conversation going on was now classified and probably beyond his full understanding anyway. He found Stan and the two had lunch together, talking about what might be coming next.

"Bruce, you remember last time… battle is battle and nobody knows how it will turn out. These Jap kamikazes are plain nuts… it becomes a fight between men that want to live and one that wants to die. Well… me… I'll do what I can to help him get his wish. On a ship, close counts. A bomb, or a plane, doesn't have to hit us directly to do damage… an explosion nearby can cave in our hull with the pressure, just as bad as exploding on the deck."

Bruce told his friend that he'd be in sick bay, helping the doctor as Commander Becton ordered. Stan said that was probably a safer place than any of the gun mounts, most of which were outside and not as well protected. The two friends finished eating and headed topside just as the ship got underway again. As the *LAFFEY* steamed out of the harbor, they passed a dozen or so other destroyers which had been on picket station and wore the damage wrought by the enemy. Several had suffered terribly; one was missing the entire bridge and the front 5" mount. The *LAFFEY*'s crew lining the rail were pointing out their own battle stations on the other ships. Everyone knew no one would be absolutely safe... wherever they were when the battle began.

Conversation for the remainder of the day centered on what each sailor had seen of the crippled destroyers. Later, in the wardroom, the officers were no different; that is, until Commander Becton entered and took his seat. Bruce noticed the immediate shift of emotion from shock to a firm resolve as the captain began to speak. His words hardly acknowledged the scene they had sailed through in the afternoon. Instead he queried each officer on the readiness status of their respective departments. Bruce appreciated his leadership style; cool and calm on the eve of battle. Every junior officer reported and Becton asked pointed questions, showing his own knowledge and understanding of each system on the ship.

"So, gentlemen, after hearing your reports... and knowing the determination of our crew... I have to say a small part of me looks forward to an encounter with the Japanese. You know I've had a ship go down once... I'll never have that happen again. We will fight as long as one gun is firing and one man is standing! Understood?"

There was an excited hum of agreement around the table, heads nodding their consent. Bruce felt the confidence of the officers and it was contagious. Looking at the Doctor, Bruce smiled and nodded; the determined look he was returned brought him back to reality. Tomorrow might prove to be a very long day indeed.

A knock at the door was answered by one of the junior officers. He took a message from someone and turned to hand it to the captain. Commander Becton read the message and, with a very sad expression, announced that President Roosevelt had died that day. The mood in the room changed immediately; tears welled up in Bruce's eyes as he pondered the news. He had almost no recollection of any other president. Becton rose and left the wardroom; soon his voice was announcing the news for the entire crew over the intercom.

Bruce thanked the officers for their hospitality and left for his own bunk, wanting to spend some time alone. Stan was already in their compartment and the two found a bit of solace in each other's company, reminiscing about the warmth and congeniality of the man whose voice all Americans recognized. The war seemed a bit further away for the moment; still, a determined resolve to see through to victory crept into their minds and words.

The next morning brought calm seas and a bright sun. Bruce was up early as he followed his friend make the rounds, checking on gun mounts and ammunition lockers. Afterward, the two visited the mess deck for breakfast; powdered eggs and bread with Spam. Plenty of coffee was downed before Stan returned topside and Bruce checked in on the bridge. Commander Becton was in his chair on the bridge wing going over the latest dispatches and daily orders. He smiled and nodded at Bruce, motioning for him to approach.

"It appears quiet this morning, Bruce… at least to this point. The President will be buried in a couple of days; I hope to have a short memorial service at the same time if the Japs cooperate. If not… I'm sure the President will understand."

"Yes, sir. It's hard to think of him gone, Captain."

A sailor came off the bridge to Becton's side, saying his presence was requested in the communications office. The Captain excused himself and Bruce watched as he quickly walked away. The sailor looked at Bruce and shrugged, though both could guess the quiet morning was slipping away.

A minute later the claxon made its whooping sound and a voice announced General Quarters over the intercom. Bruce made his way as quickly as he could to sick bay, finding the Doctor already there and the wardroom doors being removed and placed as tables around the room. The two nodded to each other and Bruce helped line the chairs up against a bulkhead. Then all they could do was wait…

Suddenly Bruce felt the ship pick up speed and begin a sharp turn to starboard, so sharp a few chairs began to slide across the floor. He looked at Doctor Darnell who shook his head. The ship straightened and began to juke to port, nearly sending Bruce off his feet. Darnell was standing, braced against his desk, feet wide as he swayed with the ship's movement. Bruce shifted his feet apart and realized how much easier it was to balance, smiling at the result.

"You'll get your sea legs yet, Bruce. Took me quite a while myself… and a whole bunch of bruised shins and elbows.

The sound of the 5-inch guns firing filled their ears and made both jump. Then the 40 mm pom-pom guns joined in and Darnell made the sign of the crucifix. Bruce's heart was pounding as he, too, prayed… and fought a sudden urge to urinate.

An enormous concussion threw both men to the deck as the lights flickered but stayed on. The smell of cordite from the guns mixed with a hot metallic taste in every breath. The door burst open and two seamen rushed in, blood streaming down the shattered arm of one and the second holding hands to his forehead, crimson streaks spurting from between his fingers.

"Put a bandage on his head and press hard, Bruce. There, over there in that chair. I've got this one."

The next several hours were a continuous flow of wounded men coming in, smoky air choking him, the ship bouncing every possible direction, lights going off and coming on again. Explosions from topside threw the men around, off the tables as Darnell worked on them. More than once Bruce found himself screaming for it to stop, only to rush over to a new arrival needing attention. He tore off burning shirts and burnt shoes to expose ripped flesh and exposed bone. Sucking chest wounds that made foamy blood bubbles with each breath were covered with bandages and the men laid down on the deck where there was room. Bruce help two sailors, both wounded, carry a dead mate into the next room. Soon there were several more.

Suddenly it was quiet… or at least quieter. The ship slowed and the sounds of the guns had lessened. Stan appeared in the doorway, face blackened and his left arm bound against his chest. A bright red stain covered most of his front.

"Stan", Bruce gasped.

"I'm alright, really. Just stopped to say we're still in the fight, but the ship is a bloody shambles. Anything you need here?"

"You could tell the damn Japs to leave us alone," was all Doc Darnell managed to mutter as he continued stitching up a wicked gash in a seaman's neck.

"I'd like to do that, Doc, but right now we're busy helping them on their way to hell. We've got three men trapped in a burning compartment aft and are cutting through the deck to get to them. We're shipping water bad, but the pumps seem to be keeping up for now… thought you'd like to know."

"Thanks, Chief. Want me to take a look at that arm? That your blood all over?"

"No, sir. The arm's broke, that's all. Blood's from another gunner… he won't be coming to sick bay. You OK, Bruce?"

"Thanks, Stan. I'll make it. Wish it was over so I could settle down and write about it."

"You'll do fine… I've gotta get back to the guns… those that are left anyway."

With that, his friend was gone from the doorway, replaced by another sailor helping a badly burned comrade. Darnell motioned for Bruce to set him on the desk and see to him. As Bruce took hold of the man's arm, the burned skin from the shoulder down sloughed off in his hands. Bruce bit his own cheeks to fight the urge to vomit, helped the man to the desk and worked to make him comfortable; he died sitting there, never uttering a word or sound.

A flash, brighter than the sun… a thunderous noise and air so hot it hurt the face. Bruce was thrown across the room, slamming into a chair. He opened his eyes to see nothing but the red glow of a fire outside in the passageway. He couldn't breathe and got on the floor in hopes of finding air. No sounds other than his ears ringing like a hundred church bells. He lay there for minutes when suddenly an amazing rush of cool water was everywhere, soaking him and clearing the smoke. He looked and saw two men with a fire hose where the doorway used to be. Most of the far bulkhead was gone, replaced by a view of the ocean outside. Bruce was surrounded by a dozen or more bodies, most of them not moving. He saw Darnell rising from the floor near where he'd been operating on a wounded man. The doctor was holding his own left hand, or what was left of it… fingers hanging by bits of flesh.

Bruce's legs didn't want to work quite right as he tried to get off the floor. His lower back was alive with electric pulses that made his feet twitch and his legs jerk. An officer came over and helped him move past the men with the hose. Bruce greedily gulped in fresh air and sensed the ship was not moving, just drifting slowly with the sea. He was laid down on a pile of debris, cushioned by a life preserver. As the minutes passed, Bruce regained more of a sense of where he was. The ringing in his ears subsided enough for him to hear voices of the men busy at their work. The guns had stopped firing. He saw, on the horizon, another ship sailing toward the *LAFFEY*.

#

Bruce hobbled down the aisle between rows of beds in the hospital. Stan walked alongside, his left arm in a cast supported by a sling around his neck.

"It's good to see you up and walking, buddy. The past couple of days have had me worried, I tell you. At first the doctors

326

weren't sure you'd ever walk on your own again without help. That was some hit you took on your back."

"It's feeling a little better every day, Stan. The numbness and tingling are improving, too. I think it'll be a week or more until I'm out of here... I start doing some exercises this afternoon. Right now the worst part is not being able to sit up straight. Lying down feels fine, but sitting... that's painful. Of course, I can't write on my back... I'm thinking I'll try Hemingway's trick of standing to type."

"Ha... that's a good one... wait, you mean he really does that? Who on earth would type standing when you can sit down?"

"I don't know why he does it... I didn't ask him. But I don't have much choice right now. I AM going to ask a nurse if she can locate a typewriter for me. At least I can get something done, even if it's slowly."

Aaron Steiner came walking around the corner ahead.

"Well, if it isn't the two I've been looking for. Tell me Bruce, is there any limit to the dangerous things you'll do just to get a good story? At least this time it didn't cost the Navy a good ship... well, not entirely."

"Aaron... nice to see you. No friendly hug, please... how about a hearty handshake? I don't think you've met Stan Larson yet. Stan, this is Commander... sorry, Captain Aaron Steiner of the Seabees; sorry, I didn't notice the extra stripe on your sleeve."

"Good morning, sir. Pleased to meet you."

"Aaron will do nicely, Chief. At least when we're not in public. Bruce, I arrived on Okinawa yesterday... we're starting the new airfields already, when I heard about the *LAFFEY*. I wasn't sure if you were aboard her, but thought I'd check with the ship anyway. They told me you were here. Anything you need?"

Bruce chuckled a bit and paused.

"I don't suppose you'd have another typewriter handy? Chances are pretty good I've lost one... again."

"Ahhh… no. But I could put in a request through the Papa channels if you'd like."

"Well, let's wait and see if it turns up first. I'm going to ask about borrowing one in the meantime. I'd best head back to my bed… the buzzing in my feet is telling me it's time to lie down."

"Sure, sure. Listen, I'll talk to the people here about a typewriter for you… that should be easy. How about if I also get you a chance to call Susan?"

"That would be great, Aaron… thanks. Knowing her and Marge… they've probably already heard about the ship."

"Yeah, I have a pretty amazing aunt. I'll get on both of those things right away."

"Sounds like getting things done right now, runs in your family."

Stan helped Bruce back to his bed, went to get him some coffee and came back in a few minutes. On a stand next to the bed was a typewriter, paper and pens.

"That guy doesn't mess around, does he?"

"Nope… and you haven't met his aunt Marge, either. The corpsman just left that brought this stuff… Aaron's getting someone to hook up a phone in the ward so I can call home, too. I've never met a family that can get things done like them."

"Hey, buddy, I hate to go… I've got to get back to the ship. The Skipper let me come over here to visit you again this morning, but said to make this one short. I'll be back as soon as I can get here again. Commander Becton's made it clear that we'll be sailing *LAFFEY* back to the States on her own! Emergency repairs are being made at Kerama and we'll be joining two other cripples across the Pacific to California or Washington, not sure which. He did ask if you'd be able to come out to be part of a memorial service day after tomorrow."

"Stan, tell the Skipper I wouldn't miss it for anything… and thank him for letting you visit me. I'd walk you to the door… maybe next time."

Stan left and Bruce laid back, thinking of what he would write of the battle. He hadn't seen anything of it except his own part in helping Doc Darnell. Bruce wondered how Doc was doing... he would try to visit him after his talk with Susan. A Seabee, in the usual dungarees, came in and began wiring in a phone extension for Bruce. Twenty minutes later he was speaking with Marge at their home on Point Loma.

"Bruce... how wonderful to hear your voice. Is everything all right? Susan is not here right now... she's up at the Del Mar house with your mother, but there's no phone up there."

"Thanks, Marge. I forgot my folks were there for a visit. Have you heard anything about the USS LAFFEY, a destroyer I've been on?"

"No, should I have heard anything, Bruce? The only scuttlebutt, as my father called it, is that Ernie Pyle was killed yesterday on Ie Shima. Isn't that an island near you... you're still on Okinawa?"

"Well, I'm back on Okinawa... damn shame about Ernie... I just saw him a week or so ago..."

"What about this ship, Bruce?"

"Oh, sorry, lost in thought for a moment. I've been on a destroyer with a team mate of mine. We were attacked by kamikazes, lots of them. It's a miracle the ship didn't go down... I'm OK, my back is bruised a bit... makes it hard to walk right now."

"Bruce, where exactly are you? What hospital on Okinawa? The Marines are still fighting on the island, according to the newspapers. Do we need to get you home?"

"No, no.... I'll be fine and good as new soon. I just wanted to talk to Susan. Aaron arranged for me to have access to a long distance phone line. He's something, this nephew of yours."

"Yes he is, I hope he stays in the Navy when the fighting stops... another admiral would be nice... and it wouldn't hurt him either."

"Please let Susan know I called... I'll try again. What time is it there now?"

"A little past six in the evening. Why don't you try in four hours; I'm sure she will be back by then. What hospital did you say you're in?"

"I didn't say... sorry, Marge. I'm in the 66th Portable Surgical Hospital... it's an army unit but Navy corpsman are here, too. I'm not sure why I'm not on a Navy Hospital Ship..."

"I'll let her know what you've told me. Take care and do whatever the doctors say... it's their help that will get you back covering the war... if that's what you want."

"I know... it'll just take some time, I think. Nice talking with you. Say hi to Saul."

"I'll do that, Bruce. Goodbye."

Bruce thought about Ernie Pyle. He'd never gotten close to him, only met the man a couple of times. His writing was so like Bruce's; Ernie would have been a good mentor. He seemed to prefer the Army life over the Navy or Marines. Bruce knew he'd write an article on the hospital he was in and dedicate it to Ernie Pyle. First, though, was one about his recent experience on the *LAFFEY*. He got up off the bed and lifted the typewriter on to the room's dresser next to the stand it was on. It weighed quite a bit more than his own... or so it seemed. Typing while standing was new to him and took a bit to get used to; soon, however, the rat..tat..tat of the keys were a steady rhythm.

He'd been at it for a couple of hours, with several breaks to lay down and rest his lower back. He had just finished lunch when a nurse came in to say he should pick up the phone. The hospital operator was on and quickly connected him with the incoming call from Susan.

"Bruce, sweetheart, I couldn't wait for you to call. How are you feeling, is everything all right, what happened..."

"Slow down, honey... I feel fine, almost everything is all right and I'll tell you what happened..."

330

"I'm sorry. Marge told me you'd called when I came in... she's a little concerned so I thought I'd call you right away... it's not easy getting through to Okinawa, I must say. But it worked. Tell me everything..."

"I found Bobbie and Stan again... spent a few days with the Marines on Okinawa and then got a ride to Stan's ship, a destroyer. We were attacked by Jap planes two days ago... I don't know how many times we were hit, but the ship refused to go down. I was helping with the wounded when the ship's sick bay was hit by something... a bomb or a kamikaze, I'm not sure. I remember being taken outside to the main deck and then another ship took many of us here; I'm in an Army hospital; that's about it. My lower back hurts quite a bit but it's already getting better... I can stand now. I've been typing standing up, just like Hemingway does."

"Really?!? I don't suppose it occurred to you that resting and listening to doctors might help you heal faster? Working might not be what you need right now. How are Stan and Bobbie?"

"Stan's okay... he got a broken arm but it's in a cast. He's back on the ship. Bobbie is somewhere on this island, I'm sure... I haven't heard anything. I'll try to get in touch with him before I go back to the *LAFFEY*. They're having a memorial service and the ship's Captain has asked me to be there. If the hospital says I can go for a short visit, I will. The ship will be sailing home to the States on her own power, so it can't be as bad as I make it out to be, I suppose."

They were on the phone together for another fifteen minutes before the line disconnected. Bruce tried to call her back, but the hospital operator could not connect with another overseas line. He would have to try again later. He asked if he could reach the Navy Public Affairs Office or the First Marine Division by telephone. The operator said he would try. It took another ten minutes before Bruce was speaking with a Marine officer. He was told to come and look for his friend personally; the Marines didn't run a babysitting service... punctuated with a few other remarks.

The sky was a cloudless, bright blue. The *LAFFEY* was anchored with dozens of the other wounded warriors. Scorch marks nearly covered her gray outside; several anti-aircraft gun mounts were completely gone and the aft 5" was a twisted wreck. What was left of the crew, among them many sporting bandages and casts visible with their stark whiteness, were assembled on the stern. Commander Becton spoke words of praise for those who survived… and those who did not. Bruce stood next to Doc Darnell, his left arm encased in a cast and bandaged where the hand had been removed. Some 32 shipmates were killed and more than 70 others wounded in the day's fight; all would be sorely missed. The ship was leaving within a week, bound for Seattle under her own power and crew. There was a rush of the wounded stepping forward to let Becton know that they, too, would be sailing on her.

The Captain singled out several men for special mention; Chief Larson among them. Bruce's eyes filled with tears as he heard the praise heaped on his friend for several heroic things done during the battle. Stan was everywhere that morning, helping the wounded and dying, getting guns back in the fight, fighting fires and pulling men out of certain death. He risked his own life a dozen times or more to save others. Stan came over and stood next to Bruce. Commander Becton continued…

"Another man I'd like to thank… Bruce Hollins didn't even have to be here. He refused a chance to leave before the fight, knowing the danger we all faced. Bruce is a credit to his country… his willingness to help in treating the wounded nearly cost his own life. I'll consider him a crewman of the *LAFFEY* to the end!" Becton shook Bruce's hand and the service was concluded. Stan and Bruce were surrounded by their crew mates. A sailor approached Bruce, carrying his typewriter case; scorched on one side with a corner missing.

"Bruce… I found this when we were cleaning up one of the berthing compartments. The case needs to be replaced, but the typewriter is fine; we've cleaned and oiled it for you."

"Replaced? There's no way I'm ever going to get a new case. This will forever remind me of the bravest sons of sea dogs I've ever met."

Doc Darnell spoke up, "With Bruce and Chief Larson on a team, it's no wonder they were state champs!" Three cheers were yelled by the hundred men standing around the two friends.

Stan and Bruce had a tearful goodbye the next morning. The two stood on the fantail of the *LAFFEY* before Bruce boarded a motor whaleboat taking him to shore. They promised each other to meet again back home when the war ended. Bruce watched from the pier as his friend… and a ship he would always remember with adoration, sailed slowly away, heading east.

Chapter 5
May 1945

Despite the heavy rainfall, shin deep mud and the Japanese artillery and mortar fire which tried to disrupt the festivities, Bruce and the members of Bobbie Milliken's squad celebrated the surrender of Nazi Germany. Nobody spoke of a desire for crowds of women showering kisses on Marines, barrels of beer or ticker tape parades... settling for a few minutes away from the front line and a warm bottle of Coca-Cola was the order of the day.

"What do you think, Bruce? Will this part of the war ever end?", the new replacement, a 17-year-old from Idaho, asked from under his still shiny helmet and brand new poncho.

"Yes, eventually. It may take months for our troops and equipment to get here from Europe... when it does we'll completely overwhelm the Japs. Right here, right now there are still plenty of the enemy looking to keep you from setting one foot in Tokyo."

"What he's trying to say, kid, is hope for tomorrow has to wait." Bobbie said this as he grabbed another bottle. "Today my hope is that no Jap shell lands in my lap."

Bruce smiled at his friend. He'd been back with the squad for a few days; his back was badly bruised in the *LAFFEY* fight but there were no breaks or permanent injuries. It was still a bit stiff in the mornings but the recuperative power of youth is a blessing. The Marines were part of a huge American army fighting for control of the southern end of Okinawa. They had landed on April 1st, Easter

Sunday and April Fool's Day rolled into one. Now it was more than a month later and the Japanese were as tenacious as ever, refusing each foot of ground gained. Marines and soldiers were all calling this the 'Hurricane of Steel' campaign. Nearly a quarter million Americans were battling against an enemy dug in and well concealed on one of their close islands. Hundreds of US Navy ships and thousands of aircraft offered a continual bombardment of enemy positions; yet the terrain itself favored the defense. Ridge after ridge rose up in a seemingly endless pattern of interlocking fields of fire; taking one piece of high ground resulted in enemy fire from a dozen more positions. Each had to be blasted, burned and buried to get to the next.

The news that Germany surrendered was good but had no immediate effect on individuals here. The chance to get away from the chaos and enjoy a soda, even a warm one, was what they were celebrating. Bruce planned to stay with Bobbie and his men for another week before heading north to spend time with the Seabees and the airfield under construction. From there a flight to the island of Iwo Jima would complete his own tour of the Air Force's campaign against the Japanese. Having flown in bombers, he was interested in seeing a fighter base; Iwo was home to squadrons of P-51s that flew to protect the B-29s pummeling the enemy cities.

The thought of returning home before the fighting ended in the Pacific did not occur to Bruce. He'd missed the surrenders in Italy and Germany and was not going to be gone when Japan fell. The thought that Okinawa itself would be used as the jumping off point for the next invasion simply showed the true scale of this part of the world war. Bruce had heard about the next step; invading the home islands of Japan would see death and destruction like never before. There were estimates of up to a million dead Americans in the operations planned for November, six months away. Half, or more, of the men who had just won in Europe would be transferred out here for the battles to come.

Bobbie stood and announced that the break was over; time to get back to their positions on the line. His men first scrambled to get another bottle of Coke before heading out. The veterans didn't grouch or grumble. That was done by the newer guys, those who weren't yet numbed by months, or years, of combat. As they trudged through the rain and mud a few hundred yards back to the line, the kid from Idaho was walking next to Bruce, telling him of life on a ranch near the Snake River. With a grin on his face he was reliving a fishing trip from the past fall, a time when Bruce had been with the Army crossing France in pursuit of the Germans. A mortar shell landed on the other side of the kid; his face contorted for one brief moment and he let out a yelp of surprise. He died with eyes wide open and a word half spoken, crumpling in a pile along the path. The youth's body had protected Bruce from the blast, happening so quickly that there was no need to even break stride.

"Welcome back, buddy… and you WANT to be here?", said one of the other men in the squad.

Bobbie told the Marine to shut up and take care of 'Idaho' before catching back up with the others. Moving over to the kid's body, he began rolling it over when the crack of a sniper's rifle sounded. His own corpse flopped on top of the first as the bullet went straight through his head. The surrender of Germany had less impact here than a single enemy rifle.

#

The hot shower felt so good… even in the heat and humidity of this place. Bobbie was humming "Jukebox Saturday Night" as he let the streams of steamy water rinse the soap suds off next to Bruce. The past week had left them both covered with a shell of sweat and mud that felt like the shell of some sea creature. Their clothes practically stood in a corner by themselves.

"Man, this is like heaven. The last shower I had was on the ship before we landed… cold and a mix of fresh and salt water. That was almost two months ago. Bruce, would you let the Marines know I'll be here for at least three more days?"

"Love to… but I'll have to radio them from the plane. I'm due to take off in… let's see… two hours."

"Well… I guess two more hours under this spray will have to do. Hey, remember how Coach Roberts used to make us shower after a practice? I wonder what he'd say about us when we stripped for this one…"

"Right… he'd say not to forget that hygiene was as important as teamwork."

The two friends finished showering, barely able to see each other in the cloud of steam. Bruce got permission for Bobbie to travel with him to the new Air Force base at Kadena, north of the fighting on Okinawa. Aaron Steiner had arranged for them to clean up and new uniforms were issued for Bobbie. Bruce also received another uniform, complete with his War Correspondent patch. Bobbie would be heading back to his squad shortly, after seeing Bruce off on a flight to Iwo Jima. The two day break had been good medicine for the Marine; the first chance for him to be more than a few hundred yards from the fighting since their initial assault.

Most of the island was under Allied control now; the Japanese were being squeezed down into the southern end. The Seabee's were nearly done helping the Air Force construction; new B-29 bombers were arriving daily. The Eighth Air Force, which James Hartke had been a part of back in England, would be arriving in July to add to the force destroying Japanese cities from the air.

The two friends, looking bright and shiny in their clean bodies and uniforms, enjoyed a meal together in the Seabees mess. It was nothing fancy, but a definite improvement to the K-rations they'd been living on.

#

"I don't know how much longer the war will last, but I'll try to get back here to Okinawa before we both head home. If I can't, we'll meet up in Ames with the rest of the guys."

"Bruce, thanks for everything you've done for me. I don't know how you've been able to get around the world to see all of us, but I want you to know how much I appreciate your friendship. It's going to take a long time, maybe forever, before I can feel normal about much of anything. I've seen too much crap to ignore it and just get back to living." Bobbie held out his hand; Bruce shook it and took a minute before letting go. He swung his seabag on his shoulder, picked up his typewriter case and headed up the portable stairway into the aircraft that would bring him to Iwo Jima.

Chapter 6
Summer 1945

Bruce finished typing his story on the tremendous feat America had accomplished with the air campaigns against the Axis in the war. From his travels and own participation, he had seen a new era of combat ushered in. Flying from England aboard the Yankee Clipper, seeing the growth of the Air Corps while in Naples, Florida; being a part of missions over France, Italy and Japan... his experiences had provided an insight he was finally able to put on paper. His editor in New York was pleased with the first two installments. Bruce was certain this final one would go over well, too. He gathered the pages together and walked to the base Admin Office; how many of these places had he visited over the past three and a half years would be hard to recount. The clerks were helpful to see the materials transmitted to Bennett in New York.

It was another fine day in the western Pacific, though the smell and heat of this island were, by far, the most difficult to get used to. The large, rounded mass of Mt Suribachi loomed over the landscape, dwarfing the airfield. Rows of new, shiny P-51 Mustang fighters were laid out in neat patterns and beyond them were several equally bright and shiny B-29 Superfortresses. Most of these were being refueled or repaired, as needed, before they returned to their own nests on Tinian, Saipan or Guam. The sight was awe inspiring and humbling at the same time. His own country had produced all of what he saw... and this was one small speck of the whole. The

United States, with her Allies, were nearly finished defeating the greatest threat to freedom the world had known. At what cost? The future would reveal if the lessons learned and the new technologies discovered were for good or more evil. Bruce hoped he would be around to write about it.

He returned to the Admin Office to see if a long-distance phone call to San Diego might be possible. He was surprised to see General Young walking in just ahead of him in a flight suit. Calling to his friend, he was greeted with a warm smile.

"Bruce… we keep meeting up in some of the most unlikely places, huh? What brings you to this pork chop shaped piece of the Pacific?"

"I've been here working on my final piece about the Air Force. I wanted to write on the efforts made to rescue the men flying against Japan itself. How about you, General?"

"I'm here benefiting from those very efforts. We developed engine trouble on our way from a target and landed here. I'll be flying back to Tinian on another aircraft soon… say, would you care to join me? There's some new folks arriving there; guys you met back in England a while back."

"That would be great! I finished here just this morning and was thinking of what might be next. It seems the war is nearly over and I want to be in on the end of it here. I think Tinian might offer a better place to arrange for that than Iwo Jima."

"I think you're right. With the Navy close by on Guam, you'll be better able to hitch along when the time comes… I don't think that will be a long wait, either. Why don't we meet right here in a half hour and you can join me for a meal before we head over to Tinian?"

"Perfect… I'm trying to call San Diego. I'd like to find out how my wife's doing; we're having a baby the end of September."

"Bruce, I sincerely hope the new arrival is born in peace… I think we're getting very close to it now. See you soon."

The Air Force clerk was very sorry that the overseas phone lines were not working. It was a common problem; he suggested Bruce try when he arrived on Tinian. Bruce thanked him, headed to his quarters to quickly pack up and was back at the Admin Office in time to meet General Young and fly with him.

On the flight, Bruce had an opportunity to speak with the General. Young was now Deputy Commander of the air forces stationed at Tinian. He was returning from, perhaps, his last combat mission.

"Bruce, things are ramping up quickly here in the Pacific. Japan's ability to defend herself from our air attacks is practically nil. We hit the islands pretty much when and where we decide; entire cities have, or will soon be, smoking ruins. Still they hold on, refusing to surrender. We've heard rumors of negotiations for their surrender; just a few weeks ago another attempt was made in Switzerland by our government. On the diplomatic front, everything is static... nothing's moving. The Russians have promised to enter the war against Japan soon... now at a time when we really might not need their help. It will put them in a position of influence in Asia; that's another thing we might not want in the future."

"But they are our allies... we've been helping them for the whole war."

"Ahh, true... but even now they're backing out of promises in eastern Europe. Free elections were to be held in Poland and now the Russians are stalling. In any event, you know the level of trust many you, yourself, have garnered with us. If there was one correspondent I'd be open to sharing information with... it's you."

"Thank you, General. You have no idea how much I appreciate and value the help and friendship I've received. It's opened opportunities I could never have imagined."

"Bruce... I know you'll be invited to witness a surrender of Japan when it happens. We may be weeks or months away from it; that depends on them. You'll be hearing things on Tinian... things not for publication. I'll be inviting you get an inside scoop on things you cannot write… yet. I remember you telling me once about you knowing how we first bombed Tokyo three years ago… from the Navy aircraft carrier. You were a bit disappointed in not being able to write that. This will be similar; a man you've met once, in England, will be in my office after we land. He arrived yesterday and our meeting has been delayed… by my landing on Iwo. I think it may also be so you two could meet again… anyway, I'd like to include you in that meeting."

"General, not a word will be said, or typed, by me without your approval."

"That's exactly why I'm inviting you."

Their plane touched down on a runway in the sprawling complex on Tinian. Bruce recognized an area he had stayed in before with the Seabees and Aaron Steiner. Now it housed Air Force personnel, since the Navy's part in construction was finished. He could see what Okinawa would look like in another year; if the war lasted that long. The aircraft taxied to a hardstand and was met by a staff car. General Young and Bruce rode to the administrative area of the base. As they entered the General's office, they were met by another officer.

"Colonel Paul Tibbetts, this is Bruce Hollins, a friend of mine and a correspondent from New York."

"Bruce… didn't we meet when the Eighth was a baby outside London?" asked Tibbetts.

"Yes, sir, we did. It was a day or so before you led the first mission over France."

"I've read some of your articles since then; you've been all over this war… seen things few others ever get the chance to. Maybe another opportunity will come along before it ends."

Bruce sat down with the two officers; a discussion followed that completely startled him. Colonel Tibbetts commanded a new Air Force unit, a Composite Squadron, so called because it was self-contained… it included transports, bombers and other units that normally were independent commands. Their mission was to drop a new type of weapon, one that had the potential to bring the war to a quick conclusion… IF it worked and IF they received permission to use it."

President Truman would be meeting with Stalin and the new British Prime Minister soon to discuss the end of the war. It was possible the new weapon would be tested before their meeting… it was being developed in a secret location back in the States. Tibbetts' squadron had been in training to drop it for nearly a year already. Bruce was politely, and forcefully, told that none of this information was to be spoken of to anyone… and that he need not plan on leaving Tinian in the foreseeable future.

#

First was the announcement that Okinawa had been secured by Army and Marine forces; two weeks later General MacArthur's headquarters released information that the Philippines were also secured. Bruce was, along with an entire nation, excited and relieved to hear such news. He was, however, disappointed that he would not be able to celebrate with his friend on Okinawa. He had been allowed to meet several of the officers involved in the new weapon; though he still had no idea exactly what it was or when it might be used. The meeting of the Allied leaders in Potsdam was winding down and agreements had been reached concerning the future of Europe and the determination to fully prosecute the war against Japan.

Bruce was trying to placate his editor, G Gordon Bennett of the Daily News, with articles about the continuing air assault against Hirohito. His writing went through General Young's office… there was, practically, no editing or deletion of material he wrote. All the same, Bruce was having to work hard to find much of anything substantial to write about. Most of what he heard and experienced on the base was not to be written.

Early on the morning of August 6th, Bruce was awakened by a Sergeant who was to drive him out to the airfield. There he was met by General Young and several other high ranking officers of the Navy and Air Force. They watched as a large, oblong bomb was moved from a small building down a ramp beneath a waiting B-29. All around him Bruce saw canvas walls had been erected, preventing the view of anyone outside their small contingent of observers. He saw no other reporters and the only photographs taken were by Air Force personnel. Once the weapon was loaded on the bomber, Bruce went with the group to the control tower and, from there, witnessed the takeoff of the plane, piloted by Colonel Tibbetts. He knew there was a chance to sleep now; the flight to Japan would take hours. He'd been on a couple of those himself; though, in the excitement, the thought of sleep was impossible. Packs of cigarettes were smoked and gallons of coffee consumed before the radio message, full of static, was received announcing the success of the bombing. It was then that General Young revealed to him the staggering news that this one bomb had destroyed an entire city of a hundred thousand people. It was hoped this would result in the immediate surrender of Japan. If it didn't, another bomb was available for delivery in a few days. Stunned, Bruce thought back to the views he'd witnessed on his two flights over Japan. The first of the city that looked like burning charcoal and the second of the aftermath; a city unrecognizable, full of grayness that was the ash.

The next morning, General Young cautioned Bruce about his upcoming phone call to Susan, which was finally allowed since news of the first atomic bombing was released.

"You still cannot mention that you observed anything or that you were even involved in meetings about the mission, Bruce. Make it a pleasant conversation... I know it's a damned shame... but it has to be this way for now. No one can know of your prior knowledge of the mission."

"I understand, General. Susan would agree, anyway. Thanks for the chance to talk with her... it's been quite some time. Her letters are full of good news about the baby and the house... but to hear her voice, and my mom's, will be wonderful."

Their talk was wonderful... all fifteen minutes of it. Susan was feeling fine, Mother was an angel of help, especially with getting the Del Mar house ready for his return. His father was also doing well back in Iowa and was enjoying all the attention of friends and neighbors since he was a temporary bachelor. The baby was due the middle of September and Marge was arranging for it to be born at the Naval Hospital in San Diego. She said several times that all of them expected Bruce to be there... no excuses on this one! Bruce promised he'd do everything he could to make it.

With the dropping of the first bomb, Bruce was included in a briefing on the science behind the new weapon. He learned that there were actually two types, both were atomic... the first had been a uranium bomb and another, plutonium, device was ready for use if needed. It was; on August 9th, he was, again, a witness to the beginning and end of a mission against the city of Nagasaki. The first target, Hiroshima, revealed an almost complete annihilation of everything within miles of the Aiming Point. The Japanese government had still not agreed to a surrender.

During their wait while the B-29 was in route to Nagasaki, news of a massive Soviet attack against the Japanese army in Manchuria was received. Several senior officers discussed the shame that now, even at the last minute, the Russians would garner political influence over a large area of Asia at little real cost. Bruce sensed a change in attitudes toward an ally. Again, the radioed report of the bomb drop was received with applause and relief that it had worked well. Bruce wondered, in silence, just what the future held if enemies, or countries that were now friends, also developed such destructive capabilities. His thoughts turned to his own baby, not yet born, and how these new weapons would affect his, or her, life and the future of mankind.

"Bruce," interjected General Young, "the Air Force is putting together a team to survey the two sites when the Japanese surrender... which they surely will after today. How would you like to come along? You'd have an exclusive story... the scoop of the century."

"General, I'd consider it a high point in my life... that is, as long as it doesn't interfere with my date in San Diego the middle of next month."

"Well, I will wager that a surrender ceremony won't take place for several weeks after the Japs call it quits. I think there would be time to get you to Hiroshima or Nagasaki and on to Tokyo ahead of a flight back to California. We'll wait and see... but the offer is sincere... I'd even look at it as a sort of 'Thank You' for all you've done in the war yourself."

#

The convoy of vehicles approached the brow of a hill overlooking the city of Nagasaki. Bruce was reliving the past couple of weeks in his mind. Emperor Hirohito had spoken to his people, announcing the end of their struggle with the world; though he had avoided using the word surrender. Japanese forces around the Pacific were already negotiating local capitulations. The Russians were quick in making territorial demands based on their own three-week long involvement in the fighting. A formal surrender ceremony would be held in early September in Tokyo Bay aboard US Navy warships; General Young had been right in his personal prediction. Bruce had time to accompany this survey team to Nagasaki and get to Tokyo in time for the ceremony; then he would catch a military transport back to San Diego, stopping first in Hawaii, in time for his child's birth. His plan was to take every minute aboard the flight to write; he'd send the first part out during the layover in Hawaii.

As the trucks topped the hill, a vista of uniform devastation greeted his eyes. He imagined this is what the moon's surface might look like. There were no streets, no houses, no discernible buildings or landmarks. A few concrete walls, a handful of scorched tree trunks were all he could see across the wide valley ahead. The truck he was a passenger in parked and he dismounted. Several other vehicles, mostly jeeps that could maneuver through the destruction, continued ahead. A man with a small box to measure radiation from the bomb was intently listening to the constant sharp clicking and reading a dial on the machine.

"I'd say we can stay here no more than an hour; then it would be best to leave."

Bruce looked at his own watch and began to study the landscape through a pair of borrowed binoculars. He saw a couple of people, their clothing standing out as the only color besides gray. They were digging through the ruins of what he assumed had been their house. His hour was spent, not investigating like the survey crew he was with… he spent it in wonder at the awfulness of it all. The waste of nearly four years of war… and all because a relatively few people desired power, control of things and of other people. He sat and wept, a few of the military men around him wondering at his reaction.

#

To Bruce the surrender, on the deck of the battleship *USS MISSOURI*, chosen because it was named for the home state of President Truman, was an anti-climax. It struck him as a celebratory show of force, a humiliation more than a celebration. He wanted to get away and on his flight, back to California as soon as possible. It didn't help that he'd picked up the flu along his way through Japan to the capital. He was pretty much over the fever and nausea, but a headache and general fatigue was still with him. He felt as if all the tired days of his travels around the war were lumped into today.

#

The plane touched down smoothly at the airbase in Hawaii. His view of Pearl Harbor and Ford Island had changed from the first time he'd landed here. Bruce had been unable to work too much on the flight; his stomach hadn't liked the lunch he was provided and his exhaustion was too much to fight. He had slept, fitfully, most of the hours in the air. He managed to write one article, expressing his personal views on the instant death of a city in Japan and the pending birth of his own child. He looked forward to a quick shower on the base, hoping it would revive him, before his flight resumed in a few hours. He was directed to a temporary room and was quickly under a stream of refreshing warm water. As he shaved following the shower, he noticed a couple of bruises on the back of his hand; dismissing them as he wondered what he'd bumped to get them. He looked in the mirror and saw a face that was older than that of a few years ago; the war and all the travel had matured him beyond his early twenties. No gray hair yet, but already losing some, if the evidence in his hair brush was to be believed.

#

"Susan! Mom!" The excitement of seeing them both at the Navy's airfield on Coronado brought back his old energy like a tonic. He bounded down the stairs and across the tarmac to where they were waiting.

"Bruce, darling." The last word was nearly lost in the smothering kiss she received as she spoke it. He was kissing her and trying to hug his mom at the same time. All three were laughing. Bruce held Susan at arm's length and looked at her very different figure, an outfit trying to discreetly hide a very visible package within.

"You look marvelous, Susan. How do you feel? Should you be out here in the sun and heat and all?"

Susan looked at Louise and laughed. They had wagered at what his first words would be; both had lost. They thought it would be more about any news on what had happened while he'd been on the flight.

"I'm fine... the baby's fine... we're all fine. I'll be checking in to the hospital soon; probably in three days unless the excitement speeds things up. Let me look at you; thinner, but our cooking will take care of that. You look like you haven't slept in days... are you tired?"

"Not any more. I actually slept most of the way here. I caught something like the flu in Japan, but I'm sure it's gone now. Just not hungry much."

They walked to the car all holding hands, Bruce sandwiched between the two ladies he loved. Susan and Louise sat up front and talked during the drive to Del Mar, bringing him up to date on... "well, just about everything". When they arrived, Saul and Marge were there to join in the welcoming. It was an evening full of remembrance and reunion. Bruce learned that Stan had visited when his ship arrived in Seattle for repairs. He shared details of their day on the *LAFFEY* that Bruce had been unable, or unwilling, to talk of. There were bundles of letters that had been forwarded from everywhere to him; notes of thanks, congratulations and mostly of appreciation for his writing. Those he'd get to later... Bottles of wine, good food and familiar music provided an atmosphere that Bruce appreciated on his first day home.

The next morning Susan had difficulty waking him and was alarmed by the bruises on his legs and back. She called Louise and they decided to head to the hospital right away. When the Navy doctor heard that Bruce had visited Nagasaki, he became very concerned. He took Susan and Louise in to another room and disclosed that he felt Bruce had a sickness brought on by latent radiation from the bomb used there. The news was, itself, a bombshell to Susan. Within an hour she was also admitted and preparations made for the baby's delivery. Louise shuttled between the two bedsides, taking time out to phone Marge and also Earl, back in Iowa.

The doctors took blood, skin and hair samples from Bruce as he lay in bed, too tired to get up. The bruises had begun to spread to his front and arms and the nausea returned, along with the fever. He was able to sit in a wheelchair and hold his baby the day after he was born. Susan wanted to name their son Sam; Bruce thought it was perfect. While mother and baby were soon ready to head home, the third patient was not. Doctors were simply not sure about

Bruce's prognosis; there was little information they could act on. Radiation poisoning was too rare to prescribe treatment; it was a side effect of the new weapons nobody had given enough thought about. Time would tell, but that offered them little hope for the present.

Bruce could not sit up to hold little Sam when the day came for Susan to go home. Earl had arrived the day before, flying in from Iowa. Sam laid on Bruce's chest while Susan and his folks fought back their tears at his farewell.

In a quiet voice that was barely heard by the others, Bruce looked at his baby and said, "Son... I've waited to meet you for quite some time. I know you'll grow up to love reading and writing... mom and gramma will see to it. Travel when you're older; it's fun and the best way to see things and meet people. I love you and your mommy so much."

Epilogue
March 1946

The young man from Chicago, rookie reporter for a newspaper, finished speaking with the farmer about the basketball game five years ago. He wondered, for the umpteenth time, just why his editor had sent him here, in the middle of Iowa, to cover a reunion of a high school team. He'd protested right from the start; all his boss said was a friend from New York told him the story would be worth sending someone.

As he surveyed the gym full of people, most appeared perfectly in place. There were a few, however, that didn't fit at all. An Air Force General, a high-ranking Navy officer with a sleeve full of gold stripes and others who were completely over dressed for a small mid-western town. One woman stood out; red flowered dress and holding a saucer and tea cup when everyone else carried paper cups of punch. He decided she'd be his next interview.

"Me? Oh, I'm Louise Hollins... one of the boys' moms. They're who you really want to talk to. Or maybe Frankie, that's Jimmie's wife... or Susan, Bruce's wife. Anyway, all the boys are outside, up the hill behind the school. Fred got here this afternoon from Europe and it's their first time alone together." She giggled, "Alone together... now that doesn't sound right at all. I'm sure they wouldn't mind you wanting to speak with them. After all, Bruce was a reporter, too."

The man thanked her and stepped outside. He paused as he collected his thoughts; last name Hollins, mother of... Bruce Hollins? Bruce Hollins, the star reporter for the New York Daily News? The guy everybody loved to read during the war... all about finding his high school team mates? He liked the writing style himself... studied it in high school last year, even had thoughts of becoming a War Correspondent... then the war ended.

With a quickening stride, the young reporter rounded the building's corner and saw a hill. There was a small group of people standing up near the top of... a cemetery? Why would they be gathered around a headstone? From the bottom of the hill he could see a woman with a young girl, another holding a baby... they must be the two wives Mrs Hollins mentioned. Four guy's standing there, too. Four? A basketball team has five players... the last got back today, all five here for the first time. Didn't add up... unless?

The young man stopped, his mind racing... the last article he'd read by Bruce Hollins was right after the war's end... on Nagasaki and the death of the city and birth of a baby... his baby. He remembered Hollins wrote from his own visit there and return to America. That was six months ago... Nothing from Hollins he could remember since. All the out of place people back in the gym, a General and the Naval officer... Bruce Hollins is dead?

The reporter practically sprinted up the hill. He slowed as he approached the group and noticed the two women were dressed in black, hadn't seen that in the evening light from below. He excused and introduced himself... and asked if they were the team.

"Team, wives and kids... what can we do for you, son?" replied the tallest, dressed in an Army officer's uniform. "I'm Fred Howard. This is Jim Hartke, his wife Frankie... also my sister. That swabbie is Stan Larson, the jarhead is Bobbie Milliken."

The reporter burst in, "And you're Susan Hollins and his baby... so Bruce must be..." He looked at the headstone they were standing near.

"Right behind Fred…" said a voice, as a man stood up from a bench. "I'm Bruce Hollins, pleased to meet you… feeling a bit tired and had to sit a while." Bruce held out his hand and shook that of the reporter.

"I got a call saying a young man from Chicago would be here… one I should meet. Apparently, your editor holds you in pretty high regard… wanted you to cover our reunion. I was a cub reporter right out of high school myself. I think it would be good for us to spend some time together. Never forget that history is something to look forward to."